TRAILHEAD

C. JEAN DOWNER

Praise for the works of C. Jean Downer

Under the Cold Moon

Seeped in fantastical elements and witchcraft, Downer gives readers a meticulously crafted tale of intrigue, mystery, and suspense. By defining a story world with logical, consistent parameters, readers are taken on a compelling ride of suspended disbelief. *Under the Cold Moon* is immersive, entertaining and should not be missed.

-*Women Using Words*

The writing is smooth and compelling, the (magical) world-building is well done.

-Henrietta B., *NetGalley*

Lies are Forever

Lies Are Forever is very well done. Downer provides readers with an engaging, cohesive storyline that's overflowing with rich, fluid language. The characters are well drawn and work together to weave a compelling and surprising plot. This is fresh, unique storytelling, and it deserves top marks. If you like well-written, suspenseful supernatural fiction, then you won't want to miss this one.

-*Women Using Words*

Lies are Forever is an enjoyably well written novel with plenty of twists and turns to keep the pages turning. Downer does well in creating a magical world…that we see revealed through Sloane's eyes. Mixing the magical with a whodunnit is ingenious resulting in an intriguing story.

-Della B., *NetGalley*

I absolutely loved this book! I can't wait for the next one! The characters were so much fun, and I loved how they interacted with each other. The paranormal aspect just added the right amount to the story! I definitely recommend this book to anyone who likes this genre.

-Natalie A., *NetGalley*

A great read and an amazing plot.

-Bonnie K., *NetGalley*

Other Bella Books by C. Jean Downer

Lies are Forever
Under the Cold Moon

About the Author

C. Jean Downer attributes her inspiration and creative process to living in a temperate rain forest near the eternal Pacific Ocean with her wife of twenty-plus years, their two fabulous teenage daughters, two lazy dogs, and three chill cats. When she is not writing, she and the love of her life are traveling to new destinations and checking them off their bucket list (okay, even when traveling she's writing but mostly in her head). For more information about her novels and poetry, visit her website at cjeandowner.com. You can also connect with her on Instagram and Facebook @cjeandowner and Bluesky @cjeandowner.bsky. social.

TRAILHEAD

C. JEAN DOWNER

BELLA BOOKS

Bella Books, Inc.
P.O. Box 10543
Tallahassee, FL 32302

This is a work of fiction. Names, characters, businesses, places, events and incidents are either the products of the author's imagination or used in a fictitious manner. Any resemblance to actual persons, living or dead, or actual events is purely coincidental. The publisher does not have any control over and does not assume any responsibility for author or third-party websites or their content.

First Edition - 2025

Editor: Cath Walker
Cover Designer: SJ Hardy
Photo credit: Adrienne Thiessen, Gemini Photography

ISBN: 978-1-64247-656-9

PUBLISHER'S NOTE

Acknowledgments

I have to start with Linda and Jessica Hill for providing me with another opportunity to share a story with the world. You are an amazing publisher, and I thank you for believing in my writing. To all the incredible people at Bella Books, my deepest gratitude for making *Trailhead* the best it can be.

Cath Walker, my editor, is a dream to work with. Thank you for sharing your expertise and elevating my writing, Cath. They say three times is a charm, and it sure felt like it.

Special thanks to my readers. Your support of my work and other LGBTQIA+ authors and queer books gives us reason to continue authoring our stories, and it means the world to me.

Finally, Theresa, Hayden, and Hadley, I am so grateful for your unwavering support. Love you to the moon and stars times infinity.

Note from the Author

I spent my childhood summers camping in South Dakota's Black Hills, the Pahá Sápa in the Lakota language. For two weeks, we slept in the dense forests and fished trout from mountain streams for dinner. Ours was a working-class family, often living paycheck to paycheck, and the US national forests and national parks provided an accessible and affordable haven. Decades have passed since those summers. I live in Canada now and prefer glamping and white-water rafting these days, but still love spending time in US national parks, some of the most beautifully scenic places on earth. I'm not alone. Last year over ninety-four million people visited the USA's sixty-three national parks. It is land that has been protected since 1916. Preserved for successive generations to access and enjoy.

I set *Trailhead* in Washington State's North Cascades National Park, a short hour's drive from British Columbia. My wife and I love the trails, the scenic beauty, and the jagged and rugged summits of over ninety mountains and three hundred glaciers, some reaching eight to nine thousand feet. My characters working in the park honor the incredible volunteers, park rangers, and ISB who ensure visits to US national parks are safe and enjoyable. And I've centered the action around the Pacific Crest Trail to give the hiking community a shout-out. I've never experienced a thru-hike like the 2,650-mile trail that connects Canada and Mexico along the West Coast, but I've met others who have, and I've followed countless blogs of those documenting the intense experience. In *Trailhead*, I've used the slang they use in their community, and I pay homage to the incredible feat that is thru-hiking.

Although my depiction of the North Cascades National Park is based on experience, I have fictionalized the community of Granite Creek and the ease of access around the Stehekin area of the park. Additionally, my portrayal of Reese Carter, Special Agent of the Investigational Services Branch of the National Park Service, draws on research and documentaries about the ISB, but she is an imagined character. If you want to know more about the North Cascades National Park there are many valuable resources available for all the US National Parks, Forests, Monuments, Cultural, and Recreational areas. In addition, the Pacific Crest Trail Association is invaluable if you want to spend some time on the trail for a day, overnight, or thru-hike: https://www.pcta.org/discover-the-trail/.

Finally, I finished writing *Trailhead* before the 2024 US Presidential election and the change in administration. I am devastated by the current president's executive orders dismantling the important legacy of the NPS, under the false guise of efficiency and economic gain. I plan to continue my bucket list of spending time in each of the US national parks, and I hope you consider visiting them too.

I so appreciate you for reading *Trailhead*, and, if you're a US citizen, I would be honored if you contacted your representatives in Congress and demanded they act to protect your majestic treasures.

PART ONE

For of all the hard things to bear and grin,
The hardest is knowing you're taken in.
                                  –Phoebe Cary

CHAPTER ONE

Quincy, Massachusetts 2017

Eleanor Watts had worked for the Maloney family for three years when it became clear to her that she might not leave the job alive. Bridget Maloney, the overindulged daughter she'd been hired to protect, had proved unmanageable the older she became, and tonight she was spinning out of control.

The uncomfortable banter among the men at the formal dining table ended with one abrupt comment from Bridget. Eleanor wiped her mouth with a crisp linen napkin, calmly replacing it on her lap, and glanced at her charge. Bridget glared at her stepfather, her cheeks flushing red, eyes hard. Eleanor readied, knowing the look meant trouble.

The only sound in the room for the next minute was the tick-tock of a mantle clock. The men, except for Sean, stared at their plates. Eleanor conducted a visual pat down of the eight people seated there and determined four had concealed handguns under their jackets. Five, including her. She fixed her gaze on her plate and considered her next move, then decided to do nothing. Not yet.

She glanced at her watch. They were thirty minutes into dinner, and their hosts, Sean Ryan and his wife, Fiona O'Flaherty Maloney, had yet to say why they had requested Bridget and her to attend. She sat alert and mentally formulated several escape scenarios. The room's main exit was behind her. She could flip the long mahogany table and shield herself from half the guests. The man in the tailored suit seated to her left would require a more personal effort. Then there was Bridget. She hoped her charge would willingly follow. Regardless, it was her job to protect her even if it was from her own family.

"What did you just say to me?" Sean asked, finally acknowledging his stepdaughter.

"You heard me." Bridget held his eyes, she lifted her steak knife.

"Oh, I heard you, Princess, and I don't like how you're talking to me." Sean glanced at the woman at the other end of the table. Fiona gave a tight smile, looking from him to her daughter.

"I couldn't care less." Bridget tossed her knife and fork on the fine china plate. "Stop with the innuendo about me and tell us why we're here, or Eleanor and I are leaving."

He scoffed. "All right, you little ingrate. I thought we'd let your mother eat in peace before I tell her what you've done, but we can have it out now. When I took over the family porcelain export business from your dearly departed father, Caleb, God rest his soul, I promised your mam I'd protect our lucrative dealings." He drew out the words *dearly departed* and settled his gaze on the man seated to his left. "Isn't that right, Thom?"

Thomas Walsh, the crime family's clan chief, grunted in agreement.

Eleanor cut a piece of lamb, her mind racing. What the hell had Bridget done? She wasn't aware of any new indiscretions. There had been a few new fights at Northeastern University bars, but no fallouts she hadn't already smoothed over. Was this about Bridget's ex-girlfriend? No. She had found the woman's cat in Bridget's lockup and returned it. No harm done. The ex-girlfriend was none the wiser. Besides, the incident had nothing to do with the family's business. She ate, avoiding eye contact.

"I vowed no one would ever trouble another O'Flaherty or Maloney as long as I lived," Sean continued, his voice gaining a threatening edge. "Or siphon business from the family without Paddy, here, taking care of the problem." He patted the shoulder of the squat, muscular man sitting to his right. The man straightened in his chair.

Eleanor quickly glanced at the O'Flahertys' newest reaper. Patrick Sullivan had taken over the head hitman position, but she had never met him before. He stayed behind the scenes, using several button men to carry out his orders. She burned his image in her mind, needing to remember his face. Then she sensed her charge move. The young woman clenched a knife in a tight fist. Eleanor laid her hand on Bridget's wrist.

"Don't you dare call my father by his first name. It's 'Mr. Maloney, God rest his soul' to you, *tu es un répugnant morceau de déchet*." Bridget's voice was unemotional, but Eleanor knew her charge only spoke French when she was losing control.

Sean mimicked her comment with gibberish in a comical French accent, making the other men at the table laugh, and Bridget stared menacingly at each one until the room fell silent again. Then she returned her attention to her stepdad. "You're an imbecile, and no one believes you make a difference in our business. They're right. You don't. My great-grandfather immigrated from Ireland and built this business a hundred years ago. Where have you taken O'Flaherty Porcelain in the last fifteen years? We still cast the same tiles, hide the same drugs, and send them to the same tired suppliers because you aren't smart enough to do anything different." She turned her glare to Fiona. "For fuck's sake, Mother, why you let this idiot run things for you is beyond me."

"Brie, what the hell's wrong with you?" Bridget's younger brother, Liam, gestured in frustration. Over time, Eleanor had watched the freckle-faced ginger change from a teenager who idolized his big sister to a young man who was increasingly disillusioned with her. He looked at Fiona. "Ma, do something. We can't even have a normal meal when she comes home."

"Normal meal? Jesus Christ, Liam. You're so dense." She burst into derisive laughter. "Dear old stepdad is trying to make a lesson out of me because I'm becoming something he's not. Successful."

"Don't laugh at me," Liam shouted and leaped to his feet, knocking over an ornate silver candelabra and sending its burning candles flying. Bridget burst into taunting laughter.

Sean pointed at Bridget and shouted, "Shut your mouth, you little—"

"That's enough." Fiona slammed her hands on the table and stood. She righted the candle holder and lit two snuffed-out candles with a burning one.

The energy in the room shifted. Liam dropped onto his seat, and Sean and his men squirmed uncomfortably in their chairs. Eleanor scanned them and confirmed their hands were all above the table. She watched the corners of Fiona's mouth lift slightly. The matriarch glanced at her daughter and then fixed her green eyes on her husband. "Temper, temper, Bridget." Fiona gently picked up her fork and knife from her plate. "I am not a fan of veiled threats, Sean. Please plainly tell Bridget why we are all together this evening."

"I was getting to it, *a stór*. I didn't want to ruin a delicious meal with the unpleasantness. But if you want to do this now…"

Fiona gestured with the back of her hand. "By all means, don't spare us."

Eleanor's stomach tightened at her words. She had been in Fiona O'Flaherty Maloney's presence enough to know a storm brewed behind those controlled words and placid looks, but she didn't know if the woman's anger was for her husband or daughter.

Sean cleared his throat, drawing everyone's attention. "I recently found out that your industrious daughter has more than classes in motion at her fancy university." He took a large bite of colcannon, mashing it loudly.

Bridget turned her scathing glare from her stepdad to the young man beside Thomas, the clan chief's son, Johnny. Eleanor had seen him a few times at her charge's condo. Johnny lowered his head.

Eleanor quickly parsed Sean's comment. Bridget must have ensnared Johnny into some enterprise of her own, probably selling drugs. It was a serious enough infraction to force them all to the table. Her mind raced to recall when she had seen Johnny at Bridget's condo. Parties mostly. She couldn't recall Bridget and Johnny ever being alone without her on guard, but she wasn't with her charge twenty-four seven.

"To the point, Sean," Fiona said, the slight smile from before had vanished.

Sean swallowed and chased the potatoes with a gulp of wine. "Seems she decided to open a new market on campus. But like most things, she's not any good at it. Picked an equal bonehead for a partner." His boss's comment prompted Thomas to slap Johnny on the back of the head. His son's head dropped lower like a wounded dog, and Sean laughed. "We don't know how they got their hands on any product, and Johnny isn't talking."

Fiona cut into her lamb chop. "Is this true, Bridget?"

"No, as usual, the idiot doesn't know what he's talking about. Why would I sell drugs on my campus? That's lame." Bridget clenched her knife again. "But what if I am selling? Who says I'm beholden to that *gobshite's* rules?"

"If it were true, it would be unfortunate, disloyal," Fiona answered, calmly. "Putting our reputation at risk is betraying the business and the family. As would drawing attention to us in any way."

"Isn't ruining the business disloyal, Mother?" Bridget lifted her knife, her wild eyes locked on her stepdad.

Sean's face had turned bright red. More outbursts from Bridget, and he might order Patrick to teach her some respect right then and there. Eleanor steeled her nerves and readied her hands. She chose an escape plan. The table flip. She could strike Patrick in the temple before he could get his gun out of that tight-fitting suit jacket.

"Well, I believe Bridget was probably just supplying some recreational drugs to her friends, don't you, a stór?" Fiona's voice was calm and soothing, but Eleanor sensed anger in the woman's body. "*My* daughter is an intelligent young lady. She knows being such a well-known student that any attempts to sell drugs would expose our family to even more scrutiny." She shifted her attention to Bridget. "You wouldn't get caught providing drugs to your friends again, would you, darling?"

Bridget frowned. "For God's sake, you even have to tell him what to think. When the hell is this charade going to end, Mother?"

Sean pointed his fork at Bridget and shouted, "Your mam's not telling me what to think. She's trying to soften the blow I'm about to give you, you little shit. This operation has manufactured and exported high-end, hard-paste porcelain *tiles* to Ireland for fifty years without interruption. That's kept a whole lot of people in a good amount of money. Don't think just because you're family you're more important than the bottom line."

"Yeah, Brie. Show some damn respect," Liam jeered.

Sean's eyes flashed to Liam and back to Bridget. "That's right. You need to show this family some respect. You keep up your bullshit, and you'll find this sweet little life you have come to an abrupt stop. That's not a veiled threat." He grinned at Liam and his men.

Bridget growled and drew back her hand holding the knife. Eleanor scrambled to her feet, grabbed Bridget's hand, and pulled it down. She felt the knife's edge slice through her palm.

"Now you're reining her in?" Sean directed his rage at Eleanor. "Where the hell were you when these two shitheads conspired to start their little enterprise? Or were they cutting you in?"

"Leave her out of this," Bridget yelled, still warning him with the knife. "She doesn't know everything I do." She looked at Eleanor, who was wrapping her hand with the linen napkin, red seeping through. "Oh, shit. I'm sorry, Elle." She scooted back and stood. "I can bandage it."

Sean tutted in frustration. "It's a good thing we have Liam to train up, a stór." He shot a look of disdain at Bridget. "Even with that fancy education, she'll never be able to run the business. And we know she's never marrying a man who will." He burst into laughter and the others joined in.

Eleanor pressed the napkin harder into her throbbing wound, reading the table. The men shared the joke among themselves, except for Johnny. He continued to look terror-stricken. Fiona remained silent, an ironic smile on her face, and Bridget glared at her brother. The shift in Liam's attitude toward his sister had brought him closer to Sean, unfortunately placing him on what Eleanor called Bridget's cold-foods list. Because revenge is best served… Eleanor caught Fiona nodding slightly at Bridget.

"Come on. Let's get the hell out of here," Bridget said, touching Eleanor's shoulder.

Eleanor followed her charge through a great archway. The Maloneys' dining room opened onto an expansive foyer with a black porcelain tile floor. The walls were bare, covered only in gray damask wallpaper. Six-foot weeping figs on stone pedestals flanked both sides of the entry's three archways. With nothing else to absorb noise, their footsteps across the foyer echoed in the cathedral ceiling.

Bridget led them down a narrow hallway, opening the last door, and pointing to a chair. "Sit over there. God, I hate that man. He needs to watch himself. What a fucking asshat. Can you believe he threatened me?"

"Seemed a poor move." Eleanor lifted the napkin and inspected the cut.

"That's an understatement. It'll put his ass in a grave. Trust me."

Eleanor watched Bridget gather gauze, tape, and a bottle of rubbing alcohol from a cabinet above a washing machine. Her thoughts raced. Any fallout with the Maloneys was a problem. Fiona meant it when she said selling outside the family was a betrayal. She couldn't see the mother hurting her child, though. On the other hand, the situation with the volatile Sean was unstable. He made it clear he thought little of Bridget. But would he be stupid enough to harm her? Then there was Johnny Walsh. The kid had sealed his fate by narcing on Bridget. Now she'd have to protect him from Bridget's retribution. Most importantly, she needed to figure out how the immensely irritating Irish princess had sold drugs without her knowledge.

"Let me see your hand." Bridget tossed the bloody napkin in a sink. She spread open the cut, and Eleanor winced. "That's not bad." Eleanor shrugged, and Bridget pulled her to the sink. "This'll hurt more." She poured rubbing alcohol enthusiastically over the wound.

"Jesus." Eleanor clenched her teeth against the sting.

"I said I was sorry." Bridget covered the wound with gauze and led Eleanor back to the chair. "You're mad at me. I can tell. When you get all quiet like this, you're angry."

"Yeah, a little. If Sean was telling the truth, you've been lying to me. How am I going to protect you if you aren't honest? You want me to trust you, right? So why keep me in the dark?"

Bridget finished taping Eleanor's hand and leaned against the counter. "Of course I do. You mean more to me than those people in there." She glared at the door. "I'm protecting you. The less you know, the better."

"Oh, no. That's not how this works. I'm the professional. I protect you."

"Here." Bridget offered a bowl of Dum-Dums pops, but Eleanor shook her head. "Come on, have one. It's tradition. If you have a wound patched up, you get a sucker. Like going to the dentist when you're a kid…except it's candy and not a cheap toy."

Eleanor sighed, dug through the lollipops, and grabbed a root-beer-flavored one. "Thanks." She stood and before she could react, Bridget embraced her.

"Your contract's only for one more year. I can't bear the thought of losing you," Bridget whispered in her ear.

Eleanor swallowed her discomfort and returned the hug. "I'm not going anywhere. Trust me."

Bridget stepped back with sad eyes. "I do, but I don't want to talk any more tonight."

"That's fine. We can talk tomorrow. I'll call for the car." She escorted Bridget outside, and the Irish princess hung onto her arm, batting her eyes. Eleanor chose to keep her close but knew that behind those big, blue eyes was a self-centered, dangerous young woman. To her, Bridget O'Flaherty Maloney was just a job, but it was one that had proved more difficult than she could ever have imagined.

CHAPTER TWO

Eleanor waited on a slate terrace, sipping hot tea. Fallen leaves rustled across the ground, and the breeze off the Charles River cut through her sweater. Bridget was late. Against Eleanor's better judgment, she had gone alone to see her mother. It was the second time in as many weeks. She glanced at her phone, then turned it upside down. Calling her charge would only make Fiona suspicious.

After the dumpster-fire dinner at the Maloneys', Eleanor invited Bridget to a come-to-Jesus meeting the next morning to clarify two things. First, she expected to know what Bridget was doing at all times, and second, she demanded to be part of all Bridget's business endeavors moving forward, or she would leave. Bridget had been initially forthcoming, but now, two months later, Eleanor was in the dark again. She thought about calling Mandy. Her friend's optimism might help her stick with the job. Besides, she missed hearing her voice.

Eleanor reached in her bag for her other phone when Bridget stepped onto the terrace and waved, her blond ponytail swishing behind her as she made her way to the table.

"How does a place like this allow Sean Ryan to be a member?" Bridget sat across from Eleanor. Her face wore a look of disgust. "He's milked his marriage to my mother for more than all the cow maids in Ireland can extract in a lifetime." She smiled, amused at herself.

Eleanor sipped her tea without responding.

"You're mad at me."

"You're late, and I have no idea what's going on…again."

"Mother invited me to Eryn's Bakery to talk, and I love their turnovers. She ordered me to come without you."

"And you didn't find that odd?"

"No offense, but she doesn't like you very much."

"That's not what I mean. She asked you to meet at the place where you've planned a secret meeting tomorrow with her now ex-suppliers. That seems a bit provocative, unnecessarily so." Eleanor lifted her brows, but Bridget only shrugged. Eleanor sat back, frustrated. "Well, tell me what she wanted."

"Jesus, Elle. She wanted to talk about the holidays. It's my senior year. She wants to celebrate." She grinned. "We're thinking of the Cote d'Azur. Maybe Nice."

Eleanor nodded. Her job was to question everything and gather as much information as possible. Bridget's answer sounded legit, but something about her grin was off. "All right, fine. So what are we doing here?"

Bridget looked past Eleanor's shoulder. A server in a black vest and bow tie approached. "Good afternoon, Ms. Maloney. May I bring you something to drink?"

"Earl Grey for us both and an apple crisp with two scoops of vanilla ice cream. Two spoons." She turned back to Eleanor.

"Thank you," Eleanor said to the server, and he nodded. She looked at her charge. "So? What did you want to meet about?"

"To celebrate, you big grouch. I'm about to open my pipeline. After tomorrow's meeting, the Eastern Seaboard is mine. That asshat, Sean, can have his routes to Ireland."

"Don't you think it's premature to applaud yourself? I'm still not convinced your mother and Sean don't know what you're doing. Not to mention any other families you might be pissing off. This is a busy and deadly market, and people can turn on you. How do I protect you if I don't know everything you're doing?"

"Oh my God. You're mad because I haven't told you who's making my drugs, aren't you?"

"I told you, no more secrets."

"It's a surprise, not a secret. I'll tell you, but not yet. You have to be patient."

Eleanor stared at the river and watched the crews row past. She had an endless well of patience, and she knew how to use silence.

"Come on, don't be like that." Bridget pouted. "I'm in a great mood. I just spent two hours with my mother, and I promise she's clueless about my new business. And that moron she's married to needs a snitch to tell him who's standing beside him. Since I took care of Johnny, he doesn't have one. So we're all good."

The server returned and placed Bridget's tea and the dessert on the table, filling her cup. She ignored him, but Eleanor said, "Thank you," and he quietly walked away. She disregarded her charge's last comment. Bridget had terrorized Johnny into silence. She usually resorted to physical violence as retribution, but this time, she extorted him, threatening to show his father explicit sexual photos, and outing him.

Bridget grabbed both dessert spoons. "No sweets for the frowny lady until she tells me why she's sulking."

Eleanor snatched one of the spoons away from her with ease. "I'm not sulking. I'm thinking."

"Oh, please. I know when you're unhappy. You're jealous I asked Cait to help us. She's got a talent. Not that it was hard to install a spy app on a drunk's phone but still..."

"Cute. I'm not jealous of your girlfriend. The only thing I feel for you is obligation."

Bridget frowned. "Liar. You like me...as a friend at least."

"More like a little sister."

"Aw, that's nice." Bridget spooned ice cream and crisp together. "So why don't you have a girlfriend?"

"Who says I don't?"

"Please. I'd know if you did."

"You sound pretty sure of yourself." Eleanor poured herself more tea. "Do you follow me when we're not together?"

"No. Why the hell would I do that?" She frowned. "You're with me most of the day, every day. I'd know if you had a girlfriend."

Eleanor chuckled. "Don't get mad. I'm only teasing. Truth is, I don't do relationships."

"Don't *do*? That's a heavy comment to unpack." Bridget paused. "Did you leave a girlfriend back in Chicago before you moved here to Boston?"

"I did," Eleanor said, lying. "Don't ask me to elaborate because I'm not going to." She hadn't even had a close friend since high school, except for Mandy. They might have been more once, but thankfully they remained friends. She fought the smile emerging and spooned a heaping bite of the apple crisp. The taste instantly transported her to the past. "Mmm. This is as good as my grandma's." Reminiscing and the spontaneous pleasure of the crisp forced the words out. She froze inside and tried to keep her face neutral.

"Your grandma's? Jesus, you *must* think it's incredible. You never talk about your family. Is she dead, too?"

"Nice, Bridget. And you wonder why I don't?"

"Oh, sorry. That was callous. I didn't mean it to be. It just surprised me. You never talk about your past, other than the tragedies."

"Yeah, well, Princess. Those tragedies defined me. You know me now. You know my past."

Bridget dropped her spoon. It clanked against the dessert plate. "Don't call me that, Eleanor. I don't like that fucking nickname." Her voice was loud and angry.

"All right. Calm down." She laid her hand over Bridget's. "I'm sorry. Listen…things are getting stressful, and even I have my breaking point, okay? We've been careful, but sometimes that's not enough." She held Bridget's eyes. "I'm feeling cautious because Cait's naïve. That's all. I don't trust she can handle the role you've given her, and her dad's a dangerous man." She pulled her hand back when Bridget had visibly calmed down.

"Well, stop worrying because it's pissing me off." Bridget looked at the river, and Eleanor observed the slightest twitch in her charge's upper lip. "Anyway, Paddy isn't smart enough to figure out Cait's hacked his phone." Bridget licked her spoon clean and grinned. "Cait's helping, so get used to it. She makes me feel good, and she makes you jealous, which makes me very happy."

Eleanor shook her head. "You're impossible."

"You love me for it." Bridget pointed her spoon at Eleanor. "You didn't answer my question. Is your grandma still alive? If she is, I'd love to meet her."

"She's not. You know my cousin is my only living family." Her voice was cross, hoping to end the conversation. She glanced around the patio and the street beyond. "Listen, you need to tell me your surprise, Bridget. I can't protect you if I don't know all the details. Trust me. If the disclosure has anything to do with tomorrow's meeting, you need to tell me now. We could be walking into a lion's den."

"Don't be so uptight. Everything will work out fine." She picked up her teacup. "You need to trust *me*. It's time a woman took the O'Flaherty business into the future. Create and diversify new products and markets." Bridget lowered her voice. "The drugs I'm selling are different from the usual. They're tailor-made for the Zoomers and Alphas. They're going to make dope and coke a distant memory."

Eleanor kept a neutral face and watched Bridget drink her tea. She had so many questions and needed even more answers. Time was running out. "Your mother pays me to worry," she finally said, resting her elbows on the table and leaning forward. "And because of your side hustle, I have to keep you safe from your family as well as their enemies. Not to mention the authorities. It's not an easy position to be in. How am I supposed to protect you from all the toes you're stomping on?"

"God, you're such a downer. I thought you'd be happy for me. I mean look how I've already put my education to work. With the money I'm going to make I don't need to graduate."

Eleanor stared at her without reacting. Bridget was in her last year of an honors science degree and was already a brilliant chemist. It didn't surprise her that she had designed synthetic drugs, but who was going to manufacture them? It was unlikely Bridget could make them in Northeastern's labs, certainly not in any commercial quantity. Right? Then again, she could make them herself somewhere else. She held Bridget's eyes. "You agreed to keep me in the loop. To tell me everything you were doing. Why shouldn't I get up and leave for good?"

"Because you wouldn't. You don't quit on people. Especially when they need you."

"You seem to be holding your own." Eleanor looked at her indifferently.

"Are you pouting?" Bridget grinned. "Of course I need you, Elle. Besides, if you quit, you'd be walking out on Fiona, and she'd kill you." She burst into laughter but stopped when Eleanor narrowed her eyes.

"You're designing *and* manufacturing, aren't you?" Eleanor sat back in the metal, latticed chair. "Where are you making them?"

"It's a way to keep things one hundred percent, no middle man fucking things up," Bridget growled. She tossed her spoon on the dessert dish. "I'm doing all the prep work in my spare room. I was going to show you and explain everything tonight."

Eleanor sighed. "All right. Does anyone else know?"

Bridget shook her head.

"Are you sure? No one else has gone into that room?"

"You haven't, and you crawl all over my shit more than anyone." Bridget looked around the terrace. "Don't worry about the apartment either. It's not like a meth lab. The building isn't in danger."

"I'm sure everyone living there would be relieved to hear that."

"I'm not stupid." The frustrated look on Bridget's face turned prideful. "When I secure the deal tomorrow for raw materials from the Novikovs, I'll set up a real lab to mass produce. Address to be disclosed later. Promise. Then it's game time."

"First things first. We need to work out the details of tomorrow's meeting. The Novikov family isn't known for playing nice. I'm still unsure why Sasha even agreed to this partnership."

"If she was good enough for my dad, she's good enough for me."

"It's not about you. I've learned Sean severed ties with her after your dad died, and it wasn't a friendly parting."

"I know all about that, too. Sasha knows I'm not Sean, and she knows I'm serious. Now no more work talk. Perk up before we see Cait tonight. When you're in a good mood, she's greedy for my attention. It works like a dream for me." Bridget flashed Eleanor a flirty smile. "Trust me. You have nothing to worry about. We'll work everything out tonight."

"You're sure Fiona didn't ask any suspicious questions today?"

"She didn't. Stop being so paranoid. Sean the idiot doesn't know shit either." Bridget stared at the Charles River and tapped her fingers on the tabletop. After a few minutes, she turned back. "Sorry again for my comments about your family. Why don't you take off the rest of the afternoon? I'll go home. You can walk through the Commons. Clear your head."

"Yeah, all right."

Bridget signed the bill, and a few minutes later, Eleanor shut the black town car door on her charge. "Take her straight home," she said to the driver.

The car pulled away, and she breathed deeply. She was intimately familiar with all the ways tomorrow's meeting could go wrong. Had Patrick found out his daughter, Cait, was spying on him? Was Sasha Novikov's resentment toward Sean Ryan enough to make her double-cross Bridget? What would Sean and Fiona do if they learned about the meeting and Bridget's covert business dealings? Could she salvage everything they'd worked so hard to secure if Sean and Fiona tried to stop Bridget? Things with Bridget and the Maloney family were coming to a head, and she needed more than a walk to destress. She should call Mandy, but first, she wanted to see the only person left in this world who loved her.

She stepped off the curb, waving her hand.

A white taxi swerved from the outside lane and stopped.

"JP. 34 Sedgwick, please," Eleanor said as she sat in the back and closed the door.

CHAPTER THREE

The lead glass door swung open before Eleanor reached the porch of a gray-and-white trimmed shingle-style home in Jamaica Plain. "Ellie," a woman cried, her arms extended with shaking hands. Eleanor's grandmother embraced her, holding her for several minutes before pushing her back at arm's length. "Let me look at you, my sweet girl." She eyed her from head to toe and pulled her inside.

Eleanor walked into the familiar living room. She breathed in the warmth and nostalgia of rose water and lemon cleaner. "I'm sorry it's been so long."

Her grandmother sighed. "I understand. All that matters is you're here now." She led Eleanor to a love seat and removed a heavy afghan throw and an open book. "Sit. I'll make us some tea. Or would you like something stronger?"

"Tea's good."

Her grandmother's gentle hand clung to her arm, not letting go. "Do you want a slice of pumpkin loaf to go with it? I made it yesterday."

"Yes, please." Eleanor's words caught in her throat. "I was hoping you'd baked something."

"Of course. I always have something ready just in case." She finally released Eleanor's arm. "Relax. I'll be right back. We'll have a nice chat in the same room for once." She cupped Eleanor's cheek and wiped away the tears welling. "I've missed you so much."

"It's been tough not seeing you, too, Grandma."

After her grandmother hurried away, Eleanor sat deep into the cushions. The love seat was her favorite spot in the house, and she had napped on its floral, overstuffed cushions more times than she could remember. Her breathing began to slow, and her head began to clear. No matter the risk, this was where she needed to be. She picked up a photo from the side table, a picture of her and her parents covered head to toe in puffy ski clothes in front of a lodge with heavy snow falling. It was the first time they had traveled out of state, and it was one of the best days of her life.

A tea kettle whistled, and Eleanor put the photo back. A few minutes later, her grandmother returned carrying a tray. "I heated your slice and topped it with butter. Just like you like it."

"Aw, thanks." Eleanor sat forward. "How's your garden club?"

"Oh, we're getting on fine, except for Harriet. She passed away a few months ago. Heart attack. Poor dear. I don't think she even suspected anything was wrong with her."

"I'm sorry to hear that." Eleanor carefully inspected her grandmother. "How have you been? Any health concerns I need to know about?"

"Nothing at all." She handed Eleanor a cup. "You know they say seventy is the new sixty."

"You're almost eighty."

"True. And eighty is the new seventy, but I feel as good as I did in my sixties." She sat back in her recliner. "My doctor put me on a cholesterol pill a few months ago, but my numbers weren't too high. She's just a pill pusher." She chuckled and then looked serious. "You're tired, sweet girl. It's your job. I know you won't talk about what you do—"

"I can't talk about it—"

"Of course. Of course. Even if you *can't*…I can tell your work is too stressful…too isolating to be the only thing in your life. Have you got any hobbies? Are you spending time with friends? Seeing anyone special?"

Eleanor smiled. Her grandma asked the same questions every visit. "Not at the moment. My assignment keeps me busy." That was mostly the truth. Eleanor reached for her slice of pumpkin loaf.

"Mm. That's what you said the last time we saw each other." Her grandmother sipped her tea, holding Eleanor's eyes. "You know, you're the same age your father was when he met your mother."

"Grandma, please. They're hardly an endorsement for relationships."

"Don't say that. Your parents loved each other very much." Her grandmother frowned. "It's not our business to know why God gave them such little time together, but it was long enough to bring you into the world, and you were a happy family. Full of love…" Her voice trailed off.

"Sorry. I didn't mean to upset you." Her parents were the last thing Eleanor wanted to talk about. "Things are just stressful right now. That's all."

"I'm sure they are, but don't use that as an excuse. You're in charge of your choices. Not the job. There's more to life than work, Ellie. Friendship and love are necessary too. You can't live without them."

"Apparently, you can't live with them either." Eleanor winced the second the words left her mouth. "I'm sorry. I don't know why I said that. I shouldn't have."

"I'm only sorry you could even think it." Her grandmother sighed. "Love didn't kill your father, and losing your mother wasn't the cause of his death, either. He died from mental illness. That he couldn't accept help breaks my heart every day."

"Maybe I shouldn't have come." She set her cup in its saucer.

"For heaven's sake, my concern for you isn't distress. It's love, and love is nothing to fear, sweet girl." Her grandmother smiled. "I would like you to try to visit more often, not less. You need to talk about the past. It's important."

"I'll try. I promise."

"Good. Now whatever happened to…what was her name…Mandy?"

"I told you Mandy's just a friend." Eleanor sat back into the cushions.

"You did, but things change, don't they?"

"I don't have time for a relationship."

"How about a puppy? Why not adopt some sweet little soul at the shelter?"

Eleanor sighed. "Please don't worry about me, Grandma. My assignment's almost done. When it is, I'll get a hobby. How about I join a garden club like yours and grow roses on my patio? I could even try to create my own variety."

"Wonderful idea. You might even meet a nice woman in the club to give your roses to." Her grandmother grinned and sipped her tea. "Would you like to see my latest hybrid?"

"Love to."

"She's the most stunning color I've ever seen. White with yellow tips. I've named her the Boston Tealight. I haven't entered a hybrid in the New England Rose competition in years, but this year I did. I think she's a winner." Her grandmother led them through the house to the back door, chatting nonstop.

They stepped onto the back porch and Eleanor's phone rang. She looked at the screen. It was Bridget. "Let me take this. You go ahead. I'll be right there." She waited until her grandmother had left the patio. "Hey, is everything okay?"

"No, it's not. I wouldn't be calling if it was." Bridget paused. "Where are you?"

"Doing what you told me to do. Having another cup of tea."

"Where?"

Bridget's tone made Eleanor's heart leap in her chest. "Why?"

"Because I saw you. Why would you hail a cab if you were walking to the Commons?"

"First of all, I'm the one who's supposed to be watching you, not the other way around." Eleanor thought quickly and responded without hesitation. "You suggested the Commons. I decided to go to the Waterfront."

"Fine. Whatever. Go where you want." Her words were abrupt, pitching toward anger. "Cait just called. She's on her way over and said her news couldn't wait. Thanks to your anxiety crawling all over me, I'm freaking out. What if something's wrong? Do you think Paddy found out? What if he forced her to call me? What if he's coming with her?"

"Calm down. That's not likely. Patrick isn't showing up at your door without permission. If he found out what Cait's been doing, you'd be summoned home to face your parents. They'd call me, too, and demand that I bring you. Like last time, right?"

"Maybe. Or maybe Sean has given him the okay to teach me a lesson, *right?*" she mocked. "I need you here, now."

Eleanor looked at her grandmother standing in her rose garden, waiting. "Yeah. All right. Let me wrap up here."

"I'll send the car to pick you up."

"No need. I'll be there in thirty."

"Fine. But don't take any longer." Bridget was getting her way but managed to sound even angrier.

Eleanor ended their call, ordered an Uber, and joined her grandmother in the rose garden. "Hey, I'm so sorry. I have to go in a few minutes."

"Oh, how disappointing." Her grandmother frowned and cupped her cheek. "Do you want the rest of the pumpkin loaf to go?"

"No, I won't be home for a while." Eleanor looked away, unable to keep eye contact.

After a few minutes in the garden, her grandmother led them back to the front door. "Oh, my sweet girl. Thank you for coming." She hugged Eleanor. "Please don't take so long to visit again."

Eleanor steeled herself against the sting in her eyes and the heaviness in her chest. "I won't. I'll see you soon. Promise."

"Okay. I love you."

"Love you, too, Grandma," she said, shutting the door behind her.

The Uber driver waited for Eleanor on the corner. She paid him twenty extra dollars to arrive at Bridget's Fenway neighborhood condominium faster than scheduled. She hurried through the lavish lobby and into the elevator, scanned her card to access the top floors, and knocked on Bridget's door.

"Finally. What'd you do, walk?" Bridget slammed the door behind them and marched into the open-concept room, flopping into a plush armchair.

"I'm early." Eleanor restrained the anger she felt and walked to the kitchen area. She poured herself a glass of water, keeping her back to Bridget.

"You don't have to lie to me if you're sneaking off to see a girlfriend. Like I care."

Eleanor's body tensed. Had Bridget followed her and seen her grandma's house? No. Her charge was too direct. She's fishing. Eleanor calmed herself and sat on a sofa. "Have you heard anything else from Cait?"

"No. She hasn't even texted. She texts nonstop when she's upset. It's so annoying. Why isn't she doing it now? I think Paddy must be with her."

"You're imagining things. If he were with her, he'd make Cait act normal. Make her text you to keep you from suspecting anything." Her reasoning stopped Bridget's downward spiral. She crossed her legs and got comfortable, hoping her relaxed body language would influence Bridget's mood. "Why don't you walk me through the plan for tomorrow? Locking down details calms me when I'm upset."

"Does it? How many crime rings have you started in your bodyguard career?" Bridget asked sarcastically.

"The right question to ask me is how many criminals have you kept safe while they started their illegal enterprises? The answer is more than the number of businesses you've started."

Bridget considered her for a moment and laughed. "Fine. I can't stay mad at you. Although, I don't believe you were—" The doorbell rang. "That's Cait." Bridget jumped to her feet.

"Sit down. I'll check." Eleanor looked at the security monitor on the wall next to the front door. Only Cait stood in the hallway. She scanned through the images from other cameras in the hallway and around the corner. No sign of Patrick or anyone else from the organization. "She's alone," Eleanor called and opened the door. She nodded at Cait, and after the young woman entered, she poked her head into the hallway, checking one more time for anyone tailing her.

"Oh, my freakin' God, Bridget. I got here as fast as I could." Cait dropped her backpack beside the sofa and stripped off a thick woolen sweater. "I heard my dad talking to Sean. He knows what's up. He told Sean he got a tip and would verify the information tonight. He promised the payback would be harsh. She mimicked Patrick's voice. "He said, 'nothing good ever came from her.' And that, 'he should have known.' Then he says, 'it's a good thing you're in charge.' Meaning Sean, of course—"

"Cait," Bridget yelled, stunning her girlfriend's rambling into silence. "I can't understand a fucking thing you're saying."

"I'm sorry…I'm just scared…that's all. I thought you needed to hear what they said." Cait's bottom lip trembled.

Bridget's voice became wheedling. "Sit down and take a breath. Eleanor will get you a glass of water. I just meant you don't have to recite everything you heard. You have recordings of Patrick's calls, right?"

"Yeah. Sorry. I'm just so nervous." Cait's face flushed, and she sat on the sofa. She reached into her purse and pulled out her phone. "Sean called my dad about an hour ago. I followed him into his office and listened. I only heard his side of the conversation. But that was enough to freak me out."

"Well, now would be a good time to listen to the whole thing," Bridget said, without hiding her irritation. She moved from the chair and sat beside Cait.

Eleanor returned and handed Cait a glass of water, sitting on her other side. Cait tapped her phone's screen and quickly pressed the volume button. They leaned closer as a man's voice grew louder.

"Hiya. You know the thing we talked about a couple of weeks ago?"

"Mmhmm."

"I just heard some disturbing information from one of Caleb's old associates. Now I was coaxing it out of him at the time, but he swore it was the truth."

"Mmhmm."

"He confirms we got a big problem." Patrick paused. "I'm going to verify the information tonight. If she is the problem, you can count on me to make the payback harsh. I'm sorry it's just now come to light. Nothing good's ever come from her. I should have known. She's damn good at keeping secrets."

"Mmhmm."

"You want me to take her picture if necessary?" The second voice was silent. "You want me to let it play out?"

"Mmhmm."

"Then that's what I'll do. It's a good damn thing you're in charge. I'll see you in the morning."

Cait ended the recording and looked at them with wide eyes.

Eleanor sat back. She recognized Patrick the Reaper's voice. He was the first speaker. The second voice sounded like Sean Ryan, but a few mmhmms were not much to go on.

"Are you kidding me?" Bridget sucked her teeth and moved back to her chair. "That's what freaked you out? You can't tell what the hell they're talking about. It isn't clear to me. What do you think, Eleanor?"

"It's unclear." She had heard these types of calls before and understood the nuances and the cryptic phrases. "But how likely is it that they're talking about another 'her' and a different 'old associate' when you have a meeting planned with one of your father's old suppliers?"

"Seriously? They could have been talking about anyone. If that asshat had an opportunity to make me look bad, he wouldn't be shy about it. He would have been cursing my name all over that conversation."

Eleanor's chest tightened. Sean's refusal to speak probably indicated he suspected the FBI was recording him. She looked at Bridget. "I know meeting with the Novikovs is important to you. But if Sean suspects anything, it could be too dangerous. We could put off the meeting. Change the time and place."

While Bridget seemed to consider the suggestion, Eleanor disappeared into her head. How did this information affect their plans already in place? If they went forward with tomorrow morning's operation, they would have to reevaluate each scenario and that could take all night.

"Fuck it. Sean Ryan can't touch me now." Bridget's angry voice brought Eleanor back. "I don't care if he knows or not. The meeting's on."

CHAPTER FOUR

Eleanor secured a Glock 22 in her cant holster and donned a houndstooth blazer. She stood in front of a full-length mirror and pinned a gold horseshoe on her lapel, adjusted her collar, and gave herself the once-over. Her eyes were bloodshot from spending all night and into the early morning hours fool-proofing new strategies to secure a positive outcome from Bridget's meeting with Sasha Novikov, which included keeping the Irish princess alive. She smiled. At least she got to reconnect with Mandy. "I'm all set," she said, staring at her reflection.

She poured a cup of coffee, leaned against her kitchen counter, and paged through a file folder. Bridget's plan to work with Sasha Novikov was reckless from the start. She had refused to learn anything about the essential-chemicals supply chain, and if you played with one of the oldest Russian crime families in East Boston, you'd better know their game inside and out. Fortunately for Bridget, Eleanor had compiled a dossier.

She wondered if Bridget knew the history between the Maloneys and the Novikovs. Bridget knew her father had ventured into manufacturing drugs, but did she know the Novikovs had only supplied the raw materials for a few years? Had she heard about the accusations of an affair between Caleb and Sasha? Did she know speculation was that Sasha's family, supposedly her husband, had executed the hit on Caleb outside the family home? Then less than a year later, Fiona married Sean Ryan, Caleb's clan chief, and severed all business ties with the Novikovs. The hostile breakup caused hospitalizations for both organizations.

Eleanor shook her head and closed the folder. Why would Sasha want to work with a Maloney again? It didn't make sense. It was a sticking point she couldn't get past. She topped off her coffee and stood beside her living room window, staring at the road beneath. Three years had passed since the Maloneys demanded she move from her Charleston apartment to Boston's South End, saying it was a job requirement to be near Bridget. The neighborhood was beautiful, and her apartment was generous, but it wasn't her place. Not that she needed more than a roof over her head. Her grandmother had made a home and raised her father and her. What did making a home get her? Nothing but heartache.

She breathed in deeply and exhaled. Maybe she would put down some roots after this operation. Buy a little place with a yard. Plant a rose garden. Hell, she could even join a dating app and convince Mandy to do it with her. She laughed aloud, then quickly said, "Sorry. Just relieving some tension."

Her phone buzzed. She looked down again. Bridget Maloney's driver had arrived. She rinsed out her cup and grabbed her wallet. It was showtime. A few minutes later, the driver stopped in front of Bridget's condominium building on Westland Avenue. Eleanor sent her charge a text. After fifteen minutes with no response, she called Bridget's number. Someone picked up on the first ring.

"What?" Bridget asked, sounding annoyed.

"Did you get my text? We're waiting out front."

"Yeah. I got it," Bridget fired back. "How about a 'good morning' or 'are you ready to kill it this morning?'"

"Good morning. Are you so sure your prey will still be there?"

"She'll wait on me," Bridget said confidently. "Now, chill out. That's an order. I'll be right down."

Eleanor exited the car and stood by the building's entrance. She glanced across the street and up and down the sidewalks, ruminating on why her charge was so sure Sasha Novikov would wait for her. Was Bridget keeping something from her? Fiona Maloney had hired her to protect her daughter, but she had spent the past three years shielding others from Bridget. Her charge was brilliant. Charming. But if you crossed her, or if she no longer had use for you, she became the most dangerous person in your life.

"Good morning, grumpy," Bridget said as she hooked her arm around Eleanor's and pulled her toward the car. "Haven't had enough coffee, huh? We'll have plenty at the bakery. And meat turnovers. I'm starving."

"I've had enough coffee, thank you, and I'm not in a bad mood. Someone has to take your appointment with Sasha Novikov seriously. I'm not convinced her intentions are above board, especially after the call Cait captured." She opened the car's back door for Bridget and got in on the other side.

Bridget shifted her body to face Eleanor and lifted Eleanor's jacket lapel. "You're wearing your lucky horseshoe. Jesus, you are nervous. It's nice to know my safety concerns you so much, or are you afraid my mom will kill you if anything bad happens to me?" She stared at Eleanor then burst out laughing. "I'm kidding. You are uptight. When was the last time you got laid?"

"None of your business." Eleanor straightened her blazer. "Time to be serious, please? We'll be at Eryn's in fifteen minutes. Now's the time to tell me if you've kept anything from me." She held Bridget's eyes. "I have to anticipate all scenarios. You understand, right?"

Bridget sat back in the car's soft leather seat. "Of course I do. You know everything you need to know. Sasha agreed to supply my raw materials—"

"Exactly. Why did she agree to work with you? Considering the past."

"Maybe she needs the goddamn business, Elle." Bridget raised her voice. "Why can't you accept she wants to work with me because it'll make her a shit ton of money."

"All right. Calm down. It's my job to be skeptical. I wasn't demeaning your work."

"Fine." She stared out the window. "Once we get there, you'll see. She's excited about it." Bridget turned back and held up her purse, shaking it. "Once her daughter tests my product, she'll be hooked on me."

"Only Sasha's daughter will be with her?"

"Yeah. Her name's Kira. She's taking over the business." A look of anger crossed Bridget's face, and she mumbled, "Like it should be. Family."

"We need to be ready for uninvited guests." She lowered her voice in case the driver had misplaced loyalties. "If your stepfather and his men arrive, are you prepared for me to protect you in any way necessary?"

Bridget feigned a look of panic. Then she laughed and opened her pink Louis Vuitton tote, flashing a Sig Sauer. "As if I wouldn't take him out myself. I wouldn't even need a reason." She closed her purse. "Sean Ryan isn't going to stand in the way of my success. Trust me."

"I do trust you, but I want you to keep the gun in your purse. If they show up, let me take care of Sean. It's my job." She paused. "Have you heard from Cait?"

"No. And I won't be anytime soon. I broke up with her. I can't take her drama. And that high-pitched voice. God, it drove me crazy." Bridget checked her phone. "Still nothing. I told you that the call wasn't about us. Did Paddy check you out last night? No. And no one showed up at my door either." She sucked her teeth. "Like I said, Paddy and the idiot were talking about a different *her* and another *old associate*."

They rode the rest of the way to Eryn's Bakery in silence. When they arrived, Eleanor saw two women sitting at a table near an empty playground. They wore large black sunglasses, and the older woman turned and watched their car approach.

"Why are they waiting for us in the park?" Eleanor asked.

"How should I know?"

They stepped out of the car. Eleanor saw a closed sign hung in the bakery's window and a piece of paper attached to its front door. "Did you know Eryn's was closed today?"

Bridget shook her head.

"I don't like this at all. Changing locations affects my plans for protecting you." Eleanor put on a pair of dark sunglasses and quickly scanned the park. The green space could only be accessed from the street on the left and the parking lot, and it was filled with old American beech trees, each wide enough to hide behind.

"Stop stressing me out. Jesus, let me wear your lucky horseshoe." Bridget thrust her hand out, and Eleanor stared at her, trying to remain calm. "Come on, Elle. Please. I feel nervous now."

"All right." She removed it from her lapel and pinned it on her charge's coat. It was the second thing to go awry, and she was unsure whether they could make the necessary adjustments.

"Let's do this," Bridget said. "Everything will be okay. I'll make the deal, and we'll leave. In and out." They joined the women, and a smile spread across her face. "Mrs. Novikov, I'm thrilled to meet you in person, and this beautiful woman must be your sister. You look so much alike."

Sasha chuckled. "You're charming, like your father," she said with a heavy Russian accent. "Call me Sasha. This is my daughter, Kira Novikov Rodin." She patted her daughter's arm. "Kira, this is Bridget O'Flaherty Maloney." Sasha's daughter forced her frown into a thin smile but said nothing.

"Nice to meet you, Kira." Bridget removed her coat and sat. The overcast sky reflected a glare off the metal patio table that made everyone look as if they were deeply concerned. Bridget retrieved her sunglasses from her bag and placed her folded coat on her lap. "Thank you both for meeting with me."

"I would insist we talk over a drink and pastry, but it seems the bakery is closed for a family emergency," Sasha said.

"Oh? Is that why? Let me see what I can do." Bridget scooted back.

"Don't bother," Sasha said. "I peeked inside. The display cases are empty. I think I saw someone in the back. But I doubt we'd get any favors."

"That's a shame. I was craving a turnover for lunch." Bridget scraped her chair across the stone pulling up to the table again. "Why don't we get right to business? Sasha, I'm sure my father was incredibly thankful for the relationship you and he had. Like I told you, I want to walk in his footsteps. Distributing and manufacturing. Your products will help me do that. But before we talk business, I have a personal question for you."

Eleanor tensed. Bridget said nothing about asking Sasha Novikov a personal question. She swore under her breath. *This.* This was the kind of thing she needed to know about beforehand.

"What is it?" Sasha asked in an easy voice.

"I want to know if the Novikovs had anything to do with my father's death." Bridget slipped her hand inside her bag, and Kira's hands moved under the table.

The last thing the operation needed was Bridget losing her shit, Eleanor thought, but before she could grab Bridget's arm, Sasha laid her hand on her daughter's forearm and Kira's body relaxed.

"Are you mad?" Sasha's voice was harsh. "Of course we didn't. Your father was my friend. I would never have hurt him. And I can assure you my family had no part in his murder either. God rest his soul." She crossed herself.

"That's the answer I was hoping for." Bridget removed her hand from her bag and placed her cell phone on the table. "Did you know my father was a chemist?"

"Yes. Your father was a brilliant man. He made quality products. They were safe and highly profitable. His market was so hungry for them that we supplied him monthly." Sasha pulled out a folder from her bag and handed it to Bridget. "I read your proposal and understand you are creating a much different product. Your market will be considerably smaller. This is the inventory of what you will need. We've broken down costs and included a delivery schedule. Take a look. You can let me know what you think later."

Bridget set the folder to the side. "My market will be huge. Like I told you, I'm a chemist, too. But I'm making a product not even my father could've imagined. I'm taking designer drugs to a whole new level. Whatever you based those numbers on will grow exponentially once my product hits the market." She turned her attention to Kira. "What's your pleasure?"

"Kira doesn't use drugs," Sasha said brusquely.

Bridget laid her hand on her chest. "My apologies. But I don't think you know your daughter as well as you think you do."

"My mother's correct. I don't do drugs," Kira said. "Sometimes I smoke a little weed."

"Right." Bridget grinned. "Most people consider weed a drug. But that's beside the point. I'm interested in knowing why you like to burn one?"

"Usually to sleep."

"Does it work?"

"I guess so. Most of the time. Why?" Kira's voice grew annoyed.

"Because I can make a synthetic cannabinoid with sleep properties. No smoke. No eating. No hangover effects." Bridget pulled out a small green baggie with a few white pills from her bag. "I'm not creating designer drugs. I'm creating bespoke drugs. Tailored to an individual's needs. Why should big pharma have all the business?"

Kira slid her sunglasses over her head and reached for the baggie. "Is that what this is?"

"No. These would be more than just sleep aids for you." Bridget handed her the bag. "Let's say you want to lose a little weight. Who doesn't, right? And you want to do it without a lot of effort. Why not do it while getting high and sleeping? Think of that pill as a safer version of grass and a weight loss drug like Qsymia combined."

Kira shook the baggie. "I would definitely give it a try."

"That's enough." Sasha grabbed the pills out of Kira's hand. "We supply precursors. We don't buy finished product. If I find you have confused the two and sell anything to my daughter, we will stop supplying your raw materials."

Kira glared at her mother, pulled her sunglasses down over her eyes, and sat back.

"All right. No problem. Just thought I'd share a preview of my merchandise."

Sasha examined the pills and then held out the baggie. "What is the BBB?"

"Bespoke by Bridget. Catchy, right?" Bridget smiled, and Sasha tossed the baggie back to her.

"Let me share some advice. It is unwise to sign your product with initials. A butterfly or dragon, sure. But not identifiers. If we do business, you'll have to stop marking them this way." She sighed heavily. "Take a look at our numbers. As long as you pay our retainer, we can work out the details later."

Bridget tapped her fingertips on the folder. "I have one more question before I decide if I want to do business with you."

Again, Eleanor shouted in her head. Bridget was going off script again. She kept her body from reacting.

"Oh?" Sasha gestured with her hand. "Go on then. What else do you want to know?"

"Did my mother know you and my father were screwing?"

Kira's chair scraped against the stone patio as she lunged toward Bridget, and Eleanor flung her body between her charge and Kira's hand while Sasha grabbed the back of her daughter's coat and yanked her back.

"Sit down. Don't be foolish," Sasha shouted. The head of the Novikov crime family waited for everyone to regain their composure. Then she rested her hands on the tabletop. "You have a lot of confidence for a schoolgirl. I admire that. Did you think I would deny my affair with your father? Because I won't. As for your mother, I suppose she suspected it. She might even have secured proof. But I wasn't the only one. Your father had many women."

Bridget's upper lip twitched. Eleanor knew the sign. Her charge was losing control.

"Listen, let's get back to the business proposal," Eleanor said. "The past is in the past. We need to focus on right now."

"Fine." Bridget opened Sasha's file folder and scanned the pages. After a few minutes, she pulled out an envelope from her purse. "Looks good to me. Here's the retainer." Bridget reached across the table.

A black SUV skidded to a stop on the street beside the park. Instinctively, Eleanor laid her hand on her Glock, adrenaline surging through her body.

It was Sean Ryan.

"What the hell is he doing here? Did you do this?" Bridget yelled at the Novikovs.

"I don't know what you're talking about. Who is it?" Sasha asked, a hint of panic in her voice. "What's going on?"

Sean, Thomas, and Patrick exited the SUV. Eleanor's mind raced. Who were they here for? What were they going to do?

Kira pulled a pistol from her bag and faced the men striding across the park toward them.

"Hold up, Kira," Eleanor said. "There's no need for that. Let's hear what they have to say."

Bridget's phone buzzed. She read the screen, shoved the folder and the money into her tote, and ran toward the bakery.

"Bridget? Wait!" Eleanor stood, but before she had time to follow, Sean, Thomas, and Patrick drew their guns and fired. A bullet whizzed past her head, and she pushed the heavy metal table on its side. The three women hit the ground, hiding behind it.

Suddenly several more vehicles rolled up, screeching to a stop, and people poured out of them with guns drawn, shouting commands. Eleanor heard Sean yell, "Go, go, go. It's the Feds."

"You and that little bitch will pay for this," Sasha screamed in Eleanor's face as voices closed in on them.

Eleanor had prepared for this scenario. She knew what Sean Ryan was capable of. He would kill her in a heartbeat, but would he kill Fiona Maloney's daughter? The gunfire had ceased, and she cautiously peered around the table and scrambled to her feet. Bridget had disappeared inside the bakery. The men were nearing the door. Eleanor sprinted toward the parking lot, refusing the federal agents' commands for her to stop. She might have to answer for it later. But Sean Ryan wasn't going to kill Bridget Maloney. Not on her watch.

Less than ten feet from the bakery's door, there was a blinding flash of light, a deafening roar, and then a spray of glass. The instant Eleanor was thrown backward played out in slow motion until everything around her sped up, and she slammed against something hard.

CHAPTER FIVE

A warm heaviness covered Eleanor's body. She opened her eyes to see a man leaning over her, adjusting the warmth. What was it? She searched for the word, and it finally came to her. Blanket. She stared at the man's profile. He had deep brown eyes, his expression soft. She glanced at his uniform and around the room. Stark taupe walls, a chair, and a dresser. A large window with closed blinds. It was a hospital room.

"You're awake. That's good." The nurse smiled. "You've been unconscious for a few days."

A loud whooshing sound filled her head, making the nurse's voice sound far away. Distorted. She panicked and grabbed his arm, putting her other hand over her ear.

"Do you remember the explosion?" he asked.

She let go of the nurse's arm, closing her eyes, and a blur of images flooded back. Bridget ran toward Eryn's bakery. Kira Novikov pointed her pistol at Sean, Thomas, and Patrick. Sean fired his gun. Other voices closed in. Then the images stopped. She didn't remember an explosion. Why couldn't she?

"Hey, you're okay," he said, gently touching her hand. "Your eardrums were blown apart and you've had surgery to put them back together. A bilateral tympanoplasty. Your hearing should return to normal. It might take some time." He pressed a button on a monitor, and a cuff around Eleanor's arm tightened. It brought her focus to her body. She wiggled her toes and moved her feet and legs, and then she winced at the fire in her abdomen.

"Are you in pain?"

Eleanor nodded, and the nurse pressed another button on the IV pole. "You've had some internal bleeding from the blast. Dr. Kozlowski will explain everything to you. Right now, you need to rest. You're on a basal rate of morphine, but if you still feel pain, this is your PCA, a patient-controlled analgesia pump. You can press this bolus and receive an extra dose. I just gave you one, so another won't be available for a while." He placed a small clicker on the pillow beside her head. "You can manage it from now on." The nurse gently touched her arm, and she looked at him again. "Is there anything else I can get you?"

Eleanor shook her head and watched him speak with an officer posted outside her door before he left. After their brief exchange, the officer used his cell phone. Telling someone she was awake, she thought and stared at the ceiling. What the hell had exploded? Where were Bridget and Sean? The Novikovs? Arrested? Where was Mandy?

A euphoric sensation began to cloud Eleanor's mind. She felt heavy. Her thoughts and the pain in her body began to melt away. Then her eyes grew heavy, and her eyelids fell.

Eleanor woke again later. At once she realized she had a visitor. The woman sat in an armchair beside her bed. "I've been waiting for you to come around." She looked toward the window. "I had tulips delivered to brighten up your room."

The woman's voice was muffled, and Eleanor's head felt woozy, but she made out the flower bouquet on a small table under the window. "Garcia," she said, finding her voice.

Mandy Garcia held Eleanor's hand. "You scared the crap out of me. We've been in tough situations, but that was the worst. When I saw you run after Ryan and his men…" She shook her head. "I was so pissed. That was not your order. If you had gone ten seconds earlier…"

"What?" Eleanor tried to lift herself and fell back.

"Are you in pain? Do you want a nurse?"

"No. I'm okay." She blinked slowly. "What the hell happened?"

"I was going to ask you the same question. You didn't know anything about it?"

"I don't even know what *it* is."

"There was an explosion."

"I don't remember."

"It was at Eryn's Bakery. The entire building blew right after Sean and his men ran in there to escape our sting and you'd run halfway across the parking lot." She took a deep breath and slowly exhaled. "The fire service could only contain the scene and protect the surrounding buildings. The bakery's gone. Our emergency response team had to wait a few days to collect evidence. The preliminary report is an incendiary bomb. They found accelerant patterns." Mandy hesitated. "The four civilians who went in all died. ERT is processing, but there isn't much left."

Eleanor opened her mouth and shut it. The words wouldn't come. Bridget running toward the bakery, calling for her, flashed into her mind. An explosion made no sense. Her thoughts jumbled, and she tried to focus on one thing at a time. "I didn't follow her right away because Sean Ryan started shooting at her or the team."

Mandy lifted her brows. "Sean fired on *you*. That's why we went with Omega plan and converged."

"No, that's not right." Eleanor tried to sit up again. The movement sent a searing pain through her abdomen. She had lied to Mandy. The pain was growing intense, but she needed to stay alert. The veil of the last morphine dose had lifted, and the scene's details were seeping through. If she hit the button, everything Mandy told her and anything she remembered would slip away. She couldn't risk it. She needed answers.

"I'm just thanking the universe you didn't immediately follow her," Mandy said, her voice faltering.

"There should be five," Eleanor said as Mandy walked away.

"Five what?" Mandy asked.

"Remains. There were five people inside Eryn's. Sasha Novikov said she saw an employee inside when she arrived and found the bakery shut."

"She didn't mention that in her interviews. You're sure?"

"I'm positive."

"Whoever it was must have left before the explosion. We interviewed all the bakery's employees. A few had been inside earlier that morning but had left before the explosion. No one was missing." Mandy's phone buzzed, and she read her screen. "I need to respond to this message."

A sharp sting in her gut seized Eleanor, and she grabbed the PCA.

"Is that a pump for pain?" Mandy asked, looking up from her text. "Use it, please."

"Not yet. Do we suspect the Novikov family planted the bomb?"

"Sasha and Kira lawyered up. They deny having anything to do with it. Sasha said she met Bridget for social reasons. She denies telling Sean about the meeting. We contacted sources in the Novikov organization and haven't received any intel connecting them to the explosion. Drug enforcement hasn't heard any chatter connecting them either." Mandy leaned closer to Eleanor. "It could be any number of people. Bridget had moved into a high-intensity drug trafficking area. She was about to irritate a lot of people. You know we considered something like this might happen. I just wish we would have been in front of it."

Eleanor closed her eyes and saw Bridget. Sadness overwhelmed her. Should she have stopped her? It would have kept her safe. No, it wasn't her role, but the guilt didn't lessen knowing she kept her own cover safe. What about Fiona? She and Bridget seemed to be getting along. They had planned a trip to France. Then someone takes Bridget's life. And Sean's. There was no telling what Fiona's retribution would be.

When Eleanor opened her eyes a few minutes later, she looked past Mandy's shoulder. A woman and a man stood beside the officer posted at her door, showing him their badges.

"Hey." Mandy touched her arm. "Do you need to sleep? I can come back in a few hours."

"No. I was thinking about our case."

"That's something else we need to talk about." Mandy hesitated, her hand gently rubbing Eleanor's arm. "I have to take you off the team—"

"Take me off ? Until I recover?"

"You're a witness, now, Peters. The attorney general's case against the O'Flaherty crime organization depends solely on you, especially now with Bridget—our leverage—gone, and you know enough that your life is in danger. We don't know what Fiona Maloney thinks happened at Eryn's, but we suspect Eleanor Watts has been compromised." Mandy frowned. "God, I hate this so much, but there isn't any other way." She turned to the door and gestured at the woman and man waiting there.

The woman entered, walking briskly. She wore jeans and a light-gray, long-sleeved polo top. Law enforcement, Eleanor decided. She stopped beside Mandy, glanced around, realized there were no more chairs, and settled into a comfortable stance.

"Hello, Special Agent Peters. I'm Deputy Marshal Joanna Stevens. Deputy Marshal Sam Nguyen is also here."

"Oh, come on," Eleanor said, staring at Mandy. "Are you serious?"

"Take my seat, Marshal Stevens." Mandy moved and sat at the foot of the bed. "I promise it's just until we have enough evidence against Fiona for a grand jury."

"She's right, Eleanor," Joanna said. She had a warm smile. Genuine. "May I call you Eleanor?"

"Yeah. Fine."

"Okay. You can call me Joanna. This is where we are. The attorney general has been updated on the O'Flaherty case and has signed off on your application to the witness protection program." She paused as Eleanor groaned in frustration. "I understand your reluctance. This is a lot to process, and you can talk to me about anything. I'm here to answer your questions."

"All right. Why'd the AG sign off on this?" Eleanor demanded. "What's the threat against my life?"

"Okay. Good question. As Special Agent in Charge Garcia said, you're the sole witness for the Bureau's investigation into the O'Flaherty crime ring. That's enough to place you in the witness security program. You might be thinking if you remained undercover, you could stay safe, but we believe there is credible evidence to suggest your cover has been compromised." She opened a small notebook and read. "Sean Ryan opened fire on you and the Novikovs. At this time, we do not know if they acted alone, or in coordination with Fiona Maloney. Directly after the explosion, the Bureau swept your apartment for evidence of the investigation or your identity. Less than an hour later, several known O'Flaherty operatives entered your apartment and searched it."

"Search is a nice way of putting it," Mandy interrupted. "They trashed it."

"Agreed. That would be a more accurate description." Joanna hesitated. "Finally, over the last two days, FBI and DEA sources have confirmed talk about a contract on your life. We believe Fiona Maloney put it out, but, at this time, we cannot eliminate the Novikovs."

Eleanor looked away. She recalled Cait's recording. So, Bridget was right—and wrong. Sean and Patrick's conversation wasn't about Bridget's and Sasha's arrangement—it was about her. But how did he know? She had been careful. Someone on the inside had to have given her up. But who? "It makes sense," Eleanor murmured. "They knew about me." She stared at the ceiling, fighting back the sting behind her eyes. "Fiona hasn't sent a lawyer to speak for me, right? That's another sign she's cut me loose."

"I'm so sorry," Mandy said.

"I understand you think WITSEC is an undesirable solution, but it's the only viable one we have right now," Joanna said. "Nguyen and I will move you to a safe medical location tonight, and when you are able, we'll take you to a safe house. SAC Garcia's team… your old team…gathered some of your belongings. The bag will be waiting. You'll continue to be under medical supervision, and I promise we'll make you as comfortable as possible. Hopefully, we can quickly secure arrest warrants and a trial. In the meantime, I'll be your WITSEC inspector."

"All right." Eleanor felt resigned to the situation. Her nearly three-year undercover investigation had blown up along with Eryn's Bakery. She knew these cases seldom made their way through the courts in a few months or even a few years. She wouldn't be testifying anytime soon, and there was no way to know when she would get her life back.

Mandy patted her leg. "You have one more visitor if you feel up to it. Hal Macon with the US Attorney's Office, or he can meet with you tomorrow if that's better for you."

"I'm okay. He can come now."

"Are you sure?" Mandy asked. "Your words say yes, but I can see pain all over your face."

"I'm fine. He's just coming to tell me how my screw-up… Bridget's death…set our case back, right?"

"Nobody thinks that, Peters. No one's judging you. He only wants to explain their case and your part in it. That's all."

Joanna stood. "Listen, I'm going to go. I need to finish preparations for your transfer, but Nguyen will be at the door until I return. We're not allowing anything to happen to you in our care. Okay?"

Eleanor nodded and watched her leave. Then she rolled her head side to side on her pillow. *WITSEC.* She hadn't wanted anyone's protection since she was a child. She sure the hell didn't want babysitters as an adult.

"We secured both your phones." Mandy patted Eleanor's leg and returned to the chair. "I can't give them back to you, but I have been in touch with your grandmother."

"Oh, my God. Don't tell me you sent agents to her house. It traumatized her when they came after my dad…"

"Of course not. I know that. I called her when you got out of surgery, and I've been texting her updates. I'll call and let her know you're awake. Is there anyone else you want me to contact?"

Eleanor shook her head no, and the pain in her abdomen caught her breath.

"Hey, let's take a break from this conversation." Mandy held Eleanor's hand again. "Do you remember when we went on spring break to that resort in the Yucatan? God, we had such a great time. Dancing all night."

"Yeah." Eleanor chuckled and flinched in pain.

"After the last time we went to that club on the beach, I swore off drinking ever again for the rest of my life." Mandy laughed and held Eleanor's hand tighter. "After we met at the Academy, I knew we'd be friends, but I'm not going to lie. The first time I saw you with all that messy, curly brown hair and those big brown eyes, I hoped we would be more." Her eyes welled. "I'm glad we didn't, though. I couldn't ask for a better friend."

"You're acting like I'm dying or something, Garcia." Eleanor tried to lighten the mood, but the pain made her groan softly and the meds made her feel emotional. "It wasn't just you, you know…after the Academy. But even though I felt it, I couldn't take that step. You know? After my dad…I guess something in me is broken."

"Don't say that. You love me, I know that." Mandy wiped her eyes. "I'm sorry to get so heavy. It's just…whatever happens, no matter how long it takes to bring the O'Flahertys down, you'll always be my best friend. Now push that damn button and give yourself some relief. That's an order."

PART TWO

Death is a Dialogue between
The Spirit and the Dust.
"Dissolve" says Death—The Spirit, "Sir
I have another Trust"—
                            –Emily Dickinson

CHAPTER SIX

North Cascades, Washington 2025

Kate Hall propped her backpack against a dead tree trunk. The chill in the air had dissipated with the sun, and the sky stretched blue as far as she could see. Mornings like this made life worth living. That and Jenny. Well, mostly Jenny. Sticking her thumb and finger in her mouth, she whistled a sharp trill. Jenny's low bay replied, and a burst of swallows rose from the alpine meadow.

The bloodhound's deep reddish brown and dappled gray face cleared a patch of lupine blooms.

"You got all the birds excited, sweet girl." Kate rubbed the dog's head with both hands. Then she pulled out a homemade biscuit from her backpack. "Here you go. Now stay with me. No more running off." Before Kate had stopped talking, Jenny had finished her treat and licked Kate's hand. "I love you, too."

They hiked on, and Kate searched for evidence of a southbound herd of hikers. The rangers had told her the SoBo group was halfway finished with the grueling Pacific Crest Trail's Section K and had reached the McGregor Mountain Trailhead. Thru-hikers, those hardy souls who walked the entire PCT, earned bonus miles if they reached the mountain's summit, and for eight years, Kate had provided trail magic along the path, most recently at a burned-out area off the trail where an illegal campsite had popped up. The area had no natural water source, so she brought water, soda, and juice for the hikers braving the climb.

Jenny ran farther ahead, looking back at Kate every so often. She led them to the McGregor Mountain Trail junction, passing Lake Howard, and the ascent started with long, dusty switchbacks. Their trek was about a mile to the dry campsite. Once there, Kate slipped off her pack, steadied her hobble, and filled a collapsible bowl with water. Jenny panted hard, her pink tongue lolling out the side of her mouth. "Here you go, sweet girl." She put the bowl on the ground. Then she sat on a charred log, shut her eyes, and relaxed, listening to Jenny lap water and the distant tapping of downy woodpeckers echoing through the trees.

After waiting two hours without the hikers showing up, they headed back down the trail. It was unusual not to see anyone at the dry camp, but the herd could have been farther along than she thought. Once they reached the PCT, Kate followed the park rules and leashed Jenny. Usually being on a lead irritated the old hound, but by this time in their journey, she happily walked by Kate's side. The youthful burst of energy Jenny had when they started their day had surrendered to age. "We might need to skip Tumwater and make the dry camp our only Friday destination, what do you think?" The old hound stopped and looked at her as if she understood, and Kate chuckled. "I'm only saying *we* might not get so tired if we shortened our hike."

An hour later, they neared the PCT junction at Stehekin Valley Road. Another trail angel was there, sharing magic from his old white van, and a group of hikers sat around on the folding chairs he provided. His name was Kyle from Marblemount, and he showed up once a month, but Kate did her best to avoid him. She preferred to be a low-key helper. He liked to make a splash with loud music and grilled food.

The glint of metal caught Kate's attention. An old Land Rover had pulled over. She had seen the Rover and its driver around the area for a few months. On Saturday mornings, she often saw the woman at the coffee shop in Granite Creek, not that she was taking notes. Although she had given her the once-over, and she was good-looking. Okay, that wasn't fair. She was hot. Exactly the kind of woman to avoid, Kate reminded herself, which she had successfully done for now. But how much longer could she avoid a new park ranger?

Jenny caught the scent of grilled meat and bayed. Her deep, low sounds caught Kate's attention. She had been watching the woman walk toward Kyle's van. Embarrassment heated her face, and she quickly led Jenny off the trail. There was no place in her life for someone who set her body buzzing unless they were only in the area for a day or two.

She and Jenny cut through the woods and returned to the road farther away from the group. A few minutes later, a voice called behind them, "Hey, are you Angel Hall?"

Kate turned around and saw three women trekking toward her. She recognized the bold colors of their bucket hats from the group at Kyle's van. "Hold up a minute." The tall, lanky one waved. When they caught up with Kate and Jenny, she said, "I knew when I saw Jenny it must be you. Do you remember me? I did a SoBo a few years ago and stayed at the Hall."

Kate tried to recall the woman's face. Then it dawned on her. "Oh, yeah. Chris…no, Crystal."

The woman nodded her head enthusiastically. "Yeah. That's right. I was with a friend, but she bailed and took a flight home from Seattle, and I decided not to finish solo." She pointed to the other women. "This is Josey and Arlie."

"Hi. Nice to meet you," Kate said.

Josey and Arlie were all smiles, and Crystal continued, "I told them all about Hostel Hall. How much fun we had hanging out in the communal room."

Kate patted Jenny's back. "We're heading back there right now. Are you staying with us again?"

"Not this time," Crystal said. "But we did plan to gain some bonus miles with a visit. Running into you out here saved some mileage."

The three women took turns rubbing Jenny's head. The old hound was one of the more popular destinations in this section of the PCT, and she loved the attention. Most of the thru-hikers at Hostel Hall had to leave their pets behind at home for months. Kate figured spending time with Jenny filled a need other people on their journey couldn't meet.

Crystal continued chatting about her past stay at the hostel and how the Hostel Hall's Lounge was the coolest place on the PCT to recuperate and meet other hikers. They looked like they'd heard the stories too many times but were good-humored about listening to them again.

Kate maintained a pleasant smile even though the idea that hikers talked about her when they left the area made her uncomfortable. She had made a home at the hostel because she wanted people who came into her life to be traveling through, never stopping for too long or remembering too much.

"Well, I better be getting back," Kate said at the first lull in the conversation. "You all have a great trek. I don't know if you had planned to hike the Agnes Gorge Trail, but if you did, it's closed. There are two fires in the area."

"That's terrible," Arlie said.

"We're headed to Bullion Camp for the night," Crystal said.

"That's good. Safe travels."

"Wait," Crystal said, holding a camera she had strapped around her neck. "Can we take a selfie with you?"

"Sorry. I don't take pictures."

"Oh, no problem." A smile wavered on Crystal's mouth. "It was nice to see you again."

"You, too. Have a safe journey."

Twenty minutes later, Kate followed Jenny into an old-growth forest of huge western red cedar. Their surroundings became darker and the air cooler and heavy with the scent of decomposing forest litter. She thought about Crystal and her friends, and how most people were careless with their privacy. The women probably documented every moment of their journey, posting pictures on the Internet where anyone with a little know-how could pinpoint their location. Then again not everyone had to hide where they were.

By the time they entered a brief clearing, the sun had begun to slip behind the tree line, washing the glade in an amber glow. Hostel Hall stood in the open space, looking like an old motor hotel off Route 66 had been dropped in the middle of a forest. It had an owner's house on one end, connected to a communal space and a row of dormitory-style rooms, and a smaller apartment at the other. She unleashed Jenny, and the hound ran through a blanket of pink and purple fireweed, across the hostel's yard, and onto a wide front porch that ran the length of the building.

A young woman opened the communal room's front door and shouted, "Jenny's home!" She played keep-away with a red ball, working up the old hound until she let out a deep bay, then threw the ball into the yard. Jenny bounded from the porch after it.

Kate glanced at her watch, pleased they'd returned in time to help Nicole set up the communal room for the evening Lounge. Their guests occupied all seven of the hostel's four-bed dorm rooms, and it would be busy.

"Hey, boss. How was your hike?"

"Great. How was the morning Lounge?" Kate thought about how easy it was to lie. Their hike wasn't great, it hadn't even been good. They hadn't handed out any magic. Jenny was slowing down, and the women she met left her unsettled. She hadn't felt that sickening pit in her stomach for years.

"Did you hear me?" Nicole asked. "Hey? You okay?"

"Yeah, I'm fine. I'm sorry, what did you say?"

"I said my parents are stressing me out."

"Why?" Kate opened her front door, and Jenny ran down a hallway off the main room. She followed the hound and opened a door to the butler's pantry, which connected the communal area to her home.

"They want me to come back and get a real job. Like this isn't one. Rude, right? They don't respect my decisions. It's my degree. I'll use it the way I want."

Jenny ran to her bowl, and Kate filled it with kibble. "They probably just miss you, Nic. When was the last time you visited?"

"My graduation."

"Exactly. That was two years ago. I'd want to see you, too, if I were your mother. You're so adorable."

Nicole didn't crack a smile at Kate's teasing. "They aren't asking me to visit. They want me to move back home. You sound like you're taking their side."

"Oh, no. I'm not on anybody's side."

"Sounds like you are."

"Well, I'm not, so don't pout. I don't want you to go anywhere, but I understand how your parents feel. It's hard not to see family. Worse when you don't have any left. I'm just saying don't let too much time pass before you visit." Kate opened the door leading into the communal room and grabbed a tray of brownies. "I'll help you set up for the evening Lounge."

Nicole picked up a tray of cinnabuns with thick white icing and followed Kate inside. They placed the pastries on a long banquet table draped in white linen. Behind it was an equally long counter with cupboards, refrigerated storage, and a dishwasher underneath. Kate retrieved milk and cream while Nicole removed a rack of mugs from the dishwasher and stacked them next to two large coffee urns.

"I'm sorry. I didn't mean to make you sad," Nicole said, after a long silence.

"You didn't make me sad. I just have a lot on my mind."

Jenny trudged over and sniffed along the buffet table. "Hey, Jenny-benny." Nicole squatted face-to-face with the old hound, letting Jenny cover her face in big wet slurps. "Who gives the best kisses?"

"I wouldn't let Vivienne catch you saying that."

"Oh my God, right?" Nicole laughed and stood up. "She wouldn't kiss me until I showered if she knew Jenny slobbered all over my face. I don't think she was raised with pets."

"Don't the French love their pets as much as we do?"

"Outliers exist everywhere."

That's the truth, Kate thought, trying to keep her expression neutral. The last thing she wanted Nicole to know was that something about Vivienne bothered her. "Grab a case of cold beer, and I'll restock the laundry soap. I think that'll do it." She stacked single-use laundry soap boxes at the end of the table for the free washers and dryers. It was a hostel perk that helped thru-hikers stave off hiker funk and kept the communal room's furniture smelling clean.

A few minutes later, some of their guests arrived. Kate greeted them as they walked through the buffet. Jenny had sprawled out on a rug near the gas fireplace. The hikers filled their plates and sat on the floor around the old hound, and she eagerly accepted their petting.

Kate smiled. Jenny had a way of bringing people together. "Do you need anything else?" she asked Nicole.

"We're all good."

"All right. I'll leave you to it. Send Jenny home before nine."

"Will do," Nicole said, and then she looked at the door and waved.

Kate followed her gaze. Vivienne had just entered, but she didn't wave back. She only glanced in their direction and dropped onto a sofa beside a guest strumming one of the Lounge guitars. The slight didn't surprise Kate. Nicole's girlfriend seldom wanted to be around her.

"Viv looks upset. I think she got more bad news today," Nicole said in a low voice. "You know she's been in the area for a year, right?"

"Wow, already a year."

"Yeah. Did I tell you she's here on a student visa?"

"You did. The Art Institute of Seattle."

"Yeah. About that. She stopped attending a while back."

"Oh, that's not smart," Kate said in her old law enforcement voice. Surprised, she tamped it down. She had no obligation to that world anymore.

"We know. She tried to change her visa but hasn't heard anything. The only thing is her grace period is up soon."

"So what's the plan?"

"She doesn't want to leave, and I don't want her to go." Nicole hesitated. "She'll wait for a response, but she's going to stay even if Immigration and Customs Enforcement deny her request."

"Really?" Not a bright move, Kate thought. She knew ICE wouldn't look for Vivienne. Not with her pale skin. But if she were ever pulled over for a traffic stop, she'd be deported and have a hard time returning to the country.

Nicole stared at her, waiting for a response.

"Well, I guess this is as good a place as any to disappear."

CHAPTER SEVEN

It was late afternoon when Reese Carter saw a white van in the distance. She parked her rusted-out Land Rover on the side of the road, clipped her badge to her belt, and stepped into the fresh mountain air. She had spent the last two weeks of her "downtime" interviewing people who had lived and worked in and around the North Cascades National Park during the past fifteen years, and trail angel Kyle Harris, the van's owner, was on her list.

She walked toward a group of hikers sitting in camp chairs around the van. They looked fairly rested for this section of the PCT. They were probably fresh off the Stehekin shuttle, after sleeping in a real bed for a night or two in the sparsely populated Stehekin community.

"Old Time Rock & Roll" blared from the van's speakers, but Reese could still hear the group chatting and laughing over Bob Seger's gravelly voice. The aroma of meat, onions, and peppers wafted her way, and she hoped it wasn't coming from a gas or charcoal grill. She didn't want to ruin their fun with a citation.

Off in the distance, a dog bayed. She stared in the direction of the sound and spotted them on the PCT at once. Kate Hall and her dog, Jenny. The hiking community called her Angel Hall. Seeing Kate sent a zing through Reese's body. She had been trying to meet the elusive angel since moving to Granite Creek, and now it looked like the trail would bring Kate to her.

Reese approached the back of the van. Kyle wore an aloha shirt and khaki Bermuda shorts. He side-eyed Reese and held up the tongs in his hand. "It's an electric grill, officer," he said and returned to flipping chicken breasts with flare.

"Thanks for observing the burn ban." Reese peeked over his shoulder. "That's a thing of beauty. Must have cost a fortune."

"Always happy to keep the park safe, no matter the cost." Kyle tossed a pile of veggies on a grill tray and closed the lid. "What can I do for you?"

"I'm Special Agent Reese Carter. I'm investigating the Coleen Farrell missing person's case." She held out a photo of a young woman with wide green eyes and long dark brown hair. "I understand you've lived in the area for some time."

"Yep. Been here since 1990. I owned a sandwich shop in Marblemount for fifteen years until I retired. Now I spend my time giving back to our hiking community." He stared at the photo. "What did you say her name was?"

"Coleen Farrell. She was nineteen. From the Great Falls, Montana, area." Reese thought she saw a fleeting look of recognition in Kyle's eyes. "She disappeared from the PCT in the summer of 2010. We ran a fifteenth-anniversary campaign about her disappearance two weeks ago."

"Oh, that's right. I thought she looked familiar. I must have recognized her from one of your social accounts. Those memes are great by the way." He laughed, and then his sun-kissed face looked solemn. "Well, the funny ones. Not that poor girl's."

"It's all right. I understand what you meant." Reese nodded at the photo. "If you could look at her picture again. We thought Coleen's last known whereabouts were near the Chinook Pass in Mount Rainer National Park. A northbound group she met there had found some of her belongings abandoned. They thought she left the trail and hitched a ride out of the park."

Kyle shook his head. "I wish I could help. But it was fifteen years ago, and I've never paid much attention to the news, especially if it isn't about our area."

"Sure, I understand. We've recently learned Coleen was last seen in this park. An eyewitness said she was a ride bride for him that summer. He claimed she helped him hitch a ride on Highway 9 to scenic Highway 20. He continued northbound and never saw her again."

"You don't say? Let me see her picture again." Kyle held out his hand. He studied the photo. "I don't recall any talk among hikers during that time. They usually have their finger on the pulse and know when things aren't right in the community." He tilted his head. "There's something about her, but I don't know what. Have you talked to many locals?"

"A few," Reese answered.

"Well, don't forget the ones who've moved away. People don't often move in and out of our area, but some do. You got Fred and Luann, the Morrisons, over near Granite Creek. They'd been there since the eighties, and after selling their hostel, they retired to Baja Mexico. There was another couple. They ran the coffee shop in Granite Creek. They recently moved to the Midwest, a prairie state, I think. Then there's the Widow Davis. She and her husband, Bert, ran a gift store in Stehekin. After he died, her kids moved her into a home in Seattle. You should ask all of them if they remember the missing girl." He handed back the photo.

"All right. I will. Thanks for your help." Reese held out a contact card. "Please call me if you think of anything else."

"I will. You can count on it." He pocketed her card and opened the grill's lid, removing the chicken and veggies, then he sliced the breasts. "The last of the grub's ready," he called to the hikers. A few stood up, and he filled their paper plates. "Do you care for a plate?"

"No, thank you. I need to be on my way." Reese walked across the dirt road and down to the trailhead, scanning the distance for Kate. When she spotted her and Jenny, they had left the trail and were headed west. *Damn.* She walked back to her vehicle. It had been ages since she felt this way, a kind of lust that crept up and demanded your attention when you were trying to sleep, or in the shower. Hell, she didn't even know if Kate Hall was available or even interested in women.

Kyle's trail magic made her hungry, and the near miss with Kate left her frustrated. She wanted to eat and relax at home with a vinyl and a glass of wine. That was a new feeling for Reese. Overseeing serious crime cases in the national parks meant wherever she hung her hat was temporary. It was a part of the job she had never minded because she had never wanted to put down roots. But things changed, and she found herself desiring stability. She blamed her parents' fortieth wedding anniversary. That and the fear she'd be the lonely aunt without a family, showing up at her brothers' homes for the holidays.

She drove over a loose gravel, windy road and smiled when a two-story mountain cabin nestled in a Douglas fir grove came into view. The first time she saw the neglected home with its wall of windows looking into the forest, it felt like home.

* * *

Every Saturday morning, out of the only handful of businesses in the tiny mountain community of Granite Creek, the coffee shop was the busiest. This Saturday was no different. Reese had learned over the last few months that Kate Hall ran errands on Saturday mornings, and the coffee shop was one of her stops. Reese would sit out of the way and watch the no-nonsense hostel owner breeze in and pick up bags of coffee beans and boxes of tea, sometimes leaving with a pie or two. Today, Reese was ready to stop Kate and talk to her. She could accomplish two interviews in one trip and be home by noon.

When she ran the names Kyle Harris had given her the night before, Reese discovered that a woman named Meena Singh had been the coffee shop's previous owner. She sold it to Phil and Lou Turner a year ago and relocated to Omaha, Nebraska. The Turners had moved to the area from Silicon Valley. They were most likely tech people, cashing in and checking out. They had aptly changed the business's name from An Unexpected Brew to

The Friendly Roast. Lou was an incessant teaser, often crude and off-putting, and Phil was just plain funny.

Reese also researched Fred and Luann Morrison who owned and operated the High Bridge Hostel from 1986 until seven years ago. They sold it to an employee, Katherine Hall. She had moved from Everglades City, Florida, and worked at the hostel for a year before the Morrisons retired. Kate bought the place in 2018 and changed its name to Hostel Hall. The financial information about Kate intrigued Reese even more. How did a single woman in her early thirties buy a hostel, mortgage-free?

The bells above The Friendly Roast's door chimed when Reese entered. The warm air inside smelled of coffee, cinnamon, and the remnants of a dying fire in the fireplace. A friendly voice called, "Good day, Special Agent Carter. How's the floor reno going?"

"Hi, Phil. It's going." She smiled at the burly man behind the counter and fell in line behind another customer. She glanced around, and a quick head count of twenty-two people confirmed that a quarter of the small town was there.

"Twelve-ounce drip, Special Agent Carter. Black. No cream?" Phil asked when Reese stepped up to the counter.

"That's right." She leaned against the counter. 'When are you going to start calling me Reese? I feel like we're past formalities, don't you?"

"Someone with your job deserves respect, but if it would make you feel more at ease, I'll oblige, Special Agent Reese."

She chuckled. "Do you have a minute?"

"Sure. What can I help you with?" He poured her coffee.

"I'm working a cold case, and it's come to our attention that the woman who disappeared was last seen in the park. I know you and Mrs. Turner are—"

"Oh, for God's sake, it's Lou. Call me Lou. You've been here long enough to know better. I don't respond to Mrs. Do I, Phil?"

"Only when someone gets it wrong, dear," he said, handing the coffee to Reese.

Lou had appeared from the back room carrying a tray of pastries. She crouched and placed them on the shelves under the glass countertop. "I know you aren't passing on my cinnabuns."

"No, of course not." Reese pulled her wallet from her jeans pocket again. Lou's booming voice coming from such a petite body always surprised her. "I was telling Phil I'm working a cold case. Coleen Farris. She went missing in 2010 and was last seen on Highway 20 in the park. I was hoping to ask you a few questions. You haven't been in the area long, is that right?"

"That's right. We moved here a little over a year ago." Lou crossed her arms over her chest. "What does that have to do with a missing woman?"

"I understand her disappearance was well before you moved here, but I wanted to know if you've heard gossip about disappearances in the park. Stories about past events. Or if you've heard lore from hikers who've come through town."

Lou stood up and leaned against the counter, moving her body in a way that made it seem bigger than it was. "Lore? What, like spooky stories?" She snorted. "Nah, we haven't heard any stories about missing people. Have we, Phil?"

He stood behind her and shook his head.

Lou's suspicious expression changed. "You know who you should talk to. Kate Hall. Do you two already know each other?"

Phil rolled his eyes at the way his wife said *know*. He quietly plated a cinnabun.

"No, I haven't met Ms. Hall," Reese said. Her face warmed, and she thought pumping the Turners for information about Kate was out.

"Excuse me, dear." Phil scooted Lou over and handed Reese her cinnabun. Then he called for the next person in line.

"We bought the coffee shop from Kate's friend Meena Singh," Lou continued. "She and her wife…What was her name, Phil?"

Phil was busy taking a customer's order and answered without looking, "Lainey."

"That's right. Lainey. Anyway, Meena sold the shop to us, and they moved somewhere in the heartland. Nebraska, I think. You know, the middle of the country. God knows why you girls would do that. Right, Phil?" She laughed and then focused on Reese again. "You didn't know them either?"

Reese shook her head and glanced around the shop at a quarter of the town's people, sitting there, listening. "Do you know Lainey's last name?"

Lou thought for a second. "Can't recall. Phil?"

He shook his head.

"The coffee shop was only in Meena's name. Kate can help you get a hold of them. Like I said, they were close." Lou looked over the counter and gave Reese the once-over. "I figured you and Kate knew each other. You're both good-looking, outdoorsy types. Probably have a lot in common like hiking around in the park. She donates a fortune to it and the forest, but not in her name." Lou leaned closer. "I'd be happy to introduce you if you're interested. She's single, and I didn't see you move here with anyone, did I?"

"Okay, then. I'm going to take the cinnamon roll to go." Reese's warm face lit on fire. She grabbed a napkin and took the pastry off the plate. "Thanks for your time. I'll see you again soon."

Lou straightened and held her hands up. "I'm just saying, you don't have too many choices out here. Although my sister-in-law, Janice, comes to town once or twice a month. We're having drinks at the new pub on Friday. You should come. I could set you up." She laughed and jammed her elbow into Phil's side.

Without responding, he continued pouring coffee into a cup and said, apologetically, "Have a nice day, Special Agent Reese."

CHAPTER EIGHT

Kate enjoyed the challenges of running a hostel. She had learned the business side from the previous owners. Everything from bathroom supplies, linen cleaning, taking guest bookings, financial bookkeeping, to taxes. Those were the easy parts of running Hostel Hall. The day-to-day challenges kept her on her toes. The dorm and the communal rooms were in constant need of repair. Small issues that if overlooked would turn into large problems. Then there was the morning and evening Lounge for hikers to recharge before and after hiking.

On Fridays and Sundays, she turned over the daily hostel management to Nicole while she and Jenny sprinkled trail magic on trail families. Most days the juice, fruit, candy bars, and chips they offered hiking tramilies only lasted through one or two stops. Some days they hiked in the backcountry and didn't see another person. On those days, Kate loved the undivided attention she could give her best friend. The only other time she and Jenny left the hostel was Saturday mornings to restock the butler's pantry.

So on Saturday morning after an uneventful Friday on the trails, except for the three women who wanted a picture with her,

Kate checked the cupboards, made a list, and drove into Granite Creek. A handful of shops lined the town's short Main Street, and she parked halfway between the two she needed, leashed Jenny, and headed to the superette.

An old, beat-up Land Rover approached them, and Kate stopped on the sidewalk like a deer in headlights, her body reacting with a warm sensation that started low and surged to her chest. The new park ranger slowed and gestured hello then drove past. Thank God. "Get a grip, Peters. You aren't going down that road," she said under her breath.

After grocery shopping, Kate loaded the last bag of groceries into her truck bed and looked down Main Street in the direction the new park ranger drove. She wanted some answers. Who was she? Why was she in town every Saturday? Did she live in the park? Alone? The questions broke through in rapid succession.

Jenny nudged her leg.

"Sorry, sweet girl. We'll go to the coffee shop in a minute, I need to make a call." Kate opened the driver's door, and Jenny jumped in with a slight struggle, lying across the cab's seat. Bob would know who the woman was. He was the ranger assigned to the park area near the hostel. Only he hadn't returned her messages for a few days now. Did it have something to do with the woman? Was she taking over his territory? Kate had trekked the same trails Bob patrolled for five years and had no desire to break in a new ranger, especially one who made her feel like this one did. The thought frustrated her. No, she didn't want any more change. She was still adjusting to Meena and Lainey leaving, and her grandmother… She pushed the thought away.

After several rings, Bob's voice mail picked up. "Hey, it's Kate again. I haven't seen you on the trails. Where are you? I have a question. Do you know who the new ranger is? She's tall. Sandy-blond hair, pulled back, maybe shoulder length? I keep seeing her on the trails in your area. You need to call—" Kate took a sharp breath and pressed her back against the truck. She ducked underneath the window, whispering, "Oh, my God. Oh, my God. Oh, my God." Then she slowly moved toward the truck's bed, peeked over it, and ducked again.

Across the street, a man stood by a four-door, gray sedan in front of The Friendly Roast. He had red hair and wore jeans and a button-down shirt, not your typical mountain wear. She ended the call and peeked again. He had climbed into the sedan, an unusual vehicle for this area. She leaned against the truck bed, preparing to hide if he headed toward her. Instead, he drove away in the opposite direction.

She slipped into the driver's seat and held the steering wheel, her hands trembling. Jenny whimpered and wriggled closer, laying her head in Kate's lap. "It's all right, sweet girl," Kate whispered and petted Jenny's back. The hound lifted her head, giving Kate's chin a wet kiss. But it wasn't okay. It was the first time since making a new home at the hostel she had seen or thought she had seen someone from her old life. And not just anyone.

She had just seen Liam Maloney.

Kate buried her face in Jenny's coat until the pounding in her chest slowed. She started the truck and rolled the windows down before shutting off the engine again. "You stay here. I'll be right back." She knew witness protection wasn't a one hundred percent guarantee, but the idea that after so many years Liam was there in Granite Creek was too jarring to believe. She had to verify what she saw.

The bells chimed, and Lou looked up behind The Friendly Roast's counter. "Hey, Kate. You're about ten minutes too late. Were your ears burning?"

Kate's pulse raced again. "Why would they be?"

"That hot new, *single*, ranger was here, and I might have mentioned you were unattached, too." Lou grinned. "Why don't I bring her along on my next delivery to the hostel, a special treat."

"Why don't I save you the trip and take the desserts now?" Kate asked, knowing it would stop Lou's teasing.

"You can't do that. It's my only chance to get away from Mr. Yawner. The deal is I bring your pastry order. It's nice to be in the company of other women. But not in that way, you know that, right?"

"Your sexuality is safe with me, Lou."

"Hello, Kate," Phil said, scooting his wife aside.

"Hi, Phil." She smiled at Lou's husband. He was a laid-back hippy type, probably stoned for self-preservation, the only way he could handle his wife.

"Americano, one cream?"

"Yes, please, and some answers if you have a minute."

Phil lifted an eyebrow. "Sounds intriguing."

"Depends on what you're asking." Lou muscled back beside Phil, and the defensiveness in her voice surprised Kate.

"I want to know about the red-headed man in here about twenty minutes ago. Do you know him? Has he been in here before?"

"Why, are you one of those alternating currents?" Lou laughed, but Kate stared at her blankly. "You know, switches back and forth."

Kate looked at Phil, and he smiled apologetically. "It's the first time I've seen him," he said. "He seemed like a decent guy. Quiet. Ordered a coffee and a danish."

"Did he ask any questions about the area?" Kate asked.

"He ordered. Paid. No questions or chit-chat. Which is a pleasant change." He looked at his wife as he finished Kate's coffee.

"Did he have an accent from another part of the country?" Kate struggled to keep the panic out of her voice.

"Now that you mention it, I doubt he's from here. He sure wasn't dressed for it." Phil handed her a to-go cup.

Lou crossed her arms over her chest and considered Kate. "Why are you so interested in this guy?"

"He looked familiar. Like someone I used to know. Do you have any security footage I could look at?" Kate tried to keep the anxiety rushing through her from appearing on her face.

Her question seemed to surprise them, and Lou snorted, "Yeah, right. Why would we need surveillance equipment in a Podunk town where nothing ever happens?"

* * *

Jenny smelled home in the air, sat up, and hung her head out the truck window as they made their way down the hostel's long driveway. Kate pulled into the parking area, and Jenny barked and wiggled her whole body at the sight of Nicole chopping firewood. Kate leaned over and opened the passenger's side door, and the hound bounded over to her friend, sloppily kissing her hands.

Sitting in the truck, Kate tried to process what had just happened. Normally, she prided herself on her keen observation skills and ability to read people, training she often used in her dealings with guests and hikers she met on the trails. She was less sure of her ability to recognize someone after eight years, especially a teenager who was now a young adult.

She clenched the steering wheel tightly. Had she seen Liam Maloney? Should she call Joanna? Their annual phone call was in December. Months away. No, not yet, she told herself. She had to confirm what she saw.

"Hey, you okay?" Nicole asked, leaning into the passenger's window.

"Yeah, I'm good. A little too much Lou this morning. She was in rare form." Kate released the steering wheel and climbed out of the truck, forcing a smile. "You've had a busy morning."

"Thought I'd fill up the log store early." Nicole met Kate at the truck's tailgate. Jenny whimpered and stared at her pocket with hopeful eyes. She rubbed the hound's head and pulled a treat from her pocket. "Who's the best girl? You are, Jenny-benny." Jenny sat motionless, keen eyes on the biscuit, and when Nicole finally gave it to her, she eagerly took her treat and trotted off with it dangling from her muzzle.

"You spoil her," Kate said, picking up two grocery bags. "If I'm not careful she'll leave me for you."

"She wouldn't if you took me up on my offer. The three of us could be one big happy family at the hostel." Nicole grabbed the box of coffee and tea from The Friendly Roast and followed Kate.

"I don't think Vivienne would be too pleased about that," Kate said, teasing her back.

"That's true." Nicole glanced toward her apartment as they walked past.

"Besides, you're—"

"Yeah, yeah. I'm too young for you," Nicole interrupted.

A memory of Bridget flashed in Kate's mind. It was all she could do to maintain a neutral face. She opened the communal room door.

"I'm starting to think your refusal has nothing to do with age and more to do with hiding," Nicole said.

"Oh? What am I hiding from?"

"Relationships. You haven't even dated since I've known you. And we're not counting hooking up as dating. Were you like this before we met?"

"Like this? That's harsh, don't you think?" Kate paused. "I'm not avoiding relationships. They don't interest me, Dr. Ruth."

"Who's that?"

"Oh, my God. You're such an infant."

"No, I'm not. I'm Canadian," Nicole said with a straight face.

Kate laughed and sat the bags on the back counter. She noticed the morning Lounge supplies were still on the buffet table and looked around the rest of the room. The coffee tables were full of dirty plates and glasses. The game tables hadn't been cleared. "You can't be serious? housekeeping didn't show up again?"

"Oh, crap. I was so busy chopping firewood. I didn't even notice. I'm sorry."

"That's all right. It's not your fault. But this is the last time they're a no-show. They're done." Kate looked at her watch. "Great. I wanted to work in my garden. We'll have to do the cleaning today. Sorry if you had plans with your girlfriend."

Nicole hesitated. "No problem. I planned on being here all day."

They carried the rest of the groceries inside and unpacked them in silence. "All right, out with it," Kate said finally. "I hear you banging the pots and pans in your brain from here. What are you cooking up?"

"Okay, yeah. I planned on asking you something today, but now...since the cleaners flaked again and you're firing them...I have a better plan. Remember what I said about Vivienne's visa and how she's decided to stay...to be with me? She'll have to quit her job if it's not extended, and then she won't be able to afford her apartment. So I thought she could live here with me if that's okay with you, and she could clean in exchange. Did I tell you she was a night cleaner at a hotel near the Art Institute?"

"Wow, you had all that going on in there?"

"Yeah. Sorry to spring it on you like this."

"That's a lot to consider, Nic, but I will. Right now, let's clean in here, and rooms four and seven need service for the new guests." Kate unpacked the groceries. She had grown to care about Nicole but felt ambivalent if not slightly uncomfortable about her girlfriend. Last year, Vivienne stayed at the hostel with two other young women during their hike through the park. Nicole fell for her instantly. She talked about the French art student nonstop. Then Vivienne started showing up at the hostel on the weekends. Kate tried to be friendly, but Vivienne kept her distance and never had much to say.

Kate gathered up the dirty dessert plates and loaded the dishwasher. What did she care if Nicole's girlfriend didn't like her? She wanted her assistant to be happy, and Nicole was smitten with Vivienne. That's all that mattered. She stifled a laugh, realizing she was seriously considering aiding and abetting a crime, and the only part that bothered her was having to see Vivienne every day.

After breaking for lunch, Kate and Nicole serviced the open dorm rooms and returned to the communal room. "Hey Jenny-benny," Nicole said as the hound lumbered in from the butler's pantry. She stroked Jenny's copper coat. "Are you here early to stake out your spot by the fireplace?" Jenny's ears perked, and she looked at the door just as Vivienne entered. "Hey, Viv." Nicole joined her girlfriend, kissing her lightly on the lips.

Kate hadn't heard a car, so she guessed Nicole's girlfriend had stayed the night, and by the sheepish look on Vivienne's face, she would bet on it. Jenny remained at her side, which wasn't surprising. The first time the old hound met Vivienne she reacted less friendly than she did with other strangers, and even though Jenny knew Vivienne now, she still didn't seek her attention.

Kate rubbed Jenny's head and started prepping for the evening Lounge, stocking clean mugs, plates, and silverware on the buffet table. She heard Vivienne say something in French to Nicole, and soon their conversation was lost on her. A few minutes later,

Vivienne's voice rose an octave, and she threw her arms around Nicole's neck and left.

"I told Viv about cleaning in exchange for living here," Nicole said.

"I gathered. Sounds like she approves of the idea."

"Yeah, she's excited. It really would help us out."

"Well, we have a lot of things to think through, Nic. Details we need to figure out. Simple things like how I'm supposed to communicate with her."

"She speaks a little English. And I can translate her French when you need me to." Nicole looked at Kate like a teenager wanting the car for a Friday night date.

Then the look in her young assistant's eyes changed from eagerness to one that spoke of impending broken hearts and unfulfilled dreams. "All right. Fine. You are too much. She can stay."

"Thank you. Thank you so much." Nicole hugged her tightly, and Jenny danced at their side.

CHAPTER NINE

Jenny trotted ahead of Kate, off trail, her head popping up through the wildflowers every few steps. The warmer temperatures and longer days of sunshine made the valley explode in hues of purple lupine with patches of red Indian paintbrush and yellow balsamroot. Kate nervously scanned the foothills. Usually trekking in the crisp morning air centered her but not this morning.

She had spent the night searching social media for Liam Maloney's movements over the last few days, but he only posted randomly on holidays and vacations. She studied his pictures. He had filled out, no longer a gawky teen. Liam also posted photos of Fiona's last birthday party. Eight years hadn't aged the O'Flaherty heir a bit. Seeing the Maloneys' faces further eroded Kate's sense of security and safety.

"Jenny," she shouted. The old hound had gone too far ahead. She whistled, and Jenny's head popped up and down in the wildflowers as she ran back to Kate. "You know the rules. Stay close. No attracting bears. Besides the hard part's coming." They had passed Lake Howard on their way to the dry camp. Jenny led the way over the switchbacks, staying only a few feet ahead. Kate concentrated on her footing, but worried thoughts broke through. If Liam was in Granite Creek, he was there for her. Did he know she ran the hostel? Did he know about Jenny and Nicole? Was she putting them in danger?

She remembered when she almost put her grandmother in danger, and tears stung her eyes. She looked ahead. Jenny had scrambled into a clearing where the dense undergrowth had given way to a subalpine forest of pine and firs.

The illegal camp was a few yards off the trail, and Jenny waited for her to catch up. They entered through a patch of trees. Kate stroked Jenny's long ears. "Ready for a drink, sweet girl?" She dropped her pack and retrieved an expandable bowl, but before she could fill it, Jenny put her nose to the ground and began tracking. Kate watched her zigzag across the campsite. "What is it?"

The hound bayed and bolted toward the rear of the camp.

"Jenny," Kate shouted. She lost sight of her in a grove of trees spared the ravages of the last wildfire. She whistled a shrill command, sending thrush and warbler into the air. The hound's baying stopped, and a minute later she returned carrying a black backpack in her mouth.

"Drop it," Kate ordered, and Jenny let go of the bag. Kate stared into the trees. Hikers used the dry camp to rest but didn't venture into the grove because it ended in a sheer drop. Rock climbers didn't even risk it. So why was the bag in there, and where was its owner? Jenny vibrated with excitement, hopping on her front paws. "Forget it. You're not touching it." She retrieved a pair of latex gloves from her pack.

The bag was light and had a foul odor of urine. It wasn't heavy enough to belong to a hiker unless its contents had been dumped, and it looked brand new. There were no stains or scuffs, or the personalization you'd usually see on hikers' packs.

She opened the main compartment. Empty. She unzipped the front pocket and turned the pack upside down, shaking it. A green plastic baggie full of little round tablets fell onto the ashen soil. Her heart pounded, and she dropped the pack, recognizing its contents at once. She retrieved her phone and called Bob, but the call went straight to voice mail. "Goddamn it, Bob. Where are you? I'm at the dry camp above Howard Lake. Jenny found an abandoned backpack with drugs inside. Call me back."

She paced in front of the backpack and baggie of drugs, her anxiety building. First, she sees Liam leaving The Friendly Roast. Now this. It was too much of a coincidence.

Her phone rang. "Finally, I've been leaving you messages for a week. Where are you? Are you close?"

"Hold on a minute. Take a breath. What did you find? Do I need to bring clean-up gear?"

"No. No needles. I found…well, Jenny found a backpack. It had a baggie full of tablets, not recreational, either. A distribution amount."

Bob paused. "That's it?"

His dismissiveness surprised Kate. Bob had never been indifferent toward drugs. She'd found them before a few years ago, and he was furious.

"What do you mean, is that it? This has to be a drop. New bag. Empty except for drugs. And I think it's marked with urine or something."

"A piss marker? That would be a new one." He laughed. "Why don't you and Jenny go back to the hostel? I'll take care of it."

His reaction was unexpected, and her fear quickly turned into frustration. "You can't be serious, Bob? We can't leave these drugs unattended. What if a hiker comes through here? Or an animal?"

"Okay. You're right. Calm down. I've never heard you so riled up. I was only trying to consider what's best for you and Jenny." He paused. "Is everything okay?"

"I'm fine." She stared at the green baggie. "Just get here as soon as you can."

Kate ended their call. She was angry and, although it was hard to admit, scared. After the bakery explosion, Fiona Maloney had removed all remnants of drugs from Bridget's apartment. The FBI found it clean when they arrived, and the AG failed to secure an indictment without evidence or Bridget. Jenny nudged Kate's leg. She laid her hand on the hound's thick coat and released a deep breath. "Let's wait for Bob, okay?"

She sat on a fallen pine, and Jenny lay at her feet. Kate's thoughts returned to the drugs. After ruminating long enough that Jenny fell asleep, Kate decided there were two possibilities. Fiona must have kept the drugs Bridget had developed and started manufacturing them. Maybe even adding them to their Ireland routes, a way of honoring her dead daughter. Somehow, they knew she was there and what her movements were. Liam planted the drugs. To intimidate her? Toy with her?

She scanned the tree line. The thought made her legs weak. The other scenario was it had nothing to do with them finding her. Liam had brought the drugs because the O'Flaherty organization had started a new pipeline, maybe moving into Canada via the PCT, and her finding the bag was an unfortunate coincidence.

Jenny lifted her head and scrambled to her feet. Bob had entered the campsite. He was breathing hard. His round, chubby face was bright red against his shock of gray hair. Jenny ran to him, and he patted her head. "All right. I'm here. Let's see what this good girl found." He walked over to the bag and put his hands on his hips. "I see what you mean. That's a new pack." He unloaded his backpack, put on latex gloves, squatted, and sniffed the bag. "Phew. That's urine for sure."

"Yeah. So what do you think? A one-off or something to be concerned about?" Kate stood beside him with her arms crossed.

"Hard to tell. It could've belonged to a hiker who lost it. A bear took off with it. Pissed on it."

"Seriously, Bob? No one treks with an empty backpack out here."

"They also don't pack fifty pounds like you do." He inspected the backpack. "Maybe the animal that carried it off scattered its contents."

"Then zipped it back up?"

"Oh, you found it closed?"

Kate nodded. "The drugs were in the front pocket."

Bob picked up the green baggie and squinted at the pills up close. "Look at that, marked with an L. Where'd Jenny find the backpack?"

"In there," Kate answered. She pointed toward the back tree line. "We never hike in there, but as soon as we entered the campsite, she caught the scent and took off. I whistled for her, and she came back fast enough. So it had to be close."

He stood and glanced at the woods. "You didn't go in and look around?"

"No." She stared at him. "It might be a crime scene. I wasn't going to trample all over it, right?"

"Yeah. Right. That's good." Bob glanced around the clearing without saying anything.

"Okay. What's going on?" Kate asked. "We've known each other for a long time, and I know when you're acting strange. You haven't returned any of my calls. I didn't see you on the trails last week either. Is it because of the new ranger?" Kate asked irritably. "Is there something you need to tell me?"

Bob's face drew a blank. "Do you mean Special Agent Carter?" he finally asked.

Kate nodded.

"She's not a new ranger. She's with the Investigative Services Branch." Bob stared at her. "Ah, that's why you're upset. Did you think she was taking my job?"

"I'm not upset."

"Could've fooled me." He retrieved a large plastic bag from his pack and bagged the black backpack. "Well, I'm not suggesting that you were having feelings about it, but if you were, you should know Special Agent Carter bought a cabin outside Granite Creek about three months ago. You'll see her around because she lives here, but she's also working on a missing person cold case. I'm her liaison in the park."

"Is that why you haven't returned my calls?"

"Yeah, I've been stretched thin." Bob took his phone out of its holder. "I'll get Garret up here to help me search the area. You might as well take Jenny and head back to the hostel."

"All right. Call me when you know more, okay? I don't want to worry all night that someone is in there or at the bottom of the cliff…dead."

CHAPTER TEN

Kate arrived back at the hostel, her mind racing. Jenny walked by her side through the empty yard as she had done the entire trek home, and they went inside without anyone noticing them.

After filling Jenny's bowl with cool water and pouring herself a glass, she texted Nicole, asking her to run the evening Lounge alone or, if she wanted, with Vivienne. Then she opened her laptop, sat on the couch with Jenny beside her, and searched for stories about drug finds on the PCT.

She found a similar case in Yellowstone earlier in the year. The same type of drop just off the trail, an empty bag except for the drugs, but no mention of urine. She scanned further and stopped. The lead investigator on the case was Reese Carter. She followed a link in the article to the National Parks Investigative Services Branch's website and saw Reese's picture. She read a few cases Reese had solved, and her search started to feel like stalking, so she closed her laptop and rested her head against the cushions. Her stomach knotted. The lead investigator turned up in Granite Creek. And then Liam. Then Jenny finds a similar drug drop.

After she fed Jenny and ate a microwaved chicken marsala, Kate poured herself a glass of wine and went to bed. The evening Lounge sounded like a full house. Several guests played guitars and sang, their muffled voices filtering through her bedroom wall. She stared out the French doors into the night and exhaled slowly. Her hostel was a haven, a safe place for people to recharge after surviving days, sometimes weeks, in the backcountry. She didn't ask too much from the land or her guests and tried to provide more than she received. It was her way of giving back, helping as many as she could, to make up for the one life she couldn't save.

The clock on the bedside table read eight p.m. It was eleven p.m. in DC. "Now or never," she said under her breath, placing her wineglass on a chest of drawers. She lifted a corner of an area rug, revealing a hidden compartment. Unlocking the hatch, she opened it and pulled out a box.

She closed the drapes and made herself comfortable on her bed. Jenny jumped up and lay beside her. The simple cedar box held the last traces of her past life, of Eleanor Peters. She looked through a stack of photos: her energetic mother before the ravages of cancer, her dad before death solved his numbness, and her grandmother. She stared at the picture of a gravesite with freshly turned soil and a pile of single roses and blinked back tears. It had only been a year since her grandmother died, but it felt like yesterday. Her grandmother had taught her everything she knew about homes and gardens. She had taken her in and raised her after her father killed himself. The only thing she could never learn was her grandmother's faith and unwavering commitment to love.

Kate steeled herself against her rising grief, too afraid to face it alone, in case it wrenched her into a dark despair. She set the photographs aside and removed a Glock 19 and a magazine. She raised the gun, inserted the mag, and loaded the chamber. Jenny lifted her head at the metallic click of the round. "It's okay, sweet girl," she said, soothing the old hound. The last item she pulled from the box was a cell phone. She retrieved a SIM card from the back of a large dresser.

After the phone's battery charged, she made a call. Deputy US Marshal Joanna Stevens answered on the second ring. "Kate? What's wrong?"

Hearing her voice, connecting with someone who knew the terror she felt inside, someone she could talk to about her past, made Kate's pent-up emotions release, and her voice cracked. "I have a problem."

"Are you in danger?" Joanna asked, her voice tense.

"I don't think I am right now."

"Okay. Good. That's good. What's happening?"

"I think I saw Liam Maloney in Granite Creek yesterday, and today, I found a backpack with a load of drugs at one of my hiking stops. The baggie looked identical to the one Bridget had at our meeting with the Novikovs. And the drugs had a cursive L imprinted on their fronts instead of three Bs." She waited for Joanna to respond. "Joanna, did you hear me? The day after I saw Liam, a green baggie full of little white tablets was left at one of my stops. It can't be a coincidence—"

"Slow down, Kate," Joanna interrupted. "Okay. This is completely unexpected. Let me think. You saw Liam in Granite Creek. All right. It's been eight years. He was only…what? Seventeen? Are you sure it was him?"

"I know what I saw," Kate shouted. Jenny whined and laid her head on Kate's leg. She caressed the hound's silky ears. "I shouldn't yell at you. I'm sorry. It's just too much to handle, and I'm freaked out, Joanna. If it was Liam, he knows my movements. My schedule. Why else would Jenny have found the backpack there? Today?" She closed her eyes, then shook her head. "I don't know. Maybe I'm imagining it all, and it wasn't him, but I think it was."

"Okay. Take some deep breaths. I understand you think you saw him. So let's run through what you know. When did you see this person?"

"Saturday morning coming out of the coffee shop. He got into a gray sedan. A rental."

"That's good. We can work with that. Did you get the plates?"

Kate closed her eyes again, becoming angry with herself. How could she have forgotten to look at the tags? She would have thrown the phone across the room if it were anyone else on the other end. She exhaled a deep breath. "No. I was too busy making sure he didn't see me."

"That's okay," Joanna soothed. "Your job is to live your new life. It's my job to make sure you aren't found. What about the drugs?"

"I called Ranger Bob. Jenny and I left before he searched the area, but I asked him to tell me what they found. He'll take the evidence back to headquarters at Sedro-Woolley. We need to find out if the Maloneys know I'm here." Kate wiped the wetness off her face with her free hand. "Why is this happening now? How did they find me?"

"I don't know. You've been off the radar for so many years. I haven't heard anything from the FBI or AG about the O'Flahertys' case or you. But I promise, we'll confirm your suspicion about the man. I'll reach out to the FBI tonight. They can verify Liam's movements. See if he's left the state. We'll also have them check on the drugs. See if there's any connection. Okay?"

"Is Mandy still leading the investigation?"

Joanna paused. "Yes. As far as I know."

Kate shouldn't have asked. It placed her marshal in an uncomfortable position. But seeing Liam…finding the drugs… brought her past slamming into her present, and Mandy was the biggest part of her past. Inwardly she sighed. She had many more questions about her friend.

"Okay. When do you want to have an update call?"

"Let's talk tomorrow. Eleven o'clock." Joanna paused. "We have to discuss one more thing. If you did see Liam, we need to relocate you. We should do so immediately."

Kate couldn't respond. It was a reality she didn't want to face. Losing the hostel and Nicole. Meena and Lainey. The life she'd built over the last eight years.

"It's your right to refuse to move, but you would be at great risk."

Jenny lifted her muzzle and licked Kate's chin. She pulled the old hound to her with her free arm. "I know, Joanna. It's just not going to be easy."

"It never is. Let's take one step at a time. I can send a few deputies from the Western District to keep you safe while we check on Liam's activities."

Kate glanced at the Glock beside her. "Yeah, all right. I'm taking precautions, too."

* * *

Law Enforcement Ranger Robert Tolbert sat at a table in a windowless break room. He looked up and frowned when Special Agent Reese Carter walked in. "You didn't have to have the chief order my ass in here just cause we haven't found a time to meet. It's only been two weeks for Christ's sake."

"Hello, to you, too," Reese said, pulling a chair from the table and sitting. Bob's silver-white crew cut and weathered skin surprised her. She hadn't thought Robert Tolbert was an older man. "To be clear, I didn't have you summoned and this isn't about the Coleen Farrell case. I'm here about the drugs you found on the McGregor Mountain Trail today."

"I thought ISB only showed up for major crimes," he said with a hint of contempt.

She considered him for a moment. He was rude and overly defensive, but he was technically right. Drug cases usually didn't rise to her level. Robert's find, however, piqued her interest. "That's right. But you're aware there's a flag on all seized drugs on or around the PCT?"

"Yeah," he answered sharply. "What are you implying?"

Reese studied his expression. She didn't mind a snide comment if it happened in a context that made sense, but he seemed agitated with her for no reason, which didn't sit well. Partly because she prided herself on keeping friendly relationships with her colleagues, but mostly because it suggested a much bigger backstory he wasn't sharing. "Why don't we start over?" She held out her hand. "Reese Carter, you can call me Reese."

He reluctantly shook her hand. "Bob Tolbert. Call me Bob."

"Well, Bob. Chief Nelson had wonderful things to say about you, and I've looked forward to meeting you since we received the tip for the Farrell case."

He sat back and relaxed his body. "You come with high praise, too."

She smiled. "Thanks. That's nice to say. I'm going to make a cup of decaf. A little late for caffeinated, at least it is for me. Do you want a cup?"

"Sure. I'll have a regular. Thanks."

"No problem. Cream?"

"Black is fine."

"That's how I take mine, too." Reese stood and made them both a cup. When she finished, she slid Bob's across the table. "About the drugs you found. If you knew to flag them, why didn't you?"

"I wasn't done with my report is all. I was up at the site until sundown. By the time I recorded all the evidence, it was late. I was going to finish my report tomorrow."

"So that's why your chief needed more detail on location and drug description?"

"Exactly. I would have flagged it in the morning after finishing." Bob held the mug in both hands and stared at the coffee. "I should've kept the report on my desk till then."

"The additional details you provided tonight connect these drugs to our ISB investigation. We've intercepted three similar drops on the PCT over the last year. Same backpack style. Same L-stamped white pills. But this is the farthest north the drugs have been found. That tells us the trafficking could be a Mexico to Canada route. We haven't found that the traffickers use the same spot twice, so we need to focus on areas north of this location." She held his eyes. "Are there any other details to add to your report?"

Bob lowered his head, shaking it slowly from side to side. "I'm sorry for the shoddy work. I just needed to get home. It wasn't on purpose. I've spent thirty years in the National Park Service. Patrolled three different parks. Spent the first fifteen years as a backcountry ranger. My wife and I raised two kids in the parks.

She's always sacrificed for this lifestyle. Never complained. We always knew retirement would come early enough for us to enjoy the second half of our lives." Tears gathered at the corner of his eyes. "Now, I'm close. Fifty-four. And she's got cancer."

Reese sat back. "I'm so sorry."

"I didn't tell you for your sympathy. It's just…I'm a bit distracted…and I botched up my reporting. But that's no excuse."

"Have you thought about taking a leave?"

"Marsha doesn't want me to, so I take a day here and there for her chemo and doctor appointments. She had surgery, a double mastectomy. I took a few weeks off then. Stayed at a hotel near the hospital in Seattle. She's doing better now, and I'm keeping my head down, working hard, and crossing off the days until my retirement. Hopefully, we'll have all the time we want after."

"I hope so, too," Reese said, sympathetically. "Would you like me to ask your chief to reassign my park liaison?"

"That's not necessary. Unless you don't want to work with me. But I'm damn good at what I do, and I know this park and community like the back of my hand."

"Excellent. Good to hear it." Reese picked up the file and stood. "I'll take the pack to the crime lab for processing in the morning. Did you find anything else in the area?"

"I searched where the backpack was found. There was nothing else. Not even footprints." Bob scooted his chair away from the table and got to his feet.

"Okay, we'll revisit the location tomorrow. Until then, I'll need you to tell me everything you can remember about finding it. Sound good?"

Bob adjusted his belt. "Okay."

"Oh, one more thing. Have you ever found drugs and paraphernalia near that section of the PCT before?"

"No." He nodded at the file in Reese's hand. "I need to clear up something. Another detail I didn't add to the report yet. I didn't find the drugs. A civilian did. She called me to the site."

Reese opened the folder and scanned the report. "Yeah. You omitted the name. Write up an amendment for the file. Is this person available for our investigation?"

"Oh, yeah. She lives here," Bob answered. "Her name's Kate Hall. She runs a hostel just outside the park near Highbridge. She's a trail angel."

The mention of Kate's name sparked a flicker of excitement in Reese. "Did she say what she was doing at the site?"

"She has a penchant for providing magic at illegal campsites."

"Hmm." Reese looked at her watch. It was late. "Okay, Bob. We'll pay Ms. Hall a visit tomorrow."

CHAPTER ELEVEN

Kate crawled forward and inspected several tiny buds. The hybrid rose bushes in the test row were in their second season, budding right on schedule. She had never understood her grandmother's thrill for rose gardening until she grew her own. The plants she purchased and carefully tended satisfied her, but those she created through hybridization and nurtured from seedlings to blooming bushes in her hothouse, those no one else had ever seen or smelled, made her feel like an artist.

She inched along the test row, spading up weeds. The late-morning sun warmed her back, and soft breezes brought her the faint sounds of her guests' conversations as they left the hostel and entered the woods. She sat back on her heels and stared into the trees. The memory of Sean, Thomas, and Patrick marching toward her flooded back. Would Liam and his crew appear the same way? Without warning? Guns drawn? Ready to shoot?

It had been so long since memories of that day had surfaced. She exhaled an angry breath. For years she had achieved peace in her garden and at the hostel, but in less than three days, one possible sighting had destroyed it all.

The sound of approaching vehicles alarmed Kate, and she quickly stood. At the same time, the communal room's door opened, and Vivienne stepped onto the front porch. Kate followed her gaze to the wood pile where Nicole had stopped chopping. The three watched an old Land Rover and a park-ranger SUV emerge from the woods. Vivienne rushed to Nicole's apartment, disappearing inside before the visitors reached the parking area.

Nicole joined Kate in the rose garden. "Who's that?" she asked nervously.

"Bob." Kate stared at the Land Rover, a warmth spreading up her neck. "And the woman in the Rover is a special agent in the Parks Investigative Services Branch."

Nicole ran her hand through her short dark hair and whispered, "Oh, shit. Oh, shit. Oh, shit."

"Nic, take a breath. They aren't here to ask about your girlfriend's visa. You need to relax, or you will get Vivienne caught." Kate dropped her spade into the soil and wiped her hands on her jeans. She had read enough about the ISB to know if Special Agent Carter was involved, the drugs Jenny found were connected to something bigger.

Their vehicle doors closed and woke Jenny. The old hound barked once and trotted off the porch toward them. Bob patted her head, and then the hound turned her attention to the stranger. Reese squatted eye-level with Jenny, stroking her long ears and scratching behind them. Jenny slurped her neck and chin in thanks.

"Hey, Kate. Your garden's looking good this season."

"Thanks, Bob. The 'Nearly Wilds' are full of blooms. I'll give you a dozen to take home to Marsha."

"That's real nice. She'd like that."

Reese strolled up, watching them, and seeing Jenny happily trotting beside the special agent made Kate even more uneasy.

"I don't think you all have met," Bob said. "This is Special Agent Reese Carter with the National Parks ISB."

Reese held out her hand, and Kate wiped hers on her jeans and then shook it. "Kate Hall." Tingling spread through her when their hands touched. She had imagined how the special agent's skin might feel but was completely unprepared for the real-life version.

"I've seen you on the trails and in town, but it's such a pleasure to see you up close."

What did she just say? Kate repeated Reese's words and decided she had heard them correctly. Was she flirting? Probably not. The same thought had gone through her mind. She just didn't let it slip out. She held the special agent's eyes. So enveloping. A stunning blue, like glacial water. *Glacial water?* She stepped back and quickly looked at Bob. "What can I help you with?"

"We need to ask you a few questions about the backpack you found yesterday."

"I've already told you what I know, and why didn't you call me last night?" She stepped into the garden, putting on gloves and picking up a pair of shears.

"Yeah, um, Garrett was too far away to assist, so I searched the area myself. It ended up being a long night." He glanced at Reese.

"What happened?" Nicole asked.

"Jenny found a backpack with some drugs inside." Kate continued to cut long-stemmed pink roses, clipping off their leaves, except for a few near the blooms.

"On the PCT?"

"On McGregor," Kate corrected. Her young assistant seemed to have recovered her nerves. "I'll put these in some water. You can ask me your questions inside."

"Let me do it, boss," Nicole said, and Kate gave her a glove and the roses. "I can make coffee, too, if anyone wants some?"

"Sounds good. Thanks, Nic."

Reese reached down and petted Jenny, then she looked at Kate. "So how long does it take to grow a rose garden like this?"

"I started it about six years ago. It's not work, though. Gardening relaxes me almost as much as trekking with Jenny." Kate wanted to command the hound to come to her but couldn't begrudge her sweet girl the affection the special agent was giving her.

"Don't let her be so humble. She's a rosarian award winner," Bob said.

"Impressive." Reese stopped petting Jenny and straightened. "She's a great dog. That always says a lot about the owner."

Bob shifted his weight. "You got plenty of room at old Hendrick's cabin for a dog or two."

"That's true," Reese answered, and Kate was positive a flush of red colored the special agent's cheeks.

"Well if you want a dog, I hope you adopt from one of the area shelters." Kate looked at the old hound and added, "Jenny, this's Special Agent Carter. Say hello, but don't get too friendly. She's coveting you and our garden." The hound responded to the playful sound of Kate's voice with an explosion of slurps on Reese's hand.

"Ah, thank you, Jenny. It's been a while since I've had such friendly kisses." Reese patted her head and looked at Kate. "So how long have you and Jenny lived in the area?"

"We've been here for eight years."

"You bought the hostel eight years ago?"

"Seven. I worked and lived here for a year before buying it."

"Where'd you live before moving to the area?"

Kate searched the special agent's blank face. She had been as good an agent once upon a time, keeping her cards close to her chest, but she lost that edge years ago. Now she just had an edge, and the interrogation was sharpening it. "I'm the one who turned the drugs in. Why all the questions about me?"

"Hey, now. Why don't we go inside and have that coffee?"

"Yeah. That's a good idea, Bob. Come on, Jenny."

When they entered the communal room, Bob wandered over to Nicole at the coffee urns, and Reese stood silently looking around the open space. "Nice place. I see why the Lounge is so popular. A comfy, homey room like this must be heaven after weeks on the hard ground. Safe too, I noticed some high-tech security out there."

"We try. Everyone needs soothing now and then," Kate said coolly, without looking at Reese.

"I agree, and for the record, I don't think you had anything to do with the drugs. Those were background questions. I'd ask any witness the same ones."

Kate stared into the room and told herself to relax. She had no idea if Special Agent Carter knew who the backpack belonged to. Hell, she didn't even know if it was connected to the O'Flaherty mob, not for sure. All she was doing was making herself seem suspicious. "Listen, I'm sorry for snapping earlier. It's just…I've already told Bob what happened."

"Understood. But if you would, I'd like you to tell me what you remember. You and Jenny hiked up to the burn area. Did you see anything unusual?"

"Other than the empty backpack soaked in urine and the baggie full of pills? No, nothing unusual." Kate inwardly groaned. The special agent was just doing her job, and she was being… difficult, the kind of witness who used to make her want to scream. "There was one thing. I didn't see any footprints into or out of the site, which is unusual because there's only one viable way in and back out, and thirty yards behind the camp there's a sheer rock face, an over thousand-foot plummet. So if it was a drop site, the drug mule got rid of their tracks."

Reese stared at her.

"What?"

"Do you think the backpack is a part of a smuggling operation?"

"I never said that."

"No, you didn't. But you seem to be aware there are drop sites—"

"Not really," Kate interrupted. "I'm making a logical assumption."

"So this is the first time you've found drugs in that area?"

"No, I didn't say that, either. I've found some weed. A pipe or two. Some foil and a few syringes. Not a lot for the number of day or overnight visitors we have come through the park and all recreational, never an amount for distribution. Most organized trafficking activity happens around Ross Lake, especially in the border area. But I'm sure you know how creative the runners can be smuggling product into Canada."

Reese silently stared at her again.

What was wrong with her? In eight years, she had never struggled so hard to forget she was ever in law enforcement, but something about the special agent made her respond foolishly. No, not *something*. Hormones. Awake and intense. Sensations she knew could get her in trouble. She looked at Bob. "Hey, pour me a cup, will you?"

"You got it. Do you want one, too, Special Agent Carter?" Bob accentuated her title.

"Yes, thanks." Reese pulled a card from her khaki pants pocket. "If you remember any other details, will you contact me?"

Just take the card and don't talk, Kate told herself as she pocketed Reese's information.

"What'd I miss?" Bob asked, handing them full cups of coffee.

"Ms. Hall has given me some helpful information about the area where Jenny found the drugs, and I was about to ask her about another case if I haven't overstayed my welcome."

The special agent's voice smoothed over Kate like a velvet blanket. *Definitely hormones.* It didn't help the woman was so damn polite, she thought and said, "No problem. I've got a few minutes."

"You know Meena Singh and her wife, Lainey. Sorry, I don't know Lainey's last name."

"It's Wright. Lainey Wright," Bob said to Reese. "You could have just asked me for her last name."

"I did, in a message you didn't return." Reese's tone was professional but sharp, and Bob's paunchy cheeks flushed.

Kate thought their exchange was interesting mostly because Bob hadn't returned her calls in the last few weeks either, but she was more concerned with why the special agent was interested in her friend. "What do you want to know about Meena?"

"I'm investigating a new lead on a cold case. Coleen Farrell went missing in 2010 about a month into a hiking trip on the PCT. Have you heard of her disappearance?"

Kate repeated Coleen's name to herself but it didn't jog any memories. "No. Sorry."

"I've worked her case for a few years, mostly in the Mount Rainer National Park area. She was last seen there. We ran an ad a couple of weeks ago on the fifteenth anniversary of her disappearance, and we got a credible tip that she was here, hitching a ride to Highway 20. That was after the witness statements placed her at Chinook Pass. The new sighting has established this area as her last known whereabouts, so I'm interviewing everyone who lived here during that time. I understand Meena and Lainey did."

"Yeah, that's right. I'll write their phone numbers down for you." Kate's voice softened. Fifteen years was a long time for a positive outcome, but the optimism in the special agent's voice moved her.

"Thanks. I'd appreciate that." Reese stared at the communal room's back wall of floor-to-ceiling bookcases surrounding a large stone fireplace. "That's an impressive book collection. Are they all yours?"

"The majority are, but the owners before me left a few."

"Nice. I collect vinyls. Last year I finished my Billie Holiday collection. Now I'm working on Joni Mitchell. I try to get my hands on first studio recordings."

"I understand that. I'm always on the hunt for first editions." Kate scanned the bookshelves. "I'm not dumb enough to keep any in here. My first editions are in my house."

Reese smiled. "Do you mind if I look around?"

"Knock yourself out." She was relieved when the special agent walked away.

Nicole snuck up and casually leaned against the buffet table. "So, Special Agent Reese Carter's hot. How did you miss her moving to town?"

"I didn't. I've seen her around." Kate retrieved a pen and a piece of paper from a drawer in the buffet table and wrote down Meena's and Lainey's cell numbers.

"You haven't met her until now?"

"I'm not interested in relationships, remember? If I were, I'd have hit on you long ago." She cupped Nic's cheek and winked.

"Right. Don't deflect." Nicole stared at Reese's back. "Check her out. That's me if I was older, less messed up, and blond."

Kate laughed and the special agent and Bob looked at them. "I have Meena's and Lainey's numbers for you," she said, holding the paper up.

"Great. Thanks." Reese picked up a small packet from a bookshelf on the far side of the room. "Do you start your roses from seed in your greenhouse?"

Kate drew her brows together. "Why? What's that?"

"Boston Tealight Rose seeds." Reese walked over as she read the packet and handed it to Kate.

Kate's breath caught. She eyed the packet. "Where did you find them?"

"Propped against the books." Reese held Kate's eyes. "Is everything okay?"

"Yeah. I'm fine." She glanced at her watch. "It's getting late, and I have work to do. A ton of invoices and orders." She moved everyone to the door and opened it. "Nic, will you have Vivienne clean the room again please?" She looked at the special agent. "It was nice to meet you. I'll call if I think of anything else." Then she handed Bob the pink roses wrapped in parchment paper. "Try returning my messages once in a while. Tell Marsha hello for me, and thanks for stopping by."

Kate pushed them out the door and leaned against it for support, the seed pack crumpled in her fist. *Boston Tealight roses? Who left it? A hiker? That would be a wild coincidence. Did one of the Maloneys place it there? Or someone working for them? If they did…then they knew about her grandma and her roses. A tremor shot through her. What else did they know?*

CHAPTER TWELVE

Kate crumpled to the hardwood floor, resting against her bedframe. She held the burner cell phone in one hand and stroked Jenny's back with the other. She wanted to scream and cry one minute and put her fist through the wall the other. The possibility of being found always existed, but she never considered it, not really, not thoroughly. She wouldn't be so unsure of what to do if she had.

After dwelling on the unknown had run its course, she tapped the only number on the call log. Joanna picked up on the first ring. "Kate? I thought we agreed on eleven o'clock?" She could hear the deputy marshal close a door. "Are you okay?"

"I found a packet of 'Boston Tealight' rose seeds in my hostel. They're my grandmother's hybrid roses that she created. It was left on my bookshelf, and I didn't purchase them. Someone brought them here. It was deliberate. Personal."

"Okay. Calm down and take some deep breaths—"

"Is that all you have to say? My grandmother's roses, Joanna. How the hell do the Maloneys know about her?"

"I understand you're upset. I get it. Finding a packet of her rose seeds...that must have thrown you. But listen, the FBI's task force reported that Fiona and Liam haven't left Massachusetts since January. Their investigation only surveils them, so they aren't sure about affiliated persons, but I feel confident your mystery man wasn't Liam."

Kate knocked the back of her head against the mattress. "You're confident? They spent less than a day on his whereabouts. Did they check airline passenger lists for aliases he undoubtedly uses? Did they check private airfields—"

"I hear you," Joanna interrupted. "I'll ask them to dig deeper. I also contacted the Western District, and they agree with me, you aren't under active protection, so we need to move you." She paused, letting the fact sink in. "It's not a suggestion. Relocation can take place at any time, without warning...Kate?"

Joanna's tone made her bite her lip, and after a deep breath she said, "Yeah, I know. I get it."

"I only have your safety in mind. Trust that we're doing everything possible to figure this out."

"What about the drugs Jenny found?" The old hound stood when she heard her name, and Kate stroked her long ears until she padded away into the living room.

"I've relayed your information to the task force."

"That's good. The Park's ISB is running the case. Their special agent thinks the drugs might be connected to one of their ongoing investigations. You'll have to update your contact."

"Sure, I will, if they don't already know. Let's plan another call tomorrow. Eleven my time again? Unless we're in contact with you sooner."

"Sure. Eleven's fine." Jenny returned with her favorite ball and dropped it at Kate's feet.

"Okay, talk then. Stay safe."

"Thanks. I'll try." Kate disconnected and picked up the ball, squeezing it. Jenny pranced on her front paws. "You want to play, sweet girl? All right. Let's go."

She replaced the box under the floorboard and opened the French doors. Jenny shot past her. "Give me a second. I'll be right back," Kate told the hound. She poured a glass of water in the kitchen and tucked her regular cell phone in her jeans pocket.

When she returned, Jenny was waiting patiently on the grassy lawn. Kate loaded the old, fuzzy ball into a launcher, and sent it soaring to the far side of the yard. Jenny tore after it, and Kate smiled even as her eyes stung, tears welling at their corners. She had done everything right. She took a new name, left her only family behind, and built a new life, a life she loved. And it could disappear at any minute.

Jenny ran up the porch steps and dropped the ball, racing back to the yard for another launch. Kate smiled at her. She didn't have the power to affect the future, but she could shape the here and now, and this moment with Jenny was enough. After half an hour of back and forth, Jenny climbed the stairs a little more slowly, and instead of dropping the ball at Kate's feet, curled up in her bed with it.

"Are you worn out?" The hound continued to chew on the ball, and Kate smoothed her hand over Jenny's back. She sat on a deck chair and pressed one of the few numbers in her phone's contact list. She wasn't sure if she was ready for a long, catch-up conversation, but she did know hearing her friend's voice would make her feel better.

"Hey, Kate. It's been a minute."

"Hi. I know. No excuses, though. I'm just a terrible communicator."

Meena laughed. "I know you are. That's why I always call you. But it's nice to be surprised once in a while."

"Glad I could bring some amazement to your life. Speaking of, how's it going?"

"Oh, my God. You wouldn't believe this place. We love it here. I was just telling Lainey the other day, I'm not sure why I ran from here."

"You were young, coming out, and in Nebraska," Kate said. "I would've left the second I could, too."

"True. But it wasn't such a bad place to grow up, and it's so much better now. All the university students make our neighborhood progressive. Plus, they've made the coffee shop a hit. Once we became popular with them, business took off. Lainey schedules events all month long. Poetry readings. Open mics. Music acts. Her ideas are so creative, and everyone has a good time."

"Sounds like life's great. Are things better with your parents then?" Kate rested her hand on Jenny's head, tracing little circles in the hound's fur with her fingertip.

"It's been too long since we talked. Mom and Dad moved to the beach in North Carolina."

"What? Are you kidding? What happened to 'the youngest daughter's duty is to move home and take care of her parents'?"

"Right?" Meena laughed. "As soon as the coffee shop was solidly in the black, they took off. Mom said they had no intention of staying. They just wanted to be sure our business would do okay before they left."

"Seriously? Aren't you angry?" Kate knew the question was a projection the minute it left her mouth. Meena's parents had requested them to move to Omaha, to leave their life in Granite Creek, to leave her life, for what?

"I can't be mad. They meant well. My brothers and sister were in on it, too. Ready-made babysitters, you know, and more company on holidays, but it was worth it. You should see Lainey. She's happier than I've ever seen her. She loves my big family, and my family loves her."

"That's great. I'm jealous your family sees you more than I do, but I'm happy for you." Kate meant what she said, even though she had to force the words.

"Thanks. If you'd train your adorable assistant to run the place, you could visit us once in a while."

"That's true." Kate gave a weak laugh.

"Seriously. She needs to be ready soon because you'll want to be here by next year, *Auntie* Kate."

"Are you serious? Oh, my God. That's so exciting. When? Who's carrying?"

"Slow down. Don't buy nursery presents yet. We're just starting the process, but it's all Lainey can think about, and I'm totally in. We want to have two kids. One to replace each of us."

"How ecologically sound of you," Kate teased.

"We thought so." Meena laughed and then her voice became serious. "We've decided not to wait any longer. Who knows what the right-wing zealots will do next? Lainey's been taking shots, and our first insemination will be her next ovulation if she develops big enough follicles. We're so excited."

"Wow. That's amazing." Kate searched for more words but was at a loss. "Lainey will be a great mother…so will you, obviously," she said finally.

"Thanks. I'll muddle through, but yeah, Lainey's always wanted to have children. You know how patient and caring she is. She'll be an incredible mom."

"I'm searching for words, but I'm so blown away, Meen. You'll both make great parents. I'm so happy for you, and I can't wait."

"Thanks." Meena's voice was soft and proud. "Enough about my life, how are you? Have you warmed up to the coffee shop's new owners?"

"Did you spend any time with them before you moved?"

"Not really. A brief meeting at the title company, but that was about it. Why? Are they terrible?"

"They're okay. Lou's crude, but Phil balances her out. The key is to spend as little time alone with her as possible."

"I had no idea. I'm so sorry." Meena laughed. "Tell me the hostel makes up for it."

"Thankfully. It's July, so—"

"Roses," Meena finished Kate's sentence.

"Exactly." She thought about the packet the special agent had found. "Hey, question. Did you bring me back Boston Tealight rose seeds from one of your trips to the East Coast?"

Meena thought for a moment. "We brought you back a *Cheers* sign for the Lounge, remember?"

"Oh, yeah." Kate recalled convincing Meena and Lainey to let her hang the famous bar's sign in her kitchen instead of the Lounge.

"Why do you ask?"

"Someone found a pack of them on the bookshelves in the communal room, and I was curious how it got there."

"It was probably a hiker. Everyone knows Angel Hall likes roses—and women. Which reminds me, you haven't mentioned if you're seeing anyone."

"I'm not hiding anyone. There's no one to mention."

"Really? Like nothing, nothing. In the last year?"

"Jesus. You're as bad as Nic."

"Oh, come on. Take your assistant out to a club in Seattle or put a profile on a dating app."

Kate gave a short laugh. "No, thanks. Besides, Nicole's coupled and too busy to hang out with her boss. I agreed to let her weird girlfriend move in."

"The French girl?"

"Yeah. She's really into her. God knows why? I've always thought solo hikers were a bit off. She's proof."

"Hey, now. Lainey was a solo hiker when we met."

"Oops. I didn't know that. There's always an exception." She stopped talking and listened to the sweet sound of her friend's laughter. God, she missed it. "Hey, before we hang up. I met an ISB Special Agent. Her name's Reese Carter."

"Oh, tell me more," Meena said playfully.

"There isn't more to tell. She's working on a missing person's case and asked if I had your numbers. She wants to ask you and Lainey some questions about it."

"Oh, okay. Did you give them to her?"

"Yeah, I hope that was all right."

Meena paused. "Sure, whatever we can do to help."

"All right. Well, good luck next month."

"Thanks. Fingers crossed. Send some pics of your roses. I can smell them from here."

Kate smiled. "Will do."

After finishing a stack of invoices and a late dinner, Kate poured a glass of wine and decided she deserved a mineral bath. The day had been long and stressful, and she needed an escape, so she ran hot water in the tub, sprinkled lavender-scented Epsom salts, and stripped. Steam fogged up the room like a soothing sauna. She dipped her fingers in the water, testing it. It was perfect, but just before she stepped in, a knock sounded at the front door.

Jenny growled and scrambled out of her dog bed, running from the bedroom.

Kate turned off the faucet and donned a robe. She glanced at her bedside table and considered arming herself, but she trusted Jenny's read of people and the hound had stopped barking. Even so, Kate woke up her laptop and clicked on the front door security images. Lou stood on the porch, her face inches away from the camera.

"Why are you here so late?" Kate said when she opened the door.

"Late?" Lou snorted. "It's nine-thirty, and you're what, midthirties? What are you doing in a bathrobe ready for bed?"

"It's Monday night, and I work in the morning."

"You and me, both. I left you a message. I had to close the shop for Phil."

"Well, I didn't get it."

"Obviously, but I'm here now, so help me bring in your order."

Kate sighed and sinched her robe's belt tighter. "Fine. But let's hurry up about it. I just ran a bath."

Lou stepped down the stairs, looking at the communal room. "Sounds like a good crowd."

"We always have a full house this time of the year. All the SoBos are filtering through."

"Guitar player is good. The woman singing is better. She might be good-looking. Why aren't you hanging out inside?" Lou lifted her brows, and Kate shook her head, walking past her toward the van. "I'm just saying, you haven't been involved with anyone since we met." She hurried to keep up with Kate's longer stride. "Are you celibate or something? Not that there's anything wrong with that."

"Like I've said, my love life isn't up for discussion. Christ, why is everyone suddenly so interested in personal life?"

"Jeez. Touchy. But I get it. I know how it is. Before I met Phil, I had a terrible dry spell. My electricity bill increased tenfold if you know what I mean." Her annoying grin spread across her face. "If you're in a dry spell, you just need to get right back up on that horse, or whatever you girls say."

Kate sighed. "Lou…don't, please. It's considerate of you to care about me, but you don't need to worry. I'm perfectly content with my life."

"I hear you, but that doesn't mean I believe what you're saying." Lou opened the back of the van and handed Kate a cardboard box with pies inside. "I made two rhubarb and strawberry and two peach 'n' cream."

"Nice. They smell delicious."

"Yeah, thanks. Do you know what else I'm good at? Hooking people up." Lou grabbed a tray of cinnabuns, and Kate groaned. "Come on, hear me out, and then I'll give it a rest." She hurried to keep up with Kate on their way back to the house. "Phil's sister is in town on Friday, and we're meeting at the new pub, Charlie's. I told you Janice is a looker. For your kind."

"What the hell, Lou? You can't say things like…'your kind' and 'you girls.' It's wrong." Kate placed the pies on a shelf in the pantry and ushered Lou to the front door. "You can't go around discussing people's sexuality, either. It's none of your business. Try harder, my friend. Much harder."

"I hear you. I'll try. So you'll have a drink with us? See if Janice gets anything buzzing. It's not healthy to go so long without sex."

"Goodbye, Lou." Kate closed the door and looked at Jenny. "I don't know why I bother with humans when I have you, sweet girl." She bent down and kissed the old hound's head.

Once the tub was full, she dropped her robe and sank into the hot water, letting out a deep sigh as the heat soothed her tension. She didn't care who came to the door now. Not even Special Agent Carter could interrupt her. All right, maybe the special agent could. She thought about the woman in her Blundstones and dark khakis and how good that first sexual attraction felt. Everything about the woman made a tingle climb her spine. Meeting her today only complicated her feelings. But could she trust her? Having Special Agent Carter in her life would be anything but easy.

Exactly why you need to be careful and not get involved, she told herself and slipped her head under the water.

CHAPTER THIRTEEN

Fiona O'Flaherty Maloney tapped her fingers to the time of a mantle clock's ticking. Then she leaned forward on her dark leather chair. It was the only item in Sean's office she hadn't replaced. She kept the chair to make a statement—the days of filling the O'Flahertys' captain seat with a man were over. Her father was dead. No one could force her to relinquish to a man again. She was the boss.

Pressing an intercom, she said, "Nora, I need to make a phone call, and I don't want to be disturbed."

"Yes, Mrs. Maloney."

She unlocked a desk drawer and retrieved a burner cell. Making the call on her office or personal cell phone was out of the question. The FBI had surveilled them once, and the out-of-the-blue visit from Agent Garcia made her believe they had never stopped. That arrogant, smug bitch had the nerve to show up at her office and demand to see her, treating her like a criminal after all this time.

She tapped a number on the phone's screen. "Are you home?"

"Yeah, got in last night."

"Then why haven't you called me?" she demanded.

"It was late, Ma. Like three in the morning. I deserve to sleep, don't you think?"

"Don't be smart with me, Liam." Fiona's voice was tinged with anger. "The FBI visited me this morning. They wanted to know if we've recently traveled out of the state or the country. Why would they be asking that?"

"How the hell should I know?"

"You don't think it's a curious coincidence that you traveled to Washington, and they knocked on my door asking about our movements?" She sucked her teeth. "I gave you one assignment to handle. All you had to do was ensure our first delivery was on track and stay under the radar, and you failed. I'll have to fix it."

"Don't blame me, Ma. There's no way the FBI knew about my flight. And if they did, why would they come asking you questions? They would've just stopped me at the hanger, right?"

"Or they're investigating us and collecting evidence," she replied angrily. "Did that cross your simple mind? The FBI doesn't make social calls." She sat forward and paged through an open contact book.

"What did you tell them?" Liam asked.

"That we haven't traveled since our New Year's trip to Ireland." She continued to flick through her contacts.

"And that's the truth, except for this quick trip, which they don't know about. So don't worry."

Fiona slowly blinked. She mustn't get too angry with him. It wasn't his fault he wasn't as bright as his sister. "It's my job to worry. We lost too much business after your sister's fiasco. We can't afford to lose any more," she said curtly, tapping a page and smiling. She'd found the name of an old contact in the FBI. One she hadn't leaned on in years. "I'll call an associate who owes us a favor and find out why Agent Garcia wants to know about our movements." She sat back and returned her attention to her son. "At least tell me the trip was worth it."

"Yeah, it went great. Antonio's a real prick, though, I'm surprised you even considered doing business with him."

"He might be, but we need this new market. I'm warning you, Liam, do not ruin it with your attitude."

"Jesus, Ma. Do you think I'm stupid?" He paused. "We had some drinks and dinner in Seattle, and he drove me by the ports at Harbor Island. Told me about the route on his end. It's not so sophisticated, either. Just a dude on a cargo ship carrying our product from some South African port to Harbor Island. The last thing we did was finalize the schedule. Once a month for the first year until we figure out supply and demand."

"Tell me again why we're not just driving through the Peace Arch Portal. Why I'm paying for Conner and Finn to work in Washington?"

"I told you, Ma. It's the safest way in. They've ramped up security at the Peace Arch and with the fentanyl trade it'll get tighter. More dogs. More opportunity for our goods to be discovered. You need to trust me on this. There're hardly any busts coming off the PCT. Okay. We're going to make a shit ton of money, Ma. More than enough to make up for the markets we lost in Ireland."

Fiona smiled. "Excellent. And you're certain our part of the pipeline is secure?"

"Oh, yeah. We're good. When they arrive, Stuart pays for the goods and moves them to Stevens Pass. The mules trek north on the PCT. They go through some little shithole towns in the North Cascades, then it's smooth sailing. Our ranger assured me the border patrol's top priority is surveillance for drones, vehicles, and boats on Lake Ross. Our couriers won't have any problems hiking over the border and into Manning Park. Stuart will pick up the product in the park and deliver it to our buyers in Vancouver." He hesitated. "We do have a slight setback. A week. Tops."

"What do you mean *setback*?"

"It's nothing, Ma. The park rangers found some drugs near where Antonio wants us to exchange our goods. It has nothing to do with us. Probably some useless runners let an animal take off with their product. Our associate assured me the investigation in the area would be over in a few days."

"You better be right," Fiona told him. She tapped her fingers on the desktop. "I suppose waiting a week would be best. I should know what Agent Garcia wants by then. I'll make Antonio aware of the postponement. I want you to supervise the first shipment when our route is clear. Just don't use the same ID on your next trip, and make sure you aren't followed to the hanger."

"I'm not an idiot, Ma."

"Let's hope not. Be home early for dinner tonight. We'll celebrate with drinks."

CHAPTER FOURTEEN

The rest of the week had been quiet. Nothing more had happened. No sightings of people from the past or suspicious items left in the communal room. Kate peeked from the butler's pantry door. Friday night Lounge was packed. The smell of freshly brewed coffee mingled with herbal teas. Forks clinked against dessert plates and conversation hummed over the low background music. She glanced at the buffet table. A few pieces of pie and half a tray of cinnabuns were left. That would be plenty for the rest of the evening.

Nicole and Vivienne sat with a group of women playing a heated game of Catan, and Jenny stretched out beside a tramily, enjoying their attention and nonstop petting. The rest of the guests sprawled out on sofas and beanbags. They were mostly under thirty and came from all over the world. The laughter and obvious regard for each other connected them through the shared joys and pains of hiking the backcountry.

Joanna had assured her the FBI task force would alert her if Liam or his known associates left Massachusetts, but she still didn't feel safe. It *was* Liam she saw. She knew she had to be vigilant and keep herself and everyone at the hostel safe. She quietly shut the door.

After a quick shower, Kate studied her reflection in the bathroom mirror as she smoothed moisturizer over her face. The last eight years had aged her, but the hikers looked the same. Twenty-somethings ready to experience the mind and body transformation that happens when you push yourself to complete hundreds or thousands of miles in all of nature's elements. She had been only a few years older than most of her guests when she bought the hostel and enjoyed spending time with them during the morning and evening Lounge. Occasionally, she hit it off with a guest and spent the night with her, too, but that hadn't happened in a few years.

She pulled her dark curls back in an elastic and thought about Lou's invitation. What must they think of her living alone in the middle of nowhere? What did she care about what they thought? She frowned. It did bother her, and she knew why. Lou was a cybersecurity expert and nosy. She could easily uncover her secret if she became curious enough. Kate couldn't let that happen. She tossed her pajamas on the bed and dressed in jeans and a T-shirt, deciding to shock the Turners by showing up at the town's new pub.

An hour later, she parked outside an old-mill-style building that wasn't old. Faint music whispered through its closed door, but once she opened it, the music thumped in her chest. The new pub was bigger than she expected and busier. People from every community around the park must have turned up to check it out. She spotted Lou and Phil at a table behind the dance floor.

"Hiya," Lou shouted over the music. "You made it."

Kate sat. "Yeah, I figured what the hell. An occasional night out won't kill me."

Lou grinned. "You came to meet Phil's sister. Admit it." She backhanded Phil on the shoulder, and he absorbed the hit without spilling the mug of beer he held inches from his mouth.

"I will only confess that a drink with people my age tempted me," Kate said.

Lou waved the server over. "We ordered a couple of flatbreads if you're hungry. They don't serve wings or French fries if you can believe that crap. Too hoity-toity."

Kate realized the smell of fried food and stale beer was indeed surprisingly absent. She ordered a glass of cabernet sauvignon and looked around the pub. Lou tapped her arm and pointed at a table of women. "Phil's sister is the one in the yellow shirt."

Kate had already checked out the table and was surprised the woman with the crew-cut platinum hair and starched clothes was Phil's sister. She wouldn't have guessed it if Lou hadn't said.

"She was supposed to sit with us and meet you, but she sniffed those girls out the minute we walked in. Do you want me to bring her back?"

"You can't say things like that, love."

"Like what?"

"Sniffed and girls…" Phil sighed and drank his beer.

"Why? I'd say the same thing if your little brother were here cruising chicks." Lou frowned. "I don't know why people have to be so sensitive. Bunch of orchids if you ask me."

"Please don't bother Phil's sister on my account," Kate told Lou. The server returned with her wine and the flatbreads. The aroma of spicy arugula and garlic made her hungry.

"Well, well, well," Lou said, her smile reappearing. "Never mind. Looks like she liked the choices over here more." Lou lifted her eyebrows up and down. "Hey, Janice. This is Kate. Kate, Phil's sister, Janice."

Kate extended her hand. "Hi."

"Hey." They shook hands, and then Janice gestured to the table of women. "We're heading over to Beth's cabin to play poker. Want to ditch these two and join us?"

"Thanks for the offer, but I'm only here for one drink, then I need to get home."

"Okay, no problem. It's nice to finally meet you. I've heard so much about your hostel, tucked away in the woods. Maybe I can get a tour next time I'm in town?"

"I'll be sure to invite you," Kate said.

"Sounds great." She hugged Phil goodbye and turned to Lou, but her sister-in-law looked away and gulped her beer. "Ah, don't be mad at me for leaving, Lou…okay. Have it your way."

Janice left and Lou blew out a sharp breath. "Could she be more selfish? We had a plan."

"I think you were alone in that plan," Phil said.

Kate laughed and glanced at the table of women again. They were looking at the pub's front door, and she followed their gaze. Special Agent Reese Carter had entered. A jolt of energy shot through her, and she quickly looked at the flatbread, grabbing a piece. It was a clumsy move, but it was the only way to keep from staring at the special agent who looked even better out of uniform, dressed in old, faded jeans and an open button-down shirt over a tank top.

"Okay. Here we go, sports fans," Lou said. The enthusiasm in her voice had returned, and her arm shot up catching Reese's attention. "Player number two might be headed for the bar, but she'll be right over. Trust me. Looks like you might get a homerun tonight after all." She winked at Kate.

Phil grumbled and bit into a piece of flatbread.

"Lou, seriously. Don't say anything like that in front of Reese, please. I mean it. It makes me very uncomfortable, and I'm not looking for a…anything…with anyone right now."

"Jeez. Relax. I'm only having a little fun. Don't take yourself so seriously. It's not a lesson you want to learn the hard way. Trust me." Phil gently squeezed Lou's hand, and her grin returned. "Look out, here she comes."

"Hi," Reese said. "Mind if I sit down?"

"Our feelings would be hurt if you didn't." Lou sounded like a flirty teenager. She waited for Reese to settle into a chair and added, "Do you and Kate *know* each other?"

"Oh, here we go," Phil whispered.

Reese smiled at Kate and looked back at Lou. "We met yesterday. Did you know she has an incredible rose garden? I'm truly envious."

"Thank you," Kate said. And she meant it. Not only the compliment but also the way Reese steered the conversation.

"Yeah, I know she has a rose garden." Lou leaned in. "Do you know how she keeps them alive and leafing out in May like they never went through a frigid winter?"

"She hasn't told me any of her secrets, but I'd love to hear all about that one."

"It's hardly a secret." She didn't mean to sound defensive and softened her voice. "Each plant gets mulched and fitted with a cone."

"Ah, come on. You do more than that. Every time I deliver pastries, you're in the garden. Those roses get more attention than anyone or anything in your life. Except for Jenny, obviously."

Kate was thankful for the bar's dim lighting. Her cheeks flushed hot, and she side-eyed Lou. "Growing roses is a year-round commitment."

"Last summer, I visited the garden in August," Phil said, tipping his glass at Kate. "Spectacular."

"Thanks, Phil."

"Maybe you can share some of your growing tips with me. I've designed some beds in my backyard. I'd love to make a few of them rose gardens."

"Sure. Just ask." The way Reese looked at her made a thousand pinheads prick her skin.

"Ah, that's nice. It takes a certain kind of person to keep up a yard and here at the same table sit two of you." Lou knocked Phil's arm. "Take this guy. He likes to get his hands dirty occasionally. That's why we have flowerpots in front of the coffee shop. But that's even too much gardening for me." Lou sat back as the server removed her empty glass and plate. "We'll have another round please."

"Just a glass of water for me. Thank you," Kate said.

Phil looked at Reese. "How do you like living in the old Hendrick's place?"

"I love it. The first time I saw it, I knew it had great bones."

"It's a beautiful post and beam. We looked at it when we bought the coffee house. But it needed too much work."

"Yeah. It's criminal how the last owner chopped it up for an Airbnb." Lou snorted. "Besides, it's too big. We had a sleek condo in Cupertino. Move-in ready. Brand new."

"Did you buy it last year?" Phil asked.

"In December, but I didn't move here until April. All those hurried DIYs the last owners did for the Airbnb are gone. I had it demoed back to its original floor plan. I'll do the restoration work myself. My dad's a retired contractor in Northern California. He taught me everything I know, and what I don't know, I can count on him to teach me."

"Whereabouts in Northern Cal?" Lou asked.

"Redding."

"My family's from Anderson. We were practically neighbors, neighbor. What year did you graduate high school?"

"2006."

"Oh, you're a baby. I was class of 2001. Did you stick around?"

"Not since college. I joined the National Park Services and lived in Yellowstone, Death Valley, and Yosemite until now. The rest of my family still lives in Redding. Both of my older brothers and their families. Do you remember Scott or Eric Carter?"

Lou thought for a moment. "Can't say that I do. But then again, I wasn't paying attention to other people unless they were into computers. Were they?"

"My brothers? Not hardly, they were into surfing and smoking weed."

Kate's stomach tightened like it did when people talked about their families and pasts, and the special agent watching her reactions to the conversation didn't help matters.

"We don't have people in the area any longer," Lou said. "My parents divorced after I left for college. My dad ran a fishing hatchery. He stayed in Anderson for a while but sold his business last year and moved to Florida. My mom remarried a charlatan—"

"He's a lawyer," Phil interrupted.

"Right. That's what I said. Anyway, she ran off to Monterey. Don't see them very often. We're all busy." She sat back as the server placed their drinks on the table.

"Where are you from, Phil?" Reese asked.

"My parents moved with my two older brothers from Kansas City to Fresno during the early eighties' recession. The rest of us were born in California. Now we're spread out all over the country.

Washington, Colorado, Michigan, Texas, Florida, Massachusetts, New York. Holidays are a trainwreck."

"How many siblings do you have?" Reese asked.

"Too many. His poor mom was pregnant for two decades. Four brothers and three sisters. I thought, what the shitgibbons am I signing up for? Jeez, I was so relieved when he said he didn't want kids." Lou pointed to herself with both hands. "This beautiful line stops with me."

"Really? You don't want kids?" Reese asked.

Lou frowned. "We're not all breeders."

"I think we can toast to that." Kate raised her water glass, and Phil burst out in a belly laugh, the loudest Kate had ever heard the man sound. Lou huffed and drank a long swig of her beer. Kate glanced at her watch. "Woah. I need to go. Sorry, I was so engaged in the conversation that time got away from me." She got to her feet and looked at Lou. "Thanks for the invite. I had a good time."

"I can't believe you're leaving now. It's not even eleven o'clock," Lou said, pouting. "You didn't even tell us anything about your family."

Reese stood. "I need to head home, too. Early day tomorrow."

Lou looked positively devastated. "Oh, fine. Leave me here with him. Jeez. You're a couple of lightweights."

"Safe travels home, and have a nice night," Phil said, sounding as pleasant as ever.

When they got to the door, Reese opened it for Kate. "You didn't have to leave on my account," Kate said and walked past.

"Why would I stay if the person I wanted to spend time with was leaving?"

That was the second time the special agent's comment tilted Kate's universe, but this time she steadied herself and turned around to face Reese. "You didn't even know I would be here tonight."

"I figured if Lou tried to set me up with her sister-in-law, she would also try to set you up."

"And you thought I'd agree to let Lou arrange a date for me?" Kate stepped off the curb beside her truck.

"Not at all. I only showed up hoping you'd decide to have a drink here tonight. Luckily, you did. I've been trying to run into you for months. You're not the easiest person to get to know, but I want to…get to know you. I hoped to ask you if that would be okay." She moved closer to Kate. "Will that be a problem?"

Her directness knocked Kate off balance again, and she spoke before thinking. "I can't see that it would be." The fiery attraction between them spread, and Reese pulled her close. She didn't evade the kiss, letting go just this once, melting into it. Reese's hand was firm on her lower back, her lips were soft, and Kate wanted more. She ached to deepen the kiss and feel the full length of Reese's body against hers, but Reese pulled back and held her eyes.

"That was amazing," she said, her voice low and raw.

"Mmhmm." It was the only sound Kate could make.

"I hope we get to do that again."

She regained her voice. "That's a distinct possibility, Special Agent Carter."

"Special agent? I think we're on a first-name basis now." Reese gave her an easy smile. "Drive safely."

"I will. Thanks." She watched Reese walk into the woods, then unlocked her truck and climbed inside before her shaky legs gave way. What the hell was she thinking? That was a mistake. A big mistake.

CHAPTER FIFTEEN

Reese enjoyed being on her hands and knees, measuring and laying the cabin's flooring. Each precise fit, the pneumatic nail gun's explosive charge, and the table saw's whirling were outlets for the storm of feelings brewing inside her.

She let the tape measure snap back and cut another floorboard. The demo restored the cabin's massive great room, exposed rustic timber posts and beams still in great shape, but the original flooring had to be torn out. The planks were water- and termite-damaged, buckled, and rotten. Reese opted for a dark wide-plank western pine to offset the lighter pine walls and ceiling.

She had several feet laid down when her phone vibrated in her back pocket. She checked the number and hesitated. But there was no use avoiding the call. She'd have to talk to her mom sooner or later, which meant her mom would hear *something* in her voice. She always did, no matter what it was.

"Hey, Mom," Reese answered. She turned down the volume on her stereo and lifted the turntable's arm.

"You sound winded. Are you walking back from the coffee shop?"

"I didn't go today." She poured a cup of coffee, opened the wall of stacker doors that brought the mountainside into the great room, and sat outside at a patio table.

"Oh, you're working on your floor, then."

She smiled that her mom already knew her Saturday morning routine. "Yeah. Got lost in it for a few hours and made good progress."

"I bet they look fantastic. You do such nice work. I can't wait to see your place, Reesy."

"Won't be much longer, and it'll be ready for visitors. What are you up to?"

"Oh, you know. This and that. Mostly trying to stay cool. It's hot as hell here. We've been under a heat advisory forever. So, I told your father enough's enough and booked us an Alaskan cruise in two weeks. You'll never guess what I signed us up for." She paused, then burst out, "A helicopter glacier tour that ends in a dog sled ride. Mush! Your dad's so excited."

"Sounds incredible." She loved hearing this new happiness in her mother's voice. Her parents had worked and sacrificed forty years to raise her and her brothers, helping them become solidly grounded on their paths. Now they were enjoying each other again, exploring the world.

"You wouldn't believe it. I'll email you the brochure so you can look at it. There are more shore excursions I want to sign us up for, but I'll let your dad choose a few."

"Well, that seems fair. Is Eric watching Reno for you?"

"Probably, or Scott. Why?"

"Just asking."

"Oh, Reesy. You're lonely. I can hear it in your voice." Her mom sounded heartbroken.

"You aren't hearing loneliness. I'm fine. Not lonely at all. It's just—"

"You have a home now and want to share it with someone, right? Well, our cruise departs from Seattle. We can come a day early with Reno. Leave him with you. It would be good practice for when you adopt a new pup. How's that sound?"

"That's a nice idea, but you don't need to put yourself out for me."

"I know I don't need to, but I want to. I was feeling bad about leaving during your birthday anyway."

"Mom, I'm thirty-eight. It's okay."

"You're never too old to see your parents on your birthday, and then we can see your beautiful new home in person. It's the perfect start to our escape, being in the woods and the crisp alpine air. Besides, your dad's been dying to get up there and figure out what projects he can help you with."

"Okay, slow down. You know I'd love to see you, but my place isn't ready. You have to wait until I have a guest bedroom set up at least. Okay?"

"Fine. We'll wait. But you better work on a guest room after you finish the floor. Promise?"

"I promise." Reese sipped her coffee. A bird called above her, and she looked up in time to watch the bald eagle disappear into the forest.

"Good. Then we'll eagerly wait for our invitation."

"All right. And don't worry about me. I'm too busy right now to be lonely."

"Busy? I thought you were on downtime."

"We got a lead on one of my cold cases. Her last seen whereabouts were in this area. And last week a neighbor found drugs off one of the area trails. It might be connected to one of our trafficking cases. So my work came home."

"Oh, Reesy. That sounds intense. Who's the neighbor who just happened to find them? That sounds suspicious."

Reese almost spit out her mouthful of coffee. She swallowed and laughed. "She runs a hostel just outside the park, and she hikes the trails a couple of times a week offering food and drinks to the thru-hikers. Besides, Poirot, she was the one who reported them. Immediately upon finding them." She felt a flush on her face.

"Hmm. I do love my Poirot. We can't get more Christie books, but I wish they'd create more shows. So does this trail angel have a name?"

"Her name's Kate Hall. Why?" The flush turned hotter. Her mother was an expert at diverting and striking.

"Ha, now that's a real aptronym. A name that fits an occupation. I've heard about people with them and read plenty of books with characters who have them, but I've never personally known anyone. Maybe Ed Bass. He liked to fish, but that doesn't necessarily count. If he played bass or sang bass then it would. Now Kate *Hall* and she's a hostel owner. That's fabulous. So how long have you been seeing her?"

Reese was ready for it this time. "Well, that is interesting. The aptronym." She drew out her pronunciation of the word. "I can always count on you to broaden my vocabulary."

"And?"

Reese laughed. "I'm not seeing Kate Hall."

"But you want to."

"It's that obvious?"

"To me, it is. I know when you're hemming and hawing. If it is to anyone else, to Kate Hall, who knows? You might want to tell her."

"Oh, trust me, she knows. I'm not sure what she'll do with the information. She seems keen on keeping to herself. But I respect the need for privacy. Besides, I'm too busy to think about starting a relationship."

"A relationship?" Her mom's voice notched up in excitement. "Ooh, you really like this woman. When will we meet the private Kate Hall?" she asked, no diversion, just full-on strike.

"Okay, I gotta go now, Mom. Tell Dad and everyone hi. Have fun in Alaska. Bye now."

"Fine." Her mom laughed. "We'll continue this later."

Reese ended the call. Her mom was right. She had dated plenty of women over the years. Some had even lasted a year or two, usually because they were in the same park, and it was easy. But none had started like this. With one kiss her thoughts moved right into wanting a relationship. She looked at the empty chairs around the deck table and picked up her coffee mug. Her thoughts about Kate were intense and consuming. It was time to start laying down more flooring.

* * *

Kate hauled another flat of planting pots onto the shelf. *Get a grip*, she advised herself. After a full day of gardening, she couldn't stop thinking about the kiss. It wasn't like she'd never kissed a woman, and that was the problem. It wasn't only the kiss or imagining the mind-blowing sex that would follow. She'd never physically desired or been this infatuated with anyone like this.

She lifted a bucket of potting soil and aggressively shook the dirt into the flat's pots. The day had been sunny and clear, making the greenhouse hotter than usual. She wiped the sweat off her face with a towel and drank from a water bottle. Jenny wandered through the greenhouse's door, and Kate poured water into the hound's bowl. "Where have you been?" she asked, and Jenny wagged her tail while lapping up the cool water. The old hound had been hanging out with Nicole at the woodpile the last time Kate saw her. "Are you ready to go inside?"

Kate covered the bucket of potting soil and shoved it under the shelf with her foot. Once outside, Jenny trotted to her dog door and disappeared inside the house. Kate stopped at the communal room's door and peeked her head in. Coffee percolated and a French song she didn't understand played on the stereo. Vivienne hummed along, unloading the dishwasher, and Nicole stacked mugs on the buffet table, their backs facing her. "Hey," she said.

Nicole turned around. "Hi. Did you finish prepping your growing flats?"

"They're coming along." She looked at Vivienne, whose back was still to her. "I'm staying home tonight. You all good here?"

Nicole glanced at Vivienne. "We're good."

"Great. Thanks. See you in the morning." Kate shut the door and felt relieved Nicole could manage the day-to-day operations of the hostel without her. It was even easier for her with Vivienne's help. Now all she had to do was teach Nic the business side, and she could take that trip to see Meena and Lainey and not worry about a thing…well, at least nothing about the hostel.

After a long, hot shower and microwaved lasagna dinner, Kate poured herself a glass of wine and opened her laptop. "Jenny. Come here, sweet girl." The hound climbed onto the sofa, curling up next to her. "We're researching Special Agent Reese Carter. We'll start with her job. It's a perfectly sane, nonstalkery thing to do when you have questions." She typed National Parks ISB into the search bar and hit return.

"'The Investigative Services Branch is the FBI of our national parks,'" she read aloud. That was not a comparison she wanted to pursue. She closed that article and read another, feeling a rush of energy. It described the major crimes Reese had solved, and by the end, she wanted to know everything about the special agent. She spent the next hour reading about how Reese had become one of only thirty agents investigating homicides and other major crimes in the national parks. That was a seriously stressful job. She wondered what Reese did to relax. Did she have a cat, dog, or both? It didn't take much time to want more personal information about the special agent, but none of the work-related hits provided those answers.

"Should I go full-on stalker?" she asked Jenny. The hound was already asleep. "I'll take your silence as approval." Reese's Facebook page popped up, and she scrolled through her posts. After a few minutes, her phone rang, and she jumped like she'd been caught looking at someone's diary.

Jenny sat up, becoming alert. "It's okay. Sorry, sweet girl." Kate soothed her, and the hound flopped down again. "Hey, Meena."

"Hey yourself. Do you have a second?"

"Yeah, what's up?"

"The park agent you told me about left us messages this morning. Could you tell us again what she wanted? Oh, and you're on speaker."

"Hey, Lainey," Kate said.

"Hi, Kate. Miss you."

"Miss you, too. She's working on a missing person's case. A woman named Coleen Farrell disappeared fifteen years ago. She'd been on the PCT, and the ISB received a tip a few weeks ago that she was last seen in our park. Reese is interviewing people who were in the area then. Business owners and angels. I think she's even trying to reach Fred and Luann."

"Good luck with that. What'd they tell you when they left? Don't bother calling for advice, we're retired and won't answer the phone." Meena laughed. "Seriously though, I don't know how much we can help, but we'll call her back."

"Especially since we had just started our relationship," Lainey added. "We were pretty wrapped up in each other. You know how it is."

"Yeah. It happens," Kate said, as she slowly closed the lid on her laptop.

"Oh? It does?" Meena asked.

"I think that's my cue to go," Lainey said. "Nice to hear your voice, Kate. I hope we see you soon."

"I promise you will. Bye, Lainey."

"Okay, it's just us," Meena said. "How did Special Agent Carter become Reese? And don't lie. I can hear how interested you are when you say her name."

"No, you can't."

"Yes, I can."

"Fine. You're right. I've seen her a few times. Not dates or anything. Just around. But, yeah, I'm way too interested, but I'm not sure what to do about it. I don't want a relationship."

"Relationship? Why are you jumping to marriage? Maybe Special Agent Reese Carter just wants sex."

Kate laughed. "You're probably right. She has to drop everything and take cases in any of the national parks at any time. Who'd want a relationship with that schedule?"

"She'd want one with you no matter her schedule. It took me five years to become a part of your inner circle, but I wanted to be there from day one. You're amazing and kind…and generous to a fault. I've no doubt she'd love to be in a relationship with you if you'd let her."

"Aw, Meen. That means the world to me. I'm glad we're in each other's circle, too."

CHAPTER SIXTEEN

Reese entered a clearing and called Ranger Bob on her phone. There was still no answer. She texted him details about Coleen Farrell's case to follow up on. Then, she told him the lab had returned forensics. The pills did match the chemical composition of the others in her PCT case, and information about the backpack was still pending.

She continued descending McGregor Mountain, trekking through thinning pine groves and scrambling down talus slopes. Earlier that morning, she had hiked up to the dry camp, examining it for footprints. Besides those identified as belonging to law enforcement and Kate Hall, there were no others. Kate was right. The drug runner had to have hiked to the site off-trail, which would have been difficult. It was also the only thing different from the other drops in the ISB investigation. The other backpacks were off the PCT in easy-to-find locations. That bothered Reese. Why were they so easy to discover? That was careless. When they had been found, why continue the same routine? That was risky. But most importantly, why was this last drop so different? Reese couldn't answer why, and it bothered her.

She stopped on a rocky outcrop, wiped the sweat off the back of her neck, and drank water. The sun was intense even in dry subalpine air. She continued hiking down to the PCT trailhead near Howard Lake, scouring the vegetation for signs of drug runners. After passing through the trees on the northeastern side of the lake, she neared the PCT and McGregor junction and heard the familiar baying of a hound. It caused a burst of grouse out of a clearing, and nervous excitement spread through her.

A few minutes later, Jenny zigzagged over the understory and rolled onto her back at Reese's feet. "Hey, Jenny." She rubbed the hound's stomach. "Ooh, you're hot. Let's get you some water." Jenny jumped up and kissed Reese's hand with an unusually dry tongue before turning and trotting back down the trail. Reese followed the old hound, expecting Kate wouldn't be far behind, and she was right. The trail angel appeared and waved. God, she was tall and leggy. Not that height mattered, but it was nice to stand face-to-face with a woman. At six feet tall, she hadn't had the pleasure often.

"Didn't expect to see you out here. Hope you aren't going to ticket me for having Jenny unleashed," Kate called.

"Fresh out of tickets. But don't let a better-supplied ranger catch the two of you." She waited for Kate to join them. "Jenny gave me a sweet greeting. She's pretty hot, though, and her tongue feels dehydrated. You might want to stop and let her have a drink."

"Come here, sweet girl." Kate stroked Jenny's back. "You are hot." She dropped her pack and filled a collapsible bowl with water. The hound was panting but only lapped the water a few times.

"I meant to call you yesterday," Reese said. "I was—"

"No worries," Kate interrupted. "I didn't call you either. Have you been up to the dry campsite?"

"Yeah, I took another look. You were right. I couldn't find any footprints either. So I decided to trek down through the brush to the trail like you suggested, but I didn't see anything there. I'm hiking up to Heaton Camp next."

"Why? You think the drug courier left some evidence there?"

"It's a possibility."

Kate stared into the forest and up to the summit. "I don't think so. They could've hiked up there, but it's steep with tremendous switchbacks. Not a lot of water until you get there. I doubt a runner is experienced enough to handle that trail. Even if they were, why would they? Heading east or north from there to hook up with another trail is out of the question, and there's nowhere to go except back down. It wouldn't make sense. Heading up the trail toward Heaton Camp and the summit is six or seven hours out of the way." She turned her head, staring behind them. "Makes more sense that one runner hiked section K from Stevens Pass to this point and then hitched out of the park. A second runner was probably supposed to continue to section L and into Canada. If it's a trafficking route this far north along the PCT, that's the obvious endpoint."

Reese could have been standing with a colleague the way Kate thought through scenarios, except she had never struggled so hard to maintain concentration to listen to a coworker. So much about this woman impressed and intrigued her. Distracted her. She focused and said, "Bob told me you knew the trails and area better than he did. He just didn't mention you knew about drug trafficking, too."

"I've lived here longer," Kate replied, and Reese could see her cheeks flush. "Where is he anyway? I thought he was helping you."

Reese noted the diversion. "He is, but I haven't heard from him today."

"He's been hard to get a hold of lately."

She wondered if Kate knew about his wife's cancer. If she did, she wasn't letting on. She glanced at Kate's backpack. "How often do you share magic at illegal campsites?"

"That sounds like a loaded question. The sites are unsanctioned, but they're still being used, and I know Bob only treks into that area once or twice a month, so I visit them twice a week, especially during peak months. I clean up if the hikers don't follow 'leave no trace' and call in any problems. If hikers happen to be there, I have Snickers, Dr. Pepper, and fruit to share." She grinned. "If you think about it, the park should pay me for my services." She looked at Jenny as she wobbled over to a clump of bracken fern.

Reese dropped her pack next to Kate's. "Is she okay?"

"She's too hot. I cut the distance of our Sunday trek, even so, I shouldn't have brought her out this late." Kate frantically grabbed another water bottle from her pack.

Reese grabbed two containers from her backpack and knelt beside Jenny. She checked the dog's gums and felt her armpits, then took the bottle out of Kate's shaking hand. "We have enough water to cool her down. She'll be okay." She peeled off her T-shirt down to a sports bra and soaked the shirt with one of her containers of water before wrapping it around Jenny's head. She wet the hound's paws, ears, and belly with her last bottle. Then she poured the remaining water on the back of Jenny's neck. "How old is she?"

"I'm not sure how old she is…nine or ten. I adopted her from a rescue shelter when I moved here." Kate stroked Jenny's back. "I know it's time for her to slow down. We stopped hiking to Heaton Camp last year. Her hips couldn't make the trip any longer, but it's hard to scale back all our treks. She gets so excited to come with me."

"Yeah, they'll do anything for us, even if it kills them." Reese poured the last of their water over Jenny's groin area. Then she stood and picked up their empty bottles. "I'll hike up to the waterfall and refill these."

"Are you sure?" Kate scrambled to her feet.

"Absolutely. I'll be back in a few."

"Okay." Kate caught herself staring at Reese's sinewy body. Her defined abdomen muscles. The slight curves under her sports bra. She quickly looked down and fumbled to untie a light jacket from her waist. "Here, cover up with this, so you don't get sunburned."

"Right. Thanks." She donned the windbreaker and jogged up the trail.

It took Reese less than an hour. When she returned, Jenny was lying on her side, and her tail thumped against the ground. She set three of the bottles on a flat stone in the full sun to warm the glacial water. Then she poured the fourth bottle over the T-shirt around Jenny's head. "Here's your jacket. Thanks."

Kate nodded and looked away. "How do you know so much about dogs?"

"Park visitors often bring them, so we train in first aid for all guests."

"Aw, I love that." She stroked Jenny's back.

"Are you willing to share your Dr. Pepper with the law?" Reese grinned.

"I think you can be the exception." Kate poured a collapsible cup full of pop.

"So you moved here eight years ago? From where?" Reese asked.

"You mean you haven't run a background check on me?"

"Should I have?" Reese took a drink and watched Kate's expression soften. "Ahh…I haven't had one of these in ages. Forgot how much I love the spiciness."

"Not worried about what's in those twenty-three flavors?"

"Guess I just like mysteries." She held Kate's eyes. "So, no comment on where you moved from?"

"I'm not avoiding your question." She continued petting Jenny's side. "Florida. Born and raised."

"Florida? I never would have guessed that. Alaska or Colorado. Maybe even Vermont. But you don't give off Florida vibes."

"What's that supposed to mean?"

"You just seem to fit in with the mountains and forests." She sat beside Kate. "You don't have to analyze what I say. It'll be the truth or a compliment. I don't waste my time maneuvering and lying—" Kate held her hand up, and Reese stopped talking. "Sorry, am I upsetting you?"

She shook her head. "I'm just upset about Jenny."

"I'll stay until she feels good enough to make the trip home. She's looking better already." Reese stroked Jenny's back, brushing against Kate's hand. "I'm glad you decided to make the mountains home."

"Yeah, us, too. We love it here, don't we, sweet girl?"

"Lou also told me you anonymously donate quite a bit to the park and the Baker-Snoqualmie National Forest."

Kate frowned. "If Lou knows and tells people, my donations aren't anonymous, are they?"

"She didn't mean any harm by telling me. She's just impressed. So am I. That kind of generosity is notable. How much money does a hostel generate in a season?"

"I don't depend on the hostel's income to live." Kate's voice became sharp.

Raw nerve, Reese thought. Very raw. She considered Kate's income a mystery for another time and changed the subject. "So how did an Everglades girl come to love the mountains?"

Kate seemed to search for an answer and said, "My parents took me skiing in Colorado when I was about ten. I fell in love with the snow and crisp air. The trees...they were incredible. All the peaks and valleys. Being in the Rockies was like being in another world."

"I've been to Florida. I can see why you'd think that." Reese gulped the rest of her soda and held the cup out. "Might as well lessen your load."

Kate filled her cup with more pop. "Take some fruit too." She opened her pack and tossed two apples to her.

Reese caught them and bit into one. "Does the rest of your family still live in Florida?"

"All right. What is this? Did you plan on conducting a face-to-face background check on me?"

"No. We didn't have a chance to talk much at the pub, not with Lou there. I thought now would be a good time to get to know you better. That's all."

"Well, you're making me feel like a suspect."

"I'm sorry. That wasn't my intention." Reese held Kate's dark-brown eyes. Someone or something had caused her defensiveness. It wasn't about a few personal questions, and she wasn't allowing Kate's past to hijack the conversation. "Here's my truth...the first weekend I moved to town, I saw you on the trails, and I've wanted to meet you since. This is the third time we've talked in case you weren't counting. Each conversation makes me more excited than the last, and I can't stop thinking about the next time I see you. It's been a long time since I've felt this way about someone, and Friday night outside the pub, our kiss...the energy...it was explosive...that's a compliment. How did it make you feel? Am I wrong?"

"You're not wrong." Kate's voice was barely above a whisper. She retrieved her refillable bottle from the rock and poured the warmed water over Jenny in the same places Reese had. The bloodhound angled her head and licked the water running down her neck. Then got to her feet, nudging the bottle. "Are you thirsty now?" She filled the bowl, and the old hound drank. "That's right, sweet girl. Have some more."

"It's good she's up and drinking." The way Kate cared for Jenny with such attentive love made Reese smile. "And so you know, I'm glad it wasn't just me who felt that way."

Kate looked at her. "I'm not interested in a relationship."

"Okay. That's good to hear." She grinned at Kate's surprised expression. "What? You didn't say you weren't interested in me."

Kate chuckled and rubbed the hound's head, kissing her muzzle. "Are you feeling better? Ready to go home?"

"The sun's down, but you still need to take it slow." Reese stroked Jenny's back. "You gave your human a scare, tough girl." She wanted to reach out and comfort Kate, too. But she felt Kate put a barrier up and didn't want to find cracks or a way to overcome it. She wanted to create a door that Kate would open for her and allow her inside. They stood and hoisted their backpacks. "Be careful and call me if she becomes overheated again. I'll help you carry her home."

"We will. Thanks for helping and staying with us. You be careful on your way to Heaton. There are usually tree limbs down on the trail. I haven't been there to report any, and who knows if Bob has."

"Okay. I will." Reese smiled, slow and sure. "Sounds like you're worried for me. I'll take that for a start."

"Worried *about* you." Kate whistled for Jenny to follow, then turned around and looked at Reese. "It's not a start."

CHAPTER SEVENTEEN

The journey back to the hostel was slow. Thankfully, it was mostly downhill, and the thin mountain air cooled as night approached. Kate stopped and made Jenny drink water and rest every time she panted. The relaxed pace allowed Kate's thoughts to linger on Reese, shirtless. The woman's toned upper body, the well-defined curves of her arms, the definition of her abdomen muscles, it all sent her blood racing. When they finally got home, the evening Lounge was in full swing. She stopped at the large windows and peeked inside. The buffet was still well supplied. Nicole sat at a game table, playing cards with three other guests, her free hand gesturing in enthusiastic conversation, and in one of the corner nooks, Vivienne nestled in an armchair beside the soft glow of a lamp.

Kate had created the areas for quiet reflection and reading. Vivienne had a book open on her lap, but instead of reading, she conversed with another woman. Kate watched them for a moment. She could only see the other woman's profile, really just her nose. Her raven-black hair hid her eyes. Vivienne's quick talking and the delight on her face suggested she had found another Francophone to talk to.

After leaving a message for Jenny's vet and making them dinner, Kate settled on the sofa with Jenny by her side. She didn't want to think about the afternoon and the drama of how scared she felt or how much Reese calmed her. She couldn't think about her. The special agent was dangerously close to occupying too much space in her life. So she distracted herself with a marathon of Masterpiece Theatre.

A few hours later, Kate stared at the drapes covering the patio doors and a feeling of unease came over her. She didn't want the fear of Liam or the O'Flahertys to control her. Years in hiding had taught her dwelling on what might happen only precluded living in the present moment. Just be careful, she told herself. She rinsed out her microwave dinner tray, tossed it in recycling, and cleaned Jenny's empty bowl. "Let's go to bed, sweet girl."

Jenny jumped off the sofa and followed Kate. Halfway down the hallway, the hound growled and whipped around, racing back to the living room. Kate's heart raced, and she hid at the end of the hall, looking into the living room. Jenny had nosed behind the drapes, scratching at the glass doors, snarling and barking.

Kate turned and ran to her bedside table, retrieving her gun, the heavy metal cold in her hand. It had been years since she had fired a weapon. With her heart pounding, she returned to the patio doors, pulled back the drape, and flipped on the outdoor lights, expecting to see her past on the patio, a face of retribution, but no one was there. She scanned the hostel's yard and stared into the woods. Nothing. Not even guests milling around.

"Jenny, shush." Kate stood between the hound and the patio doors, stroking her head until she settled down. "Nothing's out there now." She crouched and kissed the dog's head. "Thank you. You wouldn't let anything get us, would you? Not you. Good girl." She walked back to the bedroom, and Jenny followed. She was still on high alert and ran to the bedroom's French doors, acting like she needed to be outside. Kate returned her gun to the bedside table. "Jenny, nothing's out there. Go get your leash. I'll take you out and show you."

Jenny returned to the bedroom with the lead in her mouth. Kate attached it to her collar and opened the French doors, but the hound bolted, pulling the lead out of Kate's hands. "Jenny, stop!" Kate yelled, running after her. She stopped where the hound had disappeared into the woods and continued shouting for her to stop until she could no longer hear Jenny's barking.

Kate managed only a few hours of sleep and woke before sunrise. She walked the property's perimeter, shining a flashlight into the woods and calling for Jenny. The old hound hadn't returned, and panic hit her hard, conjuring images she had to shake out of her head to move forward.

The night sky gave way to a dark blue, and the individual trees of the once-black wall surrounding the hostel became defined. Warm amber light glowed in most of the dorm room windows. A few hikers who had checked out to leave before the morning Lounge waved flashlights at Kate as they headed toward the woods. It was five a.m., too early to call Bob, but she pressed his number on her phone anyway. He didn't answer, and her call went to voice mail. She shoved her phone in her back pocket without leaving a message.

Nicole appeared on the front porch, saw Kate crossing the yard, and jogged to her. "What's wrong? What are you doing out here?"

"Jenny heard something last night. I leashed her up to take her out, but she got away and tracked something into the woods. Did you hear anything around ten thirty?"

"No, but the guests were rowdy last night. Vivienne went home about ten. I can ask her."

"Jenny hasn't come home," Kate said, her voice tense and shaky. "I let her get too hot on the trails yesterday. She needed to rest, and I let her run off. What if she's collapsed out there?"

"Oh, boss." Nicole side-hugged her. "She'll be okay. Viv can open Lounge. We'll go look for her. I'm sure she's stopped at a campsite. You know how much she loves people." She looked at Kate's pajamas. "Go change, and I'll get a backpack ready. Meet back here in ten?"

"I'd rather have you and Vivienne open. We need two new rooms prepared and the guests checked in when they arrive." She paused, and Nicole nodded. "Thank you. You're right. Jenny's probably at a campsite, or the ranger's station."

"Are you sure you don't want me to go with you?"

"No, I need you here. I couldn't reach Bob on the phone, so I'll stop at the station. He can help me search her favorite spots."

Nicole smiled sympathetically. "It's early. He might not be at work yet."

"Yeah. I suppose not. That's fine. I'll figure it out."

"Okay, but call me with updates."

"Will do." Kate headed back to her house. She changed clothes and went to the refrigerator to fill water bottles. She spotted the business card under a Stehekin Valley magnet. Should she call her? She didn't want to bother her but knew she could help. Kate grabbed the card and called.

"ISB. Special Agent Carter speaking." Her voice sounded husky.

"Oh, I'm so glad you're awake. Are you? I didn't wake you, did I? It sounds like I woke you. Sorry, it's Kate. Kate Hall. I need some help right now, and I can't get a hold of Bob. I was hoping you were available. Are you home?"

"Slow down, Kate. I'm here. What's going on?"

She exhaled nervously. "Jenny's missing. Something outside upset her last night, and she wouldn't calm down, so I leashed her…but when I opened the door, she tore out of here…into the woods." Kate's voice cracked.

"All right. Give me thirty minutes. I'll meet you at the High Bridge campsite. We can start looking there. Sound good?" Reese's offer was immediate.

"Okay. Thank you." Kate gathered some power bars from the pantry and apples from the refrigerator, packing them with two water bottles and Jenny's collapsible bowl in her backpack.

She arrived at the High Bridge campsite before Reese and searched for signs the bloodhound might have been there but found nothing. A couple of two-person tents were pitched but no one was around or at least they didn't emerge when she arrived.

She checked the time on her phone. Thirty minutes had passed. She decided to trek back down the trail and spotted Reese hiking toward her.

"Jenny's not there, and I didn't see any sign of her," Kate said, her voice ramped up by panic.

"Are there any campers we can ask?"

"A few tents, but they're either gone or sleeping, and couldn't be bothered to ask if I needed anything."

"Hey. It'll be okay." Reese embraced her before she could refuse. For an instant, Kate allowed herself to be held, and her body released its tension. "There you go. That's better. Has Jenny done this before?"

Kate stumbled back, only her grandmother had ever calmed her with an embrace. "No. Never at night. And she always comes home."

"Was she still barking?"

"What do you mean?"

"When Jenny ran into the woods, was she still barking?"

Kate thought for a moment. "A couple of times but then stopped. No bays either."

"That's good. That probably means she didn't have an animal nearby. Do you want to check the Tumwater campsite or head up the PCT to the lake?"

"The trail. Jenny doesn't like the road."

They walked down the trail as orange and pink filled the eastern sky. "By the way, you were right about Heaton. I found several downed trees. I also found another small burn area. Looks like it happened a few months ago. It's about fifteen minutes from the site where you and Jenny found the drugs. Off the trail. Could be a new place to explore for a curious dog. Let's take the trail all the way there. You can scan the right side, and I'll take the left."

Reese was serious and commanding, and relief washed over Kate, which surprised her. She hadn't allowed herself to depend on someone since her grandmother took her in when she was eleven years old. She fell into step with Reese's long strides. Every ten minutes, they called out for Jenny and listened for a response amidst the songbirds and distant roar of the Stehekin River.

"I grew up with dogs," Reese said after nearly an hour of trekking. "My mom rescued three or four at a time. It used to drive my dad up the wall. When my brothers and I were old enough, we fed and walked them. There's a green space behind our house, thank God. The neighbors would've never allowed us to walk our pack by their yards. They had those signs with the dog squatting and a circle and slash stuck in their grass." She laughed. "When I was sixteen, my parents let me adopt a golden Lab puppy. I named him Cooper. He lived with me in two parks, and even though I trained him, he ran off a time or two on our backcountry assignments. Scared me to death. But I always found him. He liked to keep to our routes. I bet Jenny does too."

Kate nodded and continued walking.

"I loved that dog so much. He lived to be fifteen, and when he died the part he had of my heart did too. Still can't bring myself to adopt another pup." She stopped talking and shouted, "Jenny."

After they listened for a minute, Kate said, "Fifteen years. That's an amazing amount of time to have had with him. This isn't too hard for you, is it?"

"No, Cooper died almost seven years ago. It feels good to be around other dogs. Over the last couple of years, my mom has dropped off Reno, their Aussie, to babysit while they travel. They're leaving on an Alaskan cruise next week, and she threatened to bring him to me. She says to keep me company for my birthday, but I know she thinks having him around will encourage me to adopt again."

"Aw, she's worried for you, that's sweet. Not everyone has that."

"Yeah. I've never taken my parents' love and support for granted."

"That's good, and happy early birthday. When is it?"

"Next Tuesday. Hopefully, you'll tell me again on my birthday."

Heat crawled up Kate's neck. She stopped and drank from her water bottle. "Do you want a new dog?"

"Not for a birthday present." Reese smiled, and they walked on. "Eventually I do, but the hole Cooper left hasn't quite healed."

They continued calling for Jenny and scanning the woods on either side of the trail. "What about you? Did you grow up with dogs?" Reese asked.

"We had one when I was a kid. A little schnauzer. She died of old age. I was ten or eleven. I can't remember."

"Did you adopt a new one?"

"Could we just keep calling for Jenny, please?" Kate walked ahead of Reese, frustrated with the special agent's persistent prying.

"Jenny," Reese shouted and caught up to Kate. "I'm sorry. I've upset you again. Not interrogating. Just want to get to know you, but I respect boundaries so no more questions about your past."

She just wants to know you, Kate growled to herself. She never had a problem sharing her fabricated past. It became a type of therapy, making her stories believable and enriching them with each telling, creating the past she would have liked to have had, but she didn't want to continue lying to Reese. She had started with Florida, and it knotted her stomach.

They hiked to the McGregor and PCT junction near Lake Howard in silence. Jenny wasn't there. There were paw prints, but they could have been from the day before or belonged to a different dog.

"Jenny," Kate shouted. "Let's look around the lake." She walked a social path that led to a flat rock outcropping at the water's edge, they shouted for Jenny again.

"Do you want to follow the shoreline to the ponderosas?" Reese asked in a gentle tone.

Kate stared across the lake at the towering trees. "I don't think she'd go over there." She dropped her pack and retrieved two protein bars and an apple. "Here. You probably haven't eaten."

"Thanks." Reese unfastened her pack and dropped it. She yelled, "Jenny." Her voice boomed across the lily pad-filled lake, and Kate added a shrill whistle. They listened for a response, but the only sounds were a chorus of birds and the high-pitched squeaks of pikas in the brush.

Kate closed her eyes and was quiet for a long moment. "Damn it," she whispered and retrieved her phone. She called Nic, hoping Jenny was already home, and all this anxiety was for nothing.

"Have you found her?" Nicole asked.

"No. I was calling to see if she'd come home."

"Not yet. But don't worry, boss. Everyone knows Jenny is missing. They changed their plans to search for her. You have two dozen hikers and me combing the woods around the hostel. We'll find her. Jenny is loved as much as Angel Hall. We all want her back."

She fought back tears. "Thanks, Nic. Please tell everyone I appreciate them."

"No worries. I'd do anything for you two. You know that. Oh, and Vivienne is at the hostel in case Jenny returns."

"Give her my thanks, too. I'm not sure when I'll be back. We're searching the trail to Heaton campsite and back."

"Okay. Viv and I will take care of everything here. We'll call if we find her."

"I'll do the same." Kate disconnected and swallowed the ache that had made its way up her throat. Her eyes met Reese's. Before she could speak, Reese sat beside her and held her. She thought about pushing back, but she didn't. Instead, she laid her head on Reese's shoulder.

"We'll find her," Reese whispered in her ear, her hand gently caressing Kate's back.

Kate believed her. At least she believed Reese would never stop looking. She lifted her head and met Reese's eyes. "Thank you."

"We'll put out an alert." Reese kissed her forehead and made a call. "This is Special Agent Carter. We have a lost dog in the Chelan area. A bloodhound with a copper-colored coat. Leather collar with printed name tag. Her name's Jenny." She paused. "That's right. Kate Hall's dog. She was last seen in the woods north of the hostel." She listened. "Sounds good. I'll be in touch." She looked at Kate. "Staff will look for her and put the word out during their routes. They'll ask guests if they've seen her or if anyone's found her. We'll call for an update tonight if we don't find her first. Okay?"

Kate nodded and stood, hoisting her backpack. "Do you want another apple?"

"I'm good." Reese smiled. "I'll take you up on the offer when we find Jenny."

They hiked the dry, hot switchbacks north of the lake, calling and whistling. When they reached the alpine firs, they stopped and shouted, and a low bay sounded in the distance. "Oh, my God. Did you hear that? It's her," Kate cried. She shouted Jenny's name again and again. The hound's bays turned to barking and became louder as they neared the dry camp, but when they entered the burned-out clearing, they didn't see her.

"She's in the woods," Reese said, running into the grove. Jenny's barking led them close to the cliff's edge, and a few feet from the drop-off, they found the old hound ensnared in the rotting trunk of a large silver-fir snag.

Kate unhooked the lead from Jenny's collar and fell onto the ground with the large dog in her arms. "Oh, my God, Jenny. Are you okay?" She gave her a once-over. Her neck had been rubbed raw where she'd fought against the leash. "You're okay. Oh, thank God, sweet girl." Jenny licked the tears from Kate's face.

"Kate," Reese said, her voice soft but uneasy.

"What?" Kate's smile faded.

"Jenny's leash was tied." Kate hurried to the dead tree. "She couldn't have looped it and cinched it like that. It had to be unhooked from her collar, threaded through the handle, and attached again. I can't believe someone would do this. Why not take her down to the ranger's station?" Reese looked around, hands on her hips, thinking.

"She's okay now. That's all that matters." Kate reached to untie the leash.

"Wait. Don't touch it," Reese said. She retrieved a plastic glove and bag, untied the leash, and bagged it. "Has anyone else attached Jenny's leash to her collar?"

"Why? What are you thinking?"

"There's a chance a thoughtless park guest didn't do this." Reese placed the bag in her pack. "We can't rule out the possibility a drug runner saw you and Jenny at or around the drop site. When there were no drugs to pick up, they'd make the connection. Jesus, why didn't I think about this before? I'm so sorry. This could have been my fault." She pulled out a length of rope. "Here, we can use this for Jenny's lead. I'll return her leash as soon as possible."

"Yeah. No worries. I have others." Kate tied the rope to Jenny's collar, her hands trembling. Who had done this? Was it Liam? Would his fingerprints be on the leash? She bent over, hands on her knees, steadying herself.

"Hey. It's okay. Jenny's okay. I'll have the park release a statement that they found the drugs and make sure you aren't in any more danger. I promise." Reese's warm hand slid up and down her back. "Let's get you both home."

CHAPTER EIGHTEEN

Nicole waited for them on the hostel's front porch, waving as they crossed the yard. Kate waved back and untied the rope from Jenny's collar. The old hound trotted to her young friend, nudging Nicole's hands with her muzzle. "I'll take her inside for some water and a treat," Nicole called.

"I don't think we should say anything about Jenny being tied up," Reese said. "Word spreads fast in a small community like this. It'll cause animosity toward some unknown person."

They stopped at the rose-garden trellis gate, and Kate nodded.

"If it turns out a park guest did this and we can identify who it is, I'll charge them with animal cruelty and whatever else I can find."

"What do you mean if it turns out?"

"We can't dismiss a possible connection between Jenny hearing something outside and chasing after it and her being tied up where you found the drugs last week. We don't have any evidence that the traffickers under investigation have acted violently, but that doesn't mean they aren't capable."

Kate steadied herself on the gate. "That's something to think about."

"I'm so sorry you're in this position. If this happened because of the drugs Jenny found, we can keep you safe."

"So you'll find out if it's connected?" Kate asked, nearly choking on her words.

"As soon as possible. I'll send Jenny's leash to be processed today." Reese stared at the hostel's long front porch. "Do your security cameras capture the yard?"

"They're mostly set on the hostel's doors and windows. One covers the parking area. But I have two pan, tilt, and zoom cameras on the roof that reach a few feet into the yard."

"All right. I strongly suggest you put the PTZs on the entire yard and its perimeter, too." She touched Kate's clenched hand and gently removed it from the gate. "Can you send me a copy of the footage from last night and this morning?"

"The security…What's wrong with me? I didn't even think to check it."

"Hey, it's okay. Your mind was on Jenny." Reese squeezed Kate's hand, leaned in, and kissed her lips lightly, drawing her into a protective embrace. "Your flowers are stunning," she whispered. "I'm guessing rose bouquets as a romantic gesture don't impress you."

"I wouldn't turn down the gesture…or the flowers."

"I'm a big fan of both, too. You and Jenny could bring me a yellow bunch for dinner tonight. I'm a great cook."

Kate pulled back. "Oh, thanks for the offer—" The communal room door opened, and Jenny raced down the steps.

"I heard a big 'but' coming."

Kate kissed the hound's head, thanking her for the distraction. "Yeah, we should keep our routine tonight…after everything. Monday's our popcorn and BritBox night."

"I understand, but I'm not going to lie. I'm disappointed. BritBox shows are my favorite. We'll both be watching them. Alone. What's the sense in that?" Reese squatted and rubbed Jenny's neck. "What am I saying? You'll have this tough girl's company. I'm the one who'll be alone." She stood and looked at Kate. "I'm heading out of town on Wednesday until Saturday night, but you can consider it an open invitation."

"I will, and thanks again for your help."

"Any time."

"Have a safe trip." Kate watched Reese leave, silently berating herself. She was supposed to avoid the feelings stirring inside her. There was no place in her life for a romantic relationship. She had no right to put another person in danger. She had Jenny, and that's all she needed. "Damn it," she whispered and grabbed her phone from her backpack. She texted, *How about coffee? Sunday 8 am at The Friendly Roast?*

"Damn what?" Nicole asked, walking up to her.

"Nothing. I was thanking Reese again for helping me find Jenny." Her phone dinged, and she read the screen. *Sounds great. See you then.* She looked up in time to see Reese raise her hand in a goodbye wave as she entered the woods.

"You're seeing a lot of her lately." Nicole grinned. "Anything new you want to share?"

"We spent the day looking for Jenny. That's all."

"And last night?"

"What about last night?"

"Vivienne said she saw Reese here last night."

"She definitely didn't."

Nicole's brow wrinkled. "Maybe she saw a hiker that looked like her. To tell you the truth, she's paranoid right now."

"She's living with a big secret. That'll happen."

"Yeah, her idea wasn't the best. She's reached out to the art school and Immigration to fix things." Nicole followed Kate inside. "We'll take care of the evening Lounge. Why don't you and Jenny relax? You've had a rough day."

"Thanks, Nic. I don't know how I'd manage without you." She hugged her and then remembered the plans she had for her assistant. "I want to talk to you about your job responsibilities. You run the day-to-day guest services side better than I ever did. But it's time I put your college degree to work and teach you the business side."

Nicole brightened. "You got it. Whatever you need."

"Great. We'll talk about it soon." Kate looked around for Jenny, and panic pulsed through her. "Where'd she go?"

"She went through her dog door. It's all good."

"Sorry. I didn't see her leave. Thanks for tonight. We'll pop in later to thank everyone for helping today."

Kate turned the shower's hot water on until it reached its maximum heat, then slowly added cold. When the temperature was just bearable, she stepped under the rainfall spray, letting the heat start at the top of her head and cascade down. Then she allowed herself to cry the day's pent-up tears. She sobbed for her life at the hostel that could end at any time and for Jenny, her sweet girl, who would be gone too soon, and not just missing in the wilderness.

After she had exhausted her tears, she finished her shower and dressed in an old Mazzy Star T-shirt and faded jeans. Maybe she would make herself dinner, something from scratch instead of a microwave meal. It would be a nice idea—if she could cook. Her grandmother had tried to teach her, but she only managed to learn the essentials. Scrambled eggs. Toast. Heating a jar of marinara and boiling pasta. Then she thought about Reese's offer. She said she was a good cook. Kate smiled and wondered what constituted *good* for the special agent.

She stood before a near-empty refrigerator unable to conjure inspiration from the eggs, bottle of mustard, old bagels, and a jar of gherkin pickles. She shut the door and opened the freezer. A frozen entrée was less complicated. A few minutes later, she cuddled with Jenny on the sofa, sharing a few bites of a surprisingly delicious rigatoni Bolognese while they binge-watched their favorite mystery.

Her phone rang. It was Bob returning her early-morning messages. "Bob, where the hell have you been?" she asked.

"I've been busy. I have a life."

"Did this life just start in the last few months? You've never avoided me like this. What's going on?"

"I've been underwater since the chief farmed me out to ISB." He sighed. "She's like a lone wolf but still demanding."

"A lone wolf?" Kate laughed.

"Don't laugh. She doesn't tell me anything but expects me to drop everything and do what she needs. She kept me here at the station till late last night."

"You were with her last night?"

"Oh, yeah. She's driving me crazy. I've heard rumors about the hours ISB agents keep, but I haven't had to work with one until now. The rumors are all true."

Relief washed over her. Vivienne had been wrong. She couldn't have seen Reese. "Sounds like you need to sit down with her and establish some boundaries." He grumbled, and she asked, "Did you listen to my messages?"

"Sure did. I'm so sorry I wasn't available to help, but I'm glad Jenny's okay. Agent Carter told me you all found her at the illegal camp."

"Yeah. Her out in the woods all night scared me to death, though."

"She's a brave girl. She'd go after a bear if it came near you."

"Exactly." Kate petted Jenny's side. "When did you talk to Reese?"

"About an hour ago. I'm on my way to Seattle. She's insisted I drive some evidence to CLD tonight."

"The State Patrol's crime lab? What evidence? Did you find something else at the scene?"

"Hell, if I know. Like I said, she doesn't share much. I don't even know what's in the bag. Feels like some type of rope."

Kate's stomach flip-flopped. It was Jenny's leash. By tomorrow Reese could have Liam Maloney's name. "Sounds like things have been rough. I hope they lighten up, but you might need to talk to her about what teamwork means to you."

"I know. I know. You can only deal with one crisis at a time." He cleared his throat. "Listen, I need to get back on the road. I'll be home to Marsha late enough as it is."

"Okay. Drive safe." Kate ended the call and stood. "Come on, sweet girl. Let's go thank all the nice people who looked for you today."

About fifteen guests hung out on sofas and beanbags on the floor in the communal room. A few were singing and strumming the Lounge guitars. Vivienne was in a chess match with the same woman she had sat with the night before, and a handful of hikers surrounded Nicole as she played cards at one of the game tables. Kate remembered when the guests would swarm around her the same way. Now they saw her as the owner and boss and responded to her as if she were a favorite teacher. She loved them for it. For all of it.

"Jenny!" someone shouted, and everyone in the room turned to them. Jenny's tail whipped side to side, and she ambled into the room, her nose low to the ground, making her way to a group of hikers and sitting politely. Conflicting emotions swelled inside Kate as she watched them lavish affection on the one living being she had loved with all her heart for the last eight years. She had almost lost Jenny, and these strangers had come to her aid, even though she was the reason they were probably all in danger.

The clinking of glass drew Kate's attention. Nicole was standing, tapping a glass with a spoon. "Angel Hall wanted to say a few things."

The room became quiet, and Kate gave them a heartfelt smile. "I wanted to thank all of you for your help today. Nic told me you spent your morning looking for Jenny…" Her voice broke, and Nicole side-hugged her. "Your generosity means so much to me. As a gesture of gratitude, everyone's stay tonight is on me." Applause and shouts of thank you broke out.

"Aw, you're such a softy," Nicole said, squeezing her waist.

"Yeah, well, don't tell anyone," Kate whispered.

CHAPTER NINETEEN

Reese inched forward on hands and knees, fitting another wood plank. The cabin's main floor was one great room, so the boards could all run in the same direction, perpendicular to the joists and parallel to the longest wall, making the installation easier and faster than expected. She sat back on her heels and appreciated the early-morning's effort. She had awoken at four a.m. feeling disappointed and thinking about Kate, so channeling those emotions into constructive work felt good.

After putting her tools back on her workbench, she poured another cup of coffee and opened the stacked doors. She had a resolve to always see the sunrise if awake. There was something primal about seeing its power flowing into the woods, a kind of reassurance that the unknown, the darkest places on Earth, would always give up their secrets to the light.

She sat on the cabin's expansive deck and watched the blue hour fade into layers of pinks and yellows. The songbirds began singing in the forest around her, and a golden eagle called in the distance. She wondered if Kate was up watching the beautiful start to the day. Then she thought about how nice it would be if they watched the sunrise together.

Great. The minute she stopped working, she started ruminating. She sipped her coffee. The truth was, she couldn't help it. Kate was smart and sexy…and the most intriguing woman she'd ever met. Whatever the trail angel was hiding she hoped she'd trust her enough to open up someday. *Someday?* She knew she had it bad when every thought of Kate Hall included the future.

Reese shook her head and opened her laptop. Forensics on the backpack had come in the night before. She reread the report. The CLD had connected it to the other packs found on the PCT within the last year. They shared the same manufacturer on the East Coast, came from the same batch, and were most likely purchased in bulk. None of the backpacks had identifiable fingerprints. She had spent the last several days in Yosemite working with the ISB's one intelligence analyst, hoping to locate a point of sale. It was a long shot, but it would pay off big if they found when and where the backpacks were purchased.

Her computer chimed with a new email from the CLD— testing on Jenny's leash was complete. Forensics had lifted two sets of unidentified prints from the snap hook. That meant a couple of things. Kate didn't have a record, and someone else had used the hook the night she disappeared. The person could have been a park guest, but they also could have been who Jenny heard outside, the reason she tracked into the woods. They could have been there to lure the dog, and if that was the case. Why?

Reese had an urge to see Kate to make sure she and Jenny were safe, and that was how her week had gone, everything leading back to Kate Hall and her bloodhound. Even with two active cases, tons of paperwork, and a home in the throes of a remodel, she thought of reasons to call or text her. Their exchanges had been playful all week, but then Kate had texted yesterday morning and canceled their coffee date, sounding disappointed and asking to reschedule for tomorrow, which softened the letdown.

After breakfast, Reese returned to the rhythm of measuring, cutting, and nailing floorboards. As a young girl, she learned that physical projects opened her mind, allowing questions to bubble up and answers to form. She had spent the morning working on the Coleen Farrell and drug trafficking cases this way. Now she had to include Jenny's leash.

Hunger stopped her in the late afternoon. She returned her tools to the workbench and inspected the day's work. Just a few more boards to put down. The floor was gorgeous, and she smiled at the thought of how proud her dad would be. She plated some chicken piccata with lemon sauce she had made the night before and heated it in the microwave. Then she reset the record player's arm on David Bowie's *Low*, turned the volume up, and ate lunch at the kitchen island. She had just taken her first bite when her work phone rang. "ISB. Special Agent Carter."

"Hello, Agent Carter. My name is Holly Farrell. Coleen Farrell's sister."

She almost dropped her fork. "Hi, Holly. Thank you for calling. I've left a few messages for your father but haven't heard back from him." She rushed to her office for pen and paper.

"Oh, sorry. I didn't know you had left him messages. He didn't tell my mom or me much about Coleen's case, and we weren't to ask. My mom told me he kept a box under their bed with all Coleen's information." She paused. "He…um…he died in an accident out in the field about a month ago. I finally started cleaning out their bedroom and found your business card. I'd like to know what happened to my sister…please."

"Of course, I'll share everything we know." She returned to the island and wrote down Holly's name. "I'm sorry to hear about your father's passing." She hesitated, but Holly didn't respond to her condolences. "We have a recent update on Coleen's case. Would you like to hear that first?" She waited for an answer, and after a long silence, Holly responded with more of a whimpered yes than the actual word. "Okay. I can tell you that a few weeks ago, we asked the public on social media to contact our tips line if they remembered anything about Coleen—"

"I saw it on Facebook…" Her voice trailed off.

"Yes, that's right. On Facebook. We had someone with credible information come forward. He placed your sister in the North Cascades National Park. It's east of Seattle. His tip opened new avenues of investigation for us."

"Do you think she's alive?"

"I'm so sorry, Holly. I don't have that answer. But I can tell you that we're committed to finding Coleen."

"I think she's alive," Holly said in a sober voice, and that was the second time Holly Farrell surprised Reese. "I was ten when she left. I can't remember how long it took for the police to come, but when they did, they only talked to him. He wouldn't let my mom answer any questions, and no one asked me what I thought. After that, they only called him." She was silent for a moment. "I have to go now, Agent Carter. You'll keep in touch, please?"

"Wait, Holly. Can I come to talk with you about Coleen? I think what you have to say is important, and I apologize we haven't asked you before now."

"Why would you have?" She paused. "I guess that would be okay. When?"

"I can be there tomorrow afternoon. Would four p.m. work for you?"

"That sounds okay."

"All right. I'll see you then." Reese ended the call and exhaled. She had always been suspicious of Mr. Farrell. In her eyes, he never rose to the level of a worried, frantic parent, and now this. He had refused to relay information about Coleen to her mother and sister. Was that an act of coping? Or was something else going on?

After booking a flight to Great Falls, Montana, Reese sent her Assistant Special Agent in Charge an email with the update on Coleen's case. She looked at her phone. The last-minute trip meant missing the rescheduled coffee date with Kate, but she didn't want to cancel with her over the phone. The decent thing to do would be to tell her in person. There was also information about Jenny's leash that she wanted to share. So wasn't a visit to Hostel Hall reasonable?

Fifteen minutes later, Reese pulled in front of The Friendly Roast. One thing she knew about park communities was that no matter how hard you tried to keep your business your own, someone always knew about it. She figured Lou was the go-to person if you wanted information about anyone living in or around Granite Creek.

"Hey, Reese, what're you doing? Swapping Saturdays for Sundays?" Lou seemed annoyed. She stood at an espresso machine, frothing milk, and then handed the coffee to a young woman.

"Not at all. My work schedule's been hectic." Reese stepped up to the counter. "I was hoping to ask you a few questions. If you have a minute."

"Questions for me?" Lou asked as Phil appeared from the back room and stood beside her. "Did you hear that, Phil? The Special Agent has questions for us."

"Actually just a few for you." Reese looked at her with the growing feeling that this was a bad idea. "I was wondering if you knew Kate Hall very well?"

Lou slapped her hands together. "I knew it! The minute you sat down at the table in the pub a few weeks ago. I could see the smoke coming off both of you." She smacked Phil with an open palm. "Twenty bucks. You owe me. I called it."

Phil looked embarrassed, sighed, and disappeared into the back room.

"He'll pay up. Trust me." She leaned on the counter, and her face became serious. "What do I know about Angel Hall? I know she's single, keeps to herself, and hasn't had a girlfriend since we moved here. Unless she's having one-night stands with the hikers who stay at her hostel, she hasn't been bumping uglies, either."

"Stop." Reese held up her hands, instantly regretting her decision. "I'm not interested in her love life. Never mind."

"Oh, come on. Don't get your panties in a bunch. Jeez, laugh a little. What do you want to know?"

Reese exhaled. "I'm interested in her favorite flower or food."

"Snooze." Lou rolled her eyes. "You're lucky I know she doesn't like store-bought flowers. She has something against flower growers. Eco-warrior stuff. She also likes locally grown food, but there's not much to pick from." Lou spread her arms out. "You got us, the pub, the Sweet Stack, and Piggie Pie Pizza. I just happen to know she only eats our pastries and Piggie's pizzas— veggie delight is her favorite. You're welcome." Lou's face glowed with pride.

"Good to know. I appreciate your help." Reese headed toward the door.

"Any time. Not sure what you're up to, but it involves Kate, so good luck with that. She's about as easy to figure out as P versus NP."

"I have no idea what that means." Reese opened the door, and the bells sounded.

Lou shook her head. "Computer theory. Of course you don't."

CHAPTER TWENTY

The microwave beeped, and Kate pulled out a dinner tray. "Ow, crap. Crap." She dropped the hot plastic on the counter and sucked her fingertips. The blast of steam pretty much summed up the week. An atmospheric river had rained her out of the rose garden, which didn't matter because she had to help Nicole with the Lounge and cleaning since Vivienne had a last-minute trip to her old art institute.

Working at the hostel during the week meant she and Jenny couldn't trek to their favorite spots and provide trail magic, but that was fine. A break from the trails for her sweet girl was best. Kate was unsure what had happened to her but suspected someone from her past had lured Jenny out and left her tied to that snag. But she couldn't figure out why.

She opened a can of diet soda and poured it over ice. If Joanna and the FBI discovered anyone from the O'Flaherty crime ring had traveled to the area, she expected the marshals to arrive any day, and the constant fear of both things exhausted her. She removed the plastic film from her dinner and tossed it in the trash.

There was a loud knock, and Jenny barked, charging the front door. The bottom dropped out of Kate's stomach, and she ran to her phone, looking at the security camera feed. She saw Reese standing there, holding a pizza box and a bottle of wine up to the camera, and opened the door. "What are you doing here?"

"Hello to you, too. Maybe I should've called first, but I didn't think you'd hold it against me if I showed up with your favorite pizza." Reese wrapped her up in a smile. "Was I wrong?"

Kate stepped back, and Jenny bounced around Reese's feet. "I already made dinner…and I have plans."

"Are you working?" Reese asked, and Kate shook her head. "BritBox binge?"

"No…Masterpiece Theatre. BritBox is Monday nights."

Reese smiled and followed her to the kitchen. "Oh, I see now. A frozen entrée and Masterpiece Theatre." She placed the pizza box on the counter. "This will be harder than I thought. I have it on good authority Piggie Pie Pizza is your favorite, and this one's still hot. Unlike…" She sniffed the microwave dinner. "What is that anyway? Stroganoff?"

"Yes, and it's delicious." She could see Reese holding back a smile. "I admit it's not as tasty as Piggie Pie Pizza, but it's a close second. Besides, I can't waste it now."

Reese opened the box and moved the pizza back and forth under Kate's nose. "I don't think saving the stroganoff for tomorrow would be such a bad thing. How about you get two plates and glasses, and we'll dig into the clear winner? We could even have popcorn for dessert."

Somehow, Kate was plating up slices of pizza and watching Reese pour two glasses of wine as if a gorgeous woman showing up unannounced and interrupting her evening was a normal occurrence in her life. But it wasn't, and Special Agent Reese Carter casually showing up at her house was playing with fire. She should say she wasn't up for company, but the veggie delight did smell good.

Kate followed Reese to the living room. "I thought we were having coffee in the morning?"

"About that. I have to go out of town." Reese set the pizza and wine on the coffee table. "I was hoping tonight would make up for canceling."

"For the drug trafficking case?" Kate asked, moving past the cancellation comment.

"The Coleen Farrell case. Her sister, Holly, called me today. We have fifteen years of case files without any statements from her or Mrs. Farrell. ISB took an initial statement from the parents, and since then, we've only corresponded with Mr. Farrell."

Kate kept her disappointment off her face. She had learned nothing about the black backpack in her conversation with Bob and hoped Reese could tell her something…anything…that might hint at a connection with the O'Flahertys or rule them out.

"Hey, are you okay?"

"Yeah, sorry. Her poor family." She pulled the slice of pizza off her plate, twirling a stretching melted cheese around her finger. "It must be difficult for them not knowing what's happened to her for so many years. Sounds like the dad has a serious control issue or had. You're talking about him in the past tense. He's dead?"

"Died in an accident a month ago."

"And the mom?"

"She died a few years before I got the case."

"So her parents are dead. That's why she's reached out."

Reese nodded. "I asked Mr. Farrell for Holly's contact information years ago. He said she lived at the farm. So I've tried to reach her on the home phone, but no one answers or returns my messages." She sipped her wine. "I've had several cold cases, and the families never lose hope. They never stop asking questions. These folks just went radio silent. Until now."

"Are you thinking Coleen's a homicide victim, and Mr. Farrell's covered up the crime?"

"No one pursued that line of inquiry."

"Right. Because eyewitnesses placed her on the PCT."

"True. But what was happening in that home to keep two grown women from asking questions about Coleen for years? That could indicate serious levels of abuse. If Mr. Farrell was so controlling, why did he allow Coleen to hike the PCT in the first place?"

"Because she didn't ask. Was Coleen Farrell a runaway? Well, not technically a runaway at nineteen, but in that family situation, it must have felt like it."

"That's what I think, too. A man that abusive wouldn't allow that kind of disobedience. I want to find out if he left home and went after her."

"It's a good theory." Kate sipped her wine, pulled another slice from the pie, and took a large bite.

"I also have information on Jenny's leash."

Kate swallowed hard. "Already? What is it?"

"I'm worried about how easy it is to discuss my cases with you. I shouldn't be sharing this with you." Her blue-green eyes held Kate's. "Can I trust this stays between you and me—"

"Who would I leak it to? Bob? He'd be up to date on your cases anyway, right? Besides I wouldn't discuss an ongoing investigation."

Reese took an extra beat to consider. "Okay. Forensics found two distinct fingerprint pairs on the lead's hook. I assume one is yours. Do you have any idea who the other one could be?"

"No one else uses the leash."

"Not even Nicole?"

"You'd know if it was her. She's here from Canada on a work permit. Her prints are in the automated fingerprint system. You didn't get any hits?" Kate kept her expression neutral. The surprise that flashed in Reese's eyes suggested she'd said too much. "Or whatever you all call that database."

"That's it. AFIS. The most likely scenario is a hiker found Jenny and made a bad decision, but we can't rule out it was done intentionally." Reese glanced at the old hound, asleep in her dog bed. "I don't know why they would. If they knew you found the drugs, why take Jenny? Why not break into your house and look for them? Taking Jenny is personal." Reese paused. "I'll tell you this, too. We've confirmed the backpack she found is part of our larger investigation. The bags were manufactured on the East Coast. Thanks to you we're closer to finding a point of sale. The one you found had a barcode left on, an error in our favor."

Kate nodded and forced herself to take a bite of pizza, filling her mouth, so she didn't have to respond. Reese had skipped asking if there was a reason a person would want to take Jenny to hurt her. A reason the act was personal. It wasn't an oversight—not with this agent. Reese was suspicious, and it was only a matter of time before the special agent dug into her past.

"Hey, I didn't mean to come over and upset you," Reese said.

"I'm fine, really."

"Okay. Let's change the subject." Reese looked at the television. "What are we watching on Masterpiece?"

What are *we* watching? How had the informal coffee date at The Friendly Roast become an eating pizza, drinking wine, and watching television in a dark room on a comfy sofa date? She felt heat color her cheeks. "I'm watching *Astrid*."

"Perfect. Great show. I've already seen the first two seasons."

"I'm only on season one," Kate said.

"No worries. I don't mind watching it again. We can get two or three episodes in if we start now. If my math's right, it should only take a few more Masterpiece Sundays for you to catch up."

Reese grinned at her, and Kate lifted her brows. "You're inviting yourself over a few more times?"

"We could watch it at mine, too, and I could make a delicious, home-cooked meal, even better than Piggie's veggie pizza." She sat back in the cushions and turned her body slightly toward Kate's. "You're not saying no."

On the contrary, Reese's easy, confident presence had Kate internally agreeing to more than a few television dates. The distance between them on the sofa suddenly became too close, and Kate considered calling Jenny up between them, but the sweet girl was snoring, so she shoved a throw pillow in the middle and grabbed the remote.

They sat on either side of the pillow, watching the show and figuring out clues much faster than they should have. After the pizza was eaten, and the wine bottle half empty, Reese watched Kate queue up the next episode. "You know, I opted for onions on the pizza. I thought it might be the only thing to keep me from kissing you."

Kate stopped, her hand pointing the remote at the television. She paused the show's introduction and looked at Reese. "That was smooth."

"Too blunt?"

Kate lowered the remote. "I can't figure out if you just complimented me or admitted you planned for a preempted rejection. I'm fine with either. Like I said before I'm not looking for a relationship. Not that I think this is the start of one. I don't want you to get the wrong idea from me about letting you stay. I don't date, that's all. Haven't in a long time. I don't see myself changing that any time soon. The most time I've spent with a woman is two maybe three days. You've been around for three weeks…now you're bringing pizza…" She forced herself to stop talking.

"Did all those thoughts just bombard you at once? That's a lot going on up there." Reese softly trailed a finger across Kate's forehead. Then her gaze moved down to Kate's lips and back to her eyes. "For the record, I'm not looking for a relationship and haven't dated in a while either, but I hear that's how it happens sometimes. You find her when you're not looking."

No witty reply came to Kate, so she stared at the empty plate on her lap.

"How about we don't overthink things? We can take this slow. Whatever it is. See what happens. If nothing does, we can be friends. I've never been one to burn bridges." Reese moved Kate's plate to the coffee table and removed the pillow between them.

She didn't try to stop her. She wanted to smell Reese's skin and taste her breath again. Reese's lips were soft, and the moment they touched hers, heat coursed through her. She parted her lips, and Reese pulled her closer, deepening the kiss. Their tongues explored, twining and pressing.

Reese's hands slid up Kate's sides, and her thumbs softly passed over Kate's breasts. She let out a quiet gasp. Her breasts ached, and her nipples tautened. She wanted to feel the heat of Reese's hands against her skin. She moved Reese's hand under her sweatshirt. The warmth of her skin made Kate's lower body clench.

Reese pulled back. "I really want to do this. Many, many times. But I'm going to need some ground rules. I feel this…we…will far exceed the next few Sundays."

"I can't think of any right now," Kate said in a breathy voice. She cupped Reese's neck and drew her into another kiss, pressing her against the cushions, trailing her hand up Reese's thighs and squeezing her waist.

Without warning, Jenny growled and charged the patio doors. She slipped behind the drapes, barking and clawing to get out. Kate and Reese leaped to their feet at the same time.

"This is what happened before," Kate whispered.

"Where are the outside lights?"

Kate pointed to a switch plate on the wall left of the patio doors and turned off the television. She ran down the hall to her bedroom. When she returned, the living room was dark, and the outside was illuminated. Reese stared into the yard, holding Jenny by the collar. The old hound continued to lunge forward, trying to get out.

"I don't see what's agitating her." Reese looked at Kate. "Whoa, that's an escalation."

Kate stood at the other side of the patio door holding a gun. "It's for protection. I have a license." She scanned the yard. She couldn't tell Reese that she was looking for signs of Liam or O'Flaherty button men, that they probably lured Jenny into the forest, dragged her to the dry camp, and tied her up to die, that she feared what they would do to her when they got the chance.

"Well, nothing's out there now. How about your security cameras? Did you have Nicole adjust the roof angles?" Reese was stroking Jenny's head, calming the hound.

"I haven't yet." She dropped the drape, turned off the yard lights, and switched on a floor lamp. "Things have been busy."

"Hey, it's okay." Reese stroked Kate's arm. "You're trembling."

"I'm fine. Whatever it was, it's gone now." She stepped back. "I'm going to put this away." She leaned against the wall in her bedroom holding off the familiar shaking and shallow breath of a panic attack. She started five, four, three in her head. *Bed. Door. Picture. Lamp. Rug. Reese. Kitchen sink. Laughter in the Lounge. My breath*. Her breathing had returned to normal by the time she brought her attention to three things she felt.

Reese was rinsing off their dinner plates and stopped to shake a box of chamomile tea at her when she returned. "How about a cup before bed?"

Kate nodded and climbed onto one of three barstools at the peninsula counter. She watched Reese tie the teabag strings to the cup handles. "I forgot to tell you. Vivienne told Nic that she saw you the night Jenny disappeared, walking toward the woods. She didn't think to say anything because she figured you were with me." She paused, watching Reese's reaction.

"Me? I was at the station until late."

"I know it wasn't you, but it means someone was. They could've been a guest, but they could've been someone watching me and Jenny."

"Are you worried she sensed the same person outside tonight?" Reese poured hot water into their cups, her hand as calm as her voice. "Do you want me to go look around?"

Kate shook her head. "No." She couldn't let her go out there if the Irish mob was waiting. For what? What the hell was Liam doing? Her heart thumped against her chest. *Cupboard. Light. Faucet. Coffee maker. Reese.* Her breathing slowed. *Teakettle hissing. Spoon against the cup. My breath. Jenny's nails on the hardwoods.*

"Okay, I'm not going anywhere. Let's text Nicole and ask her to adjust the roof cameras tomorrow to pan from the woods to the hostel. If it happens again, we'll know who or what is out there." She placed Kate's tea in front of her and sat. "If you want someone to stay with you tonight, I can…on the sofa. We could search outside in the morning before I catch my flight."

Reese's presence, her voice, mingling with the wafts of chamomile tea soothed Kate, but the special agent staying over wasn't a good idea. "I'm good, and I promise to text Nicole to set the cameras first thing in the morning."

"Good." She held Kate's eyes. "I hope you'll reconsider my offer. At least let me take Jenny out for her business. Where's her leash?"

"All right. I'll think about it. Her leads are in the pantry. Down the hall to the right." Kate looked nervous. "I should go outside with you."

"Relax. Let me do this for you." Reese returned with a lead, and Jenny jumped to her feet, her tail whipping the air. She clipped it on the hound's collar and wrapped the other end around her hand. "You're staying with me, tough girl."

After Reese and Jenny left, Kate texted Nicole. She felt uncharacteristically off-center and vulnerable. For eight years, the past lurked in the darkest recesses of her mind waiting to consume her, to crumble the life she had built as Kate Hall. Now it was here, and she had to stop it. Alone. She wouldn't ask Reese for help. Even though the special agent made her feel safe. She couldn't want her protection. Her Glock and training were enough. She sighed. She didn't need Reese's help, but she wanted it.

CHAPTER TWENTY-ONE

Reese woke to a cold, wet nose pushing against her hand. She opened her eyes and glanced around. It was dark. Then another nudge, fur this time. The sleep fog began to lift, and she petted Jenny's head. The bloodhound's tail thumped against the floor, and she dropped a leash she'd been holding in her mouth.

Reese looked at her phone. Ten after five. "Is this how early you get your mom up? Or is it a special treat for me?" She sat upright on the sofa, rubbed her hands through her hair, and scrubbed her face. "Okay, I'll take you out. Just a sec." The light jersey Christmas pajamas Kate had loaned her weren't heavy enough to keep her warm outside, but Jenny was dancing at the patio doors, her nails clicking against the hardwoods, so she pulled on her shoes and wrapped a throw blanket around her. She clipped on Jenny's lead and grabbed a flashlight with one hand on Jenny to keep her quiet. Then they slipped out the sliding doors.

In the cool mountain air, she walked Jenny around the hostel's perimeter, her mind trying to make sense of last night's incident. It was too dark to see evidence of anything in the yard, of someone watching Kate, but she figured a bloodhound didn't need light, and she was right. Jenny picked up a scent and zigzagged across the yard, nose to the ground. She tracked to the trail leading into the woods and stopped, her agitation similar to the night before.

"What did you find, tough girl?" Reese rubbed the length of Jenny's back, trying to calm her. Then she pulled Jenny back, pointed the flashlight, and looked closer at the understory where the hound was sniffing. "Okay, this might be something, good girl." She used a poop bag from Jenny's leash and picked up discarded candy wrappers.

When they returned to the house, the lights were on. Kate stood in the kitchen in a T-shirt and boxers, pouring two mugs of coffee.

Reese thought about heading right back to bed, just not alone.

"Good morning," Kate said. "I see my con artist got you out the door before your alarm went off."

"Oh, no." Reese looked at her phone on the coffee table. "I forgot to turn it off."

"That's okay. I needed to get up anyway. But it did throw me, a strange sound, growing louder."

"I'm so sorry." Reese frowned and sat at the bar.

"It's okay. Go eat, Jenny." Kate snapped her fingers, and the old hound trotted down the hallway. She slid a mug across the counter. "How'd you sleep?"

"Great. That's a nice sofa." Reese sipped her coffee. It was hot and strong. She draped the blanket on the back of the barstool. "How about you?"

"Probably better than you did. My bed's much nicer." She sat beside Reese. "I'm not going to lie. It wasn't easy knowing you were out here, especially in those adorable pajamas."

"Oh, thank God. I was hoping it wasn't just me struggling." She grinned, leaned in, and kissed Kate's cheek softly. "I'm keeping the PJs because they *are* adorable."

"What's that?" Kate asked, looking at Reese's hand.

"It's some trash Jenny found near the trail entry, a few candy wrappers. She tracked right to them. Might not be anything but litter, but hikers tend to abide by leave no trace. I'll have them sent to the lab today."

"You think someone watching me and Jenny left them."

"That's a possibility. I'll let you know if the lab pulls any prints."

Kate turned her coffee mug in circles. "I couldn't fall asleep last night thinking about everything. Granite Creek is the perfect exchange location for traffickers. Seattle's to the east. There are several trails through the park to the Canadian border. Drug mules could enter near Hozomeen or leave the park and take the PCT through Manning." Her hands had stopped, and she stared at her coffee. "There's a ranger station next door that could guarantee protection through the park to the border. Not that I'm suggesting anyone on the park's staff is bent, but wouldn't securing a ranger or two be your first move if you were running drugs?"

"I can't argue with that."

"Where were the other locations?"

"I can't say."

"Oh, right. But I can guess." Kate held Reese's eyes. "They were similarly situated in a national park, close to a ranger station, just off the PCT, near a small town with no police or first-responder services but sleeping and eating accommodations, with easy access to a larger town or city. The supplier shows up and checks the merchandise, pays the runner, and leaves drugs for the next one. I would look for the people picking up and supplying at drop sites, not the mules. The same person might have stayed in these park communities and will eventually cross the border."

Reese blew out a short breath and asked, "Did you sleep at all last night?" She paused. "I can't confirm anything you just said, but I won't dispute it either. I'm curious, though, what makes you think the traffickers would use the same point person with each shipment?"

"Cost efficiency for one thing. And control. Most strangers in these towns are hikers. Business owners and residents don't think twice about looking at guests. They're all the same person to them." She drank her coffee, and Reese nodded. "I'd check CCTV footage from hotels in the area for the same person checking in, not signatures. They'd never use the same name twice."

"That's sound advice." Reese didn't know what impressed her more—the Kate Hall who dedicated her life to her dog and a small area of a national park, or the one who could do her job as well as she did if not better. "We also need to talk about your safety. Do you want to call someone to stay with you? Parents? Sibling? It might take a few days to figure out if someone is hassling you."

"I'll be okay. Nic is here. If I need someone, I'll text her." She walked to the kitchen and brought back the coffee carafe. "More coffee?"

"Sure." That was the third time Kate had avoided talking about her family, but this time the deflection didn't have the same intensity behind it. "Having Nicole a text away isn't the same as someone in the house with you. Do you think she would stay here?"

"God, no. I wouldn't let her. She chatters incessantly. Besides, Vivienne would kill me with her death glares." She half-smiled and met Reese's eyes. "It has to be Nic and a text...I don't have any family left to call." There was a finality in her voice, but she gave it gently.

Reese covered Kate's hand with hers, entwining their fingers, and giving it a slight squeeze. "Okay. A text to Nicole, it is."

Kate looked at her watch. "I had planned to make you scrambled eggs before you left. Then I discovered I only have two eggs, which is probably best because it might have given you the impression I can cook, which I can't, but I can offer you a leftover cinnabun or a frozen breakfast burrito."

"You happen to be in luck. I know how to turn an egg into a fabulous breakfast." Reese stood and looked through Kate's cupboards and refrigerator. She found a bag of flour and sugar, a can of baking powder, an egg, a carton of coffee creamer, and a handful of takeout butter pads and salt packets.

"All right, I'm intrigued. What are you cooking up?"

"I'm making you my famous pancakes, at least they are in two national parks. My secret is to mix the batter and then add the baking powder. I don't know why it works best, but it does."

"Mmm, pancakes. I can't remember the last time I ate those." Kate glanced at the ingredients. "I had baking powder?"

"You did, and it isn't even expired. There's some good stuff in your cupboards."

"I need to thank Nic for that."

"Okay, thanks to your assistant, you're in for a treat." Reese measured out ingredients into the bowl. Then she placed a flat skillet on the stovetop and turned on the heat. "My mother taught my brothers and me how to cook and bake, even grill. She would tell us that we had to learn our way around the kitchen because the days when only one partner fed a couple or family were over."

"Sounds very egalitarian. What if neither partner wants to cook?"

"That's a good point. We brought up the same argument. She countered that nothing expresses our love more than the food we make for each other. She said, 'We hunt for it, gather it, and prepare it to keep our loved ones alive, to comfort them, celebrate them, and connect them to loved ones who have passed.' We'd laugh because no one in our house hunted. But we understood the sentiment." Reese finished mixing the batter and ran water over her fingers, flicking it at the pan. The water sizzled. "The trick to the perfect pancakes is to have the heat just right." She dipped a ladle into the batter and poured a few rounds onto its surface. "You wait until a good number of bubbles burst on the first side, then flip."

Kate sat quietly for a few minutes, and finally said, "I think it's possible some people just can't learn culinary arts. My grandmother tried to teach me. I never figured out how to do it all…adding ingredients, mixing, whisking, sautéing, baking…it's complicated."

Reese turned to face her. "Maybe you weren't ready to learn. When you are, it's easier. Why don't I teach you a few recipes?" She turned back to the stove and flipped the cakes. "Of course, sharing my wisdom has a price. My fee is a free dinner. Interested?"

"All right. I can afford that. I'll do it for Jenny. She could use an upgrade on the food I share with her."

Reese laughed. "Consider yourself officially enrolled. How about tomorrow night, I teach you how to make pasta primavera? It's easy. Lots of chopping. A quick sauté. Boiling pasta. You'll do great." Reese placed a platter of cakes on the counter. "Do you have syrup or jam?"

"I have a blackberry compote in the pantry."

"Do you make preserves?"

"Me? God, no. Lainey made them for us when she lived here, and now Lou does." She disappeared down the hall and returned with a jar. "Lou jars and freezes fresh produce all summer, so we have it in the winter. This'll be your first winter here, right? If you'd like, I can help you get some provisions in place."

"I'd like that. But you know, I've lived through several winters in Yosemite. I'm used to heavy snow and the cold." She set two plates and forks in front of the barstools.

"We don't get cold, here. We freeze. Highway twenty shuts down for four to five months. Most of the ranger roads become impassable. You can snowmobile to Marblemount, but even if you do, they won't have a great selection of fresh produce."

Reese nodded and spooned the dark purple compote over her pancakes. "Sounds like I've got a busy summer teaching you to cook and stocking my pantry with preserves. Good thing we're starting tomorrow."

CHAPTER TWENTY-TWO

Reese parked in a large dirt yard outside an old, white picket fence surrounding a faded yellow farmhouse. She'd never been to Great Falls, or the Montana plains, but the fields of wheat and the vast blue sky were what she imagined it would look like. She walked through a gate and onto the front porch. A lock clicked and the door opened before she could press the doorbell.

"Hello." A petite woman wearing old jeans, a sweatshirt, and a red bandana holding back her mousy-brown hair stood in the dim afternoon light, twisting a cloth in her hands.

"Ms. Farrell?" Reese asked in a friendly voice. "I'm Special Agent Carter."

"I know. Come in." She stepped to the side, staring at the floor.

Reese followed her down a narrow hallway. Framed photos of families and the farm in purplish-brown albumen, black-and-white, and color film lined the walls on both sides of the hall. They passed two closed doors, and then Holly opened a third on the right and stopped inside an intimate living room with floral drapes matching the wallpaper and pristine antiques. The room smelled of lemon cleaner and a faint whiff of burning wood from a large stone fireplace.

Holly pointed to a box on a coffee table. "This is it. Everything he had about Coleen's disappearance." Her voice interrupted the tick-tock of a grandfather clock, the only other sound in the room. "You're welcome to look through it or take it."

"I'd like to do both if that's okay with you?" Reese asked.

"Sure." She gestured toward the sofa and chairs. "Sit where you want. Can I get you something to drink?"

"Water if it's no trouble." Reese sat in an armchair beside the box. She could tell Holly had moved it from its usual place near the fireplace where another matching chair and side table were. Coleen's sister was nervous, but she had prepared for the visit.

"I added ice. I hope that's okay. I forgot to ask if you take ice."

"Ice is great. Thank you." Reese took the water from her and set the glass on a coaster. "I'd like to ask you a few questions before I look through the box if that's okay, and I'm happy to answer any questions you might have about Coleen's case."

Holly briefly made eye contact with Reese and nodded. She smoothed a rough-looking hand over the handkerchief on her head and sat on the sofa. "Sorry, I'm a mess. I dust and polish the house on Mondays."

"I appreciate you taking the time to talk with me, Ms. Farrell. May I call you Holly?"

"Sure," she said, picking at the dust cloth she held. It struck Reese that Coleen's sister wasn't used to visitors.

"I don't think I saw another property on the drive to your place from the highway. Does your family own all the wheat fields in view?"

Holly finally looked at Reese. "They're all ours. We have over three thousand acres. Farrell Farms is four…five generations if you count me. Our original homestead is a few miles east of here. It was my great-great grandparents' home. There's only an old root cellar left now. Our family lived there until my grandfather built this house and the barns."

"That's an amazing history, and your grandfather was a talented builder and carpenter. Your home and barns are picturesque."

She waited for Holly to speak again, but the young woman only sat silently staring at her lap. "How old were you when Coleen disappeared?"

"I was ten. Coleen was nine years older than me."

"You were so young. It must have been confusing to understand what was happening."

"Not really. You don't stay young on a farm this size, at least not for very long." Anger had replaced Holly's nervousness, just for a moment.

Reese suspected the woman still felt the years of controlling abuse that went on in this quaint farmhouse. "Do you remember much about Coleen?"

Holly thought for a moment. "She was smart and strong and had an amazing smile. I can still see it. When she smiled at me, I felt…I don't know…noticed?" She got a faraway look in her pale green eyes. "Her hair smelled like strawberries after she washed it. It was long and felt like silk. I remember she was so pretty." She leaned forward and searched through the box, pulling out a picture and handing it to Reese. "See here, a natural beauty."

Reese looked at the photo of the smiling teenager and handed it back. "What was your and Coleen's relationship like?"

Holly frowned. "She didn't have much time for me. Not on purpose. We were too busy with school and chores. I only saw her at breakfast and dinner, and we weren't allowed to talk during meals. That was time for our parents to talk to us." Her face softened. "Sometimes at bedtime, Coleen would sneak into my room and crawl into my bed. She'd ask how my day was and tell me jokes until I laughed…we'd make up stories about being movie stars or pop stars…" Her voice faded.

"It sounds like growing up was hard, but she helped make it better for you," Reese said sympathetically.

"An operation this size is nonstop physical work for one or two people. When we weren't at school, I helped our mother in the kitchen and garden and with the chickens, and Coleen was…" Holly frowned.

"Was what?"

"Helping him in the fields. My grandfather had had two sons to help him. Plus farmhands. They were cheaper back then. But after my grandfather died and my uncle moved away, my father struggled. He didn't have sons, only us, and he couldn't afford to hire more than one helper, and then only during the busy seasons."

Reese nodded. "Did Coleen like working on the farm?"

"It didn't matter if she liked it or not. It had to be done." Her voice sounded resentful. "After Coleen went missing, I had to help him…I've worked with him ever since. Life on the farm didn't stop when she disappeared. Our days still started early with chores and school and more chores after. We went on as if she had never been a part of our lives. It was the same when my mother died, we kept working." She looked out a large, mullioned window at the wheat fields surrounding them. "Now it's only me, but I can't prepare the fields, plant, monitor, fertilize, irrigate, harvest…everything that goes into growing our crop. Let alone selling it in the markets. Not alone. And I can't afford a full-time farmhand." She turned back to Reese. "I'm sorry. I told you I wouldn't be much help."

"You've been more than helpful," Reese said reassuringly. "I can't thank you enough for your time. Do you have any questions for me?" She paused, but Holly only stared at her, so she continued, "You said Mr. Farrell didn't share anything about Coleen's case with you or your mother."

"That's right. He didn't talk about it. Or let us talk about it. I'd ask, and he'd shut me down with a slammed cupboard or fist against a tabletop, and then he'd walk out of the room. I just stopped asking. Mom had quit long before me."

"Did he ever leave the farm to look for Coleen?"

"I don't remember. But it would've been impossible for him to leave without someone to take his place, and I don't recall anyone ever staying with us. Besides, I doubt he ever wanted to look for her. Over the years, Mom's and my fears about Coleen turned to sadness. But he was only ever angry right from the beginning. I don't think he ever shed a tear for her."

"That must have been hard for you to understand as you got older." She tried to hold Holly's eyes, but the woman looked away. "Did you have a chance to read through any of the information in the box?"

Holly looked at it and nodded. "There isn't much there. Contact information for agents who worked on Coleen's case. He kept their updates. Places they searched for her, the few witnesses who said they saw her…I didn't even know she went that far."

"What do you mean?"

Holly hesitated. "I thought she was spending the day on the River's Edge Trail."

"Where is this trail?"

"Northeast of town. It runs along the Missouri River over the Cochrane Dam and back toward town…it was her favorite. She liked to describe it to me. She would tell me about the prairie dogs popping out of their tunnels, then at the sound of bald eagles they'd drop back inside their holes like a whack-a-mole game, and the pelicans that landed on the river filling their gular pouches with water and fish. She made it seem so incredible." Her smile faded. "When she visited me the night before she left. It felt different. She didn't have a funny story. She told me I was the only one who understood her. That she would miss me. I didn't think it meant anything then, but now, I know it did. I know she was telling me goodbye." She stared at her red, calloused hands.

"Thank you for sharing that with me." Reese paused. "You thought your sister could be alive when we talked on the phone. What did you mean?"

Holly's shoulders slumped. "After I turned seventeen, he tried to arrange for me to marry another farmer's son. He said the farm needed a man to help and to continue it after he was gone. It upset my mother so much, she took to her room for days. His plan didn't work." She hesitated. "I think he might have tried the same thing with Coleen."

Reese suppressed her anger and sympathy and continued, "Your father also told investigators that your sister asked to hike the Pacific Crest Trail for her nineteenth birthday. A long trip like that would require planning. Do you remember any conversations about her traveling southbound on the PCT? Maybe at the dinner table? Or when you chatted at night?"

Holly shook her head, her expression neutral, but Reese could see her mind racing with questions. "When she didn't return that night, or the next day, he said he'd take care of it."

"Your dad told us Coleen phoned the house, checking in every week or so. But after about two months on her trip, she stopped calling. Did you ever answer any of those calls? Or remember your parents talking with her?"

"I can't remember." Holly looked genuinely confused. "I didn't know where she went until years later."

"Okay. Did your parents keep financial records like personal bills and utilities?"

She nodded. "His office is full of files and boxes. You can look through them. Take whatever you need."

"I'm so sorry to bring up all these memories, Holly. We have people you can talk to about your feelings—"

"I don't need anything like that," she said, interrupting.

"Okay. But if you change your mind, reach out to me please, and I'll put you in touch with someone."

"If that's all, I need to get back to work."

"I promise I'm almost done. I just have one more question, and it's about you."

"Me?" She sat back.

"Yes. When you were nineteen, would your father have allowed you to leave on a trip for four to six months?"

Holly stared at Reese, her face reddening. "Absolutely not, and I wouldn't have dared to ask."

CHAPTER TWENTY-THREE

It was early afternoon, and Reese had finished pulling out the old green shag carpet and deteriorating padding from a large room she planned to remodel into her library and office. The space had four generous walls for built-in bookcases—one wall with a large stone fireplace where she'd place a reading area and another with a picture window framing the forest.

The physical work had cleared her head. She poured a cup of coffee and sat at the kitchen island in her great room, admiring the dark pine floor she'd just completed. Holly Farrell cast doubt on the fundamental premise of her older sister's disappearance and Reese believed the proof was sitting next to her. She searched through the papers in the box Mr. Farrell kept under his bed. There were fifteen years of one-sided correspondence from the ISB. It was nothing new to her. She had the original copies of each letter. Her agency had consistently shared information with Coleen's family. With her dad. But he hadn't reciprocated, and what he had shared were probably lies.

She found the document she wanted and sat back against the barstool. Mr. Farrell's recorded statement had been transcribed into four pages, and surprisingly, ISB hadn't followed up on much of it. In all fairness, eyewitness accounts had placed Coleen on the PCT nearly seven hundred miles away. Even so, the situation called for their due diligence.

Reese reread Mr. Farrell's words, hearing them now in the voice of a dominating husband and father. He stated that Coleen left on her solo hike the day after her birthday, and she called once a week to update them. A month or so into her trip, she missed her weekly check-in. He said they thought she was probably out of range, but then ISB arrived a few days later and told them that a group of hikers Coleen had befriended found her backpack, including food, cell phone, and wallet, abandoned at Chinook Pass and contacted the Mount Rainer National Park rangers. "All right, Mr. Farrell," Reese said aloud. "Let's see if you were telling the truth."

Before Reese left the Farrells' farm, she had searched his office. It had filing cabinets lining the walls and boxes stacked high in the corners filled with personal and farm financial papers dating back to his father's stewardship in the early 1970s. The meticulous record-keeping made it easy to find the documents she needed. She started with their monthly credit card and bank statements for 2010, reading for any items to suggest they had helped Coleen prepare for a birthday hiking trip. There was nothing. No supply purchases. No bus or airfare tickets to the PCT's northern terminus, or any other trailhead. No withdrawals for spending money. Coleen might have owned the hiking equipment she needed, but it was hard to believe she didn't need *something* before embarking on such a significant trip.

She searched through the files and found their phone bills. At the time, the Farrell family had a landline and three cell phones on a family plan. She scanned the incoming calls for August and September on Mr. and Mrs. Farrell's numbers and found no calls from Coleen's number or the Washington or Oregon areas. She examined Coleen's phone usage for August and September. She made no outgoing calls and received incoming calls that lasted only seconds from Mrs. Farrell's number. *Messages?* Those calls took place up to the day the ISB arrived at the farm.

Reese spent the next few hours writing up her findings and emailed the paperwork to her boss. She was certain Mr. Farrell had lied, and Coleen had run from her life on that farm. Leaving her home without telling her family didn't change the fact that she could have been abducted and killed, but it did open up the possibility that she disappeared on purpose and had worked for fifteen years to stay gone.

She checked the time and closed her laptop. Her first cooking lesson with Kate started in an hour. If she hurried, she had enough time to shower before packing the groceries in her old Rover. It usually took time to switch gears from the grim nature of her job to her personal life, but since she met Kate, her mind moved on quickly, she felt lighter and more willing to put work away.

When Reese arrived at the hostel, Kate's door opened and Jenny ran to greet her with an excited body hug against her leg. "I'm happy to see you, too," she said, rubbing the top of Jenny's head.

"Hey. You're right on time. Let me take one of those." Kate grabbed a grocery bag, resting it on her hip. They stood face-to-face, the energy around them humming. "Let's get this lesson started," she said. Her voice was unenthusiastic, and she abruptly turned and walked away.

Reese followed her to the kitchen. She thought they had made a breakthrough last night, but Kate's wall was back, and hitting it stung. She had the means to dig into Kate's past. Something kept her on guard and living alone. Someone made her keep people at arm's length. Reese exhaled quietly. Just because she could discover what it was didn't mean she would.

The kitchen counter was bare except for an iPad on a stand. Kate took the wine from Reese. "You'll need a glass. I'm not the best student."

"Then why don't we keep our thoughts sharp and save the wine for dinner?"

Kate screwed the opener into the cork. "Drinking wine while cooking didn't hurt Julia Child."

"Aw, have you been studying? I like your attitude." Reese typed on the iPad and then pointed at the screen. "A great recipe is the foundation of good cooking. When you're more comfortable in the kitchen, you can improvise more. But for now, a recipe is your best friend. It tells you what ingredients you need, the steps to prep them, and how to cook them. So read this and collect everything it calls for." Reese smiled and took the glass of wine Kate offered. "I'll stand over here and enjoy my wine."

"All right. Pasta primavera." Kate read but started scrolling quickly. "What's up with all the pictures and ads? Why doesn't Cooking with Sherry get to the point?"

Reese laughed. "You can use the jump-to-recipe link, but you'll miss her explanations and pictures of each step."

"Isn't that what you're supposed to teach me?"

"Yeah, but if you skip hers, how will you realize how awesome I am?"

Kate chuckled and continued reading. After a few minutes, she gathered items from the grocery bags Reese brought and her own cabinets. "Okay, that's everything. We're ready to do this."

"Are you a good dancer?"

"What does that have to do with anything?"

"I'm no Julia Child, but my experience has taught me that cooking requires timing and rhythm like dancing."

"Oh, it does? I'm starting to think this is a well-rehearsed routine you have for unsuspecting novices."

Reese held her hands up. "You're the first woman I've given cooking lessons to. I swear. Now dance lessons…that's another topic." The little burst of laughter that escaped Kate made her heart swell.

"All right, then. What's next?"

"For this dish, the roasted veggies take ten minutes to prep and fifteen to roast. The water will boil in about ten minutes, and the farfalle will be *al dente* in nine. The last step is the parmesan. Grating it takes a few minutes tops."

"And that's like dancing, how?"

"You know…steps, timing, and rhythm. Trust me, the way you move around your kitchen will begin to feel like a dance." She watched her take a deep breath and smiled at the serious look on her face. "You like to be good at everything you do, don't you?"

"What gave you that idea?" Kate sipped her wine. "You make cooking sound simple."

"I promise it will be. Dinner becomes more complicated if we throw in some antipasti and dessert, but we'll keep this lesson simple." Reese set her wineglass down and placed two cutting boards and two butcher's knives in front of them. "Start the water to boil. Then we'll cut all the vegetables into bite-sized pieces." She halved a zucchini and put one half on Kate's cutting board. "You cut the piece in half again then dice it about a half inch in width, like this." Kate watched Reese's knife work, its rhythmic movements of up and down, forward and backward. "When you're done, toss the veggies in the bowl."

"You're making it look too easy." Kate slowly sliced the zucchini down the middle.

"Here, hold the blade between your thumb and index finger." Reese moved Kate's hand and guided her fingers. "That's it."

"Oh, wow. That is easier. What the heck is the handle for?" Kate asked as she started on a yellow squash.

"It has its purposes." Reese looked at Kate's board. "Those cuts are perfect."

After they finished the vegetables, Kate followed the recipe and seasoned them while Reese gathered the cutting boards and knives and put them in the sink. She took the lid off the boiling water. "Add some salt to this, then the pasta. Put the veggies in the oven. Set the timer for nine minutes. While they're cooking, grate a half-cup of parmesan and tear up those basil leaves."

Kate completed the tasks and set the timer. "I'm pretty sure I don't need to learn how to grate or tear, so if you'd do those steps, I'll feed Jenny and be back before the timer goes off." She walked out of the kitchen and disappeared down the hall.

Jenny heard the kibble hit her bowl and stood on all fours in her dog bed. After a good stretch, she lumbered toward the pantry. Kate returned and inspected Reese's work. "Looks good. What's next?"

"Well, this is a colander."

"I know what a colander is," Kate said, swatting Reese's side. "I've made my share of mac 'n' cheese."

"In that case, you're an expert at the next step." Reese placed it in the sink, and the oven's timer buzzed. "Reserve half a cup of the pasta water then drain the rest. Put the farfalle in the pasta bowl, remove your veggies in five minutes, and add them. All you have left to do is toss it together—"

"With the cheese and pasta water and top it with the basil. Yep, I got this…what a breeze." Kate finished the recipe and spooned steaming pasta onto their plates. "A toast to the teacher and hopefully a successful first lesson." She held out her wineglass and Reese clinked hers against it.

They ate at the counter. When they were finished, Reese took the dishes to the sink. "That was delicious. Your seasoning was perfect. An A-plus."

"Good to know. All thanks to you, your teaching was flawless." Kate climbed off her barstool. "I have dessert planned, so sit and I'll be right back." When she returned, she switched off the kitchen light, stepped out of the hallway, and started singing, "Happy birthday to you, happy birthday to you. Happy birthday, dear Reese. Happy birthday to you." She held out a small cake with a burning candle. "Make a wish."

Reese blew out the candle, her heart did a flip-flop. "You remembered."

"I did. You said you hoped I could tell you happy birthday on the day, so I figured our cooking lesson was part of your plan." She handed her a gift bag. "This is for you."

"And a present? I'm definitely not clever enough to have planned this. I just wanted to spend time with you." She pulled the tissue from the bag. "*Song To A Seagull*. Oh, Kate. Thank you."

"I figured, you wouldn't have this one if you're just starting your Joni Mitchell collection. It's the one recorded at Sunset Sound in Hollywood with David Crosby. I found it online at a vintage vinyl shop in Seattle. Nic picked it up for me a few days ago."

"I don't have it. It's perfect. Thank you so much. And Nicole." She gave Kate a quick hug. It was such a thoughtful gift that it had caught her off guard.

"You're welcome and thank you for tonight. I look forward to more lessons, and I'm going to practice. Hopefully, you'll make it progressively harder. I love a challenge."

"Are we still talking about culinary lessons?" Reese smiled, placing the vinyl back in the gift bag. "You know, my parents have a saying, a couple who cooks together stays together. They're going on their forty-first anniversary."

"I think the saying is a couple who plays together stays together."

"You've never seen them in the kitchen."

Kate laughed and Jenny plodded back into the room. She quickly turned her attention to the bloodhound, petting her head. Then she looked at Reese again. "Remember when you asked about my dog growing up? Her name was Lila. She was a scruffy schnauzer and a complete terror. She'd bite your ankles if you walked too close to her, but I loved her anyway. I was devastated when she died. She was my first experience with death…with losing someone I loved."

"I'm so sorry. One of our family dogs, Sammie, was my first experience with dying, too. You never forget that first gut punch, the first feeling of grief. My parents helped us process her loss, I guess. We had a funeral at the park she loved and said our goodbyes. They still have her ashes in a box in their garage…with about five other boxes."

Kate picked at a piece of cake with her fork. "We didn't have a funeral for Lila. My mother was diagnosed with aggressive leukemia and began treatment a few weeks before Lila died. It felt like one day I woke up and everyone in my home was sick. My dad took Lila to the vet and had her put down, came home, and told me she was gone. Nothing else." Her free hand continued to rub Jenny's head. "Six months later, my mom was gone too, and my dad became depressed, unable to leave the house for days at a time. I was too young to understand what was happening to him. I just thought he was angry at everyone, at me. My grandma came to live with us. When he killed himself, she took me in and raised me."

She stopped talking, and Reese let the gravity of the moment settle. "Kate. I'm so sorry." Her voice was thick. "I can't imagine the world of hurt you grew up with." She slipped her hand under Kate's, holding it just above Jenny's head.

"I didn't tell you for sympathy." Kate pulled her hand back. "I think it's just fair you understand why I can't...I haven't even imagined loving someone that much...for a day...let alone forty-one years."

PART THREE

I shall overhear you, bare-foot,
scatting off into the darkness…
I shall know you, secrets
by the litter you have left
and by your bloody foot-prints.
                    –Lola Ridge

CHAPTER TWENTY-FOUR

Fiona lit the candles in an ornate silver candelabra and sat alone at the dinner table. She was pleased with herself. Everything she had worked for and planned down to the tiniest detail was proceeding on schedule. The corners of her mouth turned up. With their newest venture, she could end the O'Flaherty's drug route to Ireland, and the Feds would never prove their family porcelain business was ever a front.

She stared at the portraits on the wall, paintings of her grandfather, father, and first husband. When Sean became the new captain, he pleaded for his likeness to be painted and hung among them. There was so much that simple man never understood. Three generations of women were the real strength behind the O'Flaherty crime ring, no matter who the family allowed to sit in the captain's chair.

The door opened, and her assistant entered. "Your dinner, Mrs. Maloney."

"Thank you, Josh." She sat back, and he placed the cloche-covered plate on the table. After cutting into a steak and revealing its red center, she said, "I don't need anything more tonight. You may go home for the evening."

Josh gave a slight bow and left.

Fiona looked at the paintings again and decided to have her portrait commissioned. She made a mental note to have Nora schedule it and frowned. Bridget had once convinced her to come out of the shadows, to take the role and title that was rightfully hers, a position she'd never pass on to her daughter.

Her cell phone rang, and she answered, "Are you there?"

"I'm here," Liam said, and she could hear him pacing. "But I'm pissed the damn car I hired isn't ready. Otherwise, I didn't have any problems."

"Good. See that it stays that way. I've worked hard to develop this relationship and opportunity for us. We can't afford to screw it up." She cut into her steak again. "Antonio is a serious businessman. He'll take his business elsewhere if he suspects we can't deliver. Do you understand me?"

"I hear you, Ma." He lowered his voice. "You need to stop riding me. I'm not the reason the FBI visited you. No one flagged my ID then or now. We both know they're never leaving us alone…not when we still have a witness out there." He paused. "There's only one person to blame for that, and it sure the hell isn't me."

"You will not speak ill of your sister, Liam. We can't change the past, but we can secure our future. That's what I'm trying to do. Divesting the business the FBI thinks we have and creating a new one. This relationship with Antonio will help—"

"Or we can just find that bitch and take care of the problem," Liam interrupted angrily. "You're dismantling *my* business. I'm to run it next as my father and grandfather did. All we have to do is silence her and none of this would be necessary."

"For God's sake, Liam. We're under enough scrutiny as it is. How do you propose we search for her without bringing the US Marshals down on us too?" She took a deep breath to calm herself and cut another piece of her steak. "I'm asking you to keep a low profile, that's all. Do our business and return without incident. Please."

"I know what I'm doing," Liam snapped.

"Of course you do. I wasn't suggesting otherwise. You've stepped in and run our operations perfectly, haven't you?" She shut and opened her eyes slowly. "And I appreciate you taking the lead with Antonio. Why don't you run me through our part again?"

"Yeah, that's right, I have, Ma. You could show me a little respect." She could hear Liam stop pacing. "I pay the ranger and pass the goods to Finn tomorrow. He'll have safe passage to Canada, and Antonio's buyer will meet him once he crosses the border."

"Excellent. And Connor and Finn are settled?"

"Yeah, Ma. I moved them to Seattle last month."

"That's perfect." She picked at the broccolini on her plate. "Then there's nothing left to worry about. You have it all worked out. Don't make any mistakes, and call me when you return. I need to finish dinner now." She disconnected. Her son wasn't her most capable child, but he had succeeded in the limited tasks she had given him.

She finished eating and snuffed the candles. When she returned her plate to the kitchen, she saw the cook had gone for the night but had left her a bowl of chocolate mousse on the island. She poured a glass of wine and carried it and the dessert to her study. There was one more piece to put in place and her plan was set.

Unlocking her desk drawer, she retrieved a burner phone and tapped the only number it held. The other line rang several times before someone picked up.

"Nice of you to finally call me back. Two months is too damn long to make me wait for your response. You're lucky I answered."

"Temper, temper. It's taken me this long to consider your proposal thoroughly."

"And?"

She hesitated. "Unfortunately, it's not the right time to diversify our business any more than we have."

"For fuck's sake. Are you kidding me? It's exactly the perfect time. What's the real reason?"

Fiona sighed. "You know what it is. Liam is a dismal failure. I might as well be operating everything on my own. How do you expect me to take on a new venture on the other side of the country?"

"You could promote someone who can get the job done and make Liam work in the fucking warehouse for all I care. I've cultivated a once-in-a-lifetime opportunity for us to move into this market, and you're willing to let that idiot ruin it. We need to consider this seriously. It's worth an absolute fortune. The traditional Chinese medicine trade and the drug lanes I've opened here could free us from the Feds. Free you from being stuck in Quincy. Isn't that what you want?"

"Of course I do, darling. It's what I've wanted for eight years." Fiona sipped her wine.

"Then prove it. Antonio won't wait much longer. There's a huge market for prohibited African wildlife ingredients in Canada. He wants a TCM pipeline on the West Coast opened and needs an answer."

"I've already told you, my answer is no, Bridget." She closed her eyes while her daughter growled and swore at her. "Can I speak now?" she asked after Bridget fell silent. "There will be more opportunities. I like the idea of entering into black-markets, but our priority should be on the European drug routes you've established. You're doing so well. Making quite a name for yourself. Just like I knew you would."

"Spare me your cajoling shit. It might work on Liam, but I see right through it."

"I'm sorry my decision disappoints you, but I'm only being realistic. We'll need more than a share in a contraband pipeline to close the family drug business. But don't despair, darling. There are other ways for us to be together."

"Oh, right. Like one weekend at New Year's after you dump Liam in Ireland." Bridget's voice was loud, acrimonious. "You're making a huge fucking mistake, Mother."

"The only one who's made mistakes here is you." Fiona licked the chocolate from her dessert fork.

"Me? You're the one who hired Eleanor Peters," Bridget yelled. "How fucking stupid were you to fall for an undercover. You brought her into our lives. Then you took my life away from me, and you're not even sorry about it. Everything that has happened is your fault, but I'm the only one being punished."

"Are you finished?" Fiona asked dryly.

"I'm far from fucking finished. I've only seen you a dozen times since you stuck me in Nice. You changed my face. My life. Liam doesn't even know I'm alive. Maybe I should tell him? Maybe I'm done letting you control everything. After he finds out you faked my death, he'd gladly help me take the business from you, especially when he learns what you really think about him."

"Are you done with the histrionics?" Fiona asked sharply. "Be a good girl and stay focused. The only thing that would happen if you resurfaced and brought your brother into your mess is jail time. Is that what you want? For all of us to go to prison?"

"We wouldn't if Eleanor was dead. You've had eight years to find her. Any leads? No. Because you aren't even looking." Bridget's voice pitched to anger again. "I know you've been lying to me."

Fiona closed her eyes, struggling to control her temper. "Do calm yourself, darling. We have been actively looking for her for years. I wanted to wait before I told you this, but remember the elderly woman you saw when you followed Eleanor to that house in Jamaica Plain?"

"What about her?"

"She sold her home last year, and we think we have an address for her in Florida. It might be a link to Eleanor. Your brother is there looking for her, as we speak. But we must be careful, darling. He was there two weeks ago, and the FBI visited me last week, asking if he had gone out of state. They are always watching us. We'll find her again and watch her home for Eleanor to show her face." She paused, hoping the fabrication appeased Bridget.

"*Arrête de dire n'importe quoi putain!* I know you've lied about everything. You're the one who told Sean about my meeting at Eryn's. What did you instruct him to do? Rough me up? Bring me home? Of course, he didn't know it was a trap. Did you think I wouldn't figure it out? That it was you, not the Novikovs. The text to me…*Sean's angry. Come through the bakery alone. I'm waiting in the alley.* Telling me to text Eleanor after I got in the car, so she'd be in the bakery when you blew it up. You already knew she was FBI. But it was a stupid plan, and it failed. If you had told me what you knew, we could have dealt with Eleanor together. I would've helped you eliminate that idiot husband of yours too, but you lied to me, and you've been lying to me ever since."

Fiona had listened to her daughter's threats before, but an edge in Bridget's voice gave her a chill. "I've heard enough, Bridget. Let me remind you that your choices got you where you are. You started a new venture without telling me and put us all in jeopardy. You told Eleanor Peters about your business and enough about our family business to ruin us. I did what I had to do. To save you and the family. I'm sorry you didn't get the answer you wanted about Antonio and the TCM materials." She unlocked the desk drawer. "I'm done discussing the matter and the past. We do need to arrange some time together when things calm down. I'll have Nora make arrangements. I'd love a trip to Nice."

"Oh, Mother. Don't bother."

Bridget ended the call, and Fiona stared at the screen. Then she dropped the phone in the drawer and locked it. Her daughter had always been undisciplined. Before, she was too young to create too much damage, but now, she worried Bridget could bring the entire family to its knees.

CHAPTER TWENTY-FIVE

The sun slipped under the tree line as Kate tended the hybridized roses she had created the year before. She had crossed a semidouble, ruffled bloom in a deep red with a double, wavy bloom in a light salmon. The bushes had grown well, surviving their first winter. This year, they budded and bloomed palm-sized roses in a mottled orange. They were stunning like a fiery sunset. Over the next two seasons, she would watch how they survived the weather and insects, and if they were healthy enough, she would enter them into contests. That is if she was still there.

She had been safe at the hostel for years. The current situation caused her to speed up her plan to explain the financial side of the business to Nicole. Her assistant was a business honor graduate from a top-tier university in Ontario and a quick study. Knowing Nicole could run the hostel if the US Marshals uprooted her life provided a comfort that she hadn't realized she needed.

She wiped her hands on her jeans and glanced at her watch. Reese expected her by six. Over the last few weeks, Reese had given her cooking lessons, and she was learning everything she could about the special agent—her favorite holidays, music, people, food, and how she felt about politics, the environment, and her family. Reese was incredibly forthcoming and didn't push Kate to share more than she felt comfortable revealing.

She cut the last of the garden's long-stem yellow roses. Yellow roses symbolized friendship, nothing more or less, which was good because she couldn't offer Reese anything more. It was too dangerous. Even though she wanted more. She enjoyed Reese's company. Being with her was exciting and made Kate feel like an agent again. Then there was the kissing. Her skin tingled. God, that woman could kiss.

"Hey, boss," Nicole called out.

Kate straightened and looked at the porch. Nicole took long strides toward the garden, and Vivienne swung a pack over one shoulder and walked toward the parking area. "What's wrong with your girlfriend now?"

Nicole stared at Vivienne's car as it drove off. "Nothing. Why?"

"So it's just me she avoids?"

"She's not avoiding you. You intimidate her because you're the boss. That's all." Nicole followed Kate to the porch. "So do you have a cooking lesson tonight?"

"Actually, Reese is making me dinner instead of teaching me."

"How romantic, and you're bringing roses. Do you plan to be gone all night?"

"It's a friendly dinner, and they're yellow." She frowned and looked at the flowers. "Do you think they give the wrong message?"

"Depends on what your message is."

"They're supposed to say, 'I like hanging out with you, and I'm glad we're friends.'"

Nicole looked at her, surprised. "Friends with benefits?"

"That's definitely none of your business."

"No benefits? Are you seriously friend-zoning her? What a waste."

"I like Reese, and sex would complicate things." Kate's words were unconvincing. She took the roses to the communal room and wrapped them in paper. "I planned to pick up hot cinnabuns, too. Her favorite. Is that too much?"

"Roses and dessert, but no benefits? Yeah, that might give the wrong message." Nicole leaned a hip against the buffet table. "I think Vivienne's right. You're too used to being alone. Reese would be good for you."

"It's nice of you and Vivienne to make me a topic of conversation, but you don't need to be concerned about me. I'm fine. If I wanted that kind of relationship, I'd have one." She looked at the flowers. She knew what she felt for Reese was more than friendship, but one couldn't always have what one wanted. That was a lesson Nicole had her entire life to learn. "Has Vivienne cleaned the open rooms?"

"Yeah, and I already checked in the new hikers." Nicole petted Jenny's head as the hound ambled through the door and into her and Kate's home. "She has an appointment in Seattle first thing in the morning. Something to do with her visa. That's why I asked about tonight. She won't be back until tomorrow, but no worries, I can handle Lounge alone. I might wait until tomorrow to clean up if that's okay?"

"Sure. I'll help you set up before I leave, and if I'm not too tired tonight, I can clean up when I get home."

"*If* you make it home and feel up to it, text me and I'll help."

Kate shook her head. "Goodbye, Nic."

An hour later, Kate walked out of The Friendly Roast, smiling because she only had to talk to Phil. Lou was in the kitchen baking cinnabuns and didn't hear her voice because if she had, she wouldn't have missed the opportunity to torment her about Reese.

She was five minutes late and considered texting Reese but decided against it. Showing up within ten minutes was acceptable, and she didn't need to seem eager. She hurried to her truck and placed the dessert in the back cab away from Jenny, not that the old hound would bother with it. "Told you I'd be right back, sweet girl," she said as she got behind the wheel.

She backed her truck out of its parking spot and drove down Main Street. Then she saw someone walking out of Piggie Pie

Pizza. Her heartbeat thrashed in her ears, and her chest tightened, making her struggle for breath. It was Liam Maloney holding a large take-out box. He stood beside a white sedan. She wasn't seeing things. It was him.

She glanced in the rearview mirror. No one was coming. She could flip a U-turn, but that might draw his attention. The only thing she could do was continue forward and drive past him. Her trembling hands clutched the steering wheel. She grabbed Jenny's collar, pulled the hound against her lap, and used her to block his view of her. The truck neared him, and she prayed he'd get inside the car, but he didn't move. They drove past, her breathing becoming rapid and shallow.

When she turned onto the dirt road to Reese's house, she drifted to a stop still holding Jenny against her, unable to let go. She was working herself into a panic attack. It had been a month since she found the drugs in the black backpack. Had Liam been in the area the entire time? Watching her. Had he seen her with Reese or Nicole? Why didn't the FBI know he was there? Why hadn't the marshals extracted her? Nothing made sense. All she knew was that the Maloneys had found her, and the new life she had built was over.

She inhaled deeply to slow her breathing, checking the rearview mirror every few seconds. What was Liam planning? Whatever it was, she couldn't let it involve the people she cared for. She needed to call Joanna, but first, she had to call Reese and cancel. She'd tell her that Nicole needed help with Lounge. Then she'd ask her for a rain check, a date that would never happen. Her throat tightened, and she felt the hot sting of tears.

Reese answered on the first ring. "Hey. I hope you're hungry because my stroganoff tastes amazing. I'm pretty sure you'll never eat a frozen one again."

"Hi, yourself." Kate's voice quavered, and her tears welled again at the sound of Reese's happiness. "I'm so sorry but—"

"Oh, no. Don't tell me you have to cancel?"

"Yeah…It's work. Vivienne's in Seattle, and I don't want to burden Nicole again."

"No problem. I'll pack up everything and bring dinner to you."

"That's not a good idea. It'll be busy and loud."

"Sounds like a restaurant."

Kate let her head fall against the steering wheel. "There's nowhere to eat comfortably in the communal room."

"Then we can eat it later at your place after you close."

She could hear the suspicion in Reese's voice, and her chest tightened. She didn't want to cancel, to hurt Reese. Her mind raced as she tried to think of something to say that wasn't harsh but could end the conversation. Suddenly, a car honked behind her, she jerked forward, and a startled gasp escaped her.

"What's the matter?" Reese asked, her tone concerned. "Where are you?"

Kate looked into the rearview mirror. A red truck had pulled up behind her, unable to pass. She let her foot off the brake and coasted farther onto the shoulder. Then she shoved the gear into park. Eight years of living a new life, of secrets and lying, had exhausted her, and she wept shuddering sobs.

Jenny whined and nudged Kate, licking her face.

"Kate, please tell me where you are."

"I'm…sitting in my truck…on your road…I don't know what to do."

"Then I'm glad you called because I have a plan." Reese's voice was confident and steady. "I want you to turn off your truck's motor." She hesitated. "Is it off?"

"Uh-huh."

"Is Jenny with you?"

"Yeah."

"Good. Lock the doors and wait for me. I'll be right there." Reese's house was a quarter of a mile down the road through a dense wood. A few minutes later, she jogged toward them, and Kate opened the door. Reese sat behind the wheel and gathered Kate into her arms, holding her tightly. "Hey, I have you. It's okay. Let's get you back to mine."

CHAPTER TWENTY-SIX

Reese eased Kate onto the sofa in her great room and poured a double whiskey into a thick lowball. "Here, drink this. It'll help calm your shaking." She opened the stacked doors for Jenny. The hound plodded onto the porch where her new water bowl and chew toys were.

Kate slowly sipped her drink, feeling its warmth spread down her throat and into her stomach. She closed her eyes and fought back the burning sensation of tears.

"Hey, you're okay. Whatever you were afraid of, you're safe now." Reese sat next to Kate and held her hand. "I made you a nice dinner, and we'll dine on the patio and listen to music. We can talk if you want, or if not, we'll watch the nightfall and the stars come out. Okay?" Kate nodded, and Reese kissed her lightly on the forehead. "You finish your drink. I'll put some music on and feed Jenny."

Kate watched her walk away and felt a tug. She was so patient, so good to her, to Jenny. What the hell was she doing? Why was she leading this woman on, letting her soothe her? She had nothing to offer in return. Reese didn't deserve her messed-up understanding of love. The dishonesty. Danger. She downed the rest of her drink and laid her head back against the cushion.

"Any requests?" Reese asked, holding a vinyl record. Kate shook her head. "This is a good one. Jazz instrumental, some Coltrane pieces. I hope you like it."

After a few songs, Jenny bounded back inside, placing a bright red rope-and-plastic chew toy at Kate's feet. She picked up the rope end, and Jenny clamped down on the plastic end. They played tug-of-war for a few minutes. Then Jenny ran halfway back to the stacked doors and barked.

"Looks like it's your turn to toss it," Reese called from the patio.

Kate carried the toy outside and threw it into the yard below. Jenny ran down the steps with a loud bay, retrieved it, and rushed back to her side. There were speakers on the deck, and smooth jazz filled the air. Kate leaned against the patio railing and let herself withdraw into the music's rhythms and the back-and-forth of fetch with Jenny.

"We're ready," Reese said. "Thank you for these. They're beautiful." She had arranged the yellow roses in a vase. She smiled at Kate and set the flowers on the patio table. "While you're over there, look to the left. Do you see the tilled plot? I've decided this place needs a rose garden. Now I need a rosarian to teach me how to grow them. Maybe I'll produce champion blooms here one day."

Kate looked at the dirt patch, twice the size of her garden. Her chest clenched, and she pushed off the rail.

"Come sit down." Reese poured two glasses of wine. She handed Kate a basket of warm rosemary bread. "You probably don't feel like eating, but I promise you'll feel better if you do. Start with the bread."

The bread was warm. Kate tore off a piece, small at first, and chewed. Her stomach churned, rebelling. Her throat tightened as she swallowed. But she ate, and it became easier with each bite. Everything was delicious, but her mind was miles away. Her thoughts picked through the train wreck of her life, her former career. The memories of each time she believed Bridget Maloney would get her killed, and the irony of it happening the other way around. She thought about all the losses in her life—Mandy, and her parents and grandmother.

When Kate finally became present again, the sky had turned indigo, and the woods were fading into a black wall. A nearly full moon was the only light. She placed her silverware on her empty plate. Reese had stayed true to her word, and they had eaten their meal in silence. She wondered if it was Reese's training or her genuine concern and good heart that kept her from pressing for answers. Whichever, she appreciated it. "Dinner was delicious. Thank you so much," she finally said.

"You're welcome." Reese smiled at her with a warmth that covered her. "I'm glad you liked it. I enjoyed making it for you."

"I was thinking about that. What you said before…about cooking for others. Right after my grandmother took me in, she broke her wrist. She taught me how to do a few things in the kitchen out of necessity. Mostly I was her other hand, but it felt so good helping her. I realize now preparing food was always a celebration for her, especially her baking. God, she could bake."

"She sounds like an incredible person."

"She was the best. Whenever I was upset, she made stroganoff. That's why I have a stack of frozen ones." Kate looked at her empty plate. "It was her way of opening me up. I had bottled everything inside. Still do, I guess." She paused, and Reese nodded, encouraging her to go on. "When I was a child, I believed my dad's suicide was because he loved my mother too much. It was the story I told myself for so long that I began to think that's what happens when you love too deeply. You become subsumed by the other. When they leave you, you're not whole. Unable to live…"

Reese reached across the table and held Kate's hand, saying nothing.

"Doesn't take therapy to understand why I don't do relationships." Kate's breath caught at the tender expression on Reese's face, and she thought, God this woman deserved so much better than her. "I don't want to lead you on, and if we continue this…I can't give you what you want…not with my past."

"You can't lead me where I don't want to go. I'm staying right here." Reese pulled Kate to her feet and held her. "*We* can handle your past."

Kate stiffened then slowly eased into the embrace's tenderness and warmth, the panic of seeing Liam subsiding. She didn't need to depend on anyone else to comfort or make her feel safe. She had trained to take care of herself and to use a weapon but being in Reese's arms made her want to.

Reese leaned her head back. "Can I kiss you?"

Kate met her gaze and lifted her chin, lightly brushing Reese's lips with hers. The kiss was gentle and slow, tongues twining and exploring, their bodies pressing against each other. She began to lose awareness of where her body ended, and Reese's started.

Reese pulled back and nestled her mouth in Kate's hair. "Stay with me tonight," she whispered. Her husky, eager voice sent a rolling wave of arousal from Kate's core. She responded with soft kisses along Reese's jaw, behind her ear, and down her neck, pressing her tongue harder until Reese moaned, "Come with me."

Without hesitation, Kate followed Reese upstairs. If this was a mistake, she was willing to make it. She'd acted cautiously for so long. No one had ever made her want to take a risk. Maybe it wasn't fair, but at least she'd have tonight if the marshals removed her tomorrow.

They undressed each other in the soft moonlight. Reese unbuttoned Kate's shirt, gently removing it, looking at her body intently. She trailed her fingers along Kate's bare shoulders and brushed her thumbs over her taut nipples. "I want to savor every moment with you." Reese's voice sounded thick, and she kissed the length of Kate's collarbone, down to her chest, circling her nipples with her tongue before taking them into her warm mouth.

Kate's head lolled back, a moan sounding deep within. She pulled Reese's T-shirt over her head, running her hands through Reese's hair down to the warm skin of her shoulders, then removed her sports bra, feeling Reese's breasts against her stomach. The slow pace of Reese kissing down her stomach, the brush of her thumbs across her upper thighs as she removed her jeans, made tension coil in Kate's body. She raised Reese up by the chin and kissed her, lingering there while she removed her pants, slipped her hand between Reese's legs, and slid her fingers over her wetness.

Reese pulled Kate's hips against hers, and then gently laid her on the bed, their legs twined, hands caressing each other's hips and thighs, the sensation of skin on skin sending tremors through Kate's body. "If you give me the rest of the night, there are many, many things I want to do with you, but right now if I don't taste you, I'll explode," Reese whispered in a hoarse voice.

The words sent heat flooding Kate's core, her clitoris swelling, aching to release the tension. Reese made her way down her body with slow, wet kisses, her breath hot on her inner thighs. Kate's hips arched, and Reese pressed them down with her body's heaviness. When Reese's mouth finally covered her arousal, Kate gasped, clenching handfuls of duvet, waves of heat building with each caress of Reese's tongue. Just when she thought she couldn't be brought higher, Reese dragged her fingers down and pressed deep inside her. She cried out in a voice she hardly recognized, and her contractions peaked, releasing through her like molten lava.

Reese stayed true to her word and thoroughly satiated Kate. She allowed herself to be vulnerable and receptive to the special agent, giving her as much as she received. After mind-melting orgasms had left them in tatters, they ended the night with limp bodies, spooning before drifting off to sleep.

A few hours later, Kate's cell phone buzzed, vibrating against the nightstand.

"Do you need to get that?" Reese whispered. The warmth of her breath made the little hairs on the back of Kate's neck rise.

"No. I don't want to move." She wanted to stay wrapped in Reese's arms, feeling the length of her body until morning. Their passionate night lingered, the clean smell of Reese's skin and her taste making Kate's lower body tense. But it was more than the sex. Being with Reese differed from past fiery encounters with random hostel guests. She had allowed herself to be vulnerable for the first time.

The buzzing started again.

"Sounds like they're not giving up."

Kate groaned and moved toward the nightstand, clutching her phone. She stared at the screen—almost midnight. Nicole was calling. She picked up immediately. "Nic, what's going on?"

"Boss, I need you to come home...I should call the police... Oh my God a guest woke me up about twenty minutes ago. She said the power was out. So I checked the breaker and sure enough, it was tripped. I turned it back on and that's when I saw someone running from your place and I was like who the hell was that and I ran to the communal room and that's when I saw the Lounge—"

"Nic, slow down," Kate interrupted. Her assistant's words were beginning to blur together. "You saw someone leave my house?" She sat up, and Reese got out of bed.

"Yeah...off your side porch. I found the communal room back door busted open. The Lounge is okay, but the doors to the butler's pantry and your place were opened. But not forced. I think they had a key...and they were in your house and tore it up."

"Where are you now?" Kate asked. She looked at Reese who was pulling on a pair of jeans.

"In the communal room, by the front door."

"Did you see which direction this person was running?" she asked, getting out of bed.

"Straight toward the woods. Who would go out there at this time of night? Who would break into your house? Do you want me to call the sheriff's department?"

"Take some deep breaths, Nic. I need you to calm down." She waited for the sound of Nicole's breathing to slow. "Here's what I need you to do. Go home. If you see any guests outside their rooms, tell them to stay inside and lock their doors. Then you lock your doors and windows. I'll text you when I get there." She ended their call and dressed quickly.

"What did she say?" Reese asked.

"Someone tripped the main breaker and broke into my house. She thinks they got in through the communal room and butler's pantry. And she saw them run into the woods." Kate shoved her phone in her back pocket.

"Do you want to call the sheriff's department to assist?" Reese took her service weapon out of a locked cupboard and strapped it on.

"No. I need to see what's going on first." Her heart thundered. Liam had broken into her home, thinking she'd be there, but she wasn't. Nicole was.

"What do you mean, 'I'?" Reese followed her downstairs. "We'll go together." Kate turned and started to object, but Reese cut her off. "Breaking into your home is a crime, and that's *my* official business."

"Technically. I live outside park boundaries, so it isn't." Kate leashed Jenny and fought the panic threatening to take over.

"Your land borders the park and the perp ran into my jurisdiction." Reese clutched her keys from a table beside the front door. "Let's go, I'm driving."

Kate had to refuse her help. No good would come of it. She needed to get home, gather what was most important to her, and call Joanna. The marshals would disappear her within a few hours. Reese waited for her and Jenny at the door. It would only take a few unkind words, and she could leave alone and walk away from her life in Granite Creek and Reese.

CHAPTER TWENTY-SEVEN

Reese parked her Land Rover on the side of the hostel. She exited the old vehicle, carrying a flashlight below a drawn weapon, and stood at the passenger door while Kate texted Nicole. *We're here. Stay home.*

Kate followed Reese as they moved cautiously through the yard into the communal room. They stopped inside the butler's pantry. "Stay here while I sweep your house," Reese whispered.

Kate nodded and watched her disappear around the corner. Despite her resolution, she hadn't been able to hurt Reese, to say words so nasty they'd drive her away. Accepting Reese's help had been the right thing to do, she told herself. It didn't mean she had to expose her past or her involvement with the Maloneys and the O'Flaherty organization. She glanced at the black CCTV monitors. *Security footage.* A glimmer of hope spread through her. Maybe the intruder was a stranger, a hiker needing money, a guest at the evening Lounge who realized the butler's pantry was connected to her home. She sat at the long counter and rebooted the security system.

Reese returned a few minutes later. "The perp's gone." She looked at the monitors. "Did you see anyone?"

In the screens' glow, Kate shook her head. "There's nothing. No one. It doesn't make sense. How did they get to the main electrical box without the PTZ cameras picking them up?"

"If they were familiar with the cameras' sweep, they could avoid detection." Reese squeezed her shoulder. "Why don't you check your place and see if anything's missing?"

Kate switched on the lights in her living room and kitchen. The intruder had ransacked cupboards and drawers and knocked lamps, vases, and books off tabletops. The few framed photos and rose awards she had hung on the walls were shattered all over the hardwoods. Nothing was missing as far as she could tell. It seemed the person had only wanted to destroy her things. She was certain it was Liam. Then her eyes went wide. The box.

She ran to her bedroom and turned on the lights. The rug that covered the secret compartment had been removed and the hatch busted open. Her stomach dropped as she lifted out the cedar box. "No, no, no." She knew instantly it was too light and turned it upside down. The burner phone and something small fell out.

Reese crouched beside her. "What's wrong?"

"They took everything…" She sat back with the box in her lap.

"What else was in there?"

Kate hesitated. "My gun."

"Your gun? All right. That changes things. If you don't want to involve the sheriff's office, I'm fine with that, but now we have an armed suspect out in the park. I have to alert park law enforcement."

"I know. Just give me a second to think." Kate's voice was louder and harsher than she wanted.

"Hey, I don't want to upset you. We'll go at your pace, okay?" Reese picked up a small pin. "This fell out of the box."

Kate turned it around and froze. It was a gold horseshoe. There was no doubt about it. Liam was there to kill her, and this was his warning. Her hopes that a stranger had broken into her home or that Liam was in the area trafficking drugs and unaware of her were shattered. She grabbed the phone and got to her feet. "I need to make a call."

"I can do that for you," Reese said. She stood with hands on her hips, watching Kate.

She ignored Reese and ran across the room, her frantic energy agitating Jenny. The old hound followed her, staying at her side. She shoved her chest of drawers away from the wall and tore off the hidden SIM card, placing it in the back of the phone.

Reese stopped her before she could plug in the phone's charger and held her shoulders. "Kate, please talk to me. Tell me what's going on. What else was in the box? Who do you need to call?"

"I can't tell you that. It's best if you go and focus on the park guests." She stepped around Reese and sat on her bed. After she called Joanna, what would happen next sickened her.

"No. I'm staying until I'm sure you're safe." She sat beside her and laid her hand on Kate's leg. "I know you have secrets. I've noticed all the photos in your home and communal room are only a few years old. Hell, I'd bet my life that nothing in this house is older than the day you arrived. You change the subject or outright refuse to talk whenever anyone brings up the past. I know you're hiding from someone or something, and I'm guessing it's someone." She stroked Kate's cheek with the back of her hand. "Please look at me. You can trust me. No matter what it is, now is the time to tell me. Because whoever they are, they've found you."

Kate burst into tears and leaned into the warmth of Reese's shoulder. "I'm so tired of living this way. I just want this nightmare to end." Reese wrapped her arm around Kate and held her close. When she had run out of tears, Kate calmed herself and pulled away. She scrubbed her hands over her face and exhaled a deep breath. "You're right. They've found me, but you knowing about my past won't change what has to happen next."

"Maybe it won't. But maybe it will." Reese held Kate's hand, refusing to let her physically withdraw.

For years Kate had planned for this moment, for when circumstances would force her to say goodbye. She had practiced what she would say, choosing the right words and refining her tone, but she hadn't planned for the conversation to be with someone she was falling in love with, and now the words she rehearsed were gone, and an overwhelming need for Reese to know her, know everything replaced them. "I've had to lie for so long. I don't even know where to start…"

Reese framed Kate's face with her hands. "You begin where you can. I'm here for all of it." She kissed her lips lightly. "I'm not going anywhere."

"Okay. My…my real name is Eleanor Peters, and I was born in Western Massachusetts, not Florida. My grandmother raised me in Jamaica Plain, Boston. My parents…I told you the truth about them. We did ski in the Colorado Rockies once. I fell in love with the mountains. We never lived in Florida. I've never even visited the state." She looked down at Jenny. The bloodhound rested her graying muzzle on Kate's foot. "It was part of the fictional background they gave me."

"WITSEC?"

"For the last eight years." She took a deep breath. Her secret was out. The rest of it. That was the hardest part. She met Reese's eyes. "I've never told another soul how I came to be here…it's difficult to find the words…I need a drink." Her sudden movement made Jenny scramble to her feet. "And we need to shut the drapes. We're not safe."

"It's okay, girl." Reese rubbed Jenny's head. "You sit. I'll get us a drink and close the drapes. Whoever he is, he's not getting back in here tonight."

Reese returned with two highballs filled with double scotch, and Kate slowly sipped her drink. "The FBI recruited me out of graduate school. I was eager to join and finished Quantico just after my twenty-fourth birthday. I was one of their youngest special agents. A year later, I went deep undercover in a crime family. I didn't have much of a life. Not a lot to leave behind, except for my grandma, so I was perfect for the assignment." Her hands began to tremble. "We learned the family's daughter, Bridget, was entering university. Her parents were looking for a bodyguard to live near her. Watch her on campus and off."

"And that was your in?"

Kate nodded. "We arrested one of their button men. Offered him a deal. All he had to do was tell his boss that he had someone for the job, his cousin from Chicago. A few days later, I met with the family, Fiona O'Flaherty Maloney and her second husband, Sean Ryan. I knew right away they weren't interested in me. Sean kept saying he'd never employ a female bodyguard and other sexist stuff. But I could tell his comments were making Bridget more attracted to me. She was eighteen, going on thirty, and flirted with me to piss him off. I wanted the operation to happen, so I decided to reciprocate. I gambled that Bridget had some weight with her mother and stepdad, and could get what she wanted, so I made sure she wanted me."

It was the first time Kate had admitted openly that, as Bridget had always maintained, she had toyed with her affections. She had, but only to get the job. Guilt washed over her, and she took a long drink.

"Sounds like a good move. I'm guessing it worked?"

"It did. They hired me the next week and moved me into a nice high-rise apartment near Bridget's condo. Gave us a driver. I was to keep Bridget safe and out of trouble while she attended Northeastern. Bridget thought she had gotten her way, but she hadn't. When I started, I made it clear she would only ever be a job to me."

"How'd that go over?"

"She was hurt and angry but didn't direct it at me. She suspected her stepfather had warned me off. It was another reason for her to hate him, but he earned the brunt of her anger because he was the O'Flaherty captain. She believed Fiona should have been. Fiona was the O'Flaherty heir, but women didn't run the family business. From what I could tell, Fiona sat back and watched them fight, maybe she even encouraged it, but Sean was no match for Bridget. I could barely go toe to toe with her. She was brilliant. Fluent in several languages. Cunning and vindictive. She had a drug pipeline up and down East Coast universities in development. Right under our noses."

"Sounds like a budding crime boss."

"The worst kind. She had no qualms about hurting anyone who got in her way—physically or mentally. Her senior year Sean found out she was selling drugs when the son of his clan chief, someone she had trusted and let in on the deal, betrayed her. The fallout was Sean summoning us to the Maloneys for dinner. He humiliated her in front of the family and me. Then he took cheap shots at me. I thought she'd kill the kid who narced on her, but she didn't hurt him, not physically. She blackmailed him instead. After that night, Bridget thought she had made me her loyal employee and turned me against her mother and Sean. She told me all about her drug operation. Hinted at the O'Flaherty crime ring. It was the crack we needed into their organization."

"How many years in were you?"

"Almost three. A few months later, Bridget shared her plans to manufacture and distribute bespoke drugs with me. She had set up a meeting with a precursor supplier, Sasha Novikov, another crime family in the Boston area. It was the final piece she needed for her operation. My SAC agreed we could run a quick, easy sting on the meeting. We had enough to arrest Bridget, and I was convinced she'd turn state's evidence on her parents. We had search warrants for her condo and bedroom at the Maloneys' home before a judge and plans were in place. I thought the end was near. We'd finally bring the O'Flahertys to justice. But it all fell apart." Her voice cracked.

"Hey, come here." Reese took Kate's drink and placed it on the bedside table. She sat against the pillows and eased Kate back against her body. "If you don't want to tell me the rest, I understand."

"No, I need to. It's not done."

Reese rested her cheek against Kate's head. "Okay. But stop whenever you want."

"I want you to know everything...to know why I'm here." Kate eased back and laid her head on Reese's shoulder. "We were to meet the supplier at a bakery outside Quincy. The night before, Bridget's girlfriend recorded a conversation between Sean and his enforcer, Patrick, that suggested they might know about the meeting, but Bridget didn't want to postpone. I alerted my team, and we developed contingency plans, but I should have insisted we cancel. I had too many questions about the meeting but didn't have enough information to act on them. I still don't. Sean's phone call was one red flag, and the other was Bridget taking my listening device. It was hidden in a good-luck horseshoe brooch that I always wore." Before we got to the bakery, she said she needed good luck more than I did. For a second I thought she had figured out who I was."

"Oh, shit. That's a problem."

"Yeah, but that thought passed. Bridget put the horseshoe pin on her coat, so I figured she didn't know what it was. She would have pocketed it or dropped it in her purse if she had. There was another warning sign. The bakery was closed for inventory, which never made sense to me. Bridget was a methodical planner and expected also to eat there, so the owner had to have closed that morning unexpectedly. It meant Bridget and I had to improvise and meet the suppliers in a green space on the other side of the parking lot. The Novikovs were waiting for us at a table at the park's patio area. We sat with them, and Bridget removed her coat, folded it, and put it in her lap, under the table."

"So now your team is without audio and rerouting their location."

"That's when I started to worry. I knew they couldn't hear us and would have to act on visuals. The order was to converge as soon as Bridget and Sasha exchanged money. But I had no idea from which direction they'd come. I assumed either the street side or through the park behind us. Bridget had the envelope in her hand. They were ready to finalize their deal when Sean and his men arrived."

"Jesus, so the call that Bridget's girlfriend recorded *was* about her meeting with the Novikovs."

"Our team had planned for their possible arrival." She paused. "Everything that happened next is a blur. Sean and his men exited their vehicle, and Bridget got a call or a text. I can't remember which. I only know she picked up her phone and ran toward the bakery, yelling for me to follow her, but before I could react Sean and his men started shooting, and our team converged. I thought Sean and his men were shooting at Bridget or the team, but my SAC said they were firing at me until our team moved in. Then Sean and his men changed direction and ran toward the bakery. All I remember is that the gunfire stopped, and I pursued them.

They disappeared inside the bakery…that's when…" She fell silent, reached for her glass, and took a long drink.

"You don't have to tell me the rest," Reese said, smoothing Kate's hair behind her ear. "The way you're addressing Bridget in the past tense, I understand."

"No, I want to finish. I need to tell you everything." Kate exhaled. "Before I reached the door, the bakery blew up."

"An explosion?" Reese seemed to think for a moment. "I did not see that coming."

"Neither did we. Sean and his men had just opened the door. Evidence Response identified their remains, but the fourth victim, Bridget, was at the epicenter of the blast, and the building burned to the ground."

"No one else was in the bakery?"

"Sasha Novikov said an employee was inside when she and her daughter arrived, but they left before the explosion because all the bakery employees were accounted for." She hesitated. "The blast hospitalized me. When I was stable, the US Attorney's office, Hal Macon, put me in protective custody. The US Marshals took over and relocated me here." She held out the phone. "This is how I contact my marshal, Joanna Stevens. I called her last month. Told her I saw Liam in town. Liam Maloney is Bridget's younger brother, and must be working for the organization these days. I asked her to make certain it was him before we considered relocation, so she contacted the Bureau. They told her neither Fiona nor Liam had been out of state, but I know I saw him. And he's back."

"Are they still under the FBI surveillance?"

"She said they are."

Reese paused. "Then how would Liam make his way here again, undetected?"

"I don't know. Fake IDs. Ditched his detail." Kate sat up and turned her body to face Reese. "I need to call Joanna."

"Hey, you're safe right now." Reese gently pulled Kate against her body again. "Let's talk this out first, okay? What about the explosion? Did the Bureau figure out who set the bomb?"

"They suspected the Novikovs. Bridget's father, Caleb, had had a relationship with Sasha before his death. He was murdered.

Word on the street was the Novikovs carried it out in retaliation. Sean and Fiona naturally severed the business partnership with them. That might have done more damage to their organization than Sasha let on, and this was payback, but the Bureau didn't find a link between them and the bomb. I don't think they've arrested anyone for it. Joanna would have told me."

"Okay. Let's focus on the break-in. Why would Liam Maloney take what was in your box?"

"He wanted my gun."

"The Glock?"

"Yeah. I lied before. It's not registered, but I marked the back strap with an x, so it's identifiable." Kate paused and shook her head. "The rest of the box's contents was all I had left of my past. Pictures of my parents. My grandma. Her funeral program. I have no idea why he'd want those things."

"You had your grandmother's funeral program. The one who died last year?"

Kate nodded. "It broke my heart to leave her…to have no contact for all these years. I couldn't take care of her when she got sick, and when she died, I couldn't attend her funeral." She blinked away the sudden sting of tears. "It was almost too much for me to handle."

"I'm so sorry," Reese whispered, stroking Kate's hair.

"Joanna felt horrible for me. She attended her service and sent me the obituary and program." Kate's shoulders slumped, and she nestled her head in the crook of Reese's neck. That was all there was to tell. She felt raw and exposed, and tears sprung into her eyes. At least now when she had to say goodbye and disappear, Reese would understand why. "I'm so sorry I've put your life in danger. I shouldn't have."

"Hey, don't say that. Shoulds are shit. That kind of thinking robs us of our autonomy. And don't apologize if you've done nothing wrong. You did your job, and you did it well. Circumstances put you here, but that doesn't mean you have to live less than a full life. The marshals are supposed to keep you safe, but you're not. We need to consider why. You could call Joanna and start over somewhere new, but what's to say it won't happen again? This is your home. You've made a life here filled with people who care about you. I care about you." She kissed the top of Kate's head. "I'm falling in love with you."

Kate lifted. "Please don't say that. No one has ever said that to me." Her tears broke, and panic settled, fast and hot. "It doesn't matter how we feel. I can't stay. It's too dangerous. Joanna will insist I relocate, and she'll be right. The O'Flahertys must silence me to protect themselves. Everyone around me is collateral damage. I can't do that to you or Nic or anyone else."

"Hey, breathe." Reese wiped Kate's cheeks with her thumbs and held her face. "Before you call Joanna, think about what's happening. Okay? My investigation can place the O'Flaherty operation here, trafficking drugs. The first time you saw Liam was over a month ago, but he didn't try to make contact with you, right? When someone lured Jenny out to the burned-out campsite, it was a week later. Did you see him during that time?"

"No, but he could've been careful, avoiding me."

"Maybe, but he's risked traveling here while under FBI surveillance. So why steal your dog and burglarize your home instead of just killing you? It doesn't make sense. My gut tells me something else is going on here."

Kate opened her fist. "It has to be him. He left this. It looks just like my horseshoe pin. He and Fiona must have known it was a listening device. It's a warning. They know I'm here, and they want more than me dead. They want revenge."

CHAPTER TWENTY-EIGHT

Deputy US Marshal Joanna Stevens stopped at the guard gate and held out her badge. "Eight a.m. appointment with Special Agent in Charge Garcia."

The security attendant turned to his computer. A minute later he returned her ID badge, and the gate opened. "Have a good day."

She half-smiled and mumbled a response. A summons to FBI headquarters in Chelsea, just outside Boston, didn't make for a great start to any day. She parked in a visitor spot and reread Garcia's email. The formality of a face-to-face meeting rubbed her the wrong way, but there was no sense in guessing why the SAC insisted they meet in person. Thinking through possible scenarios only stressed her out.

After she passed through security, Joanna stood with arms crossed, waiting for the elevator doors to open. She stepped inside and pressed the button for Garcia's floor. At least she knew the meeting was about the O'Flaherty family, which meant tangentially it was about Kate Hall. Had they uncovered information about

Liam? Had he been in Northern Washington? She took a deep breath and released it. The elevator opened. Relax, she told herself as she strode onto the busy floor.

SAC Garcia waited for her. "Hello, Joanna. It's good to see you. Thanks for coming in."

"No problem. Nice to see you too, Special Agent Garcia. How've you been?"

"No need for formalities. Mandy's fine. Can't complain. And you?"

"Spread a bit thin, but I'm sure you know how that feels." Joanna followed her down a long hallway to the last office. They sat at a conference table, and Mandy opened a file, sliding it in front of Joanna. "After you contacted us about Liam Maloney, we placed stricter surveillance on him and Fiona. This included widening the scope of our electronic monitoring. As I said, we didn't find evidence Liam left Massachusetts on the dates you provided, but we've learned some troubling information since."

Joanna read the report.

"How is Eleanor?" Mandy asked.

"You know I can't talk about her." Her heartbeat quickened, and she continued to read, without looking up.

"I understand, but I'm not asking for secure information. I just want to know if she's okay. She was a good friend. It'd be nice to know she's happy."

Joanna looked up. "Right now, I can say she's upset. She's adamant she saw Liam. Based on your intel, I told her she was mistaken. I hope that's still the case." Her voice was surly, and she dropped her gaze back to the page she was reading. She hadn't yet read the troubling information Mandy had hinted at, and the anticipation had her on the verge. Play nice, she told herself, and she met Mandy's eyes. "Besides this scare, Eleanor's doing well. Really well."

Mandy smiled. "That's good to hear." She nodded at the file. "You want to look at page four, cell phone surveillance. Over the last month, Fiona has received calls from two different burner phones on her cell phone and another burner we believe is in her possession. It took a bit, but we pinpointed the numbers. Next page. The calls originate in the area circled on the map."

Joanna stared at the map. Northern Washington was circled in red. Her body tensed, and she fought to keep a blank expression.

"Here's the rub. An ISB special agent has roped us in on a drug case. Page seven. Their last seizure was in the same area as the cell locations. ISB's forensics traced the purchase of the backpacks used to traffic the drugs to the Boston area. The pills look like the description Eleanor gave of Bridget Maloney's drugs back all those years ago. Now we're way past coincidence, don't you think?"

She paused, but Joanna only shook her head and paged through the rest of the file.

"We're providing the ISB with our full cooperation under the theory that the O'Flaherty ring is trafficking drugs along the West Coast now. Two days ago, we followed Liam Maloney to a Boston apartment. His car is still in the parking garage, and we haven't seen him leave. It's possible he slipped by us. We can't be sure."

Joanna calmly closed the file and steadied her voice. "I only ask that you alert me if Liam leaves the state and where he goes."

Mandy hesitated and sat back. "Listen, I'm not asking if Eleanor lives in the area. But if you suspect the calls to Fiona Maloney are connected to her in any way, you have our complete cooperation, just say the word."

"They're not." Joanna scooted back in her chair and stood. "Thanks for the update, Mandy. I'm glad you have another opportunity to bring the O'Flaherty family to justice, and you can be sure I'll keep Eleanor Peters safe."

"Good to hear." Mandy picked up the file and opened the door. "We'll find Liam today. You have my word. Thanks again for coming in."

Joanna left the FBI building and drove south onto Everett Avenue. At the first red light, she beat her steering wheel with her fists. "Fuck, fuck, fuck." The light turned green, and she checked her rearview mirror. Would the FBI interfere with her case? She shook her head at the thought. No one was following her. She was being paranoid.

"Call Sarah," Joanna said to her car's phone system. She listened nervously as the other phone rang.

"Hey, Mom. What's up?"

Relief washed over her at the sound of her daughter's voice. "Nothing much. Just work. Everything okay at home?"

"Yep. I got my schedule for the fall semester. Jamie and I are buying our books tomorrow."

"That's great. I can't believe you're a senior already. I'm so happy for you."

"Aw, thanks, Mom. Couldn't have done it without you."

"Sure you could have." Joanna paused to steady her voice. "So listen, I need to go out of town for work for a few days. Do you have enough money in your account for dinner and gas?"

"Sure."

"Okay, then. I'll see you in a few. I love you, Sarah."

"Love you, too. Be careful."

"I will. Bye, sweetheart."

Sarah ended their call, and Joanna drove straight to the airport. No one had seen Liam Maloney for two days, and she needed to confirm he wasn't in Granite Creek.

* * *

Early the next morning, Joanna sipped a cup of black coffee in the Lake Chelan café outside the North Cascades National Park. The emergency to-go bag she kept in her trunk had a change of clothes and a US Marshal's jacket, but she needed to blend in with the tourist crowd. She had bought a hoodie and ball cap at the airport with Seattle splashed across them and tucked her hair up into the hat, pulling it low on her forehead.

When she finished her breakfast, she walked to the dock. A misty rain had settled over the area, and dense fog in several shades of gray crept over the mountains into the valley. She waited with a handful of tourists for the morning ferry to take them up lake to Stehekin. From there, she could hike into Granite Creek and investigate if Liam Maloney was there.

Her cell phone rang, and she looked at the screen. It was an unlisted number. "Deputy Marshal Joanna Stevens speaking."

"Good morning, Marshal Stevens. It's been a while since we've chatted. How've you been?"

Joanna abruptly turned away from the other ferry passengers and walked to the end of the dock. "Why are you calling me?"

"That's a very unfriendly greeting. I would think you'd appreciate a check-in from me now and then. You know, to make sure I'm okay. You're okay. Everyone we love is okay."

"I did what you asked me to do, and we had a deal. You got what you wanted and now you leave us alone. So why are you calling me?"

"You don't have to remind me. I know what we agreed to, word for word. I often listen to the recording of our conversation when I need a pick-me-up. To hear how easily someone in your position is bent. God, it works wonders for me. Restores my faith in humanity. When you strip away the hypocrisy, we're all selfish, self-centered creatures who'll choose to save ourselves, or in your case, your daughter, every time."

"Get to the point, Bridget. What do you want?"

"So cynical. I guess we know why. If you can't trust yourself, how can you trust anyone else? I get it, but you'll be happy to know I don't want anything from you. I found myself feeling melancholy today and wanted to chat with an old friend. You wouldn't begrudge me that, would you?"

The tone of Bridget's voice spread goosebumps over Joanna's skin. "Where are you?"

"We never agreed on disclosing that information, did we?"

"We never agreed to speak again, either."

"Fair enough. Let's just say I'm far away from you and your family. *Aucun souci.*"

Joanna scanned the lakefront for anyone using a phone. There was no one else. Don't be paranoid, she told herself. Bridget couldn't know she was in Washington. "So where are you? In the US?"

"That's enough about me. The topic seems to be riling you up. I heard the FBI visited my mother last month. You wouldn't know anything about that, would you?"

"Of course not. They still have your family under surveillance. You know that." She closed her eyes, calming her breathing. "Our dealings are over, Bridget. You will leave my daughter alone and never contact us again. Do you understand me?"

"I think we can agree our business is only over if you stay out of my family's way. I hope for you and your daughter's sake you haven't made any contact with the FBI."

"I'm telling you the truth. I haven't been involved in the investigation of your family." Joanna shoved her free hand into the hoodie pocket. "But since we're asking questions, I'd like to know if you sent Liam to kill Eleanor." Bridget was silent, and Joanna raised her voice. "Did you?"

"Why would I send that idiot to kill the bitch who ruined my life?" She laughed hysterically, then abruptly stopped. "I thought you knew me better than that, Marshal Stevens. I did not send Liam to Washington to kill Eleanor Peters. When the time comes and life drains from her eyes, that pleasure will be all mine."

"I have to go. Please don't call me again." Listening to Bridget had turned Joanna's stomach.

"Once more, you're so unsociable. I did call for a reason, but if you must go…"

"Damn it, then, just tell me what you want."

"Fine, if you insist. Two bodies will be found near Eleanor Peter's or should I say Kate Hall's hostel today. Call the tip a goodwill gesture and a thank-you. Thanks to you, my life is about to change for the better."

CHAPTER TWENTY-NINE

Ranger Bob paced the length of the dry camp. The gray misty rain released the acrid, sulfur scent of the blackened surroundings. He wiped the sweat from his forehead. He had not put a toe over the line in all his years of service. Now this. How did he let things get out of control? So close to retirement. He only wanted comfort for Marsha. A new home on the beach. Sunsets on the ocean.

He took a long, deep breath and told himself to relax. It wasn't like the merchandise hurt anyone. All he had to do was watch it safely through the park. In a year or two he'd retire with the money he needed—Marsha needed. He stopped and strained to listen. Someone was approaching.

A tall, lean man with shocking red hair stepped into the campsite, and Bob forced a smile. "Hey, Liam, good to see you again. I hope the hike was okay."

"Of course it was." Liam scanned the area, his hands resting on his hips. "I met with Antonio. He doesn't want to change locations. We'll keep the exchange between runners here, but I think it's a bad idea. What did you do about the drug investigation?"

"Nothing I could do. It's out of my hands. The ISB connected the backpack to another case. Most likely a new West Coast trafficking operation. But that's okay, it works better for us. ISB is looking for drops in other locations along the PCT. I understand they don't believe the traffickers would use this location twice." He stared into the trees. "The park's big enough for us to share. Whoever's running drugs won't disrupt your organization's trade route."

"That's good." Liam followed Bob's gaze. "What's in through there?"

"A hundred feet in, there's a cliff face…a sharp drop. It's probably why Antonio wants this spot. One way in, one way out."

"Makes you wonder why this new organization running the length of the West Coast doesn't have safeguards in place. Like we do. Right?" Liam held Bob's eyes. "You don't suspect one of the park rangers is helping the drug traffickers and screwing up, do you?"

Bob thought about Liam's question for a minute. It hadn't crossed his mind that one of his colleagues would do what he was doing. "I only know I'm not involved. I don't get the sense the ISB special agent on the case suspects park rangers are assisting. Think about it. It's an easy task. I'm not allowing our exchange to go unsupervised long enough for a civilian or an animal to find the package. But that's what's happening with the drugs. Doesn't make sense to me that a ranger would be involved. They'd make sure the drugs were never found."

"Good point." Liam dropped his backpack. "If I thought this merchandise was left out here alone while we were paying you to look after it, I'd be extremely unhappy."

"Lucky for you, that'll never be an issue. This is my patrol area. Everyone expects me to be out here. I'll make sure each exchange happens without incident."

"That's good. We'll wait together for Connor to pick this pack up today. But for the next shipment, Finn will hike the PCT from the south. When he reaches the park, he'll text you. You'll ensure his passage here, watch the exchange, and secure Connor's travel north to the Lightning Creek Trail. He'll go east to the PCT from there. Finn and Connor should never be more than an hour apart for the exchange. If they take longer, you need to let me know. Immediately."

"Yeah, yeah. I'll let you know. But like I said, no one will think twice about me being out here if it takes longer."

Liam frowned. "It better never take longer. I've worked hard to set up this operation, and I have to trust that the people I have in place won't disappoint me. Everyone needs to execute their part perfectly. I won't tolerate anything less. Do you understand me?" He removed an envelope from his jacket pocket, and Bob nodded. "That's good. Here's your retainer. We'll wire the remainder to your Mauritius account when the shipment leaves the park."

Bob counted the money, his hands shaking. It equaled half a year's salary and would pay off Marsha's medical debt and then some. He tucked it into the inside pocket of his vest.

Loud clapping echoed through the campsite, coming from behind a blackened Douglas fir. They turned toward the noise, and a woman in a baseball cap with chin-length black hair stepped out from behind the tree. "Nicely delivered, Liam. You've become quite the businessman. So in control. Those big green eyes are set on the captain's chair, aren't they?"

Liam stared at the woman, confused. "Who…What the fuck…Bridget?" he asked in a voice pitching toward hysteria. "Oh my God, you're alive? How? Where'd you come—?"

"Straight from hell, little brother." She drew closer, her hands deep in her hoodie's front pocket.

"Bridget?" Bob asked, drawing his weapon and aiming it at her. "What's going on? Do you know her?"

"This doesn't concern you, old man." Bridget faced Liam. "Tell your little helper to stop pointing his gun at me. I'd hate to be the cat that kills you busy mice and your best-laid plans."

"Put your gun away, for God's sake. She's my sister."

Bob scrutinized Bridget from head to toe. The woman sent a shiver up his spine, but he trusted Liam and holstered his weapon.

"Not fast enough, little mouse." She pulled a gun from her pocket and fired once. Bob dropped. The shot reverberated in the air and a flock of common ravens took flight from the surrounding trees, answering the noise with shrill caws.

"Son of a bitch," Liam yelled. The bullet had entered one side of Bob's head and on exiting had blown off the other, blood and brain spraying the charred ground. "Jesus Christ. You killed him. Oh, my God. What are we going to do now?"

"I think you know what has to happen next."

"I don't. I don't know what the hell's going on. We had a funeral for you. We go to your grave—" His voice broke.

"Obviously the ashes in the casket aren't mine. I didn't die in the explosion. Some woman off the street died for me. Mother arranged all of it."

"Why…Why do you look like that?"

"She made me change my face. We can't have the dead walking around, can we? So I spent a year in and out of hospitals with doctors cutting me up. It took another year to recover." Her voice grew louder. "The pain was unbearable."

"What the fuck, Brie? Why would she do that to you?"

"Come on, little brother, you convinced me you've grown into something other than an idiot, don't prove me wrong now. I disappointed her. The family. The FBI built a case against us, using me. Eleanor used me. Mother devised a plan to make their evidence useless. Eleanor and I had to die." Liam stared at her, his mouth open, but no words came out. "But it wasn't only us. She told Sean I was meeting with Sasha Novikov and ramped him up to rein me in. She laid a trap, and he and Thomas and Patrick ran right into it."

"Wait. You think Ma planted the bomb?"

"Jesus Christ, you are as clueless as ever. You've no idea who our mother is, do you?" Bridget strolled over to Bob's body. "She's a ruthless bitch who's only wanted one thing. To be in charge. *She* killed Dad. Found out he was screwing Sasha and seduced Sean into taking him out. But her plan backfired when Grandpa O'Flaherty made Sean captain. She finally got her way, though, didn't she?"

"This is all so messed up. Where've you been?"

"I live in Nice." He stared at her. "France, you moron."

A look of recognition crossed his face. "That's why Ma goes there at New Year's. She leaves me in Ireland and says she's shopping in France. She's lied to me all these years. What've you been doing?"

"I've kept our family business afloat. Manufacturing drugs. Establishing new distribution routes in Europe. Creating new opportunities for the family. I've also been waiting."

"For what?"

"You know, for Eleanor Peter's death. Mother promised me that you and she have been looking for her. Because with her dead, the FBI has nothing on us, and I can stop hiding. Mother said you've been looking for her yourself. How's that going? Any luck in Florida?"

Bridget knelt beside Ranger Bob and took his gun from its holster.

"What are you doing?" Liam stepped back, his hands in the air. "Listen, I had no idea about any of this. Ma never asked me to look for your old bodyguard. I'm telling you the truth. I'm the one who said we should look for her and take the bitch out. But Ma said we have too much attention on us, and we can't draw anymore. I swear."

"Maybe you should've taken some initiative."

"Yeah, I should've, but I didn't fucking know you were alive. And Ma keeps me busy. She gave me this new business on the West Coast." His voice stammered. "I'll damn sure look for her now."

"It's too late. I've already found her, and newsflash, the new traditional Chinese medicine venture keeping you so busy is mine." She laughed at Liam's expression. "There's that look of dumb surprise I've missed." She paused. "I brought Antonio's offer to Mother as a new enterprise for the family but according to her, we couldn't expand our portfolio because she's too busy, and you're too inept. Yet here you are paying off a park ranger to get things done with the very same TCM materials."

"I swear, Ma never told me. How would I know it was yours?"

"Ignorance is no excuse. If you had been interested in what happened to me, you could've figured out what Mother did. It only took me a few months. She didn't cover her tracks well."

"I'm sorry, Brie."

"Fortunately for me, Antonio is a loyal businessman. You have to trust everyone in your circle when you kill endangered species and smuggle their body parts. He's also a good sport and played along with my plan. Unfortunately for you, I never intended to share my business." She pointed Bob's gun at him.

"Bridget, stop, please. You're freaking me out," Liam cried.

She fired once, hitting him in the chest, and then she watched as adrenaline kept him on his feet until he struggled for breath and fell to his knees, gasping and reaching out to her. She put on plastic gloves and wiped her prints off Bob's gun, positioning the dead man's hand around the grip, his finger on the trigger, and firing again in Liam's direction.

Liam lay still, his eyes open. She wiped her prints off the gun she had stolen from Eleanor and placed it in Liam's hand. "As if you could've made that shot on your first try." She fired again toward Bob and laughed away an urge to close her brother's eyes. He hadn't helped her when she was alone, in pain.

Pleased with how her plan was unfolding, she smiled and removed the black backpack she wore, dropping it beside Liam's body. It had another full bag of her bespoke drugs inside. Connor would arrive soon and find his boss dead. He'd leave the backpack with the drugs and Bob's retainer money alone for fear Fiona would kill him over such a petty theft. Once he was safely out of the park, he'd anonymously call in the murders to law enforcement. They would find the drugs she planted, connecting them to the O'Flahertys now. It was only a matter of time before the FBI would inform Fiona of Liam's death at the same time they arrested her for trafficking drugs on the PCT. God, how she wished she could be there to see Fiona's face. The repeat of history was so fitting, except this time her child *was* dead, and she couldn't avoid prosecution.

Bridget doubled over, laughing hysterically. When she regained her composure, she hoisted Liam's backpack full of their first shipment—bezoar and ground bone from proboscis monkeys.

In a day or two, the bureau would alert Marshal Stevens about the murders and Fiona's arrest. They'd ask her to prepare Eleanor for the attorney general's office to give evidence in Fiona's trial. Bridget grinned and concealed her footprints. It was time to return home and finish her plan.

CHAPTER THIRTY

Reese woke to a whimper behind her. She turned to find Jenny standing beside the bed with her leash in her mouth, her tail thumping against the floor. She pulled her arm from under Kate's neck and checked her phone. Six a.m. They'd only been asleep for a few hours. She crept out of bed not wanting to wake her.

The sky was overcast with misty rain, and thick fog crept over the mountains into the trees. Wearing boxers, an old T-shirt, and a baseball cap, Reese walked Jenny around the perimeter of the hostel's yard. The old hound pulled against her leash. "Sorry, girl. Can't take it off this morning." She turned, surprised to hear hushed voices.

Two hikers walked toward the tree line and disappeared into the woods. Reese shook her head. Some people considered themselves invincible. Last night and into the early morning hours she had questioned all the hostel's guests and warned them an armed person of interest was in the area and that hiking the trail at this time was dangerous. She wanted to yell at the pair who had left the grounds. Tell them not to be idiots. To wait.

She exhaled a long breath. It wasn't the hikers she was angry with. Sleep had eluded her. She had held Kate all night, considering how Liam Maloney happened to be in the same area as the FBI's sole witness against his family. It was a needle-in-a-haystack occurrence that she didn't believe was coincidental. Someone who knew Kate's location had compromised her safety, and only a handful of people at two organizations had that information—the US Marshals and the Department of Justice. Her gut told her they needed to begin their inquiry with Deputy Marshal Joanna Stevens.

Jenny lumbered back to Reese. "All done, tough girl? If you'd been here last night, no one would've broken in, right?" She briskly rubbed the top of the hound's head. "That's right. Let's go feed you some breakfast."

When they returned, Kate was pouring water into the coffee machine. "Thanks for taking her out. I don't know why she decided to wake you up first."

"No worries." Reese leaned a hip against the counter. "Thanks for making coffee. Is her dog food in the pantry? I'll feed her while you finish."

"No." Kate's voice was sharp. "Sorry, you've done too much already and she's my responsibility. I'll do it. Just let me start this…" She fingered the filters, trying to pull one off the stack, her frustration reddening her face. She succeeded and jammed it into the basket.

Reese stepped close to her. "I'll keep doing as much as I can—everything I can. I know you're scared, but you don't have to push me away." She stroked Kate's arm, pulled her near, and kissed her forehead. Kate nestled into Reese's shoulder. "You don't have to face the O'Flahertys alone. I want to help you. You just have to let me." Kate slowly nodded against her. "Okay, that's good. Now I'm feeding Jenny. Then we'll figure out our next move."

Reese had spent several hours last night processing fingerprints. Black-and-white dust covered the butler's pantry doors, computer equipment, and countertop. It would take time to clean the fine particles from everything. She found the cans of wet dog food in a bottom cupboard and mixed one with two cups of kibble. Jenny wiggled beside her. "Here you go, girl."

When Reese returned, the coffee machine beeped, the aroma of a full pot filling the air. "You look tired. I'm sorry you didn't get enough sleep last night," Kate said, handing her a cup.

"I'm good. This coffee will help."

"Going back to bed is what we both need."

"I like how you're thinking."

"I mean for sleep. But I don't have time. I need a shower before Nic gets here to set up the morning Lounge, which is an entirely different problem."

Reese hauled her close. "I'm feeling like a shower. Maybe we can conserve water."

Kate wrapped her arms around Reese, moving a hair's breadth away from her lips. "Let's definitely do that another time." She kissed her, gently at first, then with an intensity that sparked flames in Reese's center. They lingered there for a moment then Kate pulled back.

"That's probably the best rejection I've ever had."

"I'd bet it's the only one." Kate laughed, and her happiness engulfed Reese like a warm embrace.

They returned to the bedroom. Reese washed her face and brushed her teeth while Kate stripped beside her and stepped into a steamy shower. "You really are testing my ability to respect boundaries." She heard Kate chuckle and then begin to hum. She wiped the fogged-up mirror and stared at her reflection. Oh, yeah, she thought, you've fallen.

A few minutes later, Kate walked naked from the bathroom to her dresser and put on a pair of polka-dotted boy-short panties and a sports bra. "What should I do about the morning Lounge?"

Reese sat on the side of the bed watching her, taking in every curve of her beautiful body.

"Hey? Eyes up here."

Reese looked up. "Sorry. Can you blame me? I say you skip Lounge for the rest of the weekend, and we spend it in bed." She wrapped her arms around Kate's waist.

"That's a tempting offer, but I can't cheat my guests out of their breakfast." She slipped from Reese's arms and shimmied into a pair of jeans. "We can't set up in the communal room, not with all the crime scene residue. Nic and I could take food and drinks to everyone. But then we risk waking up guests who want to sleep in," she rambled as she pulled a sweat top over her head. "We could leave a note under their doors and ask them to call when they're ready for breakfast. Then Nicole and I could deliver it to their rooms. That might be best. They're probably exhausted after being questioned last night. I'm sure being sequestered at a hostel is the last thing they thought would happen on their hike."

"Not everyone heeded our warning. When I took Jenny out, I saw some hikers leave the yard."

"You can't be serious?"

"Afraid so."

"I thought you were clear that no one should leave. Liam is dangerous. Why did they do that? God…if anyone gets hurt…" Her voice faded.

"Don't worry, we're protecting park guests. Even if Liam escapes our rangers, he isn't leaving the area. The sheriff's office is searching surrounding hotels and businesses for him." Reese gently swept her hand over Kate's cheek. "Hopefully, we'll find him in the park with your gun and arrest him on Federal crimes. It won't take long to connect him to the drugs. Then we can hand deliver the Bureau a case to bring down his family, and you won't have to hide anymore." She lifted Kate's chin and lightly kissed her lips.

"We should call Joanna, too. She can update the FBI, and we could have Bureau and marshal support within the hour."

"I still don't think that's a good idea, and not because I selfishly want you to stay, which I do." She followed Kate to the kitchen. "From what you told me, I think Joanna acted suspiciously after you called with your concerns about Liam."

"What do you mean?"

"She didn't tell the Bureau about the drugs Jenny found. When I contacted the Chelsea division, they hadn't heard anything about it or our drug investigation. She told you that she would, right?" She poured them fresh cups of coffee and sat beside Kate at the counter. "Another problem is why didn't she send a marshal to check on you, to search the area when you were adamant you saw Liam Maloney?"

"Because I told her I didn't want to relocate until we were sure it was Liam."

"Maybe I'm wrong, but I don't think you have that much power in the relationship. You can leave the program, but unless you do, they are bound to ensure you're safe. She didn't."

"She's just trying to help me. She's been so good to me over the past few years during my grandmother's illness and death." The conversation agitated Kate. "She might have acted outside protocol but only because I asked her to."

Someone knocked, and Jenny charged the front door, barking. "It's me." Jenny wagged her tail at Nicole's voice and jumped on the door until Kate opened it. "Hey, boss. Did you get any sleep?" Her young assistant stepped inside and petted Jenny's head.

"A few hours. How about you?"

"Yeah. A few."

"Come inside. I made coffee." Nicole followed Kate to the kitchen.

"Hi. How are you feeling?" Reese asked Nicole. She learned how capable and reliable Kate's assistant was in the overnight hours. Nevertheless, she was young and had confronted an armed intruder, and that would rattle anyone.

"I won't lie. I've felt better. I brought the master key back. Everyone locked their doors last night." She returned the key to its hook in the utility closet and took a mug of coffee from Kate.

"I'm so sorry, Nic," Kate said.

"I'd be worried if you weren't upset," Reese said. "He violated your home and threatened your security, but you're safe now. Park law enforcement and Forest Services are looking for him, and we'll find him."

"Right now, I need you to put that fancy business degree to work and help me make some decisions." Kate put her arm around Nicole and guided her to the barstool beside Reese.

"About what?"

"The Lounge. I've never closed it before, not once in seven years, and I don't want to start now because some asshole broke into our home, but we don't have time to clean, even if Vivienne were here."

Nicole sipped her coffee and thought for a minute. "Easy solution. We set up on the patio."

"I like the idea. How exactly?"

"We set the buffet table against the wall. That'll leave enough space for everyone to walk through and serve themselves. There are extension cords in storage. I'll run them out the window. We'll set up groups of folding chairs along the porch. The trail families in two, five, and seven will want to hang out together."

"Excellent. That's what we'll do."

Less than half an hour later, the coffee urns stopped sputtering with a last burst of steam, and the morning Lounge was open on the hostel's long front porch with coffee, tea, fruit, granola, yogurts, bagels, and Lou's cinnabuns.

Guests began to emerge from their rooms and congregate at the buffet table. Kate and Reese sat across from them on the porch area in front of Kate's home. Nicole carried a chair over and joined them. They watched Jenny with a trail family. The old hound wiggled side to side on her back as the hikers scratched her belly.

Kate looked at Reese. "Can we clean before the evening Lounge?"

"Yeah. I'm done. I need to send the evidence over to the lab. I might drive it there myself."

"All right." Kate looked at Nicole. "What about Vivienne, will she be home to help?"

"Yeah. She's supposed to be back in a few hours. I told her what happened last night, and she was upset. I had to convince her the guy wasn't one of our guests, but she was still freaked out. Said she thinks we should move back to town."

"We? I hope you told her, she's welcome to go back." Kate abruptly stood and retrieved the coffee carafe.

Nicole frowned, hurt settling in her eyes.

"Don't worry about Vivienne," Reese said, reassuringly. "It's normal to be scared. You can tell her we're searching the area, and we'll find him. In the meantime, I'll have Bob patrol the woods near the hostel, okay?"

Nicole nodded.

"I'm not saying she's using the break-in as an excuse, but I don't think Vivienne has ever wanted to live here," Kate said, refilling their mugs.

"What's that supposed to mean?" Nicole's voice sounded upset enough to make Kate pause.

"I'm just saying living here was a convenient solution for Vivienne's problem. If you had moved to town with her, she would have been happier with that arrangement."

Nicole looked like she'd been sucker punched. "That's not true."

Reese took a large bite of cinnabun and thought no good would result from this conversation, but it wasn't her place to intervene.

"Well, it looks like the truth from my side. You'd been with her for almost a year, and I only met her a few times before she moved here. Even now that she works for me, we've only talked once or twice, if you can call them conversations. Doesn't that seem strange to you?"

"You're our boss, and you intimidate her. I already told you that. She's shy."

"I'm not just your boss. We're friends. Who doesn't want to know their partner's friends?"

Nicole's cheeks flushed red. "I'll start collecting dishes."

"Don't go. Talk to me." Kate watched her walk away and sighed. "That didn't go well."

"She's in love. Always tricky ground."

"Why did I start that? I'm such an idiot." Kate closed her eyes.

"No, you're not. You care about her, and she's lucky to have you." Reese's cell phone rang. "Special Agent Carter."

"Reese, it's Nelson. We received a call about two bodies off McGregor trail. I've pulled some rangers off the armed-man search and sent them to the location. I'm heading that way now. Can you meet us?"

"Send the coordinates. I'll be there in thirty minutes. Please secure the area and don't let anyone contaminate the scene." Reese ended the call and lowered her voice as she stood. "Two bodies off the McGregor trail."

"Oh my God," Kate whispered. "My guests? Do you think Liam killed them?"

Reese cupped her face. "Calm down. We don't know who they are or what's happened, but I'll find out. I need you and your guests to stay inside until Bob arrives, okay?"

"All right," Kate said. "Please be careful."

CHAPTER THIRTY-ONE

The park rangers had cordoned off the burned-out illegal campsite with yellow caution tape. Chief Nelson and three other rangers stood several feet away from the bodies. Reese noticed the shock and discontent on their faces at once.

Nelson approached her but the others continued to whisper among themselves. "One of the victims is Bob Tolbert."

"Son of a bitch," Reese said.

"The other body could be the armed man who broke into Kate Hall's place. Maybe Bob found him hiding here. Approached him…" He bit his lip and lowered his head. "I'm going to need you to keep us involved. He's family."

"I understand completely. Every step of the way. You have my word." Reese dropped her backpack. She was the outsider intruding on the park law enforcement in their worst hour and taking over command of the investigation. Every case she worked put her in this position, and she had learned to tread lightly.

"Should I call off the search?"

"Not until forensics verifies this is the man." She looked at the huddled rangers and softened her voice. "I understand this is a shock, but I need you to remove everyone from the crime scene. We need to minimize contamination. I'd appreciate it if you could leave me a couple of rangers at the entry, and we need to have several patrolling the boundary near Hostel Hall."

"Yeah. Of course."

"When I finish forensic collection, we need to coordinate body removal. It'll take at least four of us to bring them down. I'll contact the coroner's office and have them meet us at Lake Howard."

"Just let me know when. I need…" His voice faltered, and he cleared his throat. "I need to inform Marsha."

"Sure. I'll update you soon." Reese lowered her head. She'd notified the next of kin in the past, and it was torture. The pain in their faces stayed with her, their anguished sobs a reminder death never ends for the living.

After the scene cleared, Reese gloved her hands and retrieved a digital camera and an evidence kit from her backpack. Ranger Robert Tolbert lay on the ground a few feet away from a second man. She knelt beside Bob. He had a clean bullet entry to the left side of his head and an exit wound on the back right side. A significant blood spray pattern and pooling covered the ground, turning the ashen soil black.

She identified the second man as Liam Maloney from pictures Kate had shown her. His death hadn't been instant. It appeared Bob shot him once in the chest. He'd bled out, probably over several minutes, long enough to know he was dying.

She took pictures of Liam first, the position of his body, his hand holding the gun, and the bullet wound in his chest. Then she enlarged her circle and captured the blood pattern around his body, his footprints, two spent cartridges, and the black backpack beside him. The backpack looked like the others in the drug trafficking case.

The only item in the backpack was a baggie of white pills stamped with a cursive L. Her pulse quickened. This was all they needed to connect Liam Maloney and the O'Flaherty organization to the other backpacks and the PCT drug trafficking case. She bagged everything and checked Liam's pockets. He only carried a hotel key for the Marblemount Inn. She motioned for the ranger posted at the site's entry. "Find out what room this is and who's staying in it. Make sure the front desk uses a glove and handles the card carefully. Send me back the ID they have on file then secure the room. No one goes in without my authorization."

The ranger nodded and left.

Reese returned to Liam and examined the gun. A Glock 19. She lifted the grip. There it was on the back strap. The small x Kate had scratched into the metal. "So you did break into Kate's house." She checked the mag's witness hole; two bullets were missing.

She stood and texted Kate, *Was your gun's mag full?*

Kate's response came immediately. *Yes.*

Liam found deceased. Had your gun in his possession. I'll share more tonight.

Okay. So they do know I'm here.

It appears he did. We'll figure out our next move tonight. She waited for a response, but nothing came. *Trust me, please.*

Three dots pulsated, and she waited nervously until Kate replied, *Okay.*

Reese texted Chief Nelson that a witness identified the deceased man as the man who broke into Kate's home, and they could end their search. She decided to look for the first bullet Liam fired. It would give her a minute before examining Bob's body, which she needed. Looking at a stranger's corpse was one of the hardest things to do, but dealing with an acquaintance's body was an entirely different level.

A tall Douglas fir behind Bob to the left had a large chunk of bark blown off its side. It had to be the second bullet. The exposed vascular cambium was still moist. She examined the tree but was unable to locate the slug. After taking pictures of the damage, she returned to Bob's body. She searched his pockets and found a folded picture of a sailboat and an envelope of money. "What did you get yourself involved in?" she whispered.

She stood back and reasoned that Bob and Liam had arranged a meeting. The way they faced each other showed no one surprised the other. There was no scuffed dirt or other signs of a struggle. She was sure the cash and envelope would have Liam's fingerprints. Most likely it was a payment for protecting the trafficking corridor in the park. The first drop went south when Jenny found the drugs, so she figured this time Liam decided to make the exchange with the runner in person. He demanded Bob meet them to discuss the O'Flahertys' expectations of no mistakes going forward. That made sense.

"Why would you shoot?" she asked aloud as she took photos of Bob's wounds and body position. "If you chose to protect their pipeline, why pull out when you were so close to retirement, to taking Marsha away?"

Then she looked at Liam. "Why would you steal Kate's gun, bring it to your meeting with Bob, and kill him if you needed him to protect your merchandise?" She stepped back and took pictures of the ground around the bodies. Something looked off. Areas of the ashen dirt had a pattern, one that didn't match the rest. She moved farther back and discerned a wide swath of the disturbed soil led out the side of the campsite.

Several hours later the sun had slipped behind the mountains and the crime scene darkened. Reese and three rangers made two trips carrying Liam and Bob in white body bags down the switchbacks to Howard Lake where a helicopter waited for transport to the Skagit County Coroner's office. What had transpired at the illegal campsite made little sense to Reese. Her gut said there was more to the double murder than a business deal gone wrong, and she hoped the coroner's reports and the forensic evidence she collected would fill in the blanks.

* * *

Kate's phone dinged. It was a text from Reese.
On my way. 30min.
She pressed the message and sent a thumbs-up emoji. Then she reread Reese's earlier text. Liam was dead. Her gun was found on his body. Her first instinct had been to call Joanna, but she trusted Reese, and even though panic kept her from thinking clearly, she knew something wasn't right. Why would Liam break into her home and take her gun and photos? Why didn't he quietly wait

for her to return home and kill her? Or kill her out on a hiking trail? A chill ran down her spine. Fiona had to know she was there if Liam did. The minute she learned of Liam's death the matriarch would send as many button men as it would take to kill her.

Kate paced, stopping every few minutes to peek behind the drawn drapes. Fiona would never stop. She would exact scorched earth on her and everyone…everything she loved. It was a threat Kate couldn't idly stand by and allow. The only solution was to call Joanna, to remove herself from the hostel and anyone in her life. She struggled for breath, feeling as if she was underwater. She bent over with her hands on her knees, and Jenny rushed her, licking her cheek. "Thank you, sweet girl." Kate sat and the old hound fell into her. "It's okay. I'm okay." After a few minutes of petting Jenny's back, her breath was steady, and her thoughts slowed.

She checked her watch. Reese would be there any minute and would probably appreciate a hot meal. She'd cooked pasta primavera earlier and had already eaten. She filled a bowl for Reese. Then she placed a tea kettle on the stove. Her phone dinged. *I'm outside. Don't want to make Jenny bark.* She read Reese's text and ran to open the front door. "I'm so glad you're here."

"Me, too." Reese pulled her into a gentle embrace. "I'm sorry you had to sit with that news all day. Are you holding up?"

"Trying. Not going to lie. It's hard." Kate stepped back and returned to the kitchen. "Are you hungry? I made pasta and can warm it up, or we could just have a cup of tea?"

"I'd love all of it. Thank you." She rubbed the top of Jenny's head and sat on a barstool at the counter.

Kate tied chamomile bags around the handles of two mugs. The teakettle whistled, and she quickly removed it. "Are you sure it was Liam?"

"He reserved his hotel room under the name Brad Walsh from Boston Massachusetts, but I'm positive he's the person in the pictures you showed me."

"Let me see the photos. I can verify it's him." She poured hot water into two mugs and returned the kettle to the stove.

"Are you sure?"

"I've seen bodies before, not just photos."

"That's not what I meant." Reese paused. "Come sit with me."

Kate set their tea on the counter. "What is it? I can hear it in your voice. Something's wrong."

"I'll show you a picture of the man I think is Liam. But there's something else I need to tell you." She held Kate's eyes. "The other deceased is Bob."

Kate sat back like the wind had been knocked out of her. She covered her mouth with her hand and her eyes welled.

"Before you beat yourself up, his death wasn't your fault. I don't think he's an innocent victim." Reese accessed the photos on her camera. "Look at the scene. See how their bodies are positioned. One of them was waiting, and the other walked in. They stood together, talking. There's no indication of a surprise or struggle. No scuff marks on the ground." She swiped through the pictures and showed her a closeup of the unknown man. "Is this Liam?" Kate nodded. Reese enlarged the photo of the mark on the gun. "Is this your Glock?"

"Yeah, that's mine."

"Are we going to trace it back to your father?"

"You might get a hit on an old registration with his name. But as far as I know, he didn't have any paperwork for it either."

"Okay. Look at this one." Reese stopped on the backpack and baggie of drugs. "The pack was beside Liam's body. They're similar to the ones you found." Reese swiped past a few more photos and stopped. "And this is an envelope with a considerable amount of money I found in Bob's vest pocket."

"Why would Bob get involved with them?"

"Sometimes people find themselves in stressful situations and make bad choices." Reese hesitated. "Bob told me his wife had cancer—"

"Marsha has cancer?"

"He didn't tell you?"

"That must be why he's been…was…acting so strange lately. That and becoming a bent ranger." She sighed. "Poor Marsha. Does she have to know any of this?"

"We need to confirm his involvement first. Then it's up to the AG's office, but yeah, she'll probably find out."

Jenny lumbered up and sat between them, and Kate stroked her head, lost in thought. "If Liam knew I was here, so does Fiona. He wouldn't have taken Jenny and broken into my house on his initiative…at least not the kid I remember."

"I agree. We have to assume she knows. With Liam dead, she might get away with distancing herself from the drugs just like she did with Bridget's death. The AG will struggle to build a case against her, but if we can prove she solicited your whereabouts, we'll have her on another federal charge. One that will stick."

"Easier said than done. It could be anyone involved in my enrollment in WITSEC." She looked frustrated. "I'm sorry. I shouldn't snap at you."

"There you go with the shoulds again. You're upset and rightfully so. Someone with the marshals or the Department of Justice betrayed you. Only a handful of people from those offices knew you went into WITSEC and fewer know where you were placed. Unless there's anyone else?" Kate shook her head. "What about your boss? Special Agent Mandy Garcia."

Kate's body stiffened, and Jenny rested her head on Kate's knee. "No way. Don't even say that. Mandy would never. I trust her with my life. I did trust her with my life, and I'm still here when I could have been dead."

"We have to keep all possibilities open until we can close them, right? You know that. She'll be the first person we cross off our list. I have a call with her tomorrow to discuss the drug case." Reese held Kate's hand. "We can do this. You'll be able to stop hiding and living in fear. I have a tech friend at ISB. He's a wiz, and I trust him. We can ask him to help us and only tell him what's necessary. We need to start with Fiona's phone records."

"No." Kate looked at her and gave a decisive head shake. "Lou. We'll ask Lou to help us."

"What's her background?"

"She was a cybersecurity icon."

"Seriously? Okay, but you're talking about Lou. Are you sure?"

"I'm sure. She's abrasive, but she's trustworthy. And not involved with any agency at all."

"Okay. Lou, it is. We'll talk with her tomorrow."

CHAPTER THIRTY-TWO

Kate pulled on a pair of gauntlet gloves and deadheaded roses. Her early bloomers had one more flowering before she had to winterize them. She moved down the rows and carefully snipped above the first five-leaflet sets on her hybrids. Working in her garden felt like therapy. The bags of clippings reinforced her need to clear away the wreckage of the past. The healthy, blooming rose bushes proved that point. She breathed in perfumed air and wiped the sweat from her face and neck. Jenny lay on her side in a deep sleep under a three-tiered water fountain. If the hound wasn't drinking out of its bottom basin, she was sleeping to the soft trickling of its water.

The work in the warm sunshine usually distracted Kate, but today the early-morning hours crept back into her mind. The feeling of Reese holding her from behind, nestling and kissing her neck, flooded her body with heat. She straightened and moved her gardening bench to the next bush. How had she let herself become so emotionally involved? *Emotionally involved?* Was that what she was calling it? She laughed aloud, and Jenny looked over from her sunning spot by the garden gate. "I'm fine, sweet girl. Go back to sleep."

The first time Kate stood in the garden talking with Reese she knew a casual relationship with the special agent would be difficult, but she had tried it anyway. Now she was falling in love for the first time, which was terrifying and wonderful. And even though she had feared giving Reese a place in her life, doing so hadn't made her lose her sense of self like she thought her father had. She still felt whole.

Chatter on the porch caught Kate's attention, and she stood. Nicole and Vivienne were in an animated conversation, but she couldn't make out their words. Then Vivienne glanced in her direction, abruptly turned, and headed for Nicole's apartment.

"What's wrong with her," Kate asked as Nicole entered the garden.

"It's not you if that's what you think." Jenny lazily rose and trotted to Nicole. "She's still freaked out. Room four's tramily showed up early, and we let them hang out while we set up Lounge. They heard there was a murder near Howard Lake. That and the break-in. She's upset she was out there with a killer, and she's ready to leave. I don't know how to convince her she's safe when I'm not even sure we are."

Her young assistant stared at her with desperate eyes. For some reason, the angsty French woman made Nicole happy, and she needed to be supportive, so she resisted the urge to encourage Vivienne's departure. "It's a lot to process. You can tell her the man who broke in is dead, and the threat is over." She paused. "Ranger Bob shot him."

"Holy shit. Is that what happened at the lake?"

"Not exactly." Kate rubbed Jenny's long, silky ear and blinked back the sting of tears. "Bob was also killed. It appears they shot each other."

"Oh my God. Was he trying to stop the guy?"

"It looks that way," Kate lied. Bob had chosen to work for Liam, but Marsha hadn't, and she didn't think the woman needed any more pain than she already had.

"Who was the guy? Why'd he break into your house?"

She was overcome with guilt and shame and had trouble looking Nicole in the eyes. "Reese thinks he might be connected to the drug case they're working on—the drugs Jenny found. Maybe you should think about taking Vivienne to meet your parents, just until the ISB confirms they've stopped the trafficking in this area."

"No way. I'd never leave you here, alone. Besides, Vivienne can't travel to Canada right now."

"I forgot about that. How about Seattle for a couple of weeks?"

"Does the ISB think there are more people involved?"

"All I know is the man who broke in knew I found the backpack, and he believed I kept something for myself, but I didn't, and he found that out. If others are involved, they'll know I don't have their merchandise, and I'm safe." The words tumbling out of her mouth were crap, and made no sense, but she said what she needed to say to remove the worry from Nicole's face.

"Then, I'm safe, too."

"Please, Nic. If something bad happened to you, I could never forgive myself. Visit your folks or take Vivienne to Seattle. For me?" Kate held Nicole's arms and pulled her into a tight hug.

"Hey, it's okay, boss. I'll think about it."

Kate released her. "Thank you. Now go...tell your girlfriend what's happening."

* * *

At the Skagit County Coroner's Office, Reese had insisted the FBI use facial recognition in the Next Generation Identification database on Brad Walsh after his prints didn't score a hit on AFIS. She had argued that the ID they found in his hotel room was fake and because of ISB's ongoing drug investigation, she needed a timely identification. While she attended the man's autopsy, news came from the regional FBI field office that she was right. The man was Liam Declan Maloney of Quincy, Massachusetts.

Reese reviewed the pathologist's initial report and asked the coroner to allow the forty-eight-hour notification period to elapse before contacting the Quincy police. She needed time to talk to Kate. They had to decide on a plan to keep her safe.

The hostel's communal room and most of its dorm rooms were dark when Reese arrived. She drummed her fingers on the old Land Rover's steering wheel. Working a case had never been quite like this, but now she tip-toed along a wobbly line she never thought she'd cross. Keeping Kate safe had become her top priority. Her cell phone rang. "Special Agent Reese Carter."

"Hello, Agent Carter, this is Kyle Harris. You visited my trail-angel BBQ off the PCT on Stehekin Road a while ago and we spoke about a young lady who went missing. Coleen Farrell. I never could get those green eyes out of my head and was telling my Mrs. about her. We got to looking at old photos from our shop in Marblemount back in the day, thinking maybe we'd see a picture of her. We didn't see her in any of the photos, but Julie, my Mrs., remembered a young woman we picked up on the scenic highway. She recalled we gave her a ride and let her off near Granite Creek. Julie thinks it could have been her. To tell you the truth, I don't have any recollection, but Julie's got a sharp memory. She thought about the woman because she didn't have a backpack or anything, and she thought it was strange for her to be hitching rides in the park without one. I tend to agree. Don't you?"

"Yes, that does seem odd, and I appreciate you calling me with this information. Could I visit with Mrs. Harris in the morning and show her Coleen's photo?"

"Oh, sure. She'd be happy to help. You know in the beginning it was Julie's idea to be trail angels. We never had kids, and she's just a helper and a giver. I'll text our address. To this number?"

"Yes, this number. Thanks again. I'll see you tomorrow." Reese ended the call. The information excited her, but tips didn't always develop into worthwhile leads, so she kept her excitement in check and walked to Kate's porch.

The front door opened before Reese could knock, and the rush from Kyle's call quickly turned into a fluttering sensation at the sight of Kate standing there.

"Hey. Jenny heard you pull in."

"Oh, she did, did she? And she knew it was me. You're quite a guard dog, tough girl." Reese scratched the bloodhound's head. Then she pulled Kate into a soft kiss. "A day in the sun looks good on you."

"Thanks. I feel good. Better." She took hold of Reese's hand and led her to the kitchen. "You look like you had a tough one. Are you hungry?"

"No, we ate after the autopsy."

"Oh, God. That's never pleasant. Thirsty?"

"I'll take a beer if you have one."

Kate opened the refrigerator and grabbed two bottles. "So what's new?"

"According to the pathologist, both Bob and Liam had gunshot residue on their hands, which supports they shot each other. Forensics on the guns are much more interesting. Bob's was clean for the most part. It had clear prints from his hand and finger positioning, but nothing else."

"On a service pistol? He'd have cleaned it routinely. Done target practice." Kate sat beside Reese at the bar.

"Exactly. Same report for your gun. Only one set of Liam's prints."

"Only one? I had handled the gun. It doesn't make sense. None of this does." She paused. "Why would they kill each other if they were in business together? What about the money on Bob? Has forensics confirmed it was from Liam?"

Reese nodded. "Liam's prints were on the money and the envelope. I agree the scenario doesn't make sense." She retrieved her camera from her backpack. "I want to show you something else. Look at the pattern of disruption in the dirt, and how it moves away from the bodies and into the trees. I don't think they were alone."

Kate stared at the screen, zooming in on the photo. "I see it. The soil does look like it's been disturbed, but it's a wide swath, if you're covering your tracks, you just focus on your footprints."

"Sure, if you're only concerned with them being traced back to you. But what if your concern is staging a crime scene, and you need to cover any evidence you were there?"

"I can see that. Who? The runner?"

"Could've been."

"Liam would've used someone from the organization, and they'd be too afraid to kill a Maloney. Besides, Liam and Bob would be expecting the runner."

"Maybe someone else showed up, and Bob and Liam panicked, thinking the other had double-crossed them." Reese drank her beer thoughtfully. A few details Kate had shared about her involvement in the O'Flaherty crime ring and the resulting explosion bothered her. "You said Bridget wore the horseshoe pin at the meeting with the Novikovs, right?"

"Yeah, but she took her coat off."

"Right, but was there time for the Novikovs to see it?"

Kate lifted her eyebrows. "I guess they could have."

"I think the pin left in your box symbolizes that day, and only a handful of people who lost something in that explosion remain. You, Fiona, Sasha Novikov, and her daughter, Kira. You put the Novikovs in the FBI and attorney general's crosshairs. They have a motive for retaliation as well as the O'Flaherty mob."

"I guess so. But what about Liam being here?"

"He's also been in every other western national park that the PCT traverses. We now know he set up their West Coast pipeline, traveling here using the name Brad Walsh and probably others. Why would he spend a year out here and avoid you until now?"

"So you think the Novikovs broke in, stole my gun, and killed Liam and Bob?"

"If they knew about the O'Flaherty expansion in the West, they could've been watching Liam, waiting to take him out, or if they were here for you and saw him in town, it could've been opportunistic."

Kate sighed. "That's a lot of ifs."

"It is, but we need to consider the possibility that someone else broke in, someone who knew how to avoid your security cameras. Another person who knew about your other life and the box hidden under your floor. Someone who wouldn't think twice about killing Liam and Bob." She held Kate's eyes. "More importantly, we have to figure out how anyone found out where you are, and I think we need to start, tonight, with Joanna."

"Now?" Kate glanced at her watch. "It's almost one a.m. her time."

"If she's asleep and answers, it's a good time to catch her off guard."

"*If* she has something to hide. I'll get my phone." Kate pushed away from the counter. "I just can't believe Joanna would put my life in danger."

When she returned, she plugged in the phone she used to contact the marshal. She turned on the speaker and propped the phone against her coffee mug. It rang once before Joanna answered. "Kate?"

"Sorry it's late, but we need to talk. Did the FBI contact you yesterday or today?"

"No. Why? What's going on? You sound upset."

"It's the Maloneys. My house was broken into, and my gun was stolen. The next morning Liam Maloney and a park ranger were found dead thirty minutes away. Liam had my gun, which means he was in my house." Her voice grew shaky.

"Jesus Christ, Kate. Why are you just now calling me? This is a serious breach." She paused. "The O'Flaherty organization must know where you live. We need to get you out of there immediately—"

"You said the FBI was surveilling them. How'd Liam get here without them knowing? How'd he know I was here, Joanna?"

Reese gestured for her to slow down. Then she mouthed, "Refuse to leave."

"I don't know the answers to those questions. All I know is your life is in danger, and that's my responsibility, so I'm calling the Western District office right now. Marshals will be there in a couple of hours. They'll take you to a safe house, and I'll take the next flight out. I can be there by late morning."

"Don't call. I'm not relocating. You can consider this my voluntary termination request. But I need to know why the Maloneys found me after eight years. Unless I do, they'll just find me again."

Joanna was silent for a moment. "We can investigate what's happened. Trust me. If there was a leak, we can find it—"

"*If* there was? For fuck's sake, Liam was here and died right up the mountain from my doorstep. How much more proof do you need than that?" Her voice turned angry, and Reese squeezed her hand, calming her. "I've made up my mind. Whatever the process is for me to leave WITSEC, start it."

"Kate, please. I understand how upset you are. But I advise against leaving the program. You'll lose our protection, and any threat against you will be out of our hands. Please, sleep on it. We can talk in the morning."

"There's no need to talk again. I planned for this situation a long time ago, for the eventuality Fiona would have a mole in the right place at the right time and learn where I'm living. From now on, I'll take care of my safety. No one will know where I relocate. No one." Kate ended the call and looked at Reese. "Well?"

"Gut reaction? She was shocked to hear your voice and not because it was one o'clock in the morning. Professional read? She said all the right things but didn't try very hard to change your mind, maybe because if she's involved her hands are clean of you now." Reese held Kate's eyes. "Your last comment was risky but a stroke of brilliance."

"Thought you'd like that. Let's see what a loss of control makes her do. I figure if she's not guilty, she'll call the commissioner, or if she is, she'll call the person she sold me out to. Which means we need to call Lou."

CHAPTER THIRTY-THREE

Southwestern eggs and coffee for breakfast wouldn't make up for all Reese had done for her. The special agent had been with her since the break-in, hadn't slept well, and it was all her fault. Kate diced an onion, shedding tears before she finished. The onions caused most of them.

"Smells good in here," Reese said as she walked into the kitchen and drew Kate close.

"Mmm, glad you're up, but I hoped you'd sleep a little longer." She turned her head and met Reese's lips in a light kiss. "Grab some coffee."

"Can I help?"

"Nope. I have it covered. A remarkable teacher taught me this dish. I could give her number to you."

Reese laughed and sat on the other side of the bar. "How long have you been awake?"

"Since five. I couldn't sleep thinking about everything. That's the second pot of coffee. Do you know how many people left the WITSEC program voluntarily last year? Fourteen. Out of thousands. It's rare. Then again, my situation doesn't happen very often. No one's making a movie like *Donnie Brasco* out of my life. Not that I'd want one. Then I couldn't stop thinking about convincing Lou to help us because I Googled how to track cell phones and burners, and it's not easy. It's even harder to access their call logs. Did I mention it's illegal to do both without warrants?" She stopped chopping tomatoes and looked up. Reese sipped her coffee, patiently listening. "I don't want you to get in trouble because of me."

"I hear you, and I'd do anything to stop your thoughts from racing, but it's too late for doubts. I'm willing to take whatever steps we need to find out who betrayed you, to keep you safe." She reached across the counter and held Kate's hand. "We have a plan, and we're sticking to it, okay?" She gave her hand a little squeeze, and Kate nodded. "Good, and maybe I will take your teacher's number, you have excellent knife positioning."

Kate let out a short laugh. "I think you two would get on great."

"Oh, I know we would." She smiled and watched Kate scrape the veggies from the cutting board into a large pan. "The coroner will contact Quincy police tomorrow morning, and they'll reach out to Fiona, so we have today. I can secure a warrant for Fiona's phone records to advance the ISB drug investigation, which won't take too long, but a faster route is to reach out to Mandy. She's been surveilling Fiona's and Liam's phones and communication in Fiona's office in case she's using burners."

Kate turned to her. "They've tapped Fiona's office?"

"That was my understanding. I don't have any doubt Mandy will cooperate with my investigation unless she has something to hide."

"No. She wouldn't be involved. I know she wouldn't." Kate turned back to the sizzling veggies.

"Okay. I hear you. Once we have Fiona's records, we can let Lou do her thing."

An hour later, Reese was cleaning the dishes when the doorbell rang.

Jenny leaped from her dog bed and charged the door, barking, and Kate followed.

"Check your security first," Reese called.

Kate opened her cell phone app and saw Lou holding a box containing three pies. "Hey, come in," she said, opening the door.

"I got two trays of cinnabuns in the car. You want me to bring them in now?"

"They can wait." Kate took the pies from her. "Take a seat. Do you want coffee?"

"Sure. Well hello, Special Agent Carter. Pretty early for a visit, huh? Unless you didn't go home last night." She sat beside Reese and broke out in her deep, throaty laugh.

"Wouldn't you love to know?"

"Yeah, not really. I'm razzing you. If you told me, it wouldn't be fun anymore." She moved her arm, and Kate placed a mug of coffee next to her. "So why'd you want me here this early? It would take a lot of alcohol to get me naughty, and I only drink at night."

"Lou, I need you to be serious." Kate sat on the other side of her.

"Jeez, don't get all upset." She looked between them. "What's going on? You look like Phil when we have to go visit my family." She smiled, but it faded. "Is this about the cryptic message you left me yesterday?"

"You told me you were in cybersecurity, right? Were you a hacker?" Kate asked.

"They used to call me the female Kevin Mitnick, which was bullshit. I was as good or better, but the field's a sexist cesspool. I spent twenty years revolutionizing…never mind. I don't want to get into it."

"Could you access someone's phone records or emails?" Reese asked.

Lou snorted. "I was paid to hack organizations more locked down than the CIA. A teen with a grudge and a computer could access phones and emails."

"That's what we need you to do," Reese said.

"No can do. I left that life because it almost killed me. The stress nearly stopped my ticker. Jeez, Phil would kill me now if I got back into it."

"Lou...I had no idea," Kate said. "Never mind, we can manage."

"Hacking phones and computers?" She looked cocky. "Sure you can. What exactly do you need?"

"I'm investigating a suspected drug ring running along the PCT. I've got a warrant for one suspect's phone records, but we need to compare them to a few other suspects I can't bring forward. Not yet."

"So let me get this straight, you, an officer of the law, are asking me to access the information illegally?" She narrowed her eyes and frowned. "Just kidding. Of course I'll help." She snorted, but when she looked at Kate her face was serious. "You're in trouble, huh?"

"Yeah." Kate wanted to say more but couldn't. She started to doubt their plan. Why was she putting Lou in danger? It wasn't right.

"How'd they find you?" Lou tilted her head at their shocked expressions. "Come on, I've known for months. You wouldn't let me put your picture up in the shop. You never talk about your past. You still drop your Rs so I figure you come from somewhere in New England. You confirmed my suspicion when you ran into the shop last month asking about that guy. You were pale as a ghost. I figured what really worried you was if he saw you. WITSEC, right?"

Kate let out a long sigh. "Yeah. I'm ex-FBI. I had an undercover case that fell apart before I could testify. My identity was exposed, and I was placed in WITSEC. Now someone has leaked my information."

Reese stroked Kate's arm and looked at Lou. "The man shot dead on the McGregor Trail yesterday was from the crime family she tried to put away."

"Shit. And you think you know who disclosed your location?"

"I think my inspector did."

"What the hell, your marshal sold you out? That's outrageous. What do you want me to find out? I'll start today." She grinned. "It'll give me a reason to get away from Phil. Being with him in that shop all day drives me up the wall, but you can't tell him what I'm doing."

Kate hugged her. "Thank you, Lou."

"Yeah, yeah. Don't get handsy."

Kate squeezed her tighter. She meant it, deeply. Asking for help had been a foreign concept to her for so long. She had never wanted the vulnerability that came with it, the possibility of owing anyone, of deepening a bond. She sat back and wiped the corners of her eyes.

"Thank you, Lou," Reese said. "I'll bring you hard copies of the phone records of two people, Fiona and Liam Maloney, as well as Bob Tolbert's. We have a suspect list and need their call records and tower triangulation of any calls in this area. We need to know if any of them called Fiona, Liam, or Bob in the last year. I'd start with this month and work backward." Reese handed her a list with the names Sasha Novikov, Kira Rodin, US Deputy Marshal Joanna Stevens, US Deputy Marshal Nguyen, SAC Mandy Garcia, and Deputy AG Hal Macon.

"Gotcha." Lou read the list. "This is it? Won't take me more than a day or two. Tops."

"One more thing. Could you run a background on Lainey Wright? Birth records and known addresses."

"Lainey?" Kate asked. "What's she got to do with it?"

Reese looked at her with those light blue-green eyes. "It's a hunch I need to explore."

* * *

Bridget danced around a tiny living room, the loud music from her earbuds drowning out all external noise. She deserved to celebrate, alone with her thoughts. Her plan was perfect, and everything was right on schedule. They had found Liam's body over forty-eight hours ago, so she was certain her mother had heard the news.

An incoming call interrupted her music. She glanced at the number and shoved the phone back into her pocket. The call came again, and she ignored the vibration, sending her mother to voice mail. She wanted to record the moment her mother's voice cried out in a combination of pain and shock. Real emotion. A genuine reaction to the true death of a child. She wanted to savor it.

After her playlist ended, she poured a glass of water and sat on the front porch of her hostel room. She hated it here on the West Coast. It was cold and rainy with sunless days that never ended. Thank God she could return to Côte d'Azur in a few days. She missed the warmth, the seafront, and pebbled beaches. She stared into the soaring pines. Her business needed her attention too. The captain shouldn't stay away too long, not that anyone would dare cross her, especially after she claimed the remaining O'Flaherty routes out of Quincy. The new venture with Antonio was only part of her plan to take down her mother, but maybe she'd stay in business with him. He'd proven loyal, and she didn't have to invest much to earn a decent return.

She held her cell phone and listened to her mother's voice mail. There would only be one first time, and she was ready to enjoy it. "Bridget…" She smiled. Her mother was crying the first honest tears she had ever produced. "Please call me…the unspeakable has happened. It's Liam…Bridget…Liam's dead." Her mother lost the little composure she had. Deep sobs replaced her words.

She exploded into maniacal laughter. Her mother sounded so weak, so completely gutted. She ended the message and replayed it. Liam's death had broken Fiona, and the sound was completely satisfying. Now she could call her mother back and stomach the woman's lies. A few other guests were hanging around the porch now, so Bridget left and walked toward the car park.

Fiona answered after the first ring. "Bridget. Did you listen to my message?"

"It can't be, Mother." She feigned shock. "They must be mistaken. He can't be…"

"The police came this morning…" Her voice broke. She inhaled sharply. "They showed me a picture."

"A picture. It could be someone who looks like him. You have to see him."

"I told them I wanted to…" She burst into tears.

"I won't believe it until we do." Bridget pretended to cry. "I'm coming home. I want to see Liam for myself."

"Absolutely not. You can't take the risk."

"Fuck the risk, Mother. My head is spinning, and I feel sick. This doesn't seem real. I need to see my baby brother." She paused. "What happened? Did someone order a hit on him? If that's what happened, I'm coming home no matter what you say. I'll kill the son of bitch."

"That's not what happened. He's not here…he went hiking… out West."

Bridget's eyes opened wide. Fiona was treading dangerously near the truth.

"They said he and another man were found…shot. He was murdered." Fiona whimpered. "Where was the FBI? They constantly surveil us, but when someone means to do us harm, where are they? What am I going to do?"

"You need to go there and make sure it's Liam. Then we'll find out everything we can and make whoever did this pay." Bridget waited for Fiona to speak, but her mother silently wept. "Or I'll go for you. I'll tell the authorities I'm a cousin. Tell me where he is, and I'll go."

Fiona took a sharp breath. "I said no, Bridget. Why can't you understand, you are never coming back here." She shouted in fury now. "This is all your fault. Your brother's blood is on your hands. What did you think would happen when you exposed us? Your selfish, childish need to be special ruined our lives. You're lucky I only *staged* your death. I'm warning you, stay there and don't cross me. I'll find out who's responsible, and they'll die a humiliating death far worse than what my Liam endured."

"Fine, Mother." Bridget restrained her urge to laugh. "Let me know how that goes."

CHAPTER THIRTY-FOUR

The Tuesday Skagit Valley Star featured a story about Law Enforcement Ranger Robert Tolbert's murder. Reese finished reading it and tossed the paper to the side of a long wooden table. The journalist had done her best with the little information Reese could provide, and thankfully for Marsha's sake, the piece focused on Bob's work at the park and not his possible involvement with drug traffickers.

She had returned to the sheriff's office early from her interview with Mrs. Harris. Julie had identified Coleen's picture as the young woman they picked up and dropped off at the road into Granite Creek. She had been worried Coleen didn't have a backpack, so she gave her money to pay for somewhere warm to sleep.

Reese opened a file folder, double-checking the information she would share with Special Agent in Charge Mandy Garcia when she arrived. The door to the office opened, and Reese looked up. A woman wearing an FBI windbreaker and talking on a cell phone entered. She smiled and held a finger up to Reese. So this was Kate's closest friend in her past life. Feeling a jab from the green-eyed monster, Reese wondered if friends were all they were.

The woman pocketed her phone. "Hey, I'm Mandy Garcia. Sorry about that. Some people just need that extra attention." She held out her hand, shook Reese's, and sat.

"Reese Carter. Nice to meet you. Hope your flight was good."

"No complaints."

"This is a copy of the ISB investigation for your team. Everything we have is in there." Reese handed Mandy the folder. "Our case started a year ago in Channel Islands National Park and identical drops have been found in Pinnacles National Park, Sequoia, Yosemite, Redwood National Park throughout the year, and last month here in the North Cascades."

Mandy opened Reese's file and perused the first few pages while she listened. After Reese finished talking, she stopped reading and looked up. "We've worked over a decade to bring the O'Flaherty crime family to justice. I need this to be the case that gets us there. It's personal for me. Just as I'm sure losing Ranger Tolbert is for the National Park Service."

"Oh, I understand. It's very personal for me too."

Mandy nodded and removed a folder from a document case, sliding it across the desk. "These are the phone records you requested. Do you want us to secure a warrant for Robert Tolbert's phone records?"

"I've already put in a request."

"Good. Fiona Maloney arrived in Seattle last night and identified Liam's body in Mount Vernon this morning. The deputy coroner said she was grief-stricken but angry and threw around accusations and threats. She's difficult to handle in the best circumstances, so I was hoping we could spend some time today preparing for tomorrow's interview."

"Absolutely. I was going to ask you—" Reese's cell phone rang, and she glanced at the screen. "Excuse me for a minute. I need to take this." She walked into the narrow, long hallway. "Hey, Lou."

"Hi. So listen, you got a minute 'cause I have some news."

"What is it?"

"Your request has been more complicated than I thought, but I'm getting somewhere. I've checked Fiona's and Liam's registered cell phones and Fiona's office landline, and no one from your suspect list called them. I even checked for burner purchases and found no record of Joanna Stevens, Sam Nguyen, Mandy Garcia, or Deputy AG Hal Macon acquiring burners. I did discover the Maloneys bought two burners in the last six months because instead of paying cash, the idiots sent a woman…Nora Kilpatrick…to buy them and she used her Visa card. Not too bright. But nobody from the list called their burners, either—"

"Son of a bitch," Reese whispered.

"Hey, don't interrupt. Jeez. I haven't gotten to the good part yet. I found two international numbers that connect Fiona, Liam, and Joanna. One of the international numbers appears on Fiona's registered cell phone, and the other appears on her burner. Liam's cell phone records have one of the numbers, and the other one is on Joanna's cell phone. Both of the international numbers appear on each other's call logs. I need to sort out triangulations, and I'll bring the info to the hostel tonight around nine-ish. We can work it all out then."

"Okay. Sounds good. Thanks, Lou." They'd make sense of the information later, but all that mattered to Reese at that moment was Lou had found a connection between US Deputy Marshal Stevens and the Maloneys.

After a long day at the Skagit Police Department, Reese understood why Kate had befriended Mandy Garcia. The woman was intelligent but didn't take herself too seriously, and even when she spoke directly, her dark-brown eyes were warm and calm. Before they ended for the day, she had decided to tell Kate that her old SAC was in Mount Vernon. They wouldn't be able to see each other, but at least Kate would know Mandy had made the journey to get justice for her.

Reese stopped by her home and packed an overnight bag with pajamas, clothes for tomorrow, and her personal handgun to give to Kate for protection. She tossed the bag into her Land Rover and headed out. Thirty minutes later, she pulled onto the long path winding through the woods and parked in the hostel's dirt lot.

Kate and Jenny greeted her on the front porch. "Hey. You must be exhausted."

"It's been an interesting day. Lots to tell you." She scratched Jenny's ears. "How are you, tough girl?" Jenny's tail whacked the porch's old wood slats. Evening Lounge was busy. Reese glanced inside the communal room's window. Nicole played a board game with three guests, and Vivienne sat in the reading area with another woman. "Are they doing okay today?"

"Yeah. I think I've convinced Nic to take Vivienne to Seattle for at least a week. I'm pushing them to leave tomorrow. We'll see what she says in the morning."

"I like that plan." Reese kissed her lightly on the lips and then licked her lower lip. "Mmm. You taste sweet."

"I'd like to take credit, but it's the chocolate bar I just ate." Kate smiled and took Reese's bag, dropping it on the floor. "Why don't I share a bit more." She pulled Reese into her arms, and they fell against the front door in a deep, hungry kiss. Her hands moved up the sides of Reese's body, and she slid her mouth down Reese's chin, nipping her neck.

Reese's breath caught, and her body felt like it would ignite. "Lou will be here soon. If we don't stop now, we're not stopping."

"All right. Save the last thought for later," Kate said in a sultry voice. She stepped back and grinned. "Lou will want a beer. Do you want one?"

"Sure, but ice water might help me more."

Kate let out a playful laugh.

"I want to tell you something, but I'm unsure how you'll feel about it." Reese sat on a barstool.

"Jesus, that's a stressful segue." Kate placed three beer bottles on the counter. "Just rip the Band-Aid off."

"Okay. You know Fiona arrived from Boston last night, and I mentioned SAC Garcia offered the FBI's assistance with the drug case, starting with my interview with Fiona tomorrow. Well, Mandy is the one who showed up to assist, and she made it clear the case was personal for her, that we had to bring Fiona to justice."

Kate seemed lost for words, and a moment later she said in a shaky voice, "Mandy's here? She can't know I'm involved."

"She won't. I promise. Not until it's safe."

Kate nodded, and there was a knock at the front door. She checked the security image on her phone. "It's Lou. Here open these." She placed a bottle opener on the counter and let Lou inside.

Lou glanced at the bag beside the door. "Oh, you didn't say it was a slumber party. I didn't bring my pajamas."

"I didn't invite you. You couldn't handle the party games."

Lou snorted. "Good one. I knew you had it in you." She climbed on a stool beside Reese and grabbed a beer. "I don't have all night. The old man's making me open the shop in the morning. He's had to run it alone, and you'd think he'd been abandoned in the Arctic for seventy-two hours." She took a swig and removed a stack of paper from her bag, handing it to Reese. "Information on Lainey Wright is on the first two pages. Here's the headline, it's a fake name lifted off a deceased child in Cascade, Montana."

"Fake?" Kate asked, shocked.

"Oh, yeah. The name Lainey Wright doesn't appear in any official documents. Nothing since the child's death record. No driver's license, no marriage certificate, no bank loans." She gulped her beer and looked at Reese. "Why do you think she has anything to do with Kate?"

"I don't." Reese scanned the first page. "This is great. Thanks. What about the phone records? Any progress."

"Oh, yeah." Lou gave an exaggerated exhale. "Troubling for sure. One of the international numbers belongs to Antonio Bernardi of Durban, South Africa. Not the kind of guy you bring home to meet the family. The other number is a burner purchased thirteen months ago in Grasse, France, with cash, so no name. I found Bernardi's number on Fiona's, Liam's, and the second international number's call records but not on Joanna's. Besides Bernardi's number, the second international number was on Fiona's burner and Joanna's cell phone but not on either of Liam's phones."

"So you think the calls from the international numbers have to do with me?" Kate asked.

Lou shrugged. "I'm not the detective."

Reese read the pages. "I suspect they do." She looked at Lou. "Nothing on the Novikovs?"

"Nope."

"You might as well be law enforcement. This is excellent work."

"What'd you expect?" Lou made a miffed face. "I also triple-checked for unregistered numbers on Garcia's, Ngyuen's, and Macon's numbers. They're clean unless they have burners I couldn't find. But that's not likely."

Reese looked up. "We need to know more about Antonio Bernardi. He has to be the go-between. Fiona and Liam may supply him with information, he relays it to the person with the French number, and they pass it on to Joanna."

"Oh, my God. Why would Joanna do this to me?"

Lou looked at her. "Betrayal usually comes down to greed or fear. She sold you out for money or because they're blackmailing her."

"Whatever the reason. These calls implicate her participation." Reese handed a few pages to Kate. "We need to establish a timeline—the days and times of each call. Our evidence needs to be airtight." She looked at Lou. "What about locations? Any progress?"

"That's where things get troubling. Liam's burner registered with towers in the area. We know he was here. Today both Fiona's registered cell phone and burner pinged area towers for the first time, and Joanna's phone registered—"

"Joanna was here?" Kate interrupted in surprise.

"Her phones were at least. Three days ago, her personal and work cell numbers hit towers, and she received a call from another burner. It's been harder to trace, but I'll find it—"

"It was me," Kate said to Lou. She looked at Reese, unsettled. "That's when we called her after Liam and Bob were found. She lied to us. She's been lying to me."

Lou nodded. "I'm no detective, but I'm thinking you're right about her. None of the other suspects' phones pinged towers in the area, but the international numbers have. Bernardi's phone registered with cell towers in the area a month ago but not since, and the French number has been pinging cell towers around here and down the West Coast on and off for the last year. What troubles me is Fiona had two conversations with the French number yesterday…after Liam and Bob were found dead."

"So we need to find out why. Fiona most likely hired whoever's on the other end of that phone number to kill you. It's possible Liam didn't even know you were here. Fiona could've used him just like she did Bridget. We need to expose her, and I have a plan. Lou, can you monitor phones in real time?"

"Does a whore sweat in church?"

"Lou don't say..." Kate sighed. "Just don't think like that, please."

CHAPTER THIRTY-FIVE

Kate awoke to the warmth of Reese's body behind her. The only sound in the dark room was Jenny's gentle snoring. She pulled Reese's arm draped over her waist tighter and whispered, "Are you awake?"

"Mmhmm. You okay?" Reese asked drowsily and snuggled closer.

"Can't get back to sleep." She turned over. "I can't stop thinking about Lainey. How horrible her family life must have been to change her identity. You're sure she's Coleen Farrell?"

She nodded and swept Kate's hair off her face, trailing a finger down her smooth cheek. "Her father was a controlling, abusive man. He was forcing her to marry at seventeen. She must have felt hopeless. Sometimes it's easier to bury the past, especially when it's full of things you can't change. Sometimes that's what acceptance looks like." Reese wiped a tear that gathered in the corner of Kate's eye. "I've asked Lainey to call me. I want to tell her that her abuser's dead. Maybe she'll decide not to hide any longer. She has a sister who has never stopped missing her."

"Is she facing any legal trouble?"

"I don't think so. She didn't create official documents with the name."

"Wait? She and Meena don't have a marriage license?"

"Not that Lou found."

"Oh, God. The lies they've had to keep up. It's a hard way to live." She blinked slowly. "I can't stop thinking about Joanna, either. She wouldn't have approached Fiona, not for money. They have to be blackmailing her. But how did Fiona know Joanna was my inspector?"

"Someone in the office with knowledge of her caseload could've leaked it. The Maloneys could've known who your grandmother was and watched her. It never sat right with me that Joanna attended her funeral last year. They could've seen her there. Figured out who she was."

Kate searched her memories and felt an icy pit in her stomach. "I visited my grandma a few times when I was undercover. Once Bridget seemed upset when I returned to her condo, questioning me about sneaking off to see a girlfriend. I figured she was just paranoid. What if she had followed me?"

"It's possible. She could've told Fiona. Then all the Maloneys had to do was surveil your grandmother until she led them to you. It would be easy to identify the people who attended her funeral."

"You think they watched her until she died...I can't believe I put her in that kind of danger."

"Hey, would you blame anyone else who did what you did?" She held Kate's eyes. "No, right? So stop being hard on yourself. You loved your grandmother, and you tried to keep her safe. You're not responsible for the depravity of others. Okay?"

Kate nodded and fought back the burning in her eyes. "Hold me until I fall asleep, please." She lightly kissed Reese's lips and turned over, backing up until their bodies pressed into each other. Even amid chaos, Reese quieted the chatter in her mind, and lying in her arms unfurled a growing calmness inside her. She loved this woman, and the feeling hadn't made her fall apart.

* * *

The next morning, storm clouds had rolled into the valley and darkened the sky. Reese entered a heavily perfume-filled interview room at the Skagit Valley police station, flipping on the lights. Fiona Maloney and her lawyer, a thin, gray-haired man with readers fixed on the end of his nose sat at a wooden table in the dim room. She glanced at Fiona. The O'Flaherty crime family's captain wore a severe black suit with her auburn hair pulled tight into a bun on the back of her head. She didn't turn to look when Reese entered but kept her gaze on the table.

A moment later, Mandy entered and shut the door. Her arrival caused a visceral reaction in Fiona. "Why is she here?"

"SAC Garcia is assisting the ISB in your son's murder." Reese finally met Fiona's cold green eyes. "She's familiar with your son's history, so I brought her in. We appreciate you talking with us. Any information you provide will help with the investigation."

She and Mandy sat across from them. Fiona turned her glare from Mandy to her lawyer and whispered in his ear. He cleared his throat and said, "My client has voluntarily made herself available today, despite this difficult time, but we insist SAC Garcia refrain from asking questions, or we will be on our way."

Mandy sat back, making herself comfortable. "I have no problem listening, Mrs. Maloney."

"Okay, then. If that's settled." Reese opened the file folder and removed a few photos. "I'm sorry for your loss, and I won't pretend to know how devastating losing a second child must be for you. I'm sure you want to know what happened to Liam, and I can tell you that preliminary evidence indicates he and a park ranger fatally shot each other. But we're also interested in a third person who might be involved." Reese noticed Fiona's eyes had narrowed slightly when she mentioned the loss of a second child.

"That doesn't make any sense," Fiona said. "Why would Liam carry a gun on a hiking vacation?"

Reese slid a photo of Liam's fake ID across the table. "Is that what he was doing here?"

Fiona's lawyer snatched the picture up and examined it before handing it to Fiona. She looked at it and tossed it back toward Reese. "I'm not surprised he used an alias. He couldn't use his real name because *her* people had been following him. He wanted to get away and clear his head." She held Mandy's eyes. "You caused this. Keeping us under a microscope, making his life hell. Wasn't it enough to take my daughter away from me?" Her lawyer touched her arm and leaned in, whispering.

Reese handed the next photo to her lawyer. "Why do you suppose your son would hike in the backcountry without supplies in his backpack?"

Fiona snatched the picture. "There was nothing in it?"

"I can tell you there wasn't anything you would take on a hike. Don't you think he would have brought gear, food at least?" Reese paused and watched as Fiona struggled to keep her composure.

"What do you mean, nothing you'd take on a hike? What did my son have with him?" Fiona's voice grew louder, and she leaned against the table. Her lawyer pulled her back in her seat by the arm.

"One thing we're curious about, although it wasn't on Liam, was an envelope of cash we found on the park ranger." Reese slid the picture across the table.

Fiona picked it up before her lawyer's hand could reach it. "What are you suggesting? That I know why a stranger had an envelope of money?" She turned her angry gaze to Mandy. "I've just seen Liam's lifeless body. And instead of leaving me alone to grieve, you follow me here and convince this…*park ranger*…to accuse him and me of something illegal. You're despicable."

Mandy lifted her hands. "I'm just listening."

"Mrs. Maloney," Reese said, drawing her attention. "I appreciate your concerns and can see how you might draw that conclusion, but our investigation started well before I asked SAC Garcia to be here. I'll be honest, what I need to ask you might be difficult, but I'm only trying to understand the evidence we found at the scene. That's all."

"I don't know how I can help if your questions are as ridiculous as that. I don't have any idea why."

"Okay. Do you know why Liam's prints were on the envelope and the bills? There are other fingerprints, too, but we haven't identified them yet."

The thin man abruptly scooted his chair back and stood. "I think Mrs. Maloney is done now. Is she free to go?"

Reese looked at Fiona. "You're not being detained. I assumed no matter what your son was doing here, you'd want to help find out why he and another man were found shot to death."

"Sit down, Gerard," Fiona snapped. Then she turned back to Reese. "My son is not a murderer. He would never shoot anyone. He managed business accounts for God's sake. We're in porcelain exports. Maybe he walked up on something he shouldn't have seen. Something between this crooked ranger and another person."

"That's one scenario. I have another theory." Reese handed the last photo to Fiona. "What do you think those are?"

Fiona looked at it, and Reese caught a flash of recognition in her eyes. "I have no idea." She tossed the photo back.

"Did you notice the cursive L? Remember that old television comedy, Laverne and Shirley? It reminds me of the L Laverne sewed onto her clothes." Reese paused. "Anyway, they're drugs. According to our lab, those little white pills are a synthetic blend of an almost identical composition of Qsymia and cannabis. Impressive. And trendy, too. I bet getting high and losing weight is very popular."

Gerard scrambled to his feet. "That's enough. If Mrs. Maloney is not being detained, we're leaving."

"Okay. Okay. She's free to go." Reese raised her hands and looked at Mandy. "I think we have all we need. Don't you think we're good?"

"Oh, I'm confident our investigation can move forward." Mandy nodded at Fiona. "Good to see you again, Mrs. Maloney. Take care."

* * *

Gerard held the sedan's door for Fiona, but she ignored the gesture and strode to the end of the parking lot. She had to call Bridget. The drugs. Antonio's product, now missing. Liam dead. Her breathing became shallow, rapid.

Her daughter's phone rang, and the call went to voice mail. After the beep, Fiona restrained her voice. "It's me, Bridget. I arrived in this god-forsaken place yesterday, and I saw him, Liam's dead. I feel like a black hole is swallowing me. Please return my call as soon as you can."

Halfway back to the sedan, Fiona's phone rang. "Bridget, thank God. Did you listen to my message?"

"I wish I hadn't, Mother. It's unbelievable. How'd it happen? Have you found anything out?"

Fiona hesitated. "I just left an interview with some park ranger. She told me Liam had drugs in his possession."

"So what? It was probably his personal stash. Why does she think that's important?"

"She believes he intended to sell them."

"Jesus. You're kidding. Little brother betrayed the family? I didn't think he had it in him. You must be so conflicted. But look at it this way, at least he saved you the hassle of faking his death."

Fiona fell silent. The drugs had to be Bridget's doing. She was the third person they were looking for. She had to be the one who killed Liam. Her anger seethed.

"Oh, Jesus. I bet you're scared, too. Do you think he implicated you in his side hustle?" Bridget broke out in macabre laughter.

"You evil little bitch. What have you done?" Fiona shouted, and the line went dead.

CHAPTER THIRTY-SIX

After Fiona Maloney and her lawyer left the interrogation room, Reese shut the door and shook her head. "Jesus she's a piece of work."

"Whatever you're thinking about her, she's twice as bad." Mandy sat forward.

"I think she recognized the drugs, and the idea that her prints are on the envelope and money has her head spinning." Reese sat. "I'm surprised her prints aren't in AFIS."

"She's always been in the background. Though she took over her family's business when her husband, Sean, died in an explosion about eight years ago. We've been waiting for this type of mistake. I think we can nail her for this."

"I'll do everything I can to make that happen."

"Great, so will I. What do you need from me right now?" asked Garcia.

"I've got a meeting at the US Attorney's office tomorrow in Seattle. Can you meet me there?"

"Sure, I'll be there. Text me the details."

"We need to sort out a few pieces of evidence. My intelligence analyst hit a wall on the backpacks. We could use help. Would you have your team locate the POS? Hopefully, the Maloneys used a credit card, or the store they bought them from has CCTV."

"I'll get someone on it right now." Mandy pulled her cell phone from her back pocket and started texting.

"Good. I'll have my analyst send the details to you. I expect a warrant to collect fingerprint evidence in Fiona's hotel room today. We'll compare what we find to the unidentified prints on the envelope and money." Reese's phone rang, and she looked at the screen. "Sorry, I have to take this." She walked into the hallway, closing the door behind her. "Lou, what do you have?"

"Ten minutes ago, Fiona called the French number. It lasted less than thirty seconds. I'm assuming she left a message. Her phone registered to a cell tower in Mount Vernon. Less than a minute later the French number called her back. Here's where I'm freaking out. The number pinged a tower near the Stehekin State Airport. That's too close to Angel Hall to be a coincidence. I'm heading over—"

"No, listen, that's not a good idea. Give me one second." Reese ran back into the interrogation room, holding her cell phone against her chest. "Mandy, I need to leave. I'll text you the info for tomorrow." She ran to her Land Rover. "Lou, whoever is carrying that phone has killed two people and intends to kill Kate. Don't put yourself in danger. I'm on my way to the hostel. I'll call Kate. Can you access the burner's GPS? Pinpoint its location?"

"I can try, but I'm already heading to Kate's. I'll do it when I get there. See you in a few." Lou disconnected.

"Goddamn it." Reese hit the steering wheel. Frustrated. Scared. She called Kate.

"Hey, how'd the interview go?" Kate asked.

"Listen, I'll be there in forty minutes. Please ask everyone to stay in their rooms and lock their doors. I need you to do the same—"

"What's going on?"

"I told Fiona we suspected a third person was involved in the murders. Baiting her. She bit and called the French number as soon as she was outside. Lou said the phone registered to a tower near the Stehekin Airport. Whoever is carrying the phone is close. Lou's about twenty minutes away."

"Why is she coming here? It's not safe."

"She wouldn't listen to me."

Kate sighed. "All right. I'll warn everyone. Text me when you get here."

"I will." Reese paused. "Kate, I left my personal handgun in your bedside table drawer. Carry it. Just in case."

* * *

Jenny ran through the butler pantry, scratching at the communal room's door.

"Hey, sweet girl, stop that," Kate called out. She glanced into her bedroom. The last thing she needed to do was walk around the hostel brandishing a gun.

She opened the pantry door, and Jenny rushed inside, her nose to the floor sniffing the rug and then the furniture. Kate looked around. The morning Lounge had ended an hour earlier, but Nicole and Vivienne hadn't cleaned up. An empty tray of Lou's cinnabuns, coffee urns, yogurts, and fruit remained on the buffet table. Vivienne's cleaning caddy was on the back counter.

Jenny barked and scratched at the back door. The old hound's increasing agitation made Kate's stomach churn. "Get back, sweetie." She scooted her away from the door and checked the lock. The deadbolt was engaged. That calmed her. "All right. I'm going to have to leash you. I can't have you running off."

A couple of guests sat on the front porch with their backpacks, smoking weed. "Hey, I'm so sorry, but there's another emergency in the park, and they've asked all guests to remain inside their lodging. Doors locked. So please go back inside your room. I don't even mind if you smoke inside."

"Oh, shit. What's going on?" the young man asked.

"The park rangers didn't say. They only passed on the warning." Kate knocked on the door beside them.

"They're not here. Everyone left after Lounge," the woman said.

"Everyone? Did you see Nic and Vivienne leave?"

They thought for a moment. "Nah, last time I saw them, they were in the Lounge room," the man said. He looked at his partner, and she nodded.

"All right, thanks. Go inside please." Kate ran to Nicole's apartment and knocked. "Nic?" No answer. The front blinds were closed. She and Jenny moved around the corner and checked the side windows. Blinds closed. Nicole never closed her blinds, especially on dark, stormy days. Kate's heart pounded. She ran to the back of the apartment, beat on the locked door, and yelled, "Nic? Vivienne?" *The apartment key.* She'd get the key and Reese's gun.

Kate ran home, trying to convince herself Nicole and Vivienne were fine. She grabbed the key from a hook in the pantry and headed to her bedside table. Jenny ran toward the bathroom, pulling hard on her leash as Kate opened the drawer.

The old hound snarled and began snapping and barking.

"Looking for this, Elle?"

Kate froze. The voice. The name. She spun around. The woman before her had Reese's gun pointed at Jenny. She recognized the woman immediately as the dark-haired guest who had been sitting with Vivienne in the reading nook during Lounge for the past few days. She only vaguely resembled the Irish princess, but it was definitely her.

"You look like you've seen a ghost." Bridget grinned. "It's been a long time. We've eight years to make up for. But first, put your precious Jenny in the bathroom. I'd hate to use the first bullet in Special Agent Carter's gun on her."

Kate tugged Jenny to her side and walked her to the bathroom. When she closed the door, the bloodhound lunged at it, scratching and barking.

"Time to go. I've something special planned for you." Bridget waved the gun toward the patio doors. "Put on your backpack. I wouldn't want anyone to think I'm marching you out to the woods to kill you."

Kate's backpack rested against the wall beside the sliders. She grabbed it and opened the doors. They crossed the yard and entered the woods. The rain fell lightly under the tree canopy.

"I'm not surprised to see you, Bridget. We figured out you were here. Not too smart keeping the same burner phone for so long." If she could make Bridget angry, make her lose control, maybe she could distract her long enough to have a chance. "So you've been in France all these years. Living near Grasse, I guess, where you bought the phone. Not *in* Grasse, you tried to be clever. But not smart enough. Lou and Reese are only ten minutes away. It's over for you."

"Whatever, Elle. Your girlfriend ended her interview with my mother less than fifteen minutes ago, and she's over an hour away." Bridget shoved the gun's barrel into Kate's backpack. "I'm smart enough to have watched you hike this trail for the last year. Good enough to watch you without you knowing. I know you're slackpacking, as they say, so pick up the pace."

"But you weren't bright enough to figure out I was FBI for over three years. You had to have Mommy tell you." She turned around to meet Bridget's eyes. "I'm shocked you kept control of yourself until the explosion."

"Shut the fuck up."

"Oh, my God. I assumed you knew, but you didn't, did you? Mommy kept it from you. She didn't trust you enough with her plan."

"You don't know what you're talking about. Turn around and keep going," Bridget shouted, lifting the gun. "If I have to shoot you now, we won't get to catch up."

They walked in silence. The humidity in the woods was oppressive and the rain breaking through the canopy was no relief. Kate knew they were only five minutes from High Bridge. She could hear the roar of the Stehekin River and prayed they'd run into a ranger returning to the old station.

Minutes later Bridget stopped on the bridge and threw her phone into the white rapids below. "That's because your girlfriend's tracking my phone. Or she should be if she's any good at her job. But neither of you is very good. I was sure you would recognize the Dum-Dums wrappers I left." She laughed at Kate's silence. "That's what I thought. You had no idea. We're almost at the PCT trailhead. How will the special agent guess which direction we've gone? Or did we jump?" She looked over the wooden rail and shuddered. "Now that would be a harsh way to die. But it's not how I planned to kill you." She waved Kate on with the gun.

Bridget stopped at the trailhead near Howard Lake. The Irish princess had packed a bottle in Kate's backpack for herself and drank.

"I'd share, but I think I'll need it when I have to go back down the mountain." She drank from the water bottle again.

"What's your end goal?" Kate asked.

"Revenge, obviously. But you know that. Pick it up, not far now."

"I have to ask, have you thought your plan through? I can tell you're taking me back to the dry camp. Why? There's one way in and one way out."

"You're wrong about that. There are a few other ways back down the mountain. You wouldn't survive falling off the cliff face, but you'd get back down, wouldn't you?" Bridget laughed. "There's also a primitive trail. I thought you'd know about it, but again, you're not quite as prepared as me."

They were near the end of the switchbacks, and without the tree cover, the heavy rain soaked them. "Fine. You win. Why don't you tell me what you desperately want me to know? That's what this is, right, or you would've killed me in my home?" Kate stopped and turned around. "What's your revenge plan, Bridget?"

"It's simple but effective. I'm killing everyone who betrayed me. Liam. You. My mother. After I destroy what's left of the O'Flaherty crime family, I'm returning home to run *my* organization."

"I wasn't disloyal to you. I was doing my job. You're a criminal, and I catch criminals. Nothing else. We weren't friends, so don't say I betrayed you. I tricked you."

"The last laugh's on you, though, isn't it? Thanks to Fiona, no one knows I'm alive. Oh, except for your girlfriend and Lou. So I'll need to amend my plan to include a few loose ends."

"You'll never get the chance, you psychopath," Kate shouted. Then they both turned to the sound of baying in the distance.

Bridget raised the gun. "Go, now!" She forced Kate to scramble up the rest of the trail and into the dry camp.

Kate stopped beside a charred log and dropped the backpack. "You'll have to kill me right here. You're not forcing me off the cliff. I'm not giving you the satisfaction."

Jenny's baying drew closer.

Bridget jerked the gun. "Move! Or the first sight of your fucking dog, I'll shoot it."

* * *

The old Land Rover sped over Stehekin Valley Road. Reese knew she'd lose time once she turned onto the deep, rutted path that led to the hostel. Her phone rang. "Lou, are you there? Is Kate okay?"

"She's gone, and Jenny was in the bathroom, freaking out. I opened the door, and she bolted out the bedroom sliders." Lou's voice ramped up with fear. "What do you want me to do? Should I follow her?"

"No. I want you to check the nightstand's drawer. The one closest to the bathroom. Is there a gun inside?"

"Okay. I'm looking…there's no gun. Is that good? Does it mean Kate's armed?"

"Let's hope so. Now I want you to check the parking lot for Kate's truck and then check Nicole's apartment. Kate could have left, or maybe she's with Nicole and Vivienne."

She clenched the steering wheel waiting for Lou to say something, to tell her Kate was with Nicole and Vivienne and that she had the gun. She heard knocking, and Lou shouting.

Lou came back on the line. "Her truck's here. No one's answering at Nicole's. The blinds are closed. Shit, shit, shit. You don't think they're in there, do you? Do you want me to try to get inside?"

"Listen, Lou, calm down. You need to check if they're inside. Kate has a master key in her utility closet. It's in the kitchen. Go get the key."

A minute later, Lou returned and said, "I have it. I'm going in. Promise me I won't find someone…"

"It's okay. You won't. If the gun in Kate's drawer had been fired, one of the guests would have heard and reported it." Reese tried to assuage Lou's fear, but hers was escalating.

"Nicole? Vivienne?" Lou shouted.

Reese listened to her run through the tiny apartment, calling for them.

"I heard something. It's coming from the bathroom. Jesus, I don't like this at all. What if…" Her voice trailed off.

"I hear you, Lou. This is a lot to handle. But if someone needs medical assistance, the faster we know, the better their chances."

"It's Nicole and Vivienne," Lou said, now more assured. "Someone has gagged them with gaffer tape and zip-tied them to the basin pipes."

There was a lengthy pause then muffled movement and voices. Reese could hear Vivienne crying and Nicole shouting in the background. "What's she saying, Lou?"

"It was the same person who broke in. They had on a mask. But Vivienne recognized her voice. She was a guest…a French woman." She stopped talking. "What did you say?"

"Lou, what the hell did she say," Reese shouted.

"Jesus. The woman said she couldn't have them ruining her plans. She said their boss had to pay for her past sins with a trip down a mountainside. What the hell does that mean?"

Reese threw her phone aside, her heart thundering. It all made sense now. The funeral a year ago. The drugs in the parks over the past year. The phone calls to Joanna and Fiona but not Liam. The horseshoe pin. Bridget Maloney was alive. She remembered Kate saying there was an employee at the bakery that day. Everyone assumed she was an employee. They were wrong. She could've been anyone. Fiona must have killed her to take Bridget's place in the explosion.

The heavy rain battered the Rover's windshield. Reese topped out at a dangerous speed. She knew Bridget was taking Kate to where she left the urine-soaked backpack for Jenny to find, tied up the old hound after luring her outside, and killed her brother and Bob. Taking her to the cliff face, "a trip down a mountainside."

Reese pulled off the road and grabbed her emergency backpack. She sprinted from the Rover and across High Bridge into the woods. She figured Fiona had called Bridget forty minutes ago, so if Kate slow-walked them, they couldn't be too far ahead. She could overtake them in less than fifteen minutes.

At the end of the switchbacks, she heard Jenny's baying in the distance. They were close. She took her handgun from her holster and started to run. Bridget might hear Jenny and realize she was out of time. Which meant Kate was out of time.

* * *

"All right, I'm going."

Bridget shoved the gun's muzzle between Kate's shoulders, pushing her forward.

Kate didn't have much time. Jenny would be there any minute, and Reese might be close behind. But they were walking into a trap. Bridget wouldn't hesitate to kill either of them the second they were in range. Adrenaline rushed through her body. They walked a few yards deeper into the darkening woods. She heard Jenny bark now, her tracking finished. She was there. It was time to catch her prey.

She pretended to trip and grabbed a fallen branch, raising and swinging in one fluid motion. The blow struck Bridget's side, a loud thud and an enraged cry sounded. Kate pulled the branch back, this time aiming for Bridget's head. A shot sounded, and fire seared through her knee. She dropped to the ground, the pain shooting into her chest, making it hard to breathe.

"Goddamn it!" Bridget yelled. "This isn't how it's supposed to happen. You're fucking ruining everything again!" She pointed the gun at Kate's head.

Kate winced and caught sight of a copper flash emerging from the left. Bridget swung the gun around toward the barking and snarling, and Kate screamed, "No!" She lunged at her, and a shot fired before she drove her shoulder into Bridget, knocking her off her feet. They landed in a thud. Bridget punched Kate's bloody knee. The pain forced a guttural cry from her, and Bridget seized the moment of weakness to overpower her, rolling on top of Kate and inching the gun closer to her head. Kate struggled to push it away. She wouldn't die on this mountain. She wouldn't let Jenny die either.

Then without warning, Jenny leapt on Bridget's back, making her jerk forward. The force propelled her neck into the gun. A third shot sounded, and a warm, wetness sprayed across Kate's face.

Jenny nudging her face was the first thing to break through Kate's consciousness. She gasped, crawling out from under Bridget's body and clutching the old hound. She buried her face in Jenny's coat. Her warmth and smell made Kate's eyes swim in tears. "Thank you, sweet girl. Thank you."

When Reese found them, Kate was barely conscious, hunched over Jenny's side. She heard Reese's voice, but it sounded far away. Not until a shock of pain coursed up her leg, making her cry out, did she feel Reese's hands on her.

"I'm sorry. But we need to stop the bleeding." Reese was using her belt to put a tourniquet on her upper thigh and her shirt to bandage her knee. Then she retrieved a reflective silver blanket from her backpack and covered Kate. She sat behind her, holding Kate's body against hers. "Help's on the way. You're going to be okay. Everything's going to be okay."

EPILOGUE

The sun melted behind soaring evergreens, leaving their tops under a fiery display of reds, oranges, and yellows. The air was heavy with the sweet and spicy scents of Kate's blooming rose garden, and the warm glow of party lights zigzagging above the garden lit it in the darkening evening. Reese and Kate stood inside the climbing rose-covered trellis gate holding hands.

"Over the past year, you've changed my life." Reese's voice was soft and gentle. "I'm not sure of the exact moment I fell in love with you, but having fallen, I wake up to brighter days and a lighter heart so full of love it can only make our world a better place." She swallowed back her nerves. "I want to soar with you in the good times and grow stronger, together, in bad times. As Browning penned and John Lennon sang, I want you to 'grow old along with me…The best is yet to be.'" Her voice trailed away, and she sheepishly wiped tears from the corner of her eyes.

When they joined hands again, Kate squeezed them tighter and spoke tenderly, "Under the same stars twenty-five hundred years ago, Sappho strummed a lyre and sang, 'Love, like a mountain-wind upon an oak…Falling upon me, shakes me leaf and bough.' Like Sappho's, your love has awakened my soul and led me out of a forest of darkness." Her voice caught, and she breathed deeply. "With you, I'm content under the sun again. I want to wake up with you for the rest of my sunrises, and I promise you, until my final sunset, I will cherish and love you."

Their smiles grew wide, and they looked at the woman standing in front of them.

"Kate and Reese, your family and friends have gathered on this joyous day to bear witness to your promise to join your lives in marriage. May the rings you have exchanged forever symbolize the vows you've shared today. May the love and happiness you feel be with you always." The officiant raised her arms. "By the power vested in me by the State of Washington, it is my honor to declare you married and partners in life. For life. You may seal your vows with a kiss."

They pulled each other into a sweet kiss, and applause erupted around them.

In all the excitement, Jenny and Reno, sporting matching bow ties, chased each other around the guests sitting in two groups of white wooden folding chairs. Soon after, five young children joined in the game of tag. The guests hugged and congratulated the brides as the wedding party walked to a pavilion set up in the hostel's yard.

Reese smiled when they entered the tent. She had agreed to let Lou cater and decorate the reception space and was pleasantly surprised. Bright white sparkling lights hung down from the tent's ceiling. Two buffet tables with chaffing dishes, a tiered wedding cake, and five round tables were on one side of the pavilion, and a bar and a dance floor with a disco ball were on the other. "This looks amazing," she whispered to Kate.

"It's fantastic, and the food smells delicious. Let's get the line started. I'm starving."

The brides cut the cake after dinner. A few minutes later the disco ball began to spin, refracting multicolored light around the tent, and a DJ resembling Adam Sandler in *The Wedding Singer* ran onto the platform with a microphone. "Hey, hey! The dinner hour is over, and the cake has been cut. Now it's time for you to *cut a rug* on some of my beats. We'll start with a throwback to the 2010s."

Reese looked at Kate, and they both fought the urge to laugh. "Well, everything else Lou did was fabulous," Kate said, taking hold of Reese's hand, and dragging her onto the dance floor. The upbeat rhythm of Walk the Moon's "Shut up and Dance with Me" thumped in their chests, and by the time the DJ had mixed the next song, all the guests were on the dance floor.

After several more songs, Reese shouted over the music, "I'm going to the bar. Do you want a drink?"

"A chardonnay. I'll be over in a minute." Kate smiled and continued dancing with Nicole, Vivienne, and Mandy's partner, Gale.

Reese had seen Mandy head to the bar and wanted to take the opportunity to talk to her alone. Earlier at dinner, she noticed the SAC on her phone in a text exchange, a communication too important to avoid even during her oldest friend's wedding.

"Hey." Reese joined her and turned to the bartender. "Hi, two chardonnays, please." She and Mandy took their drinks and moved away from the pounding music. "I couldn't help but notice you texting earlier. Looked intense."

"Yeah. I had planned to tell you later. Antonio's cooperation with the authorities and giving evidence against Fiona and the O'Flaherty organization earned him a pass here, but he received two ten-year sentences back home in South Africa for poaching and trafficking illegal animal parts. Antonio was clever. To protect himself, he recorded all his conversations with Bridget. For a share in her business, she had convinced him to help her retaliate against her mother. So now we also know Fiona used a sex worker to replace Bridget in the explosion—"

"Jesus…"

"Yeah, she's a piece of work. Bridget never mentioned Eleanor on the tapes. That's why Antonio never mentioned Eleanor Peters or Kate Hall in his testimony. Fiona didn't either. Bridget kept Kate's location to herself. A private revenge, I guess."

They turned their gaze to the dance floor. Kate and the others were laughing and spelling out YMCA with their arms as they danced to the Village People. "That's it then? Kate's safe?" Reese asked.

Mandy looked at her with a serious expression. "We've dismantled the O'Flaherty organization, and Fiona will die in prison, but I strongly suggest Kate stay in WITSEC."

"That's not likely. She'll never trust another marshal."

"Understood. But what Joanna did is rare. It's only happened once before in the history of the program. She knows if anyone ever threatened Kate's life again, her four-year sentence could easily turn into life in prison." Mandy drank from her beer bottle.

Reese watched the love of her life, the carefree way she danced to the music. She wanted Kate to feel this happiness in her core, to live free of fear, but as long as Fiona was alive, she would always have doubt lurking in her mind. "Okay. I'll talk to her about staying in."

"Good." Mandy smiled and set her beer on the table. "Looks like Kate is heading our way, and I'm being called to the dance floor."

"Hey, what were you and Mandy being so serious about?" Kate asked, breathless from dancing.

Reese held her tight. "About how much I love you and how you answered all my dreams when you agreed to marry me."

Kate laughed and picked up her wineglass. "I love you, too. So much so, I'll let you tell me the truth tomorrow." She rolled her eyes at Reese's grin. Then she waved at Meena and Lainey.

Reese had a private moment of satisfaction. She had shared with Lainey that her father was dead and that her sister missed her. The woman released a lifetime of pain in racking sobs during their meeting, and in time, Lainey had reached out to her sister.

"Hey, Meen, are you all having fun?" Kate embraced her and then Lainey.

"Absolutely. This is a blast." She glanced at the dance floor. "The DJ's a real throwback, right?"

"He's great. I love the music," Lainey said.

"Can I get you a drink?" Reese asked. "The bar's fully stocked, including sparkling water for the mom-to-be."

Reese returned a few minutes later, and her nieces and nephews cut right in front of her, running off their cake-induced energy. "Whoa," she said, balancing the drinks. "I'm not envying my brothers tonight."

"Are you ready for two of those at once?" Kate asked her friends.

"I guess we better be." Meena kissed Lainey's cheek. "Too late to back out now."

"Isn't that the truth?" Lainey stroked her extended belly and turned her attention to Holly. Her little sister danced with Nicole and Vivienne to ABBA's "Dancing Queen." "Look at her. I know she's never experienced this much happiness."

"How does she like Omaha?" Reese asked.

"It's an adjustment, but she's feeling better every day. We closed on the farm a few months ago. She bought a condo a few blocks from us, and she's enrolled in a nursing program at the university."

Kate smiled. "That's fantastic news."

"I'm so happy for you both. Here's to your growing family," Reese lifted her wineglass to them, and they all raised their glasses.

The DJ cut to the next song with a fade and shouted, "Everybody ready to shake your butt? Then get those tail feathers on the floor, it's time for 'The Chicken Dance.'"

"Let's go. I love this one!" Meena shouted and took hold of Lainey's hand.

Reese looked at Kate. "Do you want to dance?"

"God, no. I'm happy right here." She wrapped her arm around Reese's waist.

They watched a few guests join the group dance and some sneak off the floor. Nicole and Vivienne left for the bar, ordered shots, and joined them.

"Hey, boss. Great party."

"You have to stop calling me boss. You're the boss now."

"You'll always be the boss." Nicole's voice faded a bit, and she cleared her throat. "A shot to your happiness." She and Vivienne held out two shot glasses for them.

"Why not?" Reese took one, and Kate followed. "To us, our friends and family, and the good times ahead." They raised their shots and downed them.

"I'm glad you're having fun," Kate said. "Are your parents enjoying themselves?"

"A little too much." She directed their attention to a lanky couple flapping their arms like chicken wings and twisting low to the ground. "They love it here. The park reminds them of home, and they won't stop talking about upgrades for the hostel. I think it might be hard to keep them silent partners."

"I could think of worse business partners," Reese said.

"That's true. Don't get me wrong. I'm so grateful." Nicole held Vivienne's hand. "We both are."

"You and Vivienne will do great things at Hostel Hall, or whatever you call your hostel. Are you changing the name?"

"No way. Hostel Hall is a legend. Hikers go out of their way to stay here." Nicole's chin quivered. "Her namesake is pretty legendary too."

"Aw, Nic. You're going to make me cry on my wedding day." Kate embraced her old assistant. "Go away…you and Vivienne go dance." She waved them off with her hands.

"You are so loved," Reese said and kissed her lips lightly.

"Jeez, wait for your honeymoon, will you? There're kids around."

"Lou!" Kate turned around and hugged her. "You outdid yourself."

"I know, right? It's great." She put her hands on her hips and looked around.

Phil cleared his throat.

"Yeah, yeah. He helped too."

"Thanks, Phil. You all have made this such a special night." Kate tilted her head. "I haven't seen you on the dance floor yet. Where've you been?"

"Never left the food area. Phil got the munchies, so we've been in the corner eating cake." She winked at Reese. "Did I ever tell you how he disappeared during our wedding? He and his best man decided to burn one in the coat check room right before the ceremony and got locked in. And guess who walked up when the coat checker opened the door? My pious grandmother, that's who. She never stopped talking about the losers in the closet on my wedding day till the day she died. Thank God she couldn't see past her nose."

Kate and Reese laughed, and Phil shrugged. "What can I say? I'm charmed." He grabbed Lou's hand and asked, "Can we refresh the newlyweds' drinks?"

"Sure, I'll have another chardonnay."

"Just sparkling water for me," Reese said and looked at Kate. "I have one more wedding gift for you and need to drive you there."

"Ooh, sounds mysterious. I'm tingling."

"Oh, I bet you'll be doing that all night." Lou grinned and lifted her eyebrows.

"Come on. Let's take your comedy show on the road." Phil guided Lou toward the bar.

"Tell me more about your surprise," Kate said, crawling her fingers up Reese's chest.

"I could, but then it wouldn't be a surprise, and my parents are headed our way."

Kate jerked her hand away like a kid caught with their hand in the cookie jar.

"Reesy, this is the most wonderful wedding we've ever attended. Don't tell your brothers I said that though, okay?"

Reese laughed. "Your secret's safe with me, Mom. We're so glad you're here. And Reno. Jenny is very pleased."

"Wouldn't miss this day for the world," Reese's father said.

Her mother embraced Kate for a long moment. "I am so happy you're a part of our family. You're such a warm and loving soul, Katie." Tears spilled. "I hope you know how much we love you."

"Oh, Mom." Reese hugged her and then her dad.

"I do," Kate said, her voice shaky. "I'm so thankful to be a part of your beautiful family."

* * *

Kate took one last look at everyone on the dance floor. They were more than friends and in-laws—they were family. She and Reese had said their goodbyes. They would have one last breakfast in the communal room with their wedding guests before everyone headed home tomorrow.

Reese whistled, and Jenny and Reno trotted to their sides. She closed the old Land Rover's passenger door and climbed behind the wheel. "I hope my mom didn't overwhelm you. She cares about you so much. When you were convalescing with your knee, I had to make her go home. It wasn't easy, either."

"She's so sweet, and her food. Wow. You're a great cook, but your mom. Everything she made was incredible." Kate reached across the seat and grasped Reese's hand, the intensity of her emotions catching in her throat.

"The pain medication might have been influencing you. I mean, her food's good. Don't get me wrong. But that much better than mine?"

Reese grinned, and Kate tried to force a laugh through her closed throat. The joy she felt had opened a desire for her family. Her mother and father. Her grandmother. It had created a longing for them to see her, to share in her happiness.

"What is it? Are you thinking about your family?"

She gave a slight nod. "I wish they could've been here."

"Oh, Kate. I'm so sorry you're hurting for them." She squeezed her hand. "I want to believe they're here. You can, too. In whatever form you believe…energy…love. They're a part of you, the love you feel and receive. They always will be."

"How did I get lucky enough to find you?"

"Hmm. I'm the one who found an angel on the trails."

Kate laughed. "God, your cheesiness makes me so happy."

"I hope so. Your entire life is about to be full of it." She paused. "Are you going to miss the hostel?"

"Yeah, sure. But I'm more excited to start a new life with you, and the Peters Foundation. It'll be nice to do more for the parks."

Reese turned onto a dirt drive and parked beside her cabin.

"Is your gift something we could have done during our last night at the hostel?" Kate grinned.

"No, but I'd happily add your suggestion to the surprise."

A laugh bubbled from Kate's throat.

Reese turned on the lights inside the house. They'd spent the last year completing the remodel, choosing the finishes and furnishings together. Reese included Kate so the home felt like hers as well and it did. She opened the stacked doors and put a vinyl on the record player. A soft ethereal voice began singing.

"Is this Donna Lewis?"

"I found her album on eBay." Reese gently grasped her hand. "Follow me. Your surprise is outside."

They descended the patio steps into the yard and walked to the east side of the house. When they turned the corner, Kate first noticed the lights wrapped around a cedar pergola. They twinkled like fireflies in the night sky. Then she smelled a familiar scent, and her gaze dropped to the rose bushes that circled a three-tiered fountain with a cherub on top pouring water into the top basin.

It took a second to realize what she was seeing, but when she did, Kate gasped. "Boston Tealights. Reese. How…" She walked into the intimate garden, cupped a large white bloom with yellow tips, and breathed deeply.

"Last year I planted the seeds I found in the communal room. I had a master rose gardener unwittingly help me nurture them from sprouts in the greenhouse to healthy bushes out here. Come sit with me."

In the corner was a granite bench. Right away Kate noticed an inscription etched into its back. *In Loving Memory. Father Jasper Peters. Mother Laura Peters. Grandmother Eleanor Peters. Always in our hearts.* She burst into tears and threw her arms around Reese's neck. "Thank you so much. This is the most loving thing anyone has ever done for me…"

"I would do anything for you. This space is yours to enter and find peace and connect with your family." With a quick pop, she opened a bottle of champagne and poured two glasses. "Lou and Phil left after we cut the cake and set everything up for me. I can't thank them enough for their friendship."

Tears sprang into Kate's eyes again, this time tears of happiness. She let them slide down her cheeks. She was the same age as her father when he lost his battle with mental illness, after the loss of his love buried him under a mountain of despair. But she wasn't him. She could embrace the love given to her so freely, hold it in her heart, and let it lead her forward.

She met Reese's green-blue eyes now as dark and deep as the ocean under the night sky. "I Love You Always Forever" played over the speakers. She looked at Jenny and Reno flopped out under the fountain. "Our little family only needs one more thing," she said.

"Oh, what's that?"

"A puppy."